D0210043

ALSO BY MARGARET WEIS

Mistress of Dragons
The Dragon's Son

MASTER OF
DRAGONS

MARGARET
WEIS

TOR®
fantasy

A TOM DOHERTY ASSOCIATES BOOK
NEW YORK

This is a work of fiction. All of the characters, organizations, and events portrayed in this novel are either products of the author's imagination or are used fictitiously.

MASTER OF DRAGONS

Copyright © 2005 by Margaret Weis

All rights reserved, including the right to reproduce this book, or portions thereof, in any form.

Edited by Brian Thomsen

A Tor Book
Published by Tom Doherty Associates, LLC
175 Fifth Avenue
New York, NY 10010

www.tor.com

Tor® is a registered trademark of Tom Doherty Associates, LLC.

ISBN-13: 978-0-7653-4392-5
ISBN-10: 0-7653-4392-4

First Edition: November 2005
First Mass Market Edition: July 2007

Printed in the United States of America

0 9 8 7 6 5 4 3 2 1

To all those with dragon-magic in their blood,
this book is fondly dedicated.

ACKNOWLEDGMENTS

I would like to acknowledge the assistance of my friend and military adviser, Robert Krammes, who has been of such inestimable help to me on these novels, and to his wife and my dear friend, Mary Krammes, who has served as wardrobe mistress to Evelina.

MASTER of
DRAGONS

PROLOGUE

LYSIRA ENTERED THE ENORMOUS CAVERN THAT WAS THE ancient Hall of Parliament for dragonkind. The entrance was located in the tallest peak of a snow-capped mountain range. Gaping black against the white-shrouded crags, the opening had been carved hundreds of centuries ago by dragon-magic. No need to hide it from humans, not this far up the mountainside. The entrance was large enough to accommodate a dragon in flight. Lysira was small for her kind, and she swooped into the entryway with ease, glad to leave behind the glare of the sun glittering on the snow for the restful darkness of the Hall.

The dragon spiraled downward, drifting on the whispering air currents, listening to the silence that was dark in her mind. The Hall was empty. Parliament was not in session. She was not really supposed to be here, but she felt drawn to this place. Disturbed and troubled, she did not know what to do or where to turn for answers, and so she decided to come here. Perhaps if she were in the Hall itself, she would be able to glean some of the wisdom of those who came before her, pick up a trace of their colors. Learn from their experience. At least, that's what she'd told herself.

Gliding downward on still wings toward the floor that was far, far below her, Lysira was bitterly disappointed. She saw only darkness. The cavern was empty. If there were ghosts, they slumbered in the eternal dragon dream that was death.

Upset, Lysira was not paying attention to what she was doing, and the floor came up on her before she was ready for it. She landed with an ungraceful thud, nearly going over on her nose. Recovering, she was thankful that no one was here to have witnessed such a fledgling bumble.

She was especially glad that one particular dragon was not present—the Walker, Draconas. Her scales rippled all over in embarrassment at the thought. In truth, it was because she'd been thinking of him and everything he'd said at the last session of Parliament that she had botched her landing. But she couldn't decide if it was his words that bothered her or if it was the way his colors had so gently touched her.

Settling on the floor, tucking her wings in at her flanks and wrapping her long tail around her feet, Lysira gazed around the dark and empty cavern and sighed. She could at last admit to herself that she'd been hoping—rather unrealistically—that she would find Draconas here.

She didn't know why she expected him to be in the empty Hall.

Perhaps because he wasn't anywhere else.

Dragons communicate mentally, mind-to-mind, using images and vibrant colors to exchange ideas. A dragon may block another from entering his mind, just as a human can stop others from entering his house. But, just as the house is still there, so is the mind of the dragon. Though the colors are unreadable and prohibit entry, they shimmer like foxfire in the night. And Draconas's colors were nowhere to be seen.

Dragons dislike making hasty decisions. Lysira had been unsettled ever since the last meeting of Parliament—the meeting that had thrown the dragons into turmoil, the meeting in which Draconas had disclosed that the two children born to the human woman Melisande could communicate mind-to-mind, as could dragons. Not only that, but these humans could actually enter the minds of dragons! This was an awful, dreadful, catastrophic calamity. What's more, Draconas had told Parliament that one of their number was a traitor, one of them was feeding information to the rogue dragon Maristara and her cohort, Grald. Because of this, Draconas had hidden away the two children, and he refused to tell anyone—even Anora, the wise elder dragon, the Minister of the Parliament—where they were to be found. He'd also claimed that this same traitor had been responsible for the deaths of her father and Braun, Lysira's brother.

That meeting had taken place sixteen years ago. A long time, by human standards. A mere eye blink by dragon measuring. Lysira had spent those years dithering, wavering back and forth, trying to decide if she would talk to Draconas or not. For a couple of years, she thought she wouldn't. He was the Walker, the dragon who took human shape to walk among humans and keep an eye on them. He had, therefore, lots of humans' images in his mind, images Lysira found disturbing and distasteful. And fascinating.

It was the fascinating part that bothered her. She'd seen only a few of these images the last time he'd spoken to her, and she had since discovered that they kept cropping up in her dreams, breaking her tranquillity. Try as she might, she couldn't banish them. She didn't want to see any more of them. And yet, she did.

Once she had made up her mind that she would talk to him, a few more years passed before she found the courage to do so. She would start to approach him and then she would shy away and retreat back to her lair in a flutter of confusion.

This made her angry, and for the next year or so, she turned her anger at Draconas and blamed him as the cause of all the trouble. She knew she was being irrational. He wasn't the cause. Maristara had started it all by seizing that human kingdom and then breeding humans with dragons to produce humans with dragon magic. Lysira didn't like to admit that part.

At this point, she decided that she didn't need Draconas. She would find out who the traitor dragon was on her own. Lysira's investigations were halfhearted, however, and didn't get her anywhere. The other dragons she questioned were brusque and even rude. They obviously did not want to think about any of this. They were hoping it would all go away. They shut their minds to her and shooed her off.

Which brought Lysira right back to Draconas. She would talk to him. She was determined to talk to him. Boldly, trembling, Lysira reached out her colors to him.

Only to find that the colors of his mind were gone, as though they had been wiped away by a wet sponge.

Lysira crouched in the empty Hall of Parliament and, for the first time, she began to be afraid. Not only for Draconas, but for herself. And all of dragonkind.

Anora felt true regret that she had to kill Draconas.

Of all the walkers who had sacrificed their dragon form to take on the illusion of a human, Draconas had been the best. One of the hazards of being a walker, of living among humans, was that the dragon tended to either become too human—in which case he forgot the reason he'd been sent to walk among humans in the first place—or he remained too dragon—in which case he moped and pouted and whined about having to put up with the inconveniences of being human.

Draconas had been the first to separate the two halves of his being, maintaining a firm division between the dragon and the human. Even now, though it appeared that he was acting for the humans, siding with the humans, and protecting the humans, Anora knew better. Draconas was doing what he was doing because he firmly believed he was helping his own kind.

Admirable. Mistaken, but admirable.

She stood, masked by illusion, inside the building where she'd set her trap for Draconas. Watching him from the shadows, she pondered the idea of letting him live. She could try to explain to him that he was wrong, hoping he'd see reason. She discarded that thought with a regretful sigh.

Draconas's asset had become his liability. He was working hard to keep humans and dragons at peace, as they had been since the first human had raised himself up off all fours. Draconas would never understand why that peace had to end, and Anora knew he could never be made to understand.

He had to die.

Draconas had his back to her. She'd been spying on him from the moment he'd entered the abandoned building. He was here to set a trap for the dragon Grald, the master of Dragonkeep. Grald, disguised in his own stolen human body, was heading this direction.

Grald and Anora were in contact, the colors of their minds blending, though not very harmoniously. Anora was thinking of her own lofty goals. Grald was thinking of vengeance. But what could you expect? Grald was a dragon of the baser sort. He did not come from one of the noble families of dragonkind, who had ruled the world for centuries. In human terms, Grald was a peasant.

He'd been brought into this conspiracy by Maristara, who had chosen him because he was a peasant—rough and crude and not overly educated.

The elder female dragon, Maristara, had formed a theory—a brilliant theory—that if dragons and humans bred, they would produce offspring that would look human, but would be capable of using dragon-magic. Anora remembered how shocked and appalled she'd been at first hearing Maristara's proposal, brought to her in secret. She'd been adamantly opposed to it—not only did it break all the laws of dragonkind, it could prove dangerous for dragons. Creating humans with magical powers! It was not to be considered. When Maristara had defied her and seized a human kingdom in order to begin her experiments, Anora had vowed that she would do everything in her power to stop her.

Time passed. The dragons, with their usual ineptness and inability to make decisions, bungled any chance of halting Maristara. The experiments in breeding proceeded and went far better than even Maristara had hoped. Sadly, as time passed, Anora had come to see things Maristara's way.

These humans with the dragon-magic in their blood proved to be so powerful that they intimidated lesser humans. Thus, they made perfect rulers. And, because these humans had dragon-blood in their veins, they were easily manipulated by the dragons. Dragons ruled the half-dragon humans who ruled the humans. Perfect all around.

Maristara needed a male dragon to start the breeding program with the human females of Seth. She didn't dare choose one of the males of the noble houses, for fear word would get out. She selected a male from a family of lesser dragons, a young male, aggressive and ambitious and cruel.

His name was Grald.

She taught Grald the secret of ripping the heart out of a living human body and taking over that body, making it his own—a task far less complicated and time-consuming than casting the supreme illusion spell that changed Draconas into a human. Unlike Maristara, who used the human bodies she took to disguise her true form, Grald usurped the human bodies, giving them his name and taking over their personalities. He was on his sixth human right now, and this was his favorite. He had found something better, however, and he was looking forward eagerly to taking over the next body—that of his own son.

Before that could happen, Anora and Grald had to kill Draconas, who had done everything in his power to thwart them.

"I think you would understand," Anora said silently to Draconas, speaking to his back, as he stood across from her in the doorway of the building, sharpening his walking staff into a spear. "I think you might even take our side, but . . . I can't be sure. You have formed attachments among the humans. You hid Melisande's children away from us. If Ven had not cried out to us for help, we might never have discovered them."

"Quit sniveling, Anora. He should have died long ago."

Grald's colors intruded rudely into hers, and Anora, haughtily, didn't deign to reply. She saw no need to explain herself to underlings. Maristara let Grald take too many liberties. She should keep him in his place.

"Where are you?" Anora asked, her colors chill.

"I am in sight of the house. My son summoned me,"

Grald added with smug triumph. "He betrayed his brother, as I told you he would, to gain the female. Like father, like son." Grald chuckled.

"I don't trust him," Anora said. "Ven is devious—devious as a dragon—in many ways. I should know. I spent weeks in his company."

"All the better for me when I take over his body."

You'll acquire a brain, at least, Anora thought, but she kept that caustic comment concealed beneath the cold flow of her colors. Dissimulation was not difficult to practice on Grald, who never bothered to look beneath the surface of any conversation.

"Don't come any closer," Anora warned. "I'm about to strike."

"Take care you don't hurt Ven," Grald said. "I need his body whole and strong."

"The only one hurt will be Draconas," Anora said softly.

She began to creep up on him as he stood, unsuspecting, staring out the door. He was in his human form, holding the spear he'd fashioned in his hand. Across the street, Anora could hear the voices of the human males raised in argument, probably squabbling over the human female. Ideal cover, for they were proving a distraction to Draconas, who looked in that direction and frowned.

"Strike now!" Grald ordered suddenly. "Strike him from behind, before he knows what's hit him!"

Concentrating on Draconas, Anora had unwittingly left her mental processes open to Grald. She slammed shut the door to her thoughts and refused to answer him. He couldn't understand her strategy anyway.

It is difficult to take a dragon by surprise.

While a dragon is conscious, he can easily defend himself. Dragons must sleep, however, and when they sleep, they sleep deeply—for years at a time. There was the chance that another dragon or some enterprising human might slay the slumbering dragon. Thus, over the centuries, dragons had developed a means of self-protection. The moment Anora launched a weapon at Draconas—magical or otherwise—his dragon being would act to take defensive measures and fight back. Her plan was to reveal herself to him, let him see that the human he'd known all these years as the holy sister, was, in truth, the Head of Parliament, a venerable dragon he had long respected and trusted. She calculated that the shock of seeing her, of knowing—at the last moment—that she was going to be his doom, would suck all the fight out of him, leave him breathless, winded, amazed. Then dead.

She was quite close to Draconas now.

He was preoccupied, tense for the kill. He didn't hear a sound, didn't sense her presence.

"Draconas," said Anora gently, in her human voice.

He jumped, startled, and looked over his shoulder.

"Get out of here, Sister," Draconas told her roughly. "This is none of your concern."

"Ah, but it is," said Anora.

In that moment, Draconas knew. She saw the knowledge in his eyes as she saw her own reflection, the shadow of the dragon, rising up behind the holy sister, extending its wings and its claws.

The colors of Draconas's mind came crashing down around him.

"I don't understand . . . ," he gasped.

"I know, Draconas," said Anora softly, and her colors were gray ash. "The pity is—you never will."

Lightning crackled from her jaws . . .

1

MARCUS EXTENDED HIS HAND, POINTED BEHIND HIMSELF
to the buildings that stood at the entrance to the alley. The
magic rolled out of him, rumbled through the earth. Stone
walls shook and trembled, and with a roar like an ava-
lanche, the two buildings collapsed. Marcus heard screams
and cries and guessed that at least some of his pursuers
had been caught in the cascade of rock and debris. He
dashed out into the alley, with Evelina at his side, and it
was then he felt the weakness.

It came over him suddenly, unexpectedly, a sensation
of being exhausted, drained of energy. He could not
catch his breath. His legs and arms and hands tingled. He
stumbled and nearly fell.

Evelina caught hold of him.

"What's the matter? Are you hurt?"

He couldn't answer. He had to use his breath for
breathing. Talking required more strength than he had,
and he couldn't explain to her what was happening anyway. Nothing is free in this world. Everything has a price,
including the magic.

Conjuring pixies from dust motes had been a little fa-
tiguing, but the magic had never before sent him to his bed.
Bringing down stone buildings and raising ice storms was
apparently different. He was so exhausted, he could
scarcely move.

Behind him, he could hear behind him the monks claw-ing their way through the rubble. He had to run or give up and die.

"Dearest Marcus, sweet love, we have to keep going!" Evelina was saying, her voice trembling with fear. *"Please. Just a little ways and we are there, my heart, my own."*

She tugged at him, pleaded with him. He nodded and continued on. But he could no longer run. It took all his resolve just to walk.

"It's not far now," she said, sliding her arm around him, supporting him.

He wearily raised his head to see that they had come farther than he'd hoped. The wall was directly ahead of them. They had only to cross a street and they would be standing in front of it. Fifty, a hundred steps.

And then what? He remembered entering Dragonkeep, remembered looking back at the wall through which he'd just passed and seeing no gate, no entrance, only solid stone. On and on the wall ran, without end. Around and around the city. No break. No way out. A dragon eating its own tail . . .

"Marcus!" Evelina cried sharply, frightened.

He jerked his head up, shook his head to clear it, kept moving, kept walking. He concentrated on picking up his feet and putting them down, picking them up, putting them down.

The wall came closer. Solid stone. Fused with fire.

Marcus called again, one last time. *"Draconas . . ."*

The name echoed in the darkness of his little room. Echoed back to him.

One by one, the echoes died.

The street that ran along the wall was empty. He'd ex-pected to find a river of brown robes. If the monks were coming, they had not yet arrived.

"Yet why should they hurry?" Marcus asked himself. *"I'm not going anywhere and neither is Evelina."*

He stood in front of the guard wall, staring at it, pour-ing his whole being into that stare, wishing it, willing it to give him some hint, some clue of the way out. He risked *leaving his little room, risked roaming up and down the length of the wall, as far as he could see, risked using his magic to search for a crack, a chink in the endless stone. He stared at the wall so long that the stones began to shift and glide and he wrenched his gaze away.*

He did not call to Draconas again.

Marcus reached out his hand, touched the wall, touched stone—solid and cold. He moved his hand to another part and then another, all the while telling himself that this was stupid, futile, a last desperate attempt to stave off the inevitable.

"Marcus . . ." said Evelina urgently. "The monks . . ."

He saw them rounding the corner of the building, walking straight for him. Some held fire in their hands. Some held steel. All of it was death, so it didn't much matter.

"Tell me the truth, Marcus," said Evelina quietly. "There's no way out, is there?"

"No," he said. "There's not. I had hoped . . ." He let hope hang, shook his head.

"I'm afraid," she said and put her arms around him.

"So am I," he said, and held her close.

A hand thrust through the stone wall.

Marcus stared at it. "I'm going mad," he thought. "Like the wretched monks."

He blinked his eyes. The hand vanished and Ven stood in front of him, inside the little room.

"This is the gate," said Ven.

His blue eyes were the only color in a vast expanse of white.

"The way out!" Evelina cried. "I see it! Marcus, look!" She clutched at him. "There it is! Right in front of us! Hurry! Make haste!"

The illusion was broken and, as always when we see the truth, he wondered that he had been so blind as not to penetrate the lie at once. The gate was crudely built, constructed of wood planks and held together by iron bands. The gate stood open. From the rusted look of the hinges, the gate had not been shut for centuries. Perhaps it had rusted in place.

Beyond the gate was the forest and beyond that the river. No monks blocked the way. No dragon stood at the entrance.

Marcus looked back to the little room.

"Take care of her," said Ven. He held out his hand.

Marcus touched his brother's hand.

The gate vanished, dissolved into the wall.

The wall vanished, dissolved into illusion.

Dragonkeep was gone, and it might have never existed, but for the feel of his brother's hand, firm and warm, in his own.

Marcus guided the boat he and Evelina had stolen out into the river. Evelina sat rigid and upright in the stern opposite him, holding on to the gunwales with both hands. Her face was drawn and tense. She stared fearfully into the woods that were slowly, too slowly, sliding away. When the boat dipped slightly, as Marcus wrestled with the oars, Evelina grasped the gunwales tightly.

"Sorry," said Marcus. "I haven't rowed a boat in a long time."

"I thought I saw something!" she gasped. "Oh." She relaxed. "A deer." Evelina looked at him and managed a smile. "I'm glad you're with me. You won't let anything happen to me."

Marcus smiled back at her, trying to be reassuring, but he didn't make any promises. The shoreline was receding, though not as rapidly as he would have wished. Marcus expected to see the monks come swarming out of the forest to give chase. They would have a difficult time of it. After Evelina had plundered the boats for anything useful, Marcus had pushed each boat, one by one, out into the river, where the current caught them and carried them downstream.

He would have liked to have destroyed the boats, perhaps set them ablaze, but he lacked the strength to use any more magic. He had tried staving in the bottom of one of the boats by kicking it with his foot, but the planks were too strong and wouldn't give way. The current was slow here. The boats bobbed in the water, meandering lazily downstream. Any energetic monk could plunge in and recover them.

Marcus waited for that to happen, but no monk—energetic or otherwise—appeared.

The boat tent carrying him and Evelina rounded a bend in the river and he lost sight of the shoreline and the bobbing boats. The river was narrow at this point, the shore lined with trees, whose overhanging boughs, thickly intertwined, cut off the bright sun and made it seem as if he were rowing into a green and leafy cavern. Sparse patches of sunlight slid over his knees. The sun was directly overhead. Midday. Only noon. Presumably noon of the same day.

So much had happened, it seemed as if it should be noon of some day next year.

"I don't like this." Evelina hugged herself. "It's like a cave. Anyone could be hiding in those trees." An alarming thought occurred to her. "Speaking of caves, we're not going back there, are we, Your Highness? Back to that horrible cave beneath the water? This is the way. I remember it. I don't want to go back there. We should turn around. Travel downstream."

The sunken cave. Marcus remembered gliding through it silently, careful not to make a sound, lest Grald and the monks should hear him and Bellona. He didn't much like the idea of going back through that cave himself.

Perhaps that's why the monks didn't follow us to the shore. Perhaps they're waiting for me there. Maybe I should turn around and travel downriver, as Evelina says.

Marcus kept rowing upriver, pulling steadily for the sunken cavern.

"They're not chasing us, are they, Your Highness?" Evelina asked, peering over her shoulder. "They'd be here by now, don't you think?"

"Yes," Marcus replied. No use frightening her with his dark conjectures. "You must call me Marcus." He smiled at her. "We've been through too much for formalities."

Evelina flushed with pleasure. "Marcus—I like that. And you will call me 'Evelina.'" She sighed and let go of the gunwale. Wrapping her hands around her knees, she leaned forward and turned her attention to him. "You look tired."

"I'm all right," Marcus said. He was tired, although he'd recovered his strength somewhat after exhaustion had nearly overwhelmed him at the wall. He guessed that the exhaustion had been partly due to despair—a despair that had lifted from him when he'd felt the touch of his brother's hand.

Marcus didn't understand anything that had happened. He didn't understand why Ven had helped him escape the dragon after betraying him to the dragon. He didn't understand how Ven even came to be alive. The last he'd seen of his brother, Ven was lying in a pool of blood, a knife wound in his chest.

I don't need to understand. Not now. Now I have to concentrate on only one thing.

"You'd find the rowing to be easier, traveling downstream," Evelina pointed out for the third time.

Marcus shook his head. "Easier, but the wrong way."

"Where are we going then?"

"Home," said Marcus. His objective. His only objective.

"Your home?" asked Evelina, and she sounded troubled.

"My home."

His home, his kingdom of Idylswylde. That was why he was risking the monks in the sunken cavern. He might even find the dragon there, for that was where he had first seen Grald, the hulking human form the dragon had appropriated. Marcus was ready to risk even that to return to his home.

He could not explain this longing, but the memory came to him of another time, a time he had been away from his home for months, trapped in a world of insanity from which Draconas had saved him. When the little boy, Marcus, had seen the towers of his father's castle shining in the sunlight, he had felt the ache of longing in his heart swell so that the towers were drowned in his tears. The man, Marcus, remembered and wanted to see those sunlit towers again.

"Watch it!" Evelina cried.

Marcus jerked his head around, saw that he was steer-

ing them perilously close to a tangle of grass and dead
tree branches. He gave the oars a twitch and they cleared
the hazard, though with only inches to spare.

"You're so very tired," said Evelina. She reached out
her hand to him, bending forward still more. Her chemise
slipped a little, revealing an enticing expanse of curves
and shadows. "You would not even need to row if we
went downstream. The river would carry us—"

"I told you back at the landing, Evelina," said Marcus,
and his tone, though gentle, left no room for argument. "I
have to go home."

Seated opposite Marcus in the boat, Evelina pouted. She
was accustomed to having her own way.

"At least you have a home," she returned, sitting up
straight. By leaning forward, she had just provided him
with an enticing view of her breasts, and it all been for
nothing. He'd barely glanced at her. Therefore, she would
punish him. "Your brother took my home away from me."

This jab, meant to wound him with guilt, missed its
mark. At the mention of his brother's name, Marcus's
gaze went from Evelina's face to her blood-spattered
clothes. His eyes darkened. His lips compressed. He
looked out at the trees and continued to row.

Evelina's cheeks burned. So that was it. The blood was
Ven's, the prince's monstrous half-brother. And she'd
been the one to draw that blood. The last she'd seen of
Ven, he was lying on the floor dying, or so she hoped. She
had saved their lives. Marcus had told her that. He'd been
grateful. Now he couldn't look at her.

"What's the matter, Marcus?" Evelina demanded. She
clutched at the blood-stained bodice and tried, ineffectu-
ally, to rearrange it so that the brownish red spots did not
show. "Why do you look at me like that?"

Marcus flushed. "Like what?" He tried to sound innocent and thereby clinched his guilt.

"Like I was something ugly and disgusting that you'd
like to squash beneath your boot. You said you understood why I stabbed that beast of a brother, and now you
hate me!"

Evelina burst into tears that were not feigned—at least not much. She buried her head in her arms and sobbed stormily, lifting her head once to cry, "Your brother tried to rape me! He admitted it! And he killed my father!" Then she gave herself up to the luxury of hysterics. She felt she'd earned it.

As she wept, Evelina expected confidently that Marcus would stop rowing the boat, take her in his arms, and comfort her. He didn't. He continued to row. Admittedly, they were fleeing mad monks and a dragon, but still Evelina felt slighted. Another man—a true man—would have thrown caution to the winds in order to soothe her and pet her and try to steal a kiss or slip his hand down her chemise.

Marcus just kept rowing.

Evelina was at a loss. Hysterics were wearing, and she couldn't keep this up forever. The prince obviously wasn't going to be of any help to her. She'd have to recover on her own. She let her sobs quiet and risked a furtive glance from under her tear-soaked arms to see how he was taking it.

He was rowing steadily, his eyes fixed on her. He looked uncomfortable. Maybe he was just shy, unused to women.

I wonder how long it will take to reach this home of his? Days, maybe. Days and nights.

Nights. Alone. Together. Evelina's pulse quickened and her breath came fast at the thought. She would have to be careful with her seduction of her prince, for he believed her to be a maiden pure, as well as a maiden fair. He must be made to think that he was the one who had seduced her. Evelina's dream—dreamt from the moment she'd first met him this very morning—was to be Her Royal Highness, Princess Evelina, wife of His Royal Highness, Prince Marcus.

She knew that marriage was long odds, however. The royal mistress. She would settle for that.

Evelina had already discounted the idea of trying to convince Marcus that she was a baron's daughter, kidnapped by Ven, who carried her, fainting, from her father's castle. She was pragmatic enough to know that she could never pass for noble-born. She could neither read nor write. She could not embroider or play the lute. Her hands were not the smooth, fair hands of one who has never had to dress herself, never had to wash her own hair or scrub out her own chamber pot. Princes married farmers' daughters only in the minstrels' tales. In real life, the princes took the farmers' daughters to be their mistresses. They set them up in fine houses in the city and gave them jewels and clothes and educated their bastard sons and made them abbots.

Evelina resolved to have the house, the jewels, the bastard son. Maybe not in that order. House and jewels often came as a result of the bastard son. Her primary goal in all this was, therefore, to get herself seduced. That was the reason she'd been urging him to travel downstream, away from his home. The more time she spent with him, the better. He would not go downstream, so she would have to act fast.

Her sobs calmed to hiccups and she timidly raised her head. Her tears made her eyes shimmer, even if the lids were red. The boat slid along the surface of the sun-dappled water.

"Marcus," Evelina said, her voice quavering. "I know I am not like the well-born, accomplished women you are used to being around. My father was a merchant in the city of Fairefield. Dear man. He was respectable, kind, and gentle. Just not very practical. My mother died when I was little, and father and I were everything to each other. I'm sorry I stabbed your brother. I'm a good person. I really am. Father and I went to church every week. It's just . . . when I saw Ven . . . I saw my poor father's body, all crumpled and twisted . . ."

"Don't cry, Evelina. I understand," said Marcus. "You will have a home to go to. My home. You saved my life. My parents will welcome you for that."

Again, that cool polite tone. He looked away, searching the bank for any signs of pursuit. Evelina glowered at him, annoyed.

"I don't want your parents to welcome me for saving your life," she told him beneath her breath. "I want them to welcome me as the mother of their first grandson. And whether they do that with open arms or cold shoulders doesn't really matter. I'll have you, my love, and I'll have your baby, and there won't be a damn thing your parents can do about either."

The thought cheered her. She had plenty of time to coax him into loving her. She had never failed yet, with any man.

"Thank you, Your Highness," Evelina said softly. "I mean . . . Marcus."

Sunlight flickered through the over-arching boughs, forming ripples of gold that shone in Evelina's hair. She was dabbing her eyes with cold water. She had the loveliest face Marcus had ever seen. His gaze went from her face to the splotches of blood on her bodice and on her skirt and her chemise and the white skin of her neck. The splotches had been fresh not many hours before. They had since smeared and dried to an ugly reddish brown. Blood spots. Ven's blood.

Evelina hadn't killed him, though she had meant to. Of that Marcus had no doubt. Despite that, Ven had risked the dragon's ire to free them. He had urged Marcus to take care of her. Maybe he had acted out of guilt. He had admitted to Marcus that he'd tried to rape Evelina. Without Ven, they would be both dead now, or at least back in the clutches of Grald.

Marcus wondered how he felt about Evelina. He thought perhaps he loved her. He remembered with aching clarity the sight of her shapely legs when she'd kilted her skirts to flee the monks. As he looked at her now, seated across from him, sometimes he saw his brother's blood and other times he saw the shadow that fell enticingly between her full breasts.

Evelina looked at him as no other woman had ever before looked at him—adoring, loving, admiring. Evelina had seen him work his magic and she had not been shocked or terrified. And she had seen him work far more powerful magicks than changing dust motes into fairies. He imagined his lips touching her soft lips, his hand cupping her soft and heavy breasts, and he was filled with such burning desire that he had to firmly banish such thoughts in order to keep his mind on their peril.

Yet . . . yet . . . even as he kissed her lips in his imaginings, he saw those lips twist into a snarl of fury. He saw the hand that caressed him drive the knife into his brother's body. He saw the blood splatter onto her clothes and he saw her yank the knife free and try to stab Ven again . . .

Marcus came to a sudden, stark understanding. There was something secret and unspoken between Ven and Evelina, a truth that neither of them had shared with him. He'd heard her side of the story. He wanted, very much, to hear Ven's. His brother had tried to tell him. Marcus had jumped to conclusions and rebuffed him.

And now it was too late. Whatever had happened, Evelina wouldn't tell him and Ven couldn't, at least not now. Perhaps, in time, Marcus would be able to contact his brother, speak mind-to-mind, touch hand-to-hand, as they had done when they were little. Now he didn't dare go into the room inside his mind, the room where he could eavesdrop on dragons' thoughts and dreams. The room where he had first met his brother long, long ago.

The dragon was waiting for him in that little room.

And probably in the cavern, as well.

"I told you," Evelina was saying sharply, "I don't want to end up in that horrible cave."

Marcus gave a start. She had plucked the thoughts out of his head and spoken them aloud. "I saw him there, that man they called Grald. I didn't like the way he looked at me. Please turn around, Marcus! Go the other way! I don't want him to find me."

"I don't think that Grald will be in the cave. That explosion we heard—"

"You don't know for certain he won't be there," Evelina pointed out, and her lower lip quivered. "If we traveled south, we could spend a few days resting at a fine inn . . ."

"We're not going south."

Marcus smiled at her, to take the sting out of his refusal, and shook his head, and kept rowing, though he was aching and hurting and almost sick with fatigue.

And there it was—the argument come around to where it began. Evelina heaved a disappointed sigh, loud enough for him to hear.

If he did, he didn't let on, and Evelina ground her teeth in frustration. She needed to hide her ire from him, however, and so she bent over the side of the boat and cupped her hand for a drink of water. She caught a glimpse of her reflection. Evelina drew back, horrified. She looked a fright!

Her hair was tangled and matted with bits of twigs and leaves. Her face was covered with dirt and streaked with tears. Her nose had swelled and her eyes were red as a rat's.

"No wonder he won't have anything to do with me," she said to herself, appalled.

Not to mention those accursed red-brown splotches on her bodice and her skirt.

She couldn't do anything about her appearance now. When they stopped for the night, she'd take a bath (modestly provocative) and she would scrub those horrid spots out of her chemise and her skirt.

Which would leave her clothes sopping wet. She couldn't put them back on. She might catch her death of cold.

Which meant that she and Marcus couldn't very well continue their journey.

Not with her having nothing whatsoever to wear . . .

2

STANDING WAIST DEEP IN THE WATER, WATCHING THE boat carrying Bellona's body drift downstream, Ven turned to wade back to shore. Glancing down, he saw a thin trail of blood snaking out into the water and meandering downstream. The stab wound had reopened.

Evelina had struck in haste. The knife had glanced off bone, avoiding any organs. He'd lost a lot of blood, however, and he'd lost more blood when he'd slipped out of the city of Dragonkeep to pay his last respects to the woman who had raised him and, in her own strange way, loved him. His dragon-blood had acted promptly to start the healing process, and the wound had already partially closed. He must have torn it open during his strenuous exertions—carrying Bellona's body to the river, placing it in a boat, and casting the boat adrift, freeing her spirit to join the spirit of her life's love, Melisande— Ven's mother.

The chill of the water had kept him from noticing. The dragon-magic seemed slower to heal the wound this time. Perhaps the magical power inside him was growing weaker as he grew weaker. He needed to return to Dragonkeep quickly, before he collapsed. It would never do for him to be found outside the city walls.

Emerging from the water onto the slippery bank, he dug his claws into the mud to keep his footing and it was then he saw the footprints. Two sets, fresh: one set small, made by slippered feet; the other larger, wearing boots. He couldn't spare the time to investigate—every moment he was away was a moment his absence might be discovered. Yet, he could not help but follow the footprints with his tracker's eye to try to deduce where they had gone, the two he was risking his life to save—his half-brother, Marcus, and Evelina, the young woman who had stabbed him.

Marcus had been back and forth to the water's edge several times, dragging heavy objects along with him. Ven recalled the boats used by the monks stacked on the shore. There were none there now. He could picture Marcus dragging down one boat after another, shoving each out into the river to float away downstream. Marcus would, of course, have kept one of the boats for himself and Evelina.

Ven looked back at the river, at the bright noon sun glittering on the water. He could imagine the two of them in the boat, Marcus rowing, fearful of pursuit. Evelina sitting in the stern, gazing at Marcus with adoration.

Ven had seen the light of love burst into flame the first moment Evelina had set her blue eyes on Marcus. Well, maybe not love's light. Knowing Evelina, it was most likely the light gleaming off Prince Marcus's golden crown.

Ven pressed his hand over the wound to try to stop the bleeding.

That's why she stabbed me, he reflected. *She was afraid I would tell Marcus the truth about her, that she was not the poor, mistreated victim of my brutal advances. That she deliberately seduced me in order to trap me. That she sold me to a traveling circus to be exhibited to the gaping wonder of the crowd.*

She believes me to be dead—I made sure of that. Evelina will be sitting pretty now, thinking she's safe and secure, able to snare Marcus in her web, bind him with her silken lies and sting him with the poison of her lips, paralyzing him into stillness so that she can suck him dry.

Maybe. Maybe not.

Ven wondered if Marcus had told her that he'd communicated with his brother, that Ven was alive.

In his brother's place, Ven would not have said anything to Evelina, and he doubted that Marcus would. Both brothers had learned at an early age to keep secrets. The truth was dangerous, might be disastrous, bringing peril to themselves and those they loved. Marcus would be slow to trust, reticent about speaking his thoughts aloud, naturally cautious and reserved.

He would also be extremely confused. Ven could not help but grin wryly. It served Marcus right. He had been very quick to believe Evelina's accusation that Ven was a vicious, murdering monster. How astonished Marcus must have been when the murdering monster saved their lives.

I could tell Marcus my side of the story, Ven considered, as he gazed up river. *Marcus might even believe me.*

Ven mulled it over and decided not to. He wasn't sure exactly why. Guilt was some of it. Evelina had not entirely lied. He had meant to take her that night in the tall grass and he would have, if she had not managed to fend him off and wriggle out from beneath him. And he *was* responsible for the death of her father. She had not made that up. Ven had not killed Ramone with his own hand— the monks had done that. But they had murdered him because of Ven.

Part of his decision not to tell was vindication. Ven felt a certain satisfaction in thinking that the brother who had grown up pampered and happy and loved should fall victim to a mercenary little vixen. Ven expected this feeling to be stronger. Instead, it was uncomfortable. Ven couldn't say that he loved Marcus, but he liked his brother, and that was unexpected. Ven had looked forward to hating Marcus, who'd been given everything in life, while Ven had been given the back of life's hand. Instead, Ven found someone who understood, someone who shared his pain.

And, after all, maybe his not telling Marcus came down to the simple fact that Ven disliked interfering.

He'd said what he'd needed to say to Marcus and to Evelina. Let the two of them sort out their lives. He had his own problems.

He was thinking all this as he stood on the bank, staring at the water, when his thoughts were jolted back to earth. Voices, heading this direction.

Grald must have finally lifted the illusion that hid the city gates of Dragonkeep from the world outside. The monks were coming, somewhat late, to chase after Marcus. This meant that Grald knew Marcus had escaped. Did the dragon know *how*?

"Perhaps the monks aren't after Marcus," Ven said to himself in alarm. "Perhaps they are after me."

Ven had to retain Grald's trust. The only way to slay the dragon was to take him by surprise, catch him off guard. Grald mustn't suspect that Ven had anything to do with Marcus's escape.

Ven had been careless—that's what came of giving way to emotion. Prints of his clawed feet were everywhere, leading in and out of the water. He cursed himself for not having the foresight to cover his tracks—Bellona would have made him stand in the corner for a week in punishment. Hastily, he raked his claws over the telltale signs, rubbing out the traces that he'd been here.

He didn't have much time. The voices were growing louder, and he could hear the monks bumbling through the woods. He ran lightly and easily on his clawed feet into the trees, jumping from one grassy hillock to another, making certain that he left no more tracks.

Once safely hidden in the wilderness, he paused to consider his next move. His first thought was to race back to the city, but then the idea came to him that he might learn the answers to his questions by spying on the monks. He crouched among the foliage and waited.

Blood trickled down his side, tickling him. His wound was still bleeding. He pressed his hand over it and willed it to stop.

Three monks in their ankle-length brown robes came blundering out of the forest. They were hot and sweaty and scared, and they peered and poked about. Their eyes,

with that strange half-mad glint, went from ground to water and even sky, as if somewhere in their confused brains
they imagined that their prey might have grown wings
and taken flight.

"They're not here," said one, bewildered.

"What did you expect?" another asked. He seemed
more sane than the rest. His searching had been more me-
thodical. He'd stared a long time at the footprints. "That
they'd wait around for you?"

"I don't know. Maybe." The other two continued to
search, not with hope of finding anything, but because
they didn't know what else to do.

"The boats are gone," one pointed out.

"They used the boat to escape," said the lucid monk.

"But *all* the boats are gone," the first reiterated.

"They set the rest adrift."

"Ah!" The monk seemed to consider this an act of genius, for he stared, wide-eyed, at the sluggishly flowing
water. "I'll go find them."

He plunged into the river, splashing and floundering,
his arms flailing. The lucid monk, shaking his head,
waded in to grab hold of his companion and drag him
back to land.

"What do you think you're doing?" the monk asked
sternly. "You can't swim. You'll only end up drowning
yourself."

The monk shook free. He cast a look back at the
water—a look that was bleak and wistful—and then he
turned away. Ven shivered in the cool shadows and was
sorry he'd stayed.

"What do we do?" asked the sopping wet monk plain-
tively. "We can't go after them. We have no boats."

"We go back to Dragonkeep."

"What do we tell Grald?" The monk sounded nervous.

"That we couldn't find them. And that there were no
boats."

"Grald will be angry."

"Grald is always angry," said the leader, and he
shrugged.

The three did not leave immediately, however, as Ven

had hoped. The leader stared intently up the river, as though he were reaching out, searching with his mind. The other two continued to poke about in a desultory manner.

Ven cursed them silently and willed them to depart. The mysterious explosion had thrown the city into confusion and turmoil, but he was afraid that now his absence would be noticed. He was just thinking he would have to risk slipping off into wilderness, when the lead monk announced that they should be returning.

"Grald will be eager for our report."

"He didn't seem eager," one of the monks muttered. "Otherwise he would have opened the gate when we first reported that the two escaped."

"Grald has his reasons."

The monk who had jumped into the river spoke up. "I heard that the dragon did not open the gate because he feared that the man we've been told to find—the one Grald calls 'Draconas'—would be lost to him."

Ven's ears pricked. He wanted to hear more. Unfortunately, the monks now began walking back toward the city. Ven cursed them a second time. His dragon-blood gave him the ability to hear better than humans, and he stretched his ears to the limit.

"Grald finally did open the gate," another monk argued. "So this Draconas must have been caught."

"He wasn't," said the leader. "We have been told to keep searching for this man. Either for him or for his corpse. It seems that it was this Draconas who caused the terrible blast. They still don't know how many are dead."

"Why would he do that?" The monk sounded shocked.

"Because he is our enemy. Sent to destroy us."

"Who sent him?" The other two monks were eager listeners now, avid for news.

"The human king who has long been a threat to us. Edward, the king of a nation known as Idylswylde. You mark my words. This means war."

War against Idylswylde. War against Marcus and his father. Ven tried to picture an army of mad monks, and it was so ludicrous that he snorted in derision.

He was much more interested in finding out what had happened to Draconas.

Ven remembered the horrific blast. It had reduced the house in which he and Marcus and Evelina had been to rubble and allowed Marcus and Evelina to escape. Draconas had caused the blast and Grald was hunting for him. Which meant Draconas must still be alive.

Once the monks were well out of earshot, Ven made his way back to the city, hoping to reach it before anyone noticed that he'd been gone.

3

ANORA FOUGHT THROUGH A MIASMA OF BLACK ANGER and Grald's raging mixed with her own pain and blank confusion. She was flat on the floor, lying amidst a heap of cracked stones and splintered, smoldering timbers. Clouds of dust and smoke obscured her vision. She coughed and shook her head to clear it of the throbbing and Grald's yammering.

"What have you done?" He was howling, furious. His colors reverberated inside her aching skull. "You have destroyed half the city and nearly killed me in the process! And my son? What has become of my son?"

Anora ignored him. She tried to remember. Draconas! What had become of Draconas? She leapt to her feet and glanced swiftly about the wreckage of the building. His body must be here somewhere. He could not have escaped her. He should be dead—human bones and flesh burned beyond recognition.

A walker had never yet died while in human form, but the dragons had prepared for that eventuality. The illusion of the human body remained even in death. Otherwise, humans might come to know that dragons were spying on them. The dragons would recover the corpse in secret and then use spells to lift the illusion, so that the dead could be laid to rest in the bottom of the sea, the traditional dragon burial site, where all life began and to which all life must eventually return.

What with Grald yelling at her and shrieking humans swarming about the place and her head throbbing, Anora found it difficult to concentrate. She grit her teeth and shut them all out. Draconas was not here and he must be here.

Her illusory body possessed dragon strength, and the humans watching were amazed to see the pudgy holy sister lifting up enormous boulders and flinging them aside, heaving huge timbers out of her way, kicking and clawing at the rubble. They assumed she was searching for survivors, and they regarded her with awe and admiration.

"Shut up," she finally ordered Grald. "Where are you? I need your help!"

"Then you shouldn't have dropped a goddam building on top of me!" returned Grald, who tended to use regrettable human expressions even in his dragon thinking. "It's a good thing this human body has a thick skull, otherwise . . ." He paused, seething, then roared, "What the hell happened? You were supposed to kill Draconas, not level my city!"

Anora was silent, her colors smoldering.

"What?" Grald thundered. "Isn't he dead?"

"He must be," Anora returned coldly. "It's just . . . I can't seem to find his body."

"Perhaps it was blown to bits," Grald suggested.

"If that were the case, there would be blood, bone, hunks of flesh. There is nothing. You must help me search for him."

"I would like to," Grald stated caustically. "But at the moment I am buried under a half-ton of rubble. My magic protected me from harm, but I can't free myself. The monks are digging me out, but it's going to take some time. What about my son? What happened to Ven? The monks can't find him and neither can I."

"Ven was always adept at keeping his mind hidden from us." Anora stood in the middle of the debris, angry and frustrated. "What about his brother? The human prince? He should be easy enough to locate, and if you have one, you have the other."

"Not necessarily," said Grald. "The human managed to escape."

"He escaped the explosion?"

"The city." Now it was Grald who was on the defensive.

"How is that possible?" Anora demanded in disbelief. "The human is strong in dragon-magic, but not strong enough to penetrate the illusion of the wall. Only another dragon could do that . . ." Her voice trailed off.

"So Draconas *did* escape you," said Grald grimly. "You destroy half my city for nothing."

"I did not destroy the city," Anora returned crossly. Looking around the ruin in which she was standing, she was starting to realize what must have happened. "Draconas cast a counter-spell that caused his magic to clash with mine. It's a wonder any of us survived. You must order your monks to search for the Walker," she added, her colors sullen. "I believe he is alive after all."

"Told you so!" Grald sneered.

The monks were ordered to search for two humans: the Walker, who wore the guise of a human male in his thirties, and a human male named Marcus last seen wearing the robes of a monk. The monks were also told to look for Ven, the dragon's son, whom they all knew by sight. Unfortunately, their search for both humans and the dragon disguised as a human was hampered by the fact that the entire population of Dragonkeep had been thrown into a state of panic by the blast.

With the maddening perversity of humans, people rushed to the site of the blast instead of fleeing it, which, as Anora told Grald, any creature with common sense would have done. Before the dust had settled, humans clogged the streets and clambered over the ruins, screeching and yelling, wailing and weeping, groaning and bleeding, and none of them staying in one place, but all of them milling about in confusion.

Anora continued her search, though without much hope, for she was convinced that it must have been Draconas who had helped Marcus escape. Humans were everywhere underfoot. They scrabbled frantically through the wreckage, calling for those who would never answer. A middle-aged man hurried past carrying the bloody, broken body of a child. A young woman crouched, moaning, over the corpse of a young man as another woman was trying unsuccessfully to soothe her. The dragon paid scant attention to any of this.

There were so many humans in this world, their lives so short and fleeting, that the loss of a few dozen was no great cause for concern, especially when the future of both mankind and dragonkind was at stake.

Slowly, as the reports of the monks began to come in, Grald and Anora were able to piece together parts of the puzzle.

The monks entered the building where Ven and Marcus and the girl, Evelina, had last been seen. No one was there, although the monks did report finding a large pool of blood on the floor. They did not know whose blood. There was no body. A hole blown out the back of the building gave the monks some idea of how those inside had escaped.

Armed with dragon-magic, the monks continued their search for Marcus and Ven. Marcus could not have left Dragonkeep, for the wall surrounding the city was designed so that no human—even one possessing the dragon-magic—could find his way through the hidden gate.

Except that was exactly what happened, or so his monks reported back to Grald. Marcus had been cornered, trapped like the proverbial rat with his back against the wall. Exhausted and wounded, he could not even put up much of a fight. The human female with him had no magic and was no threat. Suddenly, without warning, Marcus walked straight through the solid rock wall and he took the girl with him.

The monks were baffled. Grald was not.

"This proves it. Draconas is responsible," he said accusingly to Anora. "You bungled the job."

Disguised in their respective human forms—Grald in the body of a large, hulking human male, and Anora in the body of a holy sister—the two dragons surveyed the midst of the ruins left by the horrific blast that had wiped out an entire city block.

"Then why haven't we seen his colors?" Anora demanded, frustrated and baffled. "If his mind is alive and active and reaching out to help Melisande's son, we would know it, for we have been watching for him. He could not hide from us."

"Someone reached out to aid Melisande's son," Grald muttered, kicking at a chunk of stone and sending it rolling. "Someone opened the gate for him. The prince could not do that by himself."

"What about your son? Ven?"

"What about him?" Grald growled.

"He was with his brother and that female. He could have opened the gate and helped them escape."

Grald snorted. "Ven hates his brother, and why not? His brother is handsome, rich, educated, and has two human legs, not two dragon ones. And Ven lusts after the girl who was with Marcus. Ven would not have permitted her to flee, especially in the company of a brother he detests. Besides, the monks theorize that Ven was injured. They think the blood was his. And, his mind remains closed to me."

"He is cagey, that one. Because he has not used the dragon-magic, his mind has no colors, like a barren field blanketed in heavy snow. Except the field is not as barren as we suppose. He has learned how to mask his thoughts from us. Where is he now? Do you know? If he's wounded, he couldn't have gone far."

"My monks continue to search for him."

"By my wings and tail, we seem to have lost everyone this morning!" Anora ground her teeth in frustration. "If you had struck Draconas from behind, slain him immediately, as I suggested, then we would not be in this mess. You had to treat yourself to your little fillip of victory. Let him know who you were—"

"Do not tell me how to fight my battles!" Anora snarled, rounding on Grald. "You have lived in that stolen body so long you do not remember what it is like to live in a body such as that inhabited by Draconas, a body created by a supreme illusion."

"And I say that you have not fought another dragon in

so long that you do not remember what it is to do battle with one," Grald returned, although in subdued tones. He could see the shadow of the elder dragon looming over him. "Draconas did with you what he did with me when I fought him—he cast a defensive spell that threw your magic back on itself, and then he turned tail and ran."

"He had seconds only," argued Anora. "He could not have gone far."

"He apparently went far enough to help the son of Melisande escape through the magical gate," Grald retorted.

"Enough of this bantering," Anora said, suddenly weary. "We go round and round, like a fledgling chasing its tail, and we get nowhere. Here comes one of your mad monks. Perhaps he has something to report."

The monk bowed obsequiously.

"Honored One—" the monk began.

"Yes, yes," Grald interrupted impatiently. "Get on with it. What have you to report?"

"Honored One," the monk continued, cringing, "your son has been found."

"Ven? Where?" Grald demanded, tense, alert.

"In the Abbey, Honored One. He made it that far before he collapsed."

"Collapsed?" Grald repeated. "Out with it, you ninny! What is wrong with him? Is he hurt?"

"He was stabbed, Honored One," replied the monk in grave tones. "We found him lying on the floor of his room in a pool of blood. We do not know if he will survive."

Grald cast a triumphant glance at Anora. "That rules out Ven having anything to do with Marcus's flight!"

Anora cast him a withering glance. "I should think you would be much more concerned about the fact that this precious body of yours is bleeding to death."

The dire reminder had the desired effect. Grald hastened off in alarm, leaving Anora alone. Once he was gone, she spoke to the third dragon of their triumvirate, Maristara, the dragon of Seth, who had started it all.

"I have to face facts," Anora said reluctantly. She hated admitting to her mistakes. "Draconas has escaped me."

"You know what he will do," Maristara returned. "He will summon the Parliament and he will tell them everything. He will tell them about Dragonkeep, about the children. He will tell them about you, Anora, and how you have betrayed them."

"I'm not betraying them," Anora retorted. "I'm trying to save them! If they could only see that!"

"Now is the time for them to see. Pull the viper's fangs."

Anora pondered, thoughtful. "You're right. Once they know the truth, have seen what we have seen—"

"—then Draconas is no longer a concern."

"And while Parliament is in an uproar, ranting and raving and flapping their wings—"

"—we will prepare to strike. And once the first human kingdom is conquered and held firmly under our claws, our people will come to see that we are right. That our way is the only way."

"And what of Draconas?" Anora still wasn't convinced.

"It would be a shame if he were to fly into the side of a mountain and break his neck . . ." replied Maristara.

4

ANORA SHOULD HAVE BEEN PAYING MORE ATTENTION TO the despised humans. She would have found Draconas. He was carried out of the ruins right under her nose and she never noticed.

Anora made the mistake of searching for Draconas in the human form he was most fond of adopting—that of a human male of undetermined years, strong and lean, with long black hair and dark eyes. It never occurred to either her or Grald that, as Draconas saw death crackling before him, he would use his last fleeing seconds to do two things: first, as Anora had postulated, Draconas cast a defensive spell that acted as a shield, causing Anora's magic to bounce off him like a thrown spear bounces off steel. Second, as the lightning flared and sizzled around him, Draconas shifted form, choosing an illusion that he had found to be useful to him in the past.

He had just managed to take on this form when the power of Anora's magic clashed with Draconas's magic, erupting in a blast that destroyed the building and brought it down on top of both of them.

Anton Hammerfall and his wife, Rosa, were workers in the city of Dragonkeep. As his name implied, Anton was a blacksmith. His wife Rosa worked as a weaver. Despite the fact that they lived in the city that had been founded as a haven for children with dragon-magic in them, Anton had nary a drop. His was the third generation to grow up in Dragonkeep, and if the men in his family had ever had the magic, it had long since dwindled out of them. Anton gave secret thanks daily that such was the case. He felt nothing but pity for those wretched monks whose blood burned with the magical fire that drove them insane.

Rosa had some dragon-magic in her, as did all the women of Dragonkeep, though not enough to make her valuable to the dragon, and thus she was a lowly weaver and not one of the holy sisters. The blood bane, as the magic was known, was not so bad in women as in men. It did not drive them insane. And thus Anton and Rosa had been proud to discover that their only daughter, Magda, was strong in the dragon-magic. She had been summoned by the dragon to live in his palace, and though they missed her, they were pleased for her.

Anton and Rosa resided in a small, one-room house in the city of Dragonkeep, not far from the site of the terrifying blast that had shaken the ground and knocked all the crockery off the shelves. The time was early morning. Anton had just fired up the forge when the blast hit. He had joined his neighbors in running to the scene, and he had proven to be invaluable in the search for survivors, for his strong smith's arms were needed to lift the fallen stones and move heavy wooden beams. Rosa had gone with her husband, bringing with her bolts of new-made woolen cloth to be used as bandages for the living and shrouds for the dead.

Both Rosa and Anton worked throughout the morning and into the late afternoon, doing what they could to help. There had been a great deal of confusion at first, as the people of Dragonkeep flocked to the site, either to help or to gawk or to conduct frantic searches for friends and relatives. Anton gave the Blessed credit for swiftly restoring order. The Blessed (as the monks were known) served as the dragon's eyes and ears and enforcers of the law. This, and the fact that some of the Blessed were quite mad, caused the ordinary, "unblessed" citizens of Dragonkeep to go in healthy fear of the monks and to be quick to obey their commands.

The Blessed ordered the majority of the citizens home, keeping only those who had proven to be useful. Anton and Rosa were among these, comforting, bandaging, lifting and hauling, rejoicing when survivors were discovered, grieving when they came upon bodies of the dead. By sundown, both were exhausted. The Blessed concluded that there was not much more to be done, especially now that night was falling. Rosa went home to "have a good cry," as she said, and to give thanks to the dragon that their dear daughter was safe from harm inside the palace beneath the mountain. One of the dead Rosa had so gently covered with a blanket had been a young woman near her daughter's age.

Anton was also weary; his arms and his back and his heart ached. He could not bring himself to leave, however, not when there was the chance of finding someone still alive. He continued to search through the rubble and the last gleam of failing sunlight gave him a reward—he saw a child's dusty hand protruding from beneath a pile of stones.

At first, Anton feared he'd found another corpse. He knelt down and touched the child's hand and, to his astonishment, found it warm, with a weak but steady pulse. Hope and elation burned away his weariness. Experience cautioned him not to immediately try to free the victim, much as he longed to pull her out from under the mound of rock. He first took a careful look at the debris pile. Shifting the wrong stone might cause the rocks to slide and bury the child deeper.

"Damn, this is odd," he muttered to himself, eyeing the strange way the stones and beams had settled. But then, he'd noted a lot about this disaster that was very odd.

He thought at first of calling for help. He thought then that he wouldn't. He could manage by himself. Considering the oddity of the situation, that might be best. And it would save precious time. He dug the child out of the debris using his bare hands and, within moments, had freed her.

She was unconscious. She had a head wound. Blood gummed her hair and covered her face and her clothes so that it was hard for him tell where else she might be hurt. Her breathing was easy, not labored or shallow. He felt her limbs to see if they were broken. Arms and legs appeared to be intact. He could not see the wound on her head for all the blood and did not want to start probing, fearing his clumsy touch might make her injuries worse. The girl was about twelve years old. She was dressed in a woolen shift and that was all—no stockings, no shoes.

The building was empty. No furniture, no sign that people lived here. The girl was alone in an abandoned dwelling. Odder and odder still.

Anton took no more time to speculate. Questions would be answered if and when the girl survived. He lifted her gently in his arms and carried her from the building. On his way out, he spotted Grald, the man who ruled Dragonkeep in the name of the dragon, talking with one of the holy sisters. Anton ducked his head, so as to escape their notice, and hurried past them as swiftly as possible. He was glad, now, he had not called for help.

He considered what to do with the child. He could take her to the healers in the Abbey, but the Abbey was a long way off and he was too tired to walk such a distance. Besides, the Houses of the Healers would be filled to overflowing. His own home was nearby. He would take the child there first, make her comfortable, and let his wife examine her injuries. Then together, he and Rosa could decide what to do with her.

Anton's home was larger than the single-room dwellings generally found in Dragonkeep. This was not because he was wealthier than the rest of the people. There were no such distinctions in the city of the dragon. Dwelling places were doled out by the Blessed based on certain considerations—number of inhabitants in the home, the type of work done by the inhabitants, etc. Rosa had her loom at home and Anton's smithy shop was attached to the dwelling, so the dwelling had to be large enough to accommodate tools and equipment for both of them.

Anton opened the door, which was never locked, with his shoulder and backed inside the house, taking care not to hit the girl's head on the door frame. Rosa was slumped over the dinner table, having her cry.

"Give me a hand here, Wife," he said, closing the door with his foot as he indicated the child in his arms. "She's hurt bad, I think, but she's alive."

Rosa lifted her tear-stained face. She was in her mid-fifties, with the deft, callused hands of one who has been sitting at the loom most of her life. Slender and small-boned, she barely came to her husband's chest. Anton was not very tall, but he was big-shouldered and massive, with powerful arms and legs. Rosa had a way of tilting her head to one side whenever she was considering anything, and Anton had a lumbering good nature about him, so that their friends nicknamed them affectionately Bird and Bear. Her amazed stare gave way to motherly compassion.

"Lay her on our Magda's bed," Rosa told her husband. "Then go fetch more water."

She had questions, Anton could see that, but she would not ask them until the child was warm and made comfortable. When he returned from the well, he found the girl tucked in bed, her face washed clean of blood and dirt, and a wet cloth on her forehead.

"How is she?" he asked anxiously, pouring the water into the kettle and then stirring up the fire beneath it.

"She'll do for the time being," Rosa answered cautiously. "Once I cleaned the wound, I found that it wasn't as bad as I'd feared. She's lost a lot of blood, though."

"Will she come around?"

"One never knows with a head wound, but I think she should be fine. Her sleep seems to be a healing one, not the bad sort from which you never wake."

Anton went to look at the girl. He regarded her thoughtfully, as Rosa waited for the water to heat so she could continue cleaning and dressing the wound. The girl had long black hair that straggled, unkempt and un-combed, over her shoulders. She lay quite still, did not groan or toss or twitch. She did, indeed, appear to be slumbering peacefully. Anton shook his head and his frown deepened.

"Where did you find her, Husband? Where are her parents? Not . . . dead?" Rosa asked, suddenly fearful.

"She was alone in an abandoned building," said Anton, seating himself with a sigh at the table. He rubbed his shoulders and stretched his aching back muscles. "No sign that anyone else lived there. The building was close to what must have been the heart of the blast."

"Truly?" Rosa was amazed. She glanced back the child. "She is lucky to have escaped with such minor wounds."

"Lucky," Anton repeated with meaningful emphasis. "I think it was more than luck."

"What do you mean?"

"She lay in the middle of a heap of debris. Heavy beams fell around her. None fell on top of her."

"You think she is one of the Blessed, then?" Rosa asked gravely.

"That would explain it. She used her magic to shield herself. She must be quite powerful."

"One of the Blessed." Rose reached down to caress the child's hand. "In an abandoned house all by herself . . ." She sighed deeply. "A runaway."

"I think so. So what do we do? By law, we're supposed to turn her over to the monks."

"Not until she is well," said Rosa firmly. "And not until we've had a chance to hear her story and talk to her. We'll tell her about our Magda, how happy she is. We'll show her some of Magda's letters from the palace."

"But do you think you can talk her into going back to the sisterhood?"

"Of course," Rosa said briskly. "The child's just confused, that's all. Girls at that age don't know their own minds. Our Magda wanted to be a blacksmith, like you, when she was twelve. Remember? What a time we had convincing her that such was not her calling!"

Anton smiled at the memory. Ten years had passed since his dearly loved daughter had left home at age twenty. She was one of the Blessed, unusually strong in the dragon-magic, and chosen by the dragon to live in the palace beneath the mountain. They had not seen Magda in all that time, but they still heard from her. Twice a year, she sent them a letter telling them that she was well and happy in her service to the dragon and describing the riches and wonders of palace life.

Being a servant of the dragon was a great honor, to be sure, but Anton often envied the men his age who had ordinary daughters, who bore ordinary grandchildren.

"If we can convince this girl to go back on her own, the holy sisters won't be hard on her," Rosa was saying. "Not like the monks."

"Keep your voice down." Anton rose stiffly to his feet and went over to peer out the window.

Although night had fallen, a few of their neighbors were still standing in the street, discussing the explosion in animated tones. No one else was around. Satisfied that they had not been overheard speaking in disparaging terms about the Blessed, Anton returned to the table.

Rosa poured hot water from the kettle to a bowl and carried it over to the child. She cleaned out the wound and then combed the long dark hair and plaited it in two tight, neat braids. The child continued to sleep.

Anton cut up bread and meat for their supper and washed it down with ale.

"You look worn out," he said to his wife. "Why don't you go to your bed? I'll sit up with the girl."

"I was tired, but I've got my second wind." Rosa smiled at him. "You're the one who looks dead on his feet."

Anton glanced at the open window, lowered his voice. "What have you heard about how it happened?"

" 'Magic gone awry,' the Blessed are saying. If so, that's not all that went awry," Rosa said softly. "Dimitri the Butcher was helping me with the wounded." She paled. "Some of them . . . some of the limbs were crushed and could not be saved. He brought his big knife—" She swallowed and put her hand to her mouth.

Anton fetched her a mug of ale and, after a gulp, she was able to go on. "Dimitri has a shop on Gate Street and before he left, he saw a battle between the monks and one of their own. This monk was crazed, seemingly. He used his magic to topple a building near the wall. This all happened right after the explosion. What is even stranger is that this monk had a young woman with him, apparently helping him! The Blessed are not talking about *that*, mind you."

"Do they think this lunatic caused the explosion that brought down the other buildings?"

"That's what everyone is saying, and the Blessed are not denying it."

"I trust they caught him."

"That is the truly strange part." Rosa dropped her voice to little more than a whisper. "The crazed monk was not so crazed but that he found the Hidden Gate and escaped! And the girl with him! Dimitri saw it with his own two eyes."

Anton frowned and shook his head. "That's impossible. The dragon would never permit it."

"I thought so, too. But then something else happened. While Dimitri was talking to me, the monks came for him."

Anton glanced at her sharply.

Rosa gave a nod and emphasized the nod with a jab of her finger. "I saw that with *my* own two eyes, Husband. The Blessed told Dimitri they had work for him to do, but what work could have been more important than what we were already doing—helping the injured? I think they took him away because they didn't like what he was saying—"

"Where am I?" came a voice.

Rosa and Anton both jumped. Rising from the table, they hastened to the back part of the house. The girl was sitting up in the bed.

"You are in our home, child," said Rosa, her voice softening. "I am Rosa and this is Anton." She sat down on the edge of the bed and rested her hand on the girl's forehead. "How do you feel?"

"My head hurts," the girl replied. She had a grave and solemn face; large, dark eyes that were clear and bright and bold. She was not shy around strangers, seemingly.

"What is your name, child?"

"Dracon—" the girl began, then stopped.

"Drake?" Rosa questioned, not certain she'd heard right.

"Draca," the girl corrected. "With an 'a.' I was named for my father. His name was 'Drake.' My parents were devoted to the dragon," she added, seeming to feel the need for explanation.

Anton and Rosa exchanged glances.

"Where are your parents, Draca?" Rosa asked. "They must be worried about you. Anton will run fetch them and bring them here."

"My parents are both dead," Draca said in matter-of-fact tones. "They died when I was little."

"The Abbey orphanage then. The holy sisters—"

At this, the girl threw off the blanket and started to climb out of bed. "You've been very kind. I don't want to be any trouble. I'll be going—"

She went very pale and her eyelids fluttered. Swaying on her feet, she put her hand to her head. "I feel sick."

"Lie down, Draca," Rosa insisted, alarmed. She rested her hands on the girl's shoulders and eased her, unresisting, back on to the bed. "I know you're afraid, but we won't tell anyone you are here. We promise. Don't we, Anton?"

He nodded, to assure her.

"We understand, you see," Rosa added, smoothing back the hair from the girl's face.

The girl regarded them both with a suspicious, wary expression, her eyes darting from one to the other. "What do you understand?"

"We know—or guess—what you are."

"You do?" Draca was astonished.

"That you are a runaway," said Rosa gently. "We won't make you go back. Not until you're ready."

"Runaway," Draca repeated. She sighed and sank down into the pillow. "My head hurts . . . Can you tell me what happened? I don't remember."

"Memory loss is not unusual with a head wound," Rosa said softly, to her husband. "Tell her what you found."

"There was an explosion. You were lying in the wreckage of an abandoned house," Anton explained. "The whole building had collapsed—the roof, the walls, everything. You should have been killed. But you weren't. You just got a bump on the head. When the beams fell down, they fell around you. Not on top of you."

Draca stared at him, unblinking. "That was lucky."

"More than luck." Anton smiled. "You used your magic to shield yourself from death. The 'blood bane.'"

"We know about the 'blood bane,'" Rosa added. "Our daughter was one of the Blessed. She was quite strong in it." Her voice softened. "And we know that sometimes it can be hard for young girls to deal with such power. We know that sometimes they run away—"

Draca lowered her gaze in confusion. Her hands plucked nervously at the blanket. "Please! Don't tell the monks—"

"We won't, dear, we won't. Now lie back and rest."

Draca nestled down among the blankets. She closed her eyes, and was soon breathing deeply and evenly.

The two stood gazing down on her.

"It's good to have a young one to care for again," said Rosa with a tremulous smile. She reached out to take hold of her husband's hand.

"We can't keep her indefinitely," Anton said, drawing his wife near. "Someone will be sure to find out, and then the monks will be coming for us."

"I know," Rosa said with a sigh. "Just a day or two. That's all. No one will miss her in the confusion."

"Now you should go to bed," said her husband.

"Not yet." Rosa pulled the stool on which she sat when she was weaving over to the side of the bed. "I'll stay up with her a bit. She might wake again and be frightened."

Her husband kissed her on the top of her head. "You're a good woman, Wife."

Rosa smiled, pleased. She drew the blanket around the girl's thin shoulders and tucked it in. Taking up some mending, she rested her back against the wall and began to hum a lullaby she had sung for their daughter.

Lulla, lulla, lulla, lullaby.
My sweet little baby, what meanest thou to cry?

Lying in their bed, Anton realized he had not heard his wife sing in a long, long time. His eyes filled with tears.

5

WHEN GRALD ARRIVED AT THE ABBEY, VEN WAS CON-
scious and alert, though he pretended not to be. He lay in
bed with his eyes closed, stirring only when he heard his
father's rough voice.

"How are you feeling, Dragon's Son?" Grald asked.

Ven did not answer immediately. Opening his eyes, he
stared around the room, as though disoriented and confused. At last, he shifted his gaze to Grald, to the dragon,
his father.

"Well enough." Ven made an effort to pull himself to a
sitting position.

"Do not move, Dragon's Son," one of the monks
warned, and laid a restraining hand on Ven's shoulder.

Ven flashed the monk a look, and the man hastily drew
back his hand.

"The monk is right. You should not be moving," Grald
said solicitously. "We must take care of that body of
yours."

A strange way to put it, Ven thought, but he let it go. He
had more urgent matters to consider than his dragon father's odd choice of words. He could hear the dragon
Grald sniffing around outside the cavern of his son's
mind; trying, as always, to find a way inside.

Ven stood in the center, wrapped in the blazing white-
ness that had no color.

Thwarted in his efforts to pry apart Ven's mind, Grald was forced to ask for information. "What happened to you, Dragon's Son? Who stabbed you? Was it your brother?"

Ven's lip curled slightly. "As if Marcus had the guts! The girl. Evelina. She stabbed me. When I went to meet with my brother, she followed me—"

"If you had not slain the monk who was given to you as guardian, that would not have happened," Grald interrupted. His heavy head lurched near, the hulking body crowded close, trying to use his bulk to intimidate.

Ven did not flinch away. He looked the dragon in its human eyes.

"Guardian!" He started to laugh, then grimaced in pain. He shifted slightly. The monks had wrapped cloth bandages around his ribs, and they constricted his breathing. "The monk was a spy. Your spy on me."

"If he was, what did you have to hide that you needed to kill him?"

Ven was silent a moment, then said quietly, "He was an annoyance. A nuisance. Mad as a rabid skunk. I didn't like him. That was why I killed him."

Far from being put out, Grald seemed to find this amusing. He gave a low chuckle and, dragging up a chair, settled himself at Ven's bedside.

"I don't like any of them," Ven continued, casting a venomous glance at the monk hovering near him. "If they want to live, they'll stay away from me."

Grald jerked his thumb and the monk left gratefully, hastening from the room. Grald looked back at Ven and his amusement evaporated.

"You sneaked off to meet your brother alone. That was stupid, as you found out. You should have been patient. I would have arranged a meeting between the two of you."

Ven stared out the window. The sun was setting, pale yellow against pale blue, its colors muted as though it were trying to slip way without anyone noticing. "Marcus is my twin brother. A twin brother I never knew I had. I wanted to meet him alone. I had things to say to him in private."

"You wanted to warn him, you mean," said Grald. "Warn him that I was going to slay him. Help him flee."

"I told you where to find him," Ven retorted. "You could have come to claim him. It's not my fault you didn't."

"I was dealing with other matters," Grald muttered.

"Such as Draconas?" Ven asked.

"What do you know of Draconas?" Grald demanded, his eyes narrowing so that they almost disappeared in the shadow of the heavy brow.

"I know that he was here in the city. I know that he saved Marcus from your assassins. I know that he was using Marcus as bait to catch you," Ven remarked coolly. "All very interesting, considering that you were using Marcus as bait to catch Draconas. What happened, Grald? Did you all end up catching each other? Is that why you blew up the city?"

The human Grald regarded Ven in grim silence. The dragon Grald, lurking outside the cave of Ven's mind, struck at him in anger and frustration. Ven stood in the white center of his mind, safe, unassailable.

"So why *did* you blow up the city, Grald?" Ven asked. "And where is my brother? Where is Evelina? I wouldn't mind seeing her again." He pressed his hand over his wound. "I owe her for this."

"You can contact your brother mind-to-mind," Grald said suddenly. "You have that power, the same as dragons. Ask him yourself where he is."

"I don't think my dear brother will be eager to open his mind to me," Ven said dryly. "Not after what happened between us. What's wrong, Grald? Have you lost the prince?"

"I'm asking the questions," Grald returned, somewhat belatedly. "And this time I want answers. What happened when you met with your brother? What did he do? What did he say?"

Ven shrugged and lay back on the pillow. "I met with Marcus. He was repulsed by the very sight of me. He loathed me from the start—a feeling that is mutual, by the way. He is what you might expect—a spoiled, pampered, royal darling. I could tell that he wanted to be rid of me, but he had to keep me around, of course, so that you could walk into the trap he and Draconas had set for you. Then Evelina showed up. She hid outside the door, eavesdropping on us, until she heard me refer to Marcus as a prince, then the mercenary little bitch nearly knocked the door down to throw herself into his arms.

"She told him what a beast I was—how I killed her father and tried to rape her. My brother believed her, of course. To give him credit, he didn't intend for her to stab me. Marcus is soft and weak. He doesn't have the balls for that sort of thing. Killing me was all Evelina's idea. She flung herself on me like a wildcat. The last thing I remember was her driving her knife into my chest."

"A knife you gave her," Grald observed.

"That was my mistake and I paid for it."

"And what happened then, Dragon's Son?"

"You tell me, Dragon Father. I heard an explosion. The next thing I knew, I woke up to find myself lying in a pool of my own blood underneath a house. Marcus and Evelina were gone. Outside, everything was in chaos, with people yelling and screaming and digging bodies out of the rubble. No one was interested in me, so I crawled out of the wreckage and came back here. I must have passed out again, because the next I know, one of your lunatic monks is bending over me, babbling at me.

"I've answered your questions, Father. Now you can answer mine. Where is my brother? Where is Evelina? Were they killed in the explosion? And where is Draconas? I think I have a right to know—considering that all three want me dead."

Grald was silent. Ven guessed the dragon was trying to decide how much to reveal, how much to keep to himself.

"You have nothing to fear from any of them, Dragon's Son," Grald said at last. "You are right about your brother. The king's son is soft and weak and gullible. He is running back to the arms of his papa, and I will let him run.

He has the girl with him. Soon"—Grald's lips twisted in what passed with him for a smile—"you will have your revenge on both of them."

"Good," Ven said, though he wondered what that meant. He waited, hoping Grald would fill in the details.

"As for any harm that might come to you," Grald continued, "the monks will protect you—if you let them."

Ven scowled and shook his head.

"Meanwhile, you must rest, return to health. When you are stronger, I will tell you everything you need to know."

The dragon departed. He sent the monk back in.

Ven ordered the monk back out, telling him to shut the door and leave him alone. The monk did as the dragon's son commanded. He didn't go far, however. Ven heard shuffling feet outside his door—two monks taking up their positions. At least two.

Ven lay back down, exhausted by the mental struggle; as drained as if he and the dragon had battled physically—an unpleasant thought that gave him pause. Someday, if he was to fulfill his oath and avenge his mother, he would have to battle the dragon, a fight that would be both physical and mental.

Ven had no idea how this was to be accomplished. He was not ready for such a battle. He knew enough about the dragon-magic to defend himself against Grald, but that was all. Ven thought back to the time when Draconas had offered to teach him about the magic. The child, Ven, had refused. He didn't want the dragon-magic that was part of him, as he didn't want the dragon legs, the dragon claws, the dragon-blood.

He still didn't want it, any of it. The monks regarded him with supposed reverence, but he could see the fear and loathing in their eyes. The same fear and loathing that he'd seen, briefly, in Marcus's eyes. The same that he saw, always, in Evelina's eyes.

Much as they loathed him, they could not loathe him as much as he loathed the dragon part of himself. He had to overcome that. The man, Ven, felt differently than the child. He had to learn how to use the magic. He would need it to destroy Grald.

One thing Ven had learned or at least guessed from his mental battle with Grald.

The dragon had no idea what had become of Draconas.

6

THIS WAS ONLY THE SECOND SESSION OF THE PARLIAMENT of Dragons the young female, Lysira, had ever attended. Anora's urgent summons to convene Parliament had come unexpectedly. Given the current crisis, the unexpected was only to be expected, or so Lysira concluded.

She was pleased at the prospect of the meeting—not so much because of the meeting itself, although she found those fascinating. She was pleased because this meant she would have another chance to see the Walker, Draconas. If Lysira had been a human female, her heart would have fluttered at the thought. Being dragon, Lysira's heart thudded calmly. Her dreams trembled.

Dragons prefer to live their lives in isolation, free to dream their dreams alone and undisturbed. They come together to mate and raise their young, and that only grudgingly, for neither much enjoys the physical process of mating, and both are glad to have it done and over with as swiftly as possible. For dragons, love is the mating of two minds, not two bodies; the blending of two wondrous dreams, the merging of fantastic colors and delightful images. The true mating ritual takes place in the minds of the pair and may go on for years, as they work together to build the nest that will house their young and create the elaborate labyrinthine illusions that baffle intruders and

keep the young safe from harm until they are old enough
to dream their own dreams.

Lysira had been enchanted by the images she saw in
Draconas's mind—so different from those of other dragons. His view of the world was different, for he saw it at
ground level. He saw the world walking. He walked with
those strange creatures—humans. He spoke to them,
touched them, had even learned to think like them. The
minds of other dragons were like her own, filled with colors that were lovely, tranquil, serene. Draconas's colors—
his human colors—were garish, jagged, jarring, ugly, and
beautiful, achingly beautiful.

She'd had a glimpse into his mind during the last session of Parliament, and she had been shocked and disturbed and intrigued, so much so that she conjured up the
images again and again as she lay dreaming in her cave.
Lysira was the first dragon to arrive in the immense cavern in which the Parliament of Dragons was held. Anora
arrived shortly thereafter.

Embarrassed by her eagerness and abashed at being
alone in the presence of this august and revered elder,
Lysira kept her thoughts carefully neutral in tone. She
paid her respects to the Minister, dipping her head and
raising her wings, then wondered uneasily what she was
supposed to do now. Was she expected to make conversation until the others arrived? Lysira could think of a great
many things she wanted to discuss, but all of them involved Draconas, and she was shy about bringing him up.

Lysira made one or two half-hearted attempts to speak
to the elder dragon. Lysira's colors were all pastel and
muted, however, and Anora, preoccupied by her own raging thoughts, never noticed the wisps of spring green and
rose pink that trailed from Lysira's mind.

Anora settled herself at the front of the cavern. She
glanced only once in the direction of the young female,
and that glance was filled with sorrow, as though she foresaw some terrible fate about to befall the young dragon.
The strange look from Anora made Lysira even more uncomfortable, and she was thankful when the elder dragon

wrapped her tail around her feet and shut her eyes, a sign that she was not to be disturbed. Lysira retreated into the darkest part of the cavern and tried to blend it with the stalagmites.

Finally the other dragons began arriving and Lysira was forced to leave her shadows and greet them. The dragons were ill at ease and nervous, their colors shifting and blurring. Of late, they had come to dread these meetings of Parliament, for the news they were given just got progressively worse. All of them looked to Anora as they spiraled down through the fathomless darkness on barely moving wings. The sight of her, clenched tightly around herself, did nothing to reassure them. Alarm flew between the assembled dragons with such rapidity that Lysira swore she could almost hear the thoughts whir through the darkness like bat wings.

Lysira dipped her head and raised her wings to each dragon in turn. She did not join in their mental conversations, however. Young dragons are, for the most part, to be seen and not heard, unless specifically invited to share their colors. Lysira might possibly have received an invitation from some of the young males; she had an impression of thoughts drifting her direction. She was distracted, however, listening for the arrival of one dragon; listening for the sound of human footfalls.

Once the last dragon had arrived, Anora came out of her dark musings and called the Parliament to order, and still Draconas did not come.

Lysira took her place among the assembled heads of the houses of Dragonkind and opened her mind to Anora's thoughts.

"I am sorry to have brought you here on such short notice," said Anora, her colors vibrant and trembling, as from some long-suppressed emotion. "But I have urgent news to impart to you, as well as a warning and . . . a confession."

"We cannot proceed. We are missing a member. Where is Draconas?" snapped Malfiesto.

Malfiesto was old and crotchety and bad-tempered, and Lysira usually found him intensely annoying. Now her heart warmed toward him. She cast the elder male a glance of gratitude that brought beautiful memories of youth to the old dragon's mind, momentarily causing him to forget what he'd been talking about. He recalled soon enough, however.

"He is late again," Malfiesto continued. "I say we issue a formal reprimand—"

"I am not sure where Draconas is," said Anora, and this was true enough. "I did not inform him of the meeting. I do not want him here."

The assembled dragons went silent, their colors quivering. Lysira felt her own colors go bounding off the walls of the cavern, and she had to seize them and keep fast hold of them, not to betray her feelings of fear and disappointment to the others.

"He hasn't got himself killed, has he?" asked Litard, a male dragon, in casual tones.

"No," Anora answered. "I do not believe he is dead."

Lysira's relief was heartfelt, if short-lived.

"I believe that he has gone rogue. Silence!" Anora blared, her colors red and blazing. "Silence, all of you, and listen to me. We don't have much time and there is a great deal that needs to be decided. Not since the Dragon Wars have we faced such a crisis. Our lives and, what is more important, the lives of our young"—here she looked again at Lysira, with that inexplicable sadness— "are in the most dire peril."

She had their attention, now. Their complete attention. Litard, for once, ceased grooming his flashy green scales and exclaimed loudly in astonishment. Mantas, his colors murky as always, was silent, unmoving, waiting for events to unfold. Jinat, who always seemed to bear some unknown sorrow, nodded gloomily as though he'd foreseen this all along. Arat grinned. He disliked humans and he disliked Draconas. Malfiesto's eyes narrowed.

Draconas came from the noble house ruled by Malfiesto, though you could not have told it, given that the elder dragon was never pleased by anything Draconas did. Lysira saw that Malfiesto was more concerned by this news than he let on. He didn't roar or rage, as she might have expected. He had gone extremely still and quiet.

The seven other rulers of the noble houses were females. Dyxtra the Silver was near the age of Anora and Maristara. Dyxtra had known both dragons in their youth and, according to her, had not been shocked by Maristara's actions in seizing and enslaving a nation of humans. Dyxtra had never seen the need for a walker and always refused to take part in the spell-casting that created the supreme illusion. She snorted, as though this was only to be expected.

Reyal was a middle-aged dragon who, far different from most dragons, thought very highly of her powers of creativity and conversation, and was always inflicting her dreams on others. She did not like humans either, having once caught a human intruder in her cave when her children were still in the egg, as the saying went. The human had never come near the baby dragons, but Reyal had been outraged and to this day would go on and on about it, if encouraged.

Alisha was also middle-aged, but far different from Reyal, being serious, grave, introspective. Alisha never spoke during a session, never demanded the Speaker's Rod, never asked a question. She listened intently and took in everything, giving no indication of her thoughts.

Nionan liked humans. She had wanted to be a walker in her youth, but had not been chosen, and it was rumored, though no one knew for certain, that she used her illusions to lure humans to her cave for the pleasure of observing them. She was, like Malfiesto, regarding Anora with grim suspicion.

The last of the rulers, Shrireth, looked half asleep. But then, she always looked that way. She was said to have a violent temper, though Lysira found that hard to credit.

"All of you know that the rogue dragon, Maristara, seized the human kingdom of Seth many hundred years ago," Anora was saying. "She has been ruling the humans secretly in the guise of a human, and she and her male consort, a lesser dragon known as Grald, experimented with the breeding of humans, mingling their blood with the blood of dragons. You all know that they produced humans who have dragon-magic in their blood. You know, for Draconas informed you at the last meeting, that he had discovered a city known as Dragonkeep, where Grald and Maristara were holding these humans, a city kept hidden from both humans and dragons by supreme illusions.

"And you know, for, again, Draconas told you, that Grald and Maristara have a spy in Parliament who is feeding them information. Thus they were prepared to repulse the dragons when they attacked Seth to try to free the humans. Thus Grald knew our secret plans for the human female, Melisande. The information the spy gave him provided Grald with the opportunity to breed with this human, a union that produced a son."

The dragons did not stir. Not a tail twitched. Not a wing rustled. The rocks in the cavern were not so still as the assembled members of Parliament.

"I am going to reveal the identity of the betrayer," Anora began.

"Draconas!" The name hissed in the minds of the assembled dragons.

Anora shook her head.

"You," said Malfiesto, and he spoke aloud, something dragons rarely do.

Lysira didn't believe him, any more than she had believed the others about Draconas. The idea was ludicrous, and she almost laughed until she saw Anora's eyes, saw the shadow of conscious guilt, pierced by glinting defiance.

"You are right," Anora replied, "I betrayed our plans to Maristara and Grald. I—reluctantly—sanctioned the killing of Brayard and his son, Braun. You condemn me now, I know that. But hear my reasons and then you will thank me."

"Never!" Lysira let go her rage in an explosion of anger and grief. Braun had been her brother, Brayard her father. "You admit to murder—"

"Silence, young one," ordered Anora sternly. "Be silent and listen."

Lysira wasn't going to be silent. She was going to bellow her rage until the walls of the cavern split asunder. She was going to fly at Anora and attack her with claw and tooth and thunderous magic. She was . . .

"Calm," came colors, blue and soothing as the cold waters of a plunge into a lake. "Keep calm and do as the Minister says. Listen."

"Draconas!" Lysira trembled inside, trembled with the force of her emotions, grief and fury vying with pleasure and confusion at reading his thoughts. "But she killed Braun—"

"Hush!" Draconas warned. "Give no sign that I am with you. Let my mind merge with yours. Keep your colors gray. I need to hear what Anora tells the Parliament, and she must not know I am listening."

Lysira obeyed, her mind in such turmoil that, while not exactly gray, her colors were so muddied that even she could not tell quite what she was thinking.

"I know this is a shock for you, Lysira," Anora was saying. "And I was truly, truly grieved that I had to do what I did. Please, listen to what I have to say in my defense."

Lysira gave an abrupt nod of her head. The other dragons would think she was barely able to control herself for her fury, and that was almost true, for anger bubbled inside her. But the ugly acid was mixed with a sweet warmth, knowing Draconas was so close to her and that he trusted her and was depending on her. Lysira dug her claws into the rock floor of the cave and waited to hear Anora.

"For thousands upon thousands of years," the Minister began, "we have watched humans evolve, grow, and develop. We have not interfered with their progress. Indeed, we passed strict laws to prevent such interference. To help enforce those laws and to keep a watchful eye upon this fragile species, we asked one of our own to sacrifice himself, to take on human form and live and walk among them. We watched over the humans, protected them, nurtured them—all without their knowledge.

"Occasionally there would be interaction between us—a young hot-blood would forget himself and carry off a few cattle or set fire to a barn—but such incidents were few and, I must admit, tended to benefit us more than harm us. For centuries, humans have feared us, held us in awe. Humans have long told stories of how their heroes attacked and even killed dragons, but those tales are just that—tales, myths, legends. No human was capable of slaying one of us."

Anora's colors grew dark and grieving. "But that is about to change."

"What are you saying?" Malfiesto demanded, scoffing. "That humans now have the power to kill dragons? Preposterous!"

"Once it was preposterous," said Anora gravely. "Not anymore. When a human first picked up a stick, we envisioned the spear. When a human flung a rock, we foresaw the catapult. When a human dug iron out of the ground, we saw the sword in his hand. Such puny weapons could never be a threat to us and so we did not concern ourselves with them. We slept in our caves and wove our dreams of tranquillity and peace. But these dreams have been shattered by the cannon's blast."

"Bah!" Malfiesto scoffed. "That puffed-up piece of ironmongery. Humans do more damage to themselves than to any of us."

"That is true now," Anora agreed. "And maybe it will be true a hundred years from now. But, inevitably, such weapons will be a threat. As we saw the spear from the stick, so I foresee a terrible human weapon that will have the capability of blowing apart a mountain, of slaughtering us while we sleep, of destroying the nests of our young, no matter how well they are hidden."

Images of fiery death flared in Anora's mind, images of caves that required hundreds of years of patient carving blown apart in an instant. Images of labyrinthine passages sliding down crumbling mountainsides. Images of eggs smashed and the young dragons crushed beneath tons of rock.

"For the first time in our long history," said Anora, "I see the possibility of our extinction. And it will be at the hands of humans."

"Is this true, Draconas?" Lysira cried in silent dismay. "Do humans have such power?"

His colors were dark for long moments and fear gripped Lysira's heart, for she knew the answer before she saw it in his mind.

"They do not have such power now. But soon."

7

THE DRAGONS WERE EITHER SHOCKED AND OUTRAGED AT Anora's words or shocked and disbelieving. Their thoughts flew about the cavern, spattering the walls and each other with the colors of fire and blood, almost as if one of the explosive devices had landed in their midst. Anora did not try to call for order. No one would have seen her colors in the storm of emotion roaring about the cavern.

"But what can we do to stop the humans?" Lysira asked Draconas.

"Humans are not ours to stop," he returned.

Lysira bristled at his tone, "I don't know how you can be so flippant—"

"Careful," Draconas warned. "She's watching you."

The tumult was dying down. Lysira saw Anora's gaze fixed upon the young female. Small tendrils of thought coiled toward her. Lysira made her own mind a flutter of confusion; not difficult, with so many conflicting emotions flapping about like birds tangled in a net. Lysira had the impression that Anora was asking for her forgiveness and her understanding. Lysira could not grant that, not yet. She hunkered down and avoided the elder dragon's thoughts.

Anora brought the meeting back to order.

"I made plans—" she began.

"Without consulting us!" Malfiesto thundered.

"I couldn't," Anora returned, blazing up. "Because of Draconas."

"The Walker? It seems to me he would be central to any plans you made regarding humans."

"The walkers were sent to live among humans in order to provide us with information about them, their habits, their way of life, and so forth. Walkers proved quite useful in this regard. I have noticed, however, that the longer they live among humans, the more human the walkers become. They begin to empathize with the humans. They lose their detachment, become emotionally involved. Usually we are able to catch walkers before they do harm to us. We remove the walker from his or her position and assign another. It is what I should have done with Draconas."

Anora sighed deeply. "But he was the best walker we've ever created. He maintained his detachment, or so I thought. I wonder now if he was lying all this time— lying to me. Lying to himself." She waved it away with a claw. "That is all past. What's done is done, as the humans say."

"So you foresee that humans are going to cannonade us into extinction," Malfiesto said caustically. "Forgive me if I fail to understand how breeding humans with dragons and thereby giving them even more power is supposed to save us."

"I will explain. It all began with Brayard."

As she spoke, Anora deliberately kept her gaze away from Lysira, who steeled herself to listen and be silent.

"Through Grald's bungling, Brayard learned about the smuggling of male babies out of Seth. He suspected the existence of a city such as Dragonkeep, although I do not think he ever found it. He told me what he knew and insisted that I bring up the matter before the Parliament. If I would not, he said that he would. That could not be allowed to happen. The revelation that we had been breeding humans to use dragon-magic would have caused an uproar among all dragonkind."

The dragons muttered, their colors black and tinged with fire.

"Hear me out!" Anora demanded, and she waited until they settled down. "He would have brought our plans to ruin. For the sake of the many, he had to be sacrificed. And so he was. No one was ever supposed to find out. Grald killed Brayard and made the murder look like an accident—as if the dragon had lost way his way in a storm and crashed into a mountain.

"All would have been well, but that Brayard's son, Braun, was the inquisitive sort. He did not believe that his father could have been so reckless. Prior to his death, Brayard assured me that he had not spoken to anyone regarding his suspicions. I now know that he must have mentioned at least some of what he suspected to his son. How much, I'm not sure, but at least enough to cause Braun to fly to Seth, with some scheme of trying to warn the humans about what was happening.

"The women of Seth, skilled in the use of dragon-magic, very nearly killed Braun. He managed to escape, and he returned and told his tale to anyone who would listen. He wanted to stir up trouble, believing that the truth about the murder of his father would then float to the surface. You know what happened. Draconas was sent to try to 'deal' with Maristara. He was to take a human male—a king of his people—to Seth to meet the Mistress of Dragons and persuade her to leave Seth.

"From that point on, nothing went right. Grald lost his nerve and sent out his magic-wielding monks to destroy Draconas. These lunatics did far more harm to us than they did to Draconas, for they alerted him to the fact that humans had been given dragon-magic. Maristara did not abandon the worn-out human body as swiftly as she should have, with the lamentable result that two humans as well as Draconas stumbled upon Maristara's secret of body switching.

"We had to act fast to repair the damage that had been done. Fortunately, Draconas provided us with the means. He came up with the idea of the human king mating with the human female—a High Priestess of Seth—producing a son that would be strong in the dragon-magic; a son who would then be sent in to deal with Maristara. Draconas later abandoned that plan, but Grald and I saw how it could be useful to us. I persuaded Draconas to go through with it. The humans mated and the female was impregnated. Then Grald also planted his seed in the human female, impregnating her with a child that would be half-human, half-dragon.

"Even that went awry. Grald's orders were to abduct the human female and carry her safely to Dragonkeep before impregnating her, but he could not control the lust of the human body in which he is housed. Still, all would have been well if Draconas had obeyed *my* orders. He was supposed to bring the two babies to me. He took it upon himself to defy me, however. He had developed a bond with these humans, and he felt guilty about being the cause of the death of the mother. And he now knew that there was someone in the Parliament in collusion with the dragons. He felt he could trust no one among us."

"He was right," Malfiesto growled.

Anora ignored him. "Grald feared that Braun had discovered the location of Dragonkeep. Whether that was true or not, we'll never know. We couldn't chance it. He argued that Braun had to die and, reluctantly, I agreed. I was afraid that Braun's death would only increase Draconas's suspicions, which it did. He tried to keep the children hidden from us—an impossible task, for they had the dragon-magic in their blood, and that meant that, sooner or later, they must open their minds to us.

"Grald and I found the half-dragon child, but Draconas intervened before we could capture him and spirit him away. Draconas warned the child against using the magic and, wonder of wonder, the child obeyed him, at least until he reached manhood and found himself in trouble. Then he turned to his father. Grald discovered his half-dragon son and rescued him from humans, who thought he was devil-spawn or some such superstitious nonsense.

"The other child, the king's son, went insane, as do so many human males with the dragon-magic, and we hoped he would die and we would not have to worry about him. But Draconas meddled in this and saved the boy. Not only that, Draconas taught him how to use the magic. The boy grew to manhood and is one of the strongest in dragon-magic we have produced. And one of the most dangerous," Anora added grimly, "for the prince has the ability to enter the minds of dragons, something no human has ever been capable of doing before.

"Worse yet, the king of this human nation, reacting out of ignorance and fear, began to develop the first human weapon built specifically to slay dragons. The weapon is not a threat to us, of course—one blast of fire will melt it where it stands. For the first time in our history, however, humans are actually daring to take a stand against us. Again, due to Draconas's conniving, the prince, Marcus, found the location of Dragonkeep. The king will undoubtedly lead his human armies against this city. Our plans are endangered. The lives of all dragonkind are threatened. We must act—"

"You keep speaking of plans, Anora," Malfiesto interrupted, using the dragon's name, not her august title of Prime Minister. "What plans are these? I think we have a right to know. And were you party to the two dragons' criminal behavior all along?"

"To answer your last question first, no, I was not party to what Grald and Maristara were planning. I was as furious as you when I heard that they had seized a human kingdom. That was before I knew the danger humans posed to us, however. When I became aware of that threat, it seemed to me that Maristara and Grald had the right idea. Use the dragon-magic in their blood to control the humans. Rule over them. Prevent them from creating these terrible weapons. Not only will this benefit us," Anora argued. "Such a prohibition will also benefit the humans. Let us face facts. Humans first invented these horrible weapons to kill large numbers of their own kind. We will stop them from harming each other, as well as ourselves. In the future, when humans come to view our intervention rationally, they will thank us."

"Thank us for enslaving them," Draconas muttered in Lysira's mind.

Some of the dragons were nodding sagely, evidently favoring Anora's position. Others glowered, not pleased with what they were hearing, among them Malfiesto, which surprised Lysira, for his dislike of humans was well known.

Lysira did not know what to feel. She was terrified of the destructive force of the humans' weapons, yet, she was troubled by the idea of dragons making humans a slave-race, as Draconas was saying. She grieved over the loss of her brother and was furious at how casually Anora spoke of slaying him. Yet, Braun had always been a troublemaker, a meddler. If only he'd let well enough alone! Now she was the last of their noble house and, if what Anora said was true, her children might be among the last dragons ever born. . . .

She momentarily lost track of what Anora was saying and caught hold of the thread in the middle.

"For two hundred years, I have been working with Grald and Maristara, developing our plans in secret. We hoped—at least I hoped—that we would never be forced to use such drastic measures. I hoped that the human inventions would fail and that they would grow weary of pursuing them. I underestimated the human desire for conquest and power. As for the nature of our plans, I cannot reveal them to you."

The dragons muttered at this. Tails snapped in irritation, wings rustled, claws scraped.

"By law, Prime Minister," said Malfiesto, "you are required to tell us."

"I have broken so many laws, old friend, that one more will not matter," Anora replied. "And I am no longer your Prime Minster. I resign from that post. Who will side with me?"

Dragons spit and snarled, snapped and roared. Heads swooped down in fighting stance, wings lifted, tails thrashed. Malfiesto bellowed, actually using his voice, something unheard of, to try to make the other dragons see reason. Three of the young males, incensed, flew off. Two of the females left with them. Others remained behind to argue and debate.

"There's nothing more you can do here," said Draconas, and Lysira, thankfully, left.

Once outside, she lifted her wings and soared into a night spattered with stars. She breathed deeply of the fresh air and felt better.

"Where are you, Draconas?" she asked, free, at last, to speak openly with him.

"I am here," he said. "In your mind. Whenever you want me, this is where you will find me."

"I mean, physically, where are you?" Lysira persisted.

"It is better that you do not know," Draconas replied. "Not that I do not trust you, Lysira, but two members of your family have already died by violence. I do not want to risk a third death, especially of someone I care about."

Lysira's colors shimmered, dazzling her with their brilliance.

"I *can* use your help, however," Draconas continued. "I need eyes to see and ears to hear. But only if you are willing."

"You mean, only if I agree with your side of things," said Lysira slowly. "I'm not sure I do agree, Draconas. What Anora said frightens me."

"Anora has been blinded by fear, Lysira. She is able to see only one path—a path that leads to doom. Many paths exist, and some are bright with sunlight."

Lysira did not immediately reply. She watched the ground skim beneath her. Humans were small as ants in her sight, and they could not see her at all. She realized, suddenly, that she'd never seen a human except from this vast distance.

"I will be your eyes, Draconas," Lysira agreed. "It is time that I looked at the world. But I want you to know beforehand that I will never do anything to betray our people. Even if that means going against someone *I* care about. What do you need me to do?"

"I need to know what has happened to the king's son, Marcus. I do not dare try to contact him, for Anora and the others are searching for him and, if they find him, they will kill him. This is what he looks like."

An image of a human came to Lysira's mind— youthful, comely, with fair hair and hazel eyes. He did not, she was forced to admit, look like a monster.

"And what do I do when I find this human?" Lysira asked.

"Warn him," said Draconas. "Warn him that he and his people are in danger."

"And he will use his cannons to try to slay us," said Lysira sadly. She shook her head. "I do not think—"

"Lysira," said Draconas gently, persuasively, "Grald does not mean to make these humans slaves. He means to slaughter them."

Lysira kept her colors to herself.

"Please, Lysira. You said yourself. Our people have gone mad with fear. We have a chance to stop the madness."

Dragons are always loath to take action.

"I will think about it, Draconas," Lysira said.

8

NIGHT STRETCHED DARK ACROSS THE RIVER. THE WATER slipped out from underneath him. The river flowed ever onward, uncaring about the vagaries of time. Marcus steered the boat nearer the sunken cavern, and his fears grew, compounded by the fact that he had no idea how far he was from the cavern.

The first and last time Marcus had traveled the river had been during the night. He had not been paying attention to his surroundings during that first journey. His attention had been divided between keeping an eye on the boats of the monks ahead and watching for snags and other dangers in the river. He had very little reckoning of the passage of time—how long it had taken him and Bellona to travel from the sunken cavern to the site of Dragonkeep. Had it been minutes or hours? He looked back on that night and he couldn't be certain.

His rowing slowed. He thought he detected a change in the air, a different smell; one that was not of green and growing things, but the smell that he remembered from the cave, a smell of wet rock and slime. He felt a change in the temperature, as well—a chill, musty breath flowing from a gaping mouth.

Evelina felt it, too, for she began to rummage about for one of the blankets she'd scrounged. Wrapping it around her shoulders, she huddled into it.

"What a horrible stench," she complained. "It smells of death."

Marcus shifted direction, rowed toward the shoreline.

"Catch hold of that branch," he told Evelina.

"Are we stopping?" she asked eagerly, unwinding herself from the blanket long enough to do as he said. She grabbed hold of the branch, and the boat swiveled around to nose gently in among a shadowy tangle of reeds and rushes and willow trees.

"Just for a little while," he answered. "I want to wait until long after midnight to enter the cave."

Evelina gave a little screech. "As if it won't be terrifying enough! You're going to make it easy for the monks to catch us."

"Hush, keep quiet," Marcus warned. "I don't want anyone to see us or hear us. I'm not going to make finding us easy for anyone."

He planned to use his magic to conceal the boat from view, cast an illusion over it, so that anyone looking at the boat would see only dark, flowing water. Such illusions never work, Draconas had once warned him. Someone always sneezes. But Marcus could think of no other way to avoid the monks, if they were in the cave.

He shipped the oars and tied the boat up securely. The boat bobbed gently in the water. He picked up one of the blankets, toyed with it a moment as he thought over what he had to do.

"I hate to ask this of you—" he began.

"Ask me," said Evelina. "Please. I will do anything."

He regarded her steadily. "I am going to use my magic to hide us and the boat."

He paused, waiting for her reaction. She continued to gaze at him.

"Yes," she said. "Go on."

"You're not afraid . . . of the magic?" he asked hesitantly.

"No, of course not," she told him. "Why should I be afraid of you?"

His heart warmed to her. No flinching, no shrinking away, no talk of "devil's work." Just calm acceptance.

"I am very tired, and I must be strong and well rested to use the magic."

"You need to sleep. Of course," said Evelina briskly. "Go ahead. You sleep and I'll keep watch."

"You don't mind?"

She shook her head. "I only wish I could do more."

Marcus drew near Evelina and kissed her on the cheek. "Thank you," he said.

Evelina blushed and lowered her eyes. Marcus lay down as best he could in the bottom of the boat. Evelina fussed over him, making a pillow of another blanket for his head and helping him to find the most comfortable of uncomfortable positions. Closing his eyes, Marcus gave himself to the rocking motion of the boat.

The confusion one feels as the mind sinks slowly into sleep stole over him, so that he was rowing again, and then he had no oars, but he was still rowing, and the boat slid into darkness . . .

Evelina put her hand to her cheek. She could still feel Marcus's kiss, as though it had burned her like the hot irons they used to brand the mark of shame on prostitutes. Evelina was pleased with herself. She had recovered in a few moments all the ground she'd lost with Marcus during the trip.

She sat with her chin in her hands, thinking back to their conversation. He'd been pleased when she'd told him she wasn't afraid of the magic. Well, she thought, why should she be afraid of it? She didn't believe it. Any of it.

"Seeing is believing" the old saw went, except that it wasn't.

Evelina had known the truth of that from the time she was a very small girl and she'd watch her father swindle the gullible with a bean under a walnut shell. *See the bean? I'll put the shell over it. Three shells. The bean's under one of them. See it? Yes, there it is. Now, I'll just switch the shells around. Are you following the one with the bean under it? Yes, sir, I can see that you are. You are a man of perception, sir. Now, I'll bet you money, sir, that you can't tell me which shell the bean is under. Of course, I'll lose, you*

*being so very perceptive, sir, but it's an honor playing with
someone so keen-sighted. That shell, sir? Are you sure, sir?
Well, well, well . . . I guess you weren't watching so closely
after all, sir. You owe me . . .*

Of course, the secret was that the bean wasn't under any
of the shells. Ramone had palmed the bean before the game
started and slipped it back before it ended, sliding it under
one of the walnut shells as he lifted it to shift it about. A
trick to fool the gullible. Nothing wrong with it. All men
and women were tricksters and liars. One had to be to
survive—even Marcus, a prince, the man Evelina loved as
she'd never loved anyone else in her short life (with the exception of Evelina). She had no illusions about him.

Evelina had seen all manner of fantastic things in
Dragonkeep: a monk with hands made of blazing fire,
snow falling on a warm day in the morning sunshine,
Marcus bringing down a building by pointing at it. She'd
seen herself walk through a solid stone wall. Wonderful
tricks, all of them. She could make a fortune with such
fakery by taking it on the road like that poor sod, Glimmershanks. She'd didn't know how the tricks were done,
but that didn't matter. Before Ramone had taught her the
secret of the shell game, she'd thought the bean had really vanished.

Evelina didn't know or care how Marcus's tricks
worked. She was determined to win this game of love,
and if this meant that she had to pretend to believe the
bean disappeared, it was a small price to pay for the jewels and the castle and her son being an abbot.

"He can lie to me about magic all he wants," murmured
Evelina, gazing at Marcus fondly as he lay sleeping at her
feet. "Just as long as he lies *with* me."

Her little joke amused her for all of several seconds and
then she yawned and slapped irritably at a mosquito and
looked around at the river, which held nothing new for
her, and at the trees, and there was nothing interesting
about them either. She heaved an audible sigh and glanced
at Marcus, half hoping he'd hear her and wake up.

He didn't stir, and she realized he was deep in slumber.

"After all, he needs his rest," she reflected. "If he's going to get us safely through that horrible cave. Why do we have to go that way anyhow? There are lots of other routes we can take to his home. His home. His castle. I wonder how many rooms it has. Dozens, probably. And food that goes on forever. Peacock tongues and suckling pig and wine from golden goblets and servants to wait on me and sweetmeats and sugared almonds and why, why, why did I have to think about food?"

Her stomach grumbled. Evelina tried to recall when she'd last eaten. She remembered Ven bringing food to her and she remembered flinging it to the floor in a fit of temper. Henceforth, she resolved, she would make certain she ate first before she flew into a rage.

And then all she could think about was being hungry. Evelina had been hungry before in her life; very hungry, sometimes, when one of her father's schemes had failed to produce any income. She looked again at Marcus. Bending over him, greatly daring, because the boat rocked alarmingly whenever she moved, she kissed him on the mouth. She let her tongue slide over his lips and was gratified to feel his lips move, ever so slightly, in response.

Evelina sighed and sat back, her blood tingling. Wrapping herself in her blanket, she gave herself up to tantalizing daydreams of their lovemaking. When even that grew boring, she yawned and yawned again and again after that. Her eyelids drooped. She slid into sleep and then sat up with a start.

"I said I'd keep watch," she reminded herself. "But I'm so tired. No one is coming for us. We're safe enough. It's not fair that he gets to sleep and I don't. I'll just shut my eyes a moment."

Having absolved herself from blame, Evelina closed her eyes and drifted into sweet slumber.

Thus it was that the dragon found them.

Fortunately for them, the dragon was Lysira.

Draconas had provided Lysira with directions to the hidden city of Dragonkeep. She couldn't see it, though she looked hard for it. She did see the boats of the monks drifting down the river, however—evidence of human habitation. He'd warned her against flying too low, a warning she ignored, for she had to fly low in order to investigate. The humans weren't in any of the boats heading downstream. Draconas thought they would be traveling the other direction, and he proved to be right.

Lysira spotted the two between a gap in the trees. Their warm human bodies glowed softly in the night.

"Your humans are not very intelligent," she reported to Draconas. "Surrounded by their foes, they are both sound asleep."

"Are they surrounded?" Draconas asked, alarmed.

"No," Lysira returned. "But, according to what you said, they could be."

"Have you seen any sign of other dragons?"

"None."

"Grald could still be hiding in the cave waiting for them," Draconas said more to himself than to her. "Are you keeping your distance?"

"Yes, Draconas," returned Lysira, her colors sharp-edged with annoyance. "I am not a fledgling."

The truth was, Lysira had decided to satisfy her curiosity about the humans. Draping herself in a simple illusion to make herself invisible, she descended from her lofty vantage point in slow, lazy circles. She kept watch as she drifted downward on her strong wings, but saw nothing to give her concern. Animals prowled the forest, birds flitted about the skies. They could not see her, and so the fox continued his rabbit-hunt and the nightjar her bug-catching without raising the alarm.

Lysira hovered above the tops of the trees and gazed down curiously on the two creatures in the boat.

Sleeping, all humans look as innocent and harmless as nestlings. And they were so fragile and vulnerable. Their bodies soft and unprotected, their soft mouths with tiny teeth, and talons with weak little claws. No wings to carry them out of harm's way. No fire rumbling in their bellies to scorch their enemies.

It was a wonder they had survived thus far. She could understand why they had to rely on terrible machines. So weak. So pitiably weak.

"What if Grald is waiting for them in the cave, Draconas?" Lysira asked. "What am I to do?"

"Nothing. You cannot fight Grald. It would be madness to try. He very nearly bested me in battle," Draconas admonished sharply. "You would have no chance against him."

"And your humans? What chance do they have?" Lysira demanded.

"More than you might think. No matter what happens, you must stay out of it. Not just for your own sake, but for the sake of our people. You are my only link with the other dragons now, Lysira. We must keep your involvement secret. Promise me you will not interfere if there is trouble. Promise."

"I don't see what right you have asking me for promises," Lysira retorted, bristling.

"I have no right," Draconas conceded. "Except as someone who cares about you. Cares very much."

Lysira's colors blurred in confusion. She didn't know what to say and so she said nothing, and by the time she thought of something, he was gone.

Lysira soared triumphantly into the evening sky. She could have fought Grald or a hundred like him in that moment of happiness. She did not forget her charges and, from her vantage point, she cast an eye on the humans, antlike, in the boat on the river that wound, snakelike, among the trees, and she thought how deceptively serene and peaceful the chaotic world of men looked from this vast distance, up among the stars.

9

MARCUS WOKE WITH A START TO PITCH DARKNESS, NOISY with the songs of frogs and crickets, to find Evelina lying across his feet. He tried to recall what had awakened him, but he'd been so deeply asleep that he couldn't distinguish dream from reality. He had either heard the swishing sound of something creeping along the shoreline or he'd dreamed it.

He froze, not moving, barely breathing, thinking that if he was quiet, whatever was out there might try to sneak up on him and he'd have the advantage of surprise.

He heard nothing except Evelina, who muttered something and rolled over, causing the boat to rock. He waited a few more moments. He couldn't wait long, however, for he was afraid that Evelina might wake and inadvertently say or do something that would reveal their hiding place.

Marcus rose up slowly and stealthily. He slid one arm beneath Evelina's head, and he placed his hand, very gently, over her mouth.

"Evelina," he said softly.

He expected her to jump and gasp or scream, which was why he had his hand over her mouth. What he did not expect was for her to nibble at his fingers, murmur something unintelligible, and nestle more deeply into his embrace.

"Evelina, wake up," he said again.

She snuggled closer. Her breath was warm and moist on his hand. "Kiss me," she whispered.

"Evelina," he said. "Please . . ."

Her eyelids fluttered. She stretched languorously, arching her back and flexing her arms behind her head. Soft, full parts of her brushed against him. Her lips licked his fingers and the touch of her lips and her body sent desire aching through his body.

"I'm awake," she said, and her eyes opened.

She gazed at Marcus, then she pushed him back and sat up with a suddenness that set the boat rocking wildly.

"Oh!" she gasped, clutching at her chemise.

"I'm sorry!" he gasped in turn. Drawing back, he felt guilt-ridden and confused. "I didn't mean . . . I was only trying . . . I was afraid you might cry out . . ."

Evelina hung her head. "No, I'm sorry," she said, her voice soft as the night. "What must you think of me! I was dreaming . . ." She blushed so deeply that he could see her flush even in the lambent starlight. "Please forgive me, Your Highness."

Not knowing what else to do, he patted her hand soothingly, all the while keeping watch in the woods.

"Is there something out there?" she asked, noticing his preoccupation and clutching his hand tightly in alarm.

"I thought I heard a noise. But it may have been an animal. I haven't heard it again." He gently disengaged his hand. "We should be going. I didn't mean to sleep so long."

"I didn't mean to sleep at all," said Evelina remorsefully. "It's just . . . I was so tired . . ."

He soothed and petted her again and thought about the spell he was going to cast on the boat.

"How do your hands feel after all that rowing?" Evelina asked suddenly.

"Like raw meat," he said ruefully.

"I'm so sorry," said Evelina, and her eyes shimmered in the starlight. "When we stop to rest, I will make a poultice to put on them. You will have to leave it on for several days and not do any more rowing, but it will heal them, and when they are healed, we can continue our journey."

"A kind thought, but we don't have time," said Marcus. He was busy constructing the magic in his mind.

"I was thinking, Marcus. This may be unseemly of me to offer, but if I tore off some strips of the hem of my chemise, you could use them to bandage your hands. It might help a little—"

"That's a good idea." He knew what he had to do and he turned his attention to her. "If you don't mind—"

"I don't mind."

Evelina lifted her skirt and folded it back over her knees. Marcus realized a bit belatedly that a gentleman should turn his head away, and he did so, but he took with him the image of shapely legs, white in the starlight. He heard fabric rip and tear, and when she told him he could turn around, she held up two long strips. She wrapped Marcus's hands herself, apologizing profusely for the fact that the cloth was travel-stained and frayed.

"That feels better already," he said, as she was carefully winding the cloth around and around his blistered palms. "I'll have my mother's seamstresses make you a new chemise when we reach my home. Made of the finest silk." He had only a vague idea what chemises were made of, but silk seemed safe. "With a hem of lace."

"I would like that, Marcus," said Evelina, and her hand stroked his hand gently as she finished her bandaging.

He was embarrassed by the adoration in her eyes and he turned away. He wished she wouldn't look at him that way, when he didn't know how he felt about her.

"We should get started."

"We're going into that cave," said Evelina, and her voice was tight.

"It's going to be all right." Marcus drew in a deep breath, then let it out slowly. "I'm going to cast a magical spell on the boat, Evelina. I'm going to make it invisible. And I'm going to make us invisible. Not to each other," he added hastily. "You'll still be able to see me and to see the boat. But no one else will be able to see us."

He was making a mess of this, but he'd never had to explain his magic to anyone before.

"I know you don't understand—" he began.

"Understand what? That you are going to make us invisible? Of course, I understand." Evelina settled herself in the stern, pulled the blanket more closely around her shoulders, and regarded him calmly. "Just tell me what I need to do."

He found himself almost loving her at that moment. "You must keep perfectly still. And not make a sound. Not a sniffle, not a gasp, not a whisper. For though they cannot see us, they can still hear us."

"They can't see us, but they can hear us. I understand, Marcus," she said.

In order to cast the magic, he would have to enter his little room, a room in his mind similar to the room where he had been locked up as a child. The danger was that whenever he entered the room, the dragons were aware of him. They would try to catch him, haul him out. And so he opened the door swiftly and ran inside and slammed the door shut behind him. Almost immediately, he could hear claws scraping and scratching outside, searching for weakness, searching for a chink, a crack.

Marcus sat on the small stool in the middle of the room, shut out the clawing, and considered what he had to do. He'd never cast a spell of such magnitude before, not in cold blood. He knew how to do it; Draconas had taught him, long ago, on the bank of a river.

There are two types of dragon-magic, Marcus. Like two types of strategy in a battle: offensive and defensive. From what I have observed watching the monks, humans can use either one or the other. The determining factor as to which they can use appears to be sex. Females can use defensive magic, males offensive. You are unique, in that you can use both.

Outside the door, the dragon snorted in frustration. Marcus forced himself to concentrate, to forget the dragon. He brought the image of the boat to mind, so that it was like a wet painting on a canvas, and he began to scrub it with water, so that the colors streamed and ran together and dribbled off the canvas in muddy droplets. He scrubbed and scrubbed until the image of the boat vanished. Looking at the painting, he saw the river and he saw the black net of tree branches catching the stars in the sky. But no boat. No Marcus. No Evelina.

He sighed deeply. He could tell by the contented warmth of pleasure that the magic had worked. The weakness and the sick feeling would come later; hopefully much later, after they'd managed to sneak through the cavern.

Marcus picked up the oars and, wincing at the pain in his hands, began to row.

Evelina opened her mouth.

Marcus shook his head, reminding her she must be silent.

"Are we invisible now?" she whispered.

Marcus nodded.

Evelina glanced around at the boat, which was plainly visible, and at herself, and at him.

"Good job," she whispered solemnly. "I can't see a thing."

Marcus smiled, thinking she was joking to relieve the tension. He continued to row and the boat rounded the bend of the river.

"There it is!" Evelina cried in a smothered voice that she remembered just in time to keep soft. She pointed.

Marcus glanced over his shoulder. The river flowed into a black maw. Chill, dank air washed over them. Evelina shivered and cast him a pleading glance that said, quite plainly, "It's not too late to turn around and go back!"

He knew those words because he was hearing them inside his head. He kept on rowing. The black maw came nearer and nearer, spewing out the river, sucking them in.

The rock cliff loomed above them, blotting out the stars. He listened, but heard only the soft gurgle of the river water, roiling around the base of the stone walls. Grald might be in there, crouched in the darkness, waiting. Or perhaps a cadre of monks, their hands tipped with fire, deadly bolts ready.

Whatever eyes were watching would not be able to see him. He reminded himself of that and continued to row. The maw came closer. He was rowing as quietly as he could, but the oars made plashing noises as they entered the water, and there was nothing he could do to muffle them. The river's flow was not very strong here, and he hoped that one mighty pull would give the boat momentum enough to coast through the cavern, so that he would not have to put the oars into the water once they were inside.

The entrance was coming up fast upon them. He had forgotten it was so low. Evelina took one frightened look, then hunched down and threw the blanket over her head.

"I can't watch!" she gasped.

Marcus gave a final pull at the oars, and then shipped them and ducked his head.

The boat skimmed over the surface and slid into the maw. He was awash in darkness so deep that it made the lambent light of stars and river seem bright by contrast. He could see nothing, and he recalled how the monks had lit lanterns on their boats when they had sailed into the cavern.

Marcus stared hard in the direction of the shoreline. He could not see it. He could see nothing in the pitch dark of the cave. He couldn't hear anything either and he began to think that the cavern was empty, that they were going to slip through unchallenged.

He did not give thanks yet. The boat was starting to lose its forward momentum. He would have to row. His heart in his mouth, he picked up the oars, moving slowly and carefully to keep them from squeaking, and slowly and carefully lowered them into the water. They made a gentle splash, and he cringed as he pulled on the oars. He feared losing his way in the darkness, and he was relieved beyond measure to see the exit—a much wider aperture than the entrance—come into view. The starlit river glimmered in the opening, and he steered the boat toward it.

The opening came nearer and nearer. Marcus was starting to think that they were going to escape after all, his heart was starting to lift, when a glimmer of light caught his attention.

The light came not from the shore, but from the dark water.

Marcus stared down into the river's depths. The light

grew in brilliance, and then there were two lights—red-gold in color, widening and expanding and drawing closer.

Marcus ceased to row. His hands clenched on the oars. Two eyes—red-gold, with black, reptilian, slit pupils—gazed up at him.

The dragon was in the water beneath them.

Terrified, Marcus stared into the eyes that followed him, unblinking, as the boat slid over the surface. The boat moved of its own volition, for Marcus's hands had gone numb, his arms had lost their strength. He sat in his small chair in his little room and quaked at the sight of the unblinking eyes and the dragon's thoughts that clawed with sharp colors at his soul.

"Come out," Grald urged. "I've your doom to show you."

Marcus stayed where he was, kept the door bolted.

"I will give you a glimpse," said Grald.

Ranks of soldiers—human soldiers, clad in armor that sparkled in the moonlight like the scales of the dragon—marched toward Marcus. The soldiers marched faster and faster, rushing up at him. Water surged around the boat, and he envisioned it capsizing, throwing him into the river, where the dragon would seize him and drag him under.

Marcus grabbed the oars and drove them deep into the water, propelling the boat toward the exit. Determinedly he rowed and kept rowing, grunting at the stinging pain in his bandaged palms.

"What is it? I can't look!" Evelina lifted her head out of the folds of the blanket, she stared, terror-stricken, around her.

Marcus didn't answer her. He lacked the breath. The boat shot out of the cave. The soldiers vanished. The dragon's eyes watched Marcus row, plunging the oars into the water, pulling, lifting, plunging, again and again, until the eyes were far behind him. Sweat poured off him.

"What's wrong?" Evelina cried.

"Didn't you see the dragon?"

Evelina glanced timidly over her shoulder, then looked back at Marcus.

"No," she said. "I didn't see anything."

"It was there, watching us."

Or was it?

Illusion. An illusion created by the dragon. An illusion meant to show Marcus that his puny magicks, of which he was so proud, were the mewling of a babe compared to the magic of the dragon.

Marcus slumped over the oars, his strength gone. His hands burned. His arm muscles jumped and twitched.

A hint of your doom. Come inside and see the rest! See the dancing girls take off their veils! All for the price of . . . your soul.

Marcus was tempted. He would open the door just a crack . . .

"Don't be a fool," said a female voice, quite clearly.

"You're right." Marcus smiled wearily at Evelina. "That would be foolish."

"Maybe it would," said Evelina, regarding him strangely. "But I didn't say anything."

10

THE MOON HAD RISEN AND, THOUGH PAST THE FULL, THE
night had shaved off only a sliver, so that its light was
bright in a cloudless sky. Marcus and Evelina continued
traveling the broad expanse of the river, keeping away
from the shore. Not even Evelina wanted to stop for the
night so near the horrible cave. She was rowing the boat
now. It was either row or linger in the place that had
driven her prince mad.

Marcus dozed fitfully in the bow of the boat. At least
when he was asleep, he wasn't talking crazy, talking
about what he'd seen in the cave or hearing the voices of
dragons in his head. There had been nothing in the cave.
Evelina had hidden her head in the blanket so she
wouldn't see anything horrible, but, consumed by a
dreadful fascination, she'd peeped out from between the
folds. She'd watched the cavern slide by, dark and empty.
And no one was talking to him, either.

"You're tired and hungry," she had told Marcus in
soothing tones. "And your poor hands! They could be
hanging in a butcher's stall, they're so red and raw. Let
me row, at least for a little while."

He argued, of course, but in the end—rather to her
surprise—he gave the oars to her, shifting position with
her in the boat. Evelina didn't do a bad job of rowing,
once she got the hang of it. She could do most things she

set her mind to; a characteristic that had carried her stubbornly through life.

Fortunately, she didn't have far to go before she steered them out of the tributary that flowed past the cave and entered the main body of the river, Aston. Here, she was rowing with the current, not against it, since the river flowed south, carrying them in the direction they wanted to go.

"We should find a place to stop," Marcus had told her before he'd fallen asleep. "It's dangerous traveling the river in the dark."

Evelina was in hearty agreement. She had no intention of spoiling her hands the way Marcus had spoiled his, and she could feel them starting to blister. Her back and shoulders ached, as did her buttocks, from the hard seat. When she saw lights ahead, bobbing up and down in the darkness, Evelina would have thanked God, had she known Him well enough to take the liberty.

The lights belonged to fishermen setting out from their small village for some night fishing. They used lantern light to lure the fish to their nets, and it was these lights that Evelina saw. She woke Marcus with a kick of her foot.

The fishermen were naturally quite astonished when a young woman rowed a boat into their midst and more astonished yet to find that she had a monk with bandaged hands for a passenger. Their confusion was cleared up when Marcus explained who he was. He didn't expect them to believe him, for he had no way to prove his identity. To his astonishment, he was greeted with smiles and good cheer and enthusiasm. The king's men, it seemed, had been here only two days before, telling the people that the prince had been lost on the river during a fishing expedition and asking them to keep a watch out for him. Not only were his people pleased to see their prince, there was a handsome reward being offered for his safe return.

"Yer Majesty," said one of the fishermen, clapping Marcus on the shoulder. "Yer the best catch we've made all year. Beggin' Yer Majesty's pardon."

The fact that he was wearing monk's robes was quickly explained by a hastily made-up tale of falling into the river and being rescued by a passing monk, who gave him dry clothes. Marcus was more vague concerning Evelina, saying confusedly something to the effect that she had found him and nursed him. The fishermen received this information with straight faces. He was, after all, their prince.

They were quick to abandon their fishing to help the two lost travelers, and within moments Marcus and Evelina were on dry land with half the village surrounding them. One of the fishermen sent his boy off at a run to inform the village patriarch of their good fortune. The patriarch met the boy on the way, for he'd heard the commotion and was heading down to see what was going on. He greeted the prince and the lady Marcus introduced as "Mistress Evelina" with calm dignity and offered them his house for the night.

"Thank you, sir," said Marcus gratefully. "I know my parents must be worried sick. If someone could carry a message—"

"No one in the village owns a horse," the patriarch replied, and seeing the prince's downcast expression, he added, "I will send our swiftest lad to find the king's men tomorrow morning."

Since that appeared to be the best Marcus could hope for, he accepted the offer with good grace. He was too exhausted and hungry to do much else.

The patriarch's wife served up a hastily prepared meal of fish stew, left over from their own dinner. Marcus won the good woman's heart by eating two helpings and swearing that he'd never tasted any food so delicious from the royal kitchen. The women of the village clucked over his injured hands and made up a poultice for him as he ate, then wrapped his hands in bandages.

Marcus, well-fed, safe, and warm, felt sleep creeping over him. He must have dozed off in his chair, for the next thing he knew, the patriarch was assisting him to a mattress on a floor in the corner—the patriarch's own bed. He fell onto the mattress and closed his eyes.

"Thank you, kind sir, but I will stay with him," Evelina said shyly. "My place is by his side."

"No," said Marcus, opening his eyes. "I cannot allow that. You are as tired as I am. Sir, I would be grateful to you if you could find a place for Mistress Evelina to stay this night."

He meant this kindly, and he was startled to see Evelina cast him an irate glance. He couldn't imagine what he'd done to upset her. She flounced out without a word, accompanying the patriarch and his wife.

He was drifting into unconsciousness when the red eyes of the dragon bore down on him, jolting him to heart-pounding wakefulness. Marcus found himself drenched in sweat. His hands stung and burned.

He was a long time going back to sleep.

Evelina, on the other hand, slept quite soundly and woke early the next morning, still burning with anger over the insulting manner in which Marcus had treated her last night. A perfectly good chance for him to get her alone and seduce her, and he'd thrown it away! True, he had been exhausted and his hands were bandaged, but any other man would have managed to overcome such minor inconveniences.

She was staying with the patriarch's married daughter, and the young woman and her fisherman husband were up with the dawn. Being in awe of their guest, they both left the house as quickly as they could in order to give Evelina some privacy. The wife went to do her laundry on the river banks, the husband went to his boat.

Evelina lay on the straw mattress, making plans and discarding them, mulling over what she needed to do in order to catch her own particular fish. Time was running out. She remembered, suddenly, that the patriarch had offered to send a message to the king's men. Already it might be too late. Evelina roused herself from her bed and walked outdoors. She found the village astir and the patriarch just leaving his house.

"Is His Highness awake?" Evelina asked.

"No, Mistress," said the patriarch. "I went to ask if he

needed anything, but he sleeps like a babe. He never knew I was there. I doubt the trump of doom could awake him."

"His Highness is exhausted. We have been through a great deal together, both of us." Evelina laid emphasis on that. With trepidation, she asked the burning question, "Have you sent the boy off to find the king's men?"

"Yes, Mistress," the patriarch answered. "Young Thom left with first light."

Evelina sighed deeply. "And how long do you suppose the king's men will be in coming?"

The patriarch frowned, considering. "When they passed through the village, they said that if we saw or heard anything of His Highness, we were to send word to Grafton, where they were camped. Now, Grafton is a day's journey on foot, longer if the weather is bad, for the roads hereabouts are in a sorry state, and I don't like the looks of the sky this morning. I'm thinking we'll have rain before noon."

Evelina clenched her fists to control the urge to slap the man. "How long, sir, before the king's men—"

"Oh," he said, pondering. "Tomorrow, but not before."

Evelina smiled to herself and prayed for torrential downpours and footpads and snakes and every other mishap that could possibly happen to a traveler to happen to "young Thom."

"I hope His Highness won't be too disappointed," added the patriarch.

"His Highness can use the rest," said Evelina, and she smiled sweetly, for, at that moment, the heavens opened up and poured rainy blessings down on her.

11

"DRACONAS . . ."

"Lysira."

"Can you talk?"

"Yes, only for a moment, though. Is Marcus safe?"

"He is with his own kind. He and the female who accompanies him—"

"Never mind her," said Draconas. "She is irrelevant."

"I trust you don't consider all females irrelevant," returned Lysira, her colors bright. She was a young dragon and excited about her first venture into the world.

"No, Lysira. I find females extremely relevant, especially those who risk their lives to help me. This one human female, however, has nothing to do with our predicament."

"I was teasing," said Lysira.

"I know you were," said Draconas "And so Marcus is safe, at least for the moment."

"He almost fell victim to the dragon. I was watching him, as you told me, and he very nearly let Grald into his mind. I warned him away. That is the first time I have ever spoken to a human. It was strange. But I liked it. I didn't think I would."

Draconas's colors warmed. He wished beyond anything in the world that he'd met this vibrant young female in a different time—a time when he could have spent years letting his dreams twine with hers.

"What do you want me to do now, Draconas?" Lysira asked, and he saw her colors shimmer and tremble. She must have seen what he was thinking.

"There's nothing you can do, not without tipping off Grald and the other dragons that you're spying on them. You are careful to keep out of sight, aren't you?"

"I am flying at such a high altitude that I have to come down every once in a while to catch my breath."

"We're about to be interrupted. I must soon leave you, Lysira. Tell me quickly, have you heard anything from Anora?"

"She has not communicated with me or with Malfiesto or the other dragons with whom I've been in contact. That is not surprising, though," Lysira added, her colors darkening, "since we are the ones who spoke out against her."

"Do not trust Anora," Draconas warned. "If she tries to talk to you, do not let her into your mind."

"She is an elder dragon, Draconas," said Lysira gently. "And very powerful. If she wants to speak to me, there is not much I can do to stop her. You know that."

Draconas did know. He'd been holding Anora at bay thus far by keeping his colors to himself as much as possible.

"Just . . . be careful, Lysira."

"I will," she promised and her colors were lovely and lingered in his mind.

"Draca." A gentle hand touched his shoulder.

Stretching, Draconas sighed and blinked up drowsily at the motherly woman bending over him.

"Draca," said Rosa, "I'm sorry to wake you, but it is noontime. You've slept the morning through. Anton is home for his meal and I thought you might be hungry—"

The illusory body of the girl that Draconas had assumed sat up in the bed and sniffed at the good smells wafting through the small house. Draconas had used this illusion before, and he was quite pleased with it. Being a human child, he'd discovered, gave him a great deal of freedom.

Human adults take a tolerant view of their offspring.

As a child, Draconas could be as curious and inquisitive as he liked, poke and pry and snoop, and adults would sigh and shake their heads and the worst they might do would be to send him to bed without his supper. He had learned that many humans, who might otherwise keep their mouths shut tighter than a clam shell when in the presence of an adult, tended to blab freely in the presence of a child.

"How are you feeling?" asked Rosa anxiously.

"Much better," said Draconas in the girl's high and piping voice. "I am hungry. What've you got to eat?"

He threw off the blankets and sat up in bed.

"Not too quickly," Rosa cautioned. "You'll make yourself dizzy."

"I'm fine, really," Draconas assured her. He reached out his little girl's hand. "Thank you for helping me, ma'am. And thank you for not telling . . ."

"I promised I wouldn't," Rosa said gently. "But you *will* have to go back to the Abbey someday soon, child."

Draconas let his face fall and his shoulders droop. He ducked his head and made a swipe at his eyes with his hand. "I don't want to," he mumbled. "I want to stay with you."

"There, there, child," said Rosa, soothing him. "Don't cry. You can stay with us a little while. Now come and eat something. You are much too thin. You need some meat on those bones."

Draconas accompanied Rosa to the table. Anton was already eating, digging his spoon into a bowl of mutton stew. He welcomed the little girl with a broad smile and shoved a chair out with his foot.

Draconas picked up the spoon and was about to eat, when colors exploded inside his head.

"Draconas!" Malfiesto barked. "What's this nonsense Anora has been spreading about her army preparing to attack a human kingdom? Is this true?"

Draconas dropped his spoon and put his hands to his temples.

"Child, what's the matter?" Anton asked, alarmed. "Look at her, Wife. She's gone white as sheep's wool."

"Army," Draconas repeated inwardly. "What are you talking about? What's this about an army?"

"That's what I'm asking you!" Malfiesto raged in ear-splitting colors.

"Look, Malfiesto, this is not a good time. I can't talk now. I'll contact you later."

"If you don't, I will," the dragon threatened. "Keep me informed! I'm taking charge, now that Anora has lost her senses. You are the Walker. You report to me."

Draconas sighed. He'd been pleased at first to find that Malfiesto was on his side. Now, he wasn't so certain. The irascible old dragon was likely to prove more hindrance than help.

"What's the matter, Draca?" Rosa hovered over him.

"Nothing, ma'am. Just a pain in the . . . head," said Draconas. "I'm fine now. This stew is really good."

He shoveled food into his mouth, and Rosa sat back, reassured. Adults, be they human or dragon, are always pleased to see children eat.

"This was my daughter's favorite meal," said Rosa, and she gave a little sigh.

"Where is your daughter? I'd like to meet her," mumbled Draconas.

"Don't talk with your mouth full, dear. Our daughter is one of the Dragon's Chosen."

"She lives in the palace," Anton added proudly.

"What does she do there?"

"She serves the dragon, of course."

Draconas looked at them, puzzled. "Huh?"

Rosa and Anton exchanged glances.

"The holy sisters must have told you about the Dragon's Chosen, Draca," Anton said.

Draconas shook his head. "No, sir, not a word."

"Don't lie, child," said Rosa. "Lying is a sin. The dragon won't like it."

"The dragon's not here," said Draconas impudently.

Anton choked on a mouthful of ale. Rising swiftly to his feet, he went to look out the window. Rosa put her hand over Draconas's, squeezed it tightly.

"You should not speak of the dragon that way," she said loudly. "It is disrespectful."

She looked at Anton, and Draconas saw fear in her eyes.

Anton sat back down. "No one's about. Perhaps it's not so surprising," he said to his wife. "The girl is young yet, after all. Maybe they don't tell them until they are old enough to be considered."

"Old enough to be considered to do what?" Draconas asked. His child's wide-eyed, innocent gaze went from one to the other.

"Oh, dear, maybe I shouldn't have said anything." Rosa's hands plucked at her dress, twisting the fabric.

"I won't tell," Draconas promised. "Is it a secret? I'm good at keeping secrets!"

"No, it's not a secret," Anton said slowly, after a moment's pause. "Everyone in Dragonkeep knows about the Palace of the Dragon. Being selected as one of the Dragon's Chosen is an honor, after all."

"When a girl is eighteen, she becomes eligible to be one of the Chosen. Our girl was selected almost immediately," Rosa said, flushing with pride. "The dragon picks only those who can demonstrate that they are strong in the magic. The Chosen leave their homes and move into the palace with the dragon. They serve him and, in return, they are given everything they want."

"What's it like inside the palace?" Draconas asked eagerly.

"My goodness, child, we don't know," Rosa said, smiling. "We've never been inside."

"But you've seen your daughter since she moved in," Draconas persisted.

"No, not in many years," Anton replied, and his face was shadowed. "Once a woman enters the palace, she's not allowed to leave. That's one of the rules. And not a very good one, if you ask me."

"But we get letters from her," Rosa said hastily, with a worried glance at her husband. "Twice a year she writes to us about how happy she is and how much she enjoys serving the dragon. As strong as you are in the blood bane, Draca, I'm sure you'll be chosen to serve the dragon."

"Maybe . . ." Draconas was cautious. "Where is the palace?"

"Now, Draca, don't be a tease," said Rosa. "Everyone knows where the palace is."

"And everyone knows that we are forbidden to go near it," Anton said sternly. "That includes children."

Draconas gave them a mischievous grin and held out the bowl. "Could I have some more to eat, please? It's really, really good."

Rosa, gratified, ladled out more stew.

Anton rose from the table. "I have to get back to the forge, Wife. I may be late for supper. We've a deal of work to do all of a sudden. A large order came in this morning. An order for weapons."

Rosa set down the bowl in front of Draconas, who watched and listened, all the while pretending to be absorbed in his meal.

"Weapons?" Rosa repeated. "What sort of weapons?"

"Throwing darts, mostly. As many as I can turn out as fast as I can turn them out. One of the Blessed came by the shop this morning to tell me. And it's not just me. Every blacksmith in the city has been told to drop all other work and turn his hand to this."

"And what are you to do with these weapons?"

"Hand them over to the Blessed."

"And what do they do with them?"

"They take them to the palace. That is what I hear. The weapons are being stored there."

"The palace . . ." Rosa wrinkled her forehead. "Maybe the rumors *are* true."

"Maybe," Anton grunted.

Rosa sighed. Her hands squeezed together tightly.

Anton kissed her cheek. "Don't fret, Wife. It's nothing to do with us, whatever may be brewing, except that it brings me more work, and that will mean extra rations. What are you doing this afternoon?"

"I should go to the market. I meant to go this morning, but I didn't want to leave Draca home alone."

"I'm fine. Truly I am," Draconas piped up. "You can go, Rosa. I don't mind being alone. I like it."

"We are out of meat," said Rosa, and she gave Anton a meaningful look. "I was thinking of going to the butcher. Dimitri, perhaps. There'll be nothing for your supper otherwise—"

"The child will be well enough on her own," said Anton, and he added in a whisper not meant for Draca to hear, "See what you can find out. If Dimitri's not around, go visit the chandler, Carlo. Tell him about the weapons. You can have the Widow Meadows look in on the girl."

Draconas's dragon ears caught every word. He picked up his bowl and went to wash it out, along with his spoon. Then he returned to his bed and crawled under the blanket. "I'm still feeling tired, Rosa. I think I'll take a nap. Don't worry about me."

Rosa kissed the girl on the forehead. "The widow will check on you, and I'll be back in time to cook your supper. Sweet dreams, Draca."

Draconas closed his eyes and nestled beneath the covers. Anton departed. Rosa washed up the dishes and left shortly after, taking her marketing basket with her.

Draconas waited until he was certain that neither was coming back, and then he slipped out of bed. Cautiously, he opened the door and peered out into the street. The forge was adjacent to the house. He could smell the acrid scent of molten iron and see Anton's broad back and shoulders silhouetted against the glare of the forge fire. The ringing sounds of Anton's hammer echoed up and down the street, which was crowded with people heading back to work after their dinner break.

Draconas dashed out the door and quickly lost himself in the crowd. Behind him, an illusion of a little girl slumbered peacefully in the bed.

12

DRACONAS ROAMED THE STREETS OF DRAGONKEEP,
mulling over in his mind his conversation with Anton and
Rosa and that pain in the backside, Malfiesto: Anora talking about armies, orders given to the blacksmith to produce large quantities of darts in a hurry. Draconas had
been in human cities on the verge of war, and he remembered clearly the forge fires of the blacksmiths burning
far into the night and the furious din of hammers pounding like war drums, turning out armor and swords, arrows
and shields. Yet, he'd seen no soldiers in Dragonkeep.

The darts were to go to the palace. Only the monks
were permitted to enter the palace. Was the army composed of mad, dart-flinging monks?

Draconas was familiar with the darts Anton was
making—one such dart had felled Bellona.

Humans had long played dart-throwing games. Draconas had watched them and even participated in a few.
He'd known humans who could throw darts with remark-
able accuracy, but he'd never known one who could throw
a small metal dart—no bigger than his index finger—
with such force that it could kill a person a furlong away.
The impetus behind the dart was dragon-magic. The
monk used his magic to increase the force of his throw.
Perhaps the monk had even been able to use the magic to
assist the dart in finding its target.

Yet, Draconas considered, most of the monks he'd seen were mentally unstable, bordering on the insane. The dragon-magic in the blood did strange things to the brains of human males. An army of insane men was not an army any rational general would want to lead. Impossible to discipline, they could not be counted upon to obey the simplest command. Turn them loose on a battlefield and they could conceivably do more damage to themselves than to an enemy.

"Unless Grald discovered how to cure the madness, just as I did," Draconas muttered. "Marcus was insane until I taught him how to master the magic, not succumb to it. If I could find a way, so could Grald. And he's had far longer to experiment. Maybe there are soldiers *and* monks in Dragonkeep. Maybe the monks are the failures. . . ."

That opened up new and extremely disquieting possibilities. Obviously, the answer lay in the palace that no one was supposed to enter.

Draconas continued his wanderings until he found what he was looking for—other children like himself.

The children of Dragonkeep were expected to make their contribution to society, and in this they were no different from the children of Idylswylde or New Bramfells or Weinmauer or countless other human communities. Those children who lacked the dragon-magic were apprenticed to craftsmen or worked in the fields. They milked goats, tended sheep, fed the chickens. Those with dragon-magic lived with the monks and the holy sisters.

Still, children were children the world over, and Draconas hoped to find some like himself who had sneaked out of the shop when the master went home for his dinner or had left the chickens to go off in search of fun. Draconas knew where to look for such rascals, and he soon came upon a group of youngsters skulking in an alley, playing at mumblety-peg.

"Can I have a toss?" Draconas asked, joining them.

"No girls," said one of the boys.

"You're just afraid I'll beat you!" Draconas sneered.

Several of the boys snickered. The speaker cast little Draca an angry glance.

"Oh, yeah? Let's see you." He handed over the knife.

Draconas had been playing mumblety-peg for several hundred years. He could have beaten his rival handily at the game, but that would have alienated the children, and he wanted them to accept him. Draca demonstrated her skill, and the match was considered a tie, with the result that she was pronounced an expert mumblety-peg player and accepted into the ranks of boydom.

Draconas and his newfound friends played at mumblety-peg until they grew bored, at which point they began to look about for other forms of amusement. The boys—six of them—ranged in age from nine to fourteen. One was an apprentice to a disreputable shoemaker, who had a taste for ale and generally took a nap about this time of day, leaving the boy to his own devices. Two were supposed to be working in the fields, but had thought better of it. Another was meant to be running errands for his mistress, an herbalist, and another was supposed to be home sick in bed.

The sixth was vague as to where he came from. The others indicated with winks and nods, whispers and nudges, that he was a "runaway"—one of those children with the dragon-magic in their blood. Draconas kept a wary eye on this boy, who was constantly mumbling to himself and who, when given the knife for mumblety-peg, made a wild swipe at Draca. When the other boys told the runaway that stabbing fellow playmates was against the rules, the boy then sliced open his own forearm. Not the least bothered by this bizarre behavior, the boys simply took the knife away and told their friend to go wash off the blood at the public fountain "or the Blessed will nab you for sure!"

This done, the boys suggested various means of passing the time. Some wanted to steal apples from the market. Others wanted to ogle the women who were doing their laundry in the creek, and still others wanted to go look at the destruction caused by the explosion, on the off-chance that they might find a dead body.

The majority was leaning in this direction, when Draconas said, "Pooh! There aren't any more dead bodies. I heard my father say everyone had been found."

Faces fell. The boy with the dragon-magic slammed his fist into the stone wall in disgust and drew back bleeding knuckles.

"I know!" Draconas said, edging away from the boy, who was looking at her oddly. "Let's go see the palace."

Dead silence fell. The boys stared at her, some with awe, others nervously.

"Why? What's the matter?" Draconas asked.

"We're not allowed," said one.

"We're not allowed to skip out of work and we're doing it," Draconas reminded them.

"This is different," said another.

"If he catches us, the dragon will eat us," said the youngest boy in a whisper.

The others scoffed and knocked him around playfully and mussed his hair, but no one made a move to go. The boy with the dragon-magic had quit talking to himself and was staring at Draca with narrowed eyes.

"I think you're all afraid," said Draconas loftily. "I dare you to come to the palace with me."

The boys looked uncertainly at each other.

"Double-dare," said Draconas, upping the stakes.

"I'll go," said the boy with the dragon-magic. He had an eager look on his thin and blood-smeared face and he couldn't seem to take his eyes off her.

"Good for you!" said Draconas. She held out her hand to him and pretended not to notice when he recoiled and backed away from her. "You and I'll go. The rest are too scared."

There was no question for the others now. Their honor had been challenged.

"We'll just go *look* at the palace," said the eldest, clarifying the rules.

"Of course," said Draconas scornfully. "You don't think I mean to go inside, do you? Who's the leader?" Her gaze went to the eldest and she smiled sweetly. "I guess you must be."

"I am," he affirmed, flattered.

"Then you lead the way." Draconas flashed a glance around at the others. "We'll follow, won't we, boys?"

All agreed, though with mixed levels of enthusiasm. The eldest boy, his head held high, started off down the alley. The rest fell in behind. Draconas was slightly disconcerted to find the boy with the dragon-magic dogging his footsteps, his mad gaze fixed on Draca with rapt attention.

Some males with dragon-magic had the ability to see through Draconas's illusion, see the dragon that he was, not the little girl he was pretending to be. He wondered uneasily if this boy was seeing Draca or the dragon . . .

The children wended their way through streets that twisted and turned, rambled into alleys, wandered uphill and down, and meandered around buildings that were all jumbled together in seemingly senseless order, judging by human standards. Grald had laid out the city and Draconas saw the dragon's instinctive need to surround and defend himself with mazes and labyrinths in every twist and turn. Draconas's dragon-brain being accustomed to mazes, he was able to keep track of the route they were taking. He now had a pretty good notion of where the dragon must have located his "palace"—somewhere near the mountain where Grald would have his lair.

The gray stone walls of the Abbey rose up in front of them. Beyond the Abbey was a broad expanse of meadow land where sheep and cattle grazed. The eldest said that they should avoid the Abbey "because that's where the Blessed hang out." The boy with dragon-magic nodded his head emphatically at this.

"The Dragon's Son lives there," he said, his voice low and reverent. He repeated this several times.

"Dragon's Son!" said one and rolled his eyes.

"It's true," claimed the youngest. "I saw him. He has the legs of a dragon. And claws instead of toes."

"And a tail, too, I'll bet," the eldest sneered.

"I didn't see a tail," said the nine-year-old.

"Pooh, you didn't see anything!"

"I did so."

"Did not."

"Careful! There's one of the Blessed!" Draconas warned, and the quarrel ended abruptly. The boys darted off down a side street. Now that they had made up their minds to this adventure, they were giving it their all.

Draconas glanced back at the Abbey. He now knew where to find Ven.

The children made a wide circle around the Abbey and were about a half-mile past it when they entered a part of the city that had the look of being very old. It was also very empty.

The stone buildings had not been kept in repair and were in various stages of tumbling down. The streets were deserted.

"I don't like this. We're not supposed to be here," said one of the boys—the shoemaker's apprentice—and he came to a halt.

"Shut up," said the eldest. "Or maybe you want to run home to your mama."

The boy looked defiantly at his leader, then looked around at the others. "You can all get eaten by the dragon if you want to. Not me." He took to his heels and went racing back the way they'd come.

"Piss yellow!" shouted the nine-year-old after him.

Emboldened by this show of cowardice and caught up in the daring of their actions, the others forged ahead, picking their way through streets littered with debris. The rows of buildings came to an abrupt end at the edge of a deep ravine. The street continued on, leading to a bridge that spanned the ravine.

"Stop here!" ordered the leader and he raised his hand. The others clustered behind him, careful to keep to the shadows.

"There it is," he said, awed.

The bridge was crude, built out of piles of boulders that had been dumped into the ravine and then fire-blasted smooth on top. On the other side, at least two miles distant, stood the Palace of the Dragon.

The palace was far different from the crudely constructed buildings of Dragonkeep. Smooth marble pillars decorated an elaborate marble portico. Marble steps flowed outward in graceful curves from immense double bronze doors adorned with the heads of dragons. Marble walls were topped by countless marble spires and battlements and turrets. The palace was very beautiful, and it was all very false.

The palace was an illusion, and not a very good one.

The illusion of the forest that surrounded the city of Dragonkeep, hiding it from the eyes of both humans and dragons was a supreme illusion and close to perfect. Draconas had not been able to penetrate it until Grald had lifted the spell, and he still had trouble seeing through it, though he knew it was there. Perhaps Grald had worn himself out casting that illusion, which, even after it was cast, required a certain amount of energy to keep in place. The palace was an ordinary dragon-illusion, meant to fool human eyes alone and it was doing a good job of that, judging by the gape-jawed wonder of the youngsters. Draconas glanced at the boy with the dragon-magic and saw that he was as wide-eyed as the rest.

Draconas saw no pillars or spires or marble stairs. What he saw, when he looked across that bridge, was the side of the mountain pierced by the dark opening at its base. Draconas crept nearer.

"Don't let them see you!" said the leader, and he reached out and dragged Draca back into the shadows.

A cadre of monks guarded the bridge on the city side of the ravine. Draconas noted, as a point of interest, that there were no guards posted on the palace side of the bridge. Apparently the dragon was concerned about people from the city entering the palace, not about those in the palace leaving to enter the city.

The Blessed did not make very good guards. They wandered about in a desultory manner, gazing with their mad, unfocused eyes at the sky or the clouds, or staring blankly into the empty city streets, or peering over the edge of the bridge into the ravine.

"Why? What would happen if they did see me?" Draconas asked. "Would the dragon really eat me?"

"No. At least, I don't think so. But the Blessed

wouldn't like it. They don't like anyone getting too curious about the palace."

"I wonder what's inside," said Draconas.

"A whole 'nother city, replied the leader. "So my father says."

"Truly?" Draca regarded him with admiration. "Tell me about it."

"No one knows," the leader admitted. "But the people who live there send letters that say how beautiful everything is."

"Someone must have gone in there and come back out again. Don't the Blessed go inside?"

"They go in," said the boy with the dragon-magic. He stood staring at the illusion with a wistful hunger in his eyes. He was biting his fingernails. "The Blessed go in and they come back out, too. Some of them. But they don't talk about it."

One of the boys pointed at the lengthening shadows. "Hey, fellows, it's almost suppertime. We better be getting back. My mistress will be hopping mad."

Having found what he sought, Draconas was more than willing to leave. He and the others started to retrace their steps, when he suddenly realized that one of them was missing.

"Hey, where's that kid?" he asked. "The runaway?"

"Don't worry about him." The others shrugged. "The Blessed'll find him and take him home."

"Either that or he'll throw himself off the cliff," said the leader, and the rest snickered.

Draconas looked back and saw the boy still standing in the shadows, leaning up against the building. Draconas wondered how many of the "blessed" children had flung themselves off that cliff onto the sharp rocks far below.

"C'mon," said the leader. "Race you home!"

Draconas proved remarkably fast, for a girl.

13

WHEN ANTON AND ROSA RETURNED FROM WORK, THEY found Draca puttering about the small house, doing chores. The widow dropped by to tell them that when she had checked on the child, Draca had been fast asleep. Rosa was pleased with Draca's unlooked-for help around the house and invited her to assist with their supper. As the two chatted and laughed while preparing the simple meal, Anton sat at the table, waiting to eat, and thought about their daughter, who had been gone so many years. It was good to see Rosa with a child again, good to hear her laugh. He sighed deeply. Rosa seemed to have put all thought of sending Draca back to the Blessed out of her mind.

After supper, Anton rose and headed for the door.

"Husband, where are you going?" Rosa asked in astonishment.

"There will be moonlight tonight," Anton returned. "Between that and the light of the forge, I can work a little longer." He paused, then said heavily, "The Blessed were not pleased by my output. They expected more."

"You are exhausted!" Rosa protested. "You cannot work this night. Come, sit and rest. You will go to work with the first light tomorrow."

Anton smiled ruefully. "I will be doing that, as well. Probably for the next few days."

"Draca," said Rosa casually, catching her husband's eye. "We need more water. Would you run to the well for me?"

Draca obediently picked up the bucket and went out the door. She ran to the well, which was close by, and then ran back. She did not enter, but leaned near the open window, looking and listening.

"This war is being undertaken for our own good, Wife. Our own defense."

"Do the Blessed think we are going to be attacked?" Rosa asked, alarmed.

"They hint as much, though they don't say outright."

"But . . . who would attack us? And why? We've done nothing to anyone!"

"I don't know." Anton shook his head. "There is no doubt that the Blessed are preparing for war."

"And who will fight? Will they? Will you? Our people? We know nothing about such things." Rosa's cheeks reddened, her eyes flashed. "Two hundred years, this city has been in existence, and all those years we've lived in peace. Why now? What has changed? We've seen no sign of any enemy—"

"I can't say, Wife." Anton raised his hands defensively, retreating from the barrage.

"I don't like this. First there's an explosion and people die and no one will say what blew up. Then people start disappearing. Dimitri has not returned to his home and his family has had no word of him. I tell you, Husband, I don't like it!"

"Don't be angry at me, Wife. I am not the one responsible. You must ask the Blessed if you want answers. Or the dragon. Where is Draca?" he asked suddenly. "She's been gone long enough to fetch five buckets of water."

"Sorry!" said Draca, bursting through the door. She was dripping wet. "I spilled the first bucket all over me."

"Sit by the fire and dry out," Rosa said, fussing over her. "I'm going to the forge with Anton. I won't be gone long."

Draca dragged her stool close to the fire, gave them both a grin, and waved.

"I don't want to scare her with talk of war," Rosa said, shutting the door.

Anton realized there was something more here. He thought he knew what it was and he braced himself.

"Husband—" began Rosa,

"Rosa," he said gently, "we must take her back."

"Why?" Rosa demanded. "She is a help to me around the house. She brings a light to your eyes that I have not seen in years—"

Just what Anton had been thinking to himself about his wife.

She laid her hand on his arm. "What if there is a war? The girl will need a safe home. Please, Husband. No one has been asking around for her. I made inquiries when I was at the market. There are no reports of a child missing. The Blessed are not making the rounds, searching for her. Maybe you were wrong about her. Maybe she does not have the blood bane."

"I saw what I saw, Wife. Her magic saved her life," said Anton. "That's the only explanation."

"No, it's not," Rosa returned briskly. Her husband was weakening and she was quick to see it. "There are quirks of fate. Happy accidents. Coincidences."

"Wife, I am behind enough as it is. I must go to work. We will speak of this in the morning—"

"I will make a bargain with you," Rosa continued, pretending not to hear. "If the Blessed announce publicly that they are looking for a lost girl, I will take her to them myself. If not, we will give her a home."

"We will speak in the morning," Anton repeated, but he knew by the set of his wife's shoulders, as she walked back into the house, that he had already lost the argument.

Draconas finished the washing up, swept the floor, and laid the table ready for tomorrow's breakfast. He gave no sign that his dragon ears had overheard every word between husband and wife. He stayed up to keep Rosa company until Anton returned. The smith came home early; the moonlight he'd expected had not materialized, for the sky clouded over and rain began to fall. All three went to bed.

Draconas lay awake, listening for Rosa and Anton to fall into slumber, which both did very shortly, for the day had been long and hard for both of them. Creeping out of his bed, he went to stand over the couple, who slept in each other's arms.

The house was dark, but his dragon eyes could see the lines of care and fatigue etched on each face, and he thought how he—the little girl—helped ease those lines, at least for a little while. Someday—maybe someday soon—he would sneak away and not come back. And they would never know why.

He would leave them as he had left other humans in his past. Others who had cared about him, cared about him deeply. Others who had never known why he had walked into their lives, only to walk right back out.

He tried to avoid saying goodbye. That always called for explanations. Easier on all parties if he just simply disappeared. As he cast the enchantment over Anton and Rosa that would insure that they sleep throughout the night, he told himself that if he could bring them news of their daughter, such news would help ease the pain of his disappearance.

It was a nice thought to carry with him.

The night was dark, for the sky was cloud-covered and drizzling. The streets were empty. The Blessed imposed a curfew on all citizens and the monks walked the streets at night, their fell presence presumably warding off whatever temptation anyone might feel to break the law.

The monks roamed the streets wherever whim or madness took them. Draconas would sometimes travel for blocks and never see one and then run into groups of them skulking about in an alley. Avoiding them proved easy, for they carried lanterns and he could see them coming long before they could see him. Sighting other shadows flitting past in the night, he guessed that he wasn't the only person in Dragonkeep out on some furtive mission. Two such shadows stood in a doorway, locked in an embrace.

Draconas had dropped the image of Draca the minute he left the house and shifted his illusory form to become one of the monks, borrowing the features of a monk who had attacked Marcus when he first entered the city. If Draconas did run into one of the Blessed, they would find his face familiar.

At the sight of the cowled figure of Draconas, the two shadows in the doorway fled.

Draconas retraced his steps of the morning. He walked past the Abbey, wondering which room belonged to Ven. Perhaps the single room on the second floor where the light burned bright. Draconas stared hard at the light, as if it could answer his many questions concerning Ven, not the least of which was why he had lured Marcus here to be given as a present to the dragon, then turned around and helped his brother to escape?

The rain came down harder. Draconas pulled his cowl over his head. The only way to answer that question and others was to talk to Ven, either face to face or mind to mind. Both those options were dangerous. The monks guarded Ven's body. Grald guarded Ven's mind.

Draconas passed other monks on the street. None spoke to him. Some gave him brief nods. Others went by without even noticing him, walking with a shuffling gait, muttering to themselves. Draconas tried to imagine an army made up of these wretched creatures and failed. The dragons were smarter than that. They must have something else planned. Which was why Draconas was on his way to the palace.

Reaching the bridge, he halted in the shadows and settled down to watch. He wanted to see monks cross the bridge, wanted to see if they were accosted by the guard and, if so, what they said and did.

The number of the Blessed on duty at the bridge was considerably reduced by night. Only three were posted on the city side of the bridge, and there were still no guards on the palace side. Draconas pondered what this might mean, but could arrive at no satisfactory answer. The only obvious one was that there was no one in the palace to guard—a grim thought, especially for the daughter of Anton and Rosa.

He waited and waited, but no one made any attempt to cross. After almost an hour, Draconas began to realize that no one was going to try to cross. When they said no one entered the palace, they meant it.

The Blessed roved about aimlessly, occasionally coming together to talk, then wandering off. Draconas considered using his magic to make himself invisible. The illusion would work with ordinary humans, but he could not count on that with these monks. Whereas another of their own trying to cross the bridge . . .

Draconas made up his mind. He set forth, walking briskly, as with purpose.

The monks guarding the bridge were apparently not accustomed to dealing with interlopers in the night, for they were startled beyond measure when Draconas materialized out of the darkness. Indeed, he was almost on top of them before they even noticed him, and then all three stared at him in such amazement that they seemed to wonder if he was real or an apparition.

"Greetings, Brethren," said Draconas pleasantly. Sweeping past them, his robes flapping around his ankles, he glanced skyward. "At least it has stopped raining for the moment. I trust I will be finished with my business and back safely in my bed before another storm breaks."

He kept walking as he spoke, as if crossing the bridge in the night was an everyday occurrence. None of the monks said a word or made a move, and he thought he was going to make it. He took another step, then one of them glided sideways to take up a position directly in front of Draconas.

"None may pass," said the monk. He was polite, not threatening, merely stating a fact. The monk's eyes were neither unfocused nor wandering. His eyes looked quite sane. All too sane.

"I have the dragon's sanction." Draconas affected surprise. "I was told to inspect the shipment of weapons that was brought into the palace this day. It seems that the dragon is concerned about their quality. He may decide to take the smith to task on the morrow."

"You need not concern yourself with this, Brother. The matter will be dealt with by those within," said the monk calmly.

"But I was told to handle this myself," protested Draconas.

"Then whoever told you that was mistaken."

The monk was calm, imperturbable, and immovable as the mountain. Less movable, maybe, for an earthquake might shake the mountain, but it seemed that nothing would shift this monk. Draconas glanced past the man to the other end of the bridge. He could always make a run for it and, with his dragon strength and speed, he could easily outdistance the human. He was turning back to the monk when his eye caught a faint shimmer of light like a fine spray of water sparkling in the sunshine—except that there was no water and no sun. He looked hard at the end of bridge and the shimmer vanished. When he looked away, the shimmer reappeared.

Draconas was thwarted. He'd been in enough dragon lairs to recognize a magical barrier when he saw it; a barrier that was undoubtedly so sensitive it would detect a rat's whisker. Draconas could use his magic against the monk and then against the barrier, but he had the feeling—looking into those all too sane eyes—that this monk knew a few magic tricks of his own, and the last thing Draconas wanted was the eruption of a magical firestorm in front of Grald's living quarters.

Draconas could think of no other persuasive arguments. Muttering that he was going to get into trouble with his superiors, he stomped angrily off the bridge and retreated up the street. Halting in an alleyway, he eyed the bridge and the stanchionlike guardian and the unseen barrier.

" 'No one may pass,' " he repeated. "Except by invitation, and only those women who are strong in the dragon-magic. No one else is admitted, not even the Blessed. What is in that palace that no one is meant to see?"

No one may pass. At least not across the bridge, and that was the only way inside the mountain.

The only way for humans . . . Not for dragons.

Draconas glanced up in frustration at the buildings that towered over him and pressed in around him. He thought of the Abbey and the broad, open expanses of grassy meadows that surrounded it, and he headed in that direction at a run.

Ven rose from his sickbed shortly after supper, and over the protests of the monks, he announced his intention of going for a walk in the cool night air. He needed to get out, to walk off his trouble, as Bellona termed it. The mind worked better when the body was active. Ven needed exercise, needed fresh air, not the stale, monk-breathed air of the sick room.

He started for the door, but at this the monks did more than protest. They told him firmly that he was not to venture out—Grald's orders.

Ven argued and even threatened. The monks were careful to keep their distance, for they feared him, but they apparently feared Grald more, for Ven was not able to shake their resolve. When he saw sparks dance on their fingertips and heard the crackle and sizzle of magic in the air, he was forced to back down.

"It is not personal to you, Dragon's Son," one of the monks told him in tones meant to be mollifying. "No one walks the streets of Dragonkeep after the Slumber Hour. Take your rest this night and I will ask Grald if you may be permitted to go forth on the morrow."

Ven was left with nothing more than the small satisfaction of ordering the monks out of his room.

Alone, he paced and paced, his claws clicking loudly on the wood floor, back and forth, back and forth— an irritating sound that he hoped was annoying the hell out of the monks.

He had much to think about, not the least of which was how he would fulfill the promise of his name— Vengeance. He had sworn an oath to the spirit of Bellona that he would avenge his mother's death. How he was to fight a dragon, when he couldn't even stand up to a half-starved, half-mad monk, was more than Ven could fathom.

He thought again of trying to learn the magic and rejected the idea. He wanted no part of the dragon within him. The human part of him would kill the father who had made him. And it was then, in his pacing and his thinking, that Ven realized a truth about himself.

He was not just avenging his mother's death. He was avenging his own accursed birth.

He dreamed about the battle with his father in all its bloody glory, but that was all it was—a dream. In reality, the only blood likely to be spilled was Ven's. He could wield a sword—Bellona had seen to that. But he did not possess a sword, and with the blasted monks dogging his footsteps, there seemed no way to acquire one.

Add to that the fact that he'd have to kill Grald twice. First he'd have to slay the huge and hulking human body—a task that might daunt even the most skilled human warrior, something Ven was not. Then, he'd have to kill the dragon.

Growing increasingly frustrated, Ven paced and kept on pacing. His route took him near the small hole that passed for a window in the crudely constructed building. He looked out this window every time he passed, longing for the freedom of the grassy sward that lay beyond it, and he vowed that tomorrow he was getting out of this room, even if he had to tear down the walls to do it.

On his hundred and umpteenth time past the window, Ven looked outside and caught sight of movement. Even a deer bounding across the hillside would be a welcome distraction to his own dismal ponderings, and he halted his pacing to stare out into the field, his dragon eyesight easily penetrating the rain-drenched darkness.

He saw a man standing on the hillside lift up his arms, and the arms became enormous wings. A huge reptilian head gazed up into the night. Powerful hind legs and a massive tail drove into the ground, propelling the body upward. The dragon's claws grabbed at the clouds and caught them, seeming to drag them down to earth, as the wings carried the massive body into heaven.

Ven was a child again, watching with vivid clarity a man take wing, take flight, soar into the sky, leaving behind a grief-stricken half-human, half-dragon, who wanted to be all human, no dragon.

Ven sprang at the window with a bound, sprang at it as

though he might spring out of it. Gripping the ledge with his hands, he stared into the night and sucked in a breath and let it out in a hiss that was also a name.

"Draconas!"

He watched the dragon wheel in the sky. Draconas was fleeing Dragonkeep, escaping. Leaving Ven behind.

Ven was tempted to call out to Draconas, to splatter the white emptiness of his cave with the red-gold stain of Draconas's name. Ven stopped himself, however. He had only once in his life cried out for help, a cry that had been answered by Grald. He would not beg for help ever again.

The dragon flew into a cloud bank and Ven lost sight of him. He continued to watch, his gaze roving rapidly over every portion of the sky. He was frustrated in his search, for the clouds gathered thickly overhead. Spatters of rain started to fall. He leaned precariously out the window, twisting his body to peer upward, but saw nothing. The rain fell harder, drops plashing on his bare head. He pulled himself back inside and continued to watch.

His patience was rewarded. A gap opened in the clouds and Ven had a clear view of the dragon.

The creature spiraled down from the sky to land on a rock ledge at a point about halfway up the mountainside. The dragon was there an instant and then disappeared from view as the clouds caught the mountain in their grasp and smothered it.

Ven drew back from the window. He no longer paced. He had worn himself out. He had a lot to think about, but he could think in his bed.

The last Ven had seen of Draconas, the dragon stood silhouetted against a lightning flash. Ducking his head and folding his wings close to his body, Draconas had entered the mountain.

14

DRACONAS HAD NO DIFFICULTY FINDING THE BACK DOOR
into the dragon's lair. He spotted the gaping gash in the
cliffs on the southern side of the mountain the moment he
flew over it. No effort had been made to disguise the
opening or conceal it. Grald was either a very lazy dragon
or a very arrogant one.

Or—very calculating.

Such an obvious door might be a trap.

Conceding that possibility, Draconas entered the cave
using extreme caution. The aperture was narrow. He had
to flatten his body and keep his wings pressed against his
flanks in order to squeeze into it, and then his shoulders
rubbed against the cavern walls. He was forced to maneu-
ver carefully to keep from tearing a wing. He peered intently at the walls as he entered. If Grald had passed this
way in dragon form, Draconas would see some sign of
it—scraped-off scales clinging to the walls, claw marks
in the rock.

No sign of either. Draconas doubted that any dragon
had walked this cavern for years, perhaps not since it was
formed. From the heaps of guano on the floor, the cavern
appeared to have been taken over by bats.

Draconas assumed that he had probably tripped some
sort of alarm upon entering. No dragon with a brain
would leave a back door unguarded. The dragon would

weave some sort of magic across it that would alert him to intruders. Draconas knew this was a risk the moment he entered the cavern. He deemed it acceptable. There was always the possibility—the hope—that Grald was not in his lair. He and his human body might be somewhere else.

The cavern narrowed into a tubelike corridor that ran for some distance straight into the mountain, then opened up into a large chamber where Draconas was able to lift his head and release his wings. He shook himself all over, scales clicking, and drew in a breath of air that reeked of bat. The creatures were out with the night, but this was evidently the chamber where they roosted. Despite the stench, Draconas breathed well and deeply. He always felt better when he was in his true form, his dragon body, and he felt better in his natural habitat—a cave.

Though his human form was just illusion—unlike Grald and Maristara and Anora, who had all seized the bodies of real humans—the illusion was so real that Draconas sometimes felt as if he were trapped in that human body, a body that was fragile, soft and unprotected—all part of the magic of the supreme illusion. The Walker had to feel human, as well as look human. He had to come to believe the lie, so to speak, for otherwise he would not be able to understand what it was to be human and so be able to pass for human.

Draconas thought what it would be like to walk inside this cavern as a human—terrified of the bats, for one thing; unable to see in the darkness; blundering into stone walls and falling over unseen obstacles; losing himself in the tangled maze of corridors. And always fearful of puncturing the vulnerable flesh or breaking one of the slender bones, knocking a hole in the skull, or poking out an unprotected eye.

In his dragon form, Draconas was armored in scales that were harder than any steel man had yet created. His eyes could spot a rodent in the pitch darkness fifty feet away. He had a massive tail that could fell a tree with one swipe, razor-sharp claws and sword-sharp teeth, and the fire of magic blazed in his blood. He was invincible to every creature in this world with the exception of his own kind.

Or at least, he had been.

King Edward's cannons. Not a threat now, but there was one thing to be said for humans—they never stood still. They were always surging forward, bashing their headstrong way through their brief lives, making progress, as they liked to call it. Dragons had watched humans advance from the point where their brutish ancestors were flinging stones to bring down small animals to the firing of cannonballs. He conceded that Anora was right. It was not difficult to predict that the crude iron ball that now flew a few hundred feet to land with a thud in a field of millet would someday be armed with such destructive force that it could blow apart this mountain.

Safe in their caves, deep beneath the earth, dreaming their wondrous dreams, the dragons and their young would, for the first time in human history, be at the mercy of humans.

Dragons could never rest safe again. Like humans, they would always live in fear.

In that moment, Draconas came very near to turning and walking out the back door. He came very near to going back to his own lair, saying, "The hell with it. The hell with them."

And then his own words to Lysira came back to him. Fine words, about freedom and doing what was right.

"Dragons will have to adapt to this new world," he said to himself. "We will have to change. Something will be lost. Something is always lost when change comes. But something will be gained, for that, too, is a given. At least, I hope so."

Wondering if the alarm had gone off and if someone was there to hear it, Draconas sent a penetrating gaze through the darkness, seeking out the tunnels that branched off from this chamber and led deeper into the dragon's lair. He found three. Draconas sniffed the air of each of them, smelling and tasting with nose and tongue. He poked his head down each of the tunnels, listening for the smallest noises. He stared deep into each of them, studying them, searching for the tiniest hint.

He could not smell dragon in any of them, and that further confirmed his belief that Grald had not been near this part of his mountain in a long time.

No reason he should be, of course. His interests lay in the world of humans. But it was an indication that the dragon had grown lazy. Even though Draconas returned to his lair only a couple of times every hundred years, he always checked it over from top to bottom. Magic spells needed to be reinforced or rewoven; traps needed to be reset; animal squatters driven out. And it was always good to know if any stranger had been prying about.

He began to wonder if there had been an alarm at the entrance or not. Given the hundreds of bats coming and going on their nightly runs, the alarm—unless specifically designed to detect only dragons—would have been going off constantly.

Bats. In a dragon's lair. Draconas's lip curled in disgust as he waded through their droppings, which were knee deep. He headed down the middle corridor. The other two were quiet and smelled bad. The middle one had an intriguing odor and, more important, intriguing noises. He was able to detect, echoing up through the halls and tunnels of the dragon's lair, the sounds and smell of humans.

The babble of human voices increased markedly as Draconas walked the corridors of Grald's "palace." To judge by the sound, the humans were engaging in some sort of celebration, for the voices would often rise in unison, making what humans termed music, something that was, for Draconas, a cacophony of ear-jarring screechings and wails. The music was followed by bursts of applause or laughter that thundered through the cavern chambers. If the noise they were making was any indication, Draconas guessed that, like the bats, there must be hundreds of humans inside the cavern.

Yet no one crossed the bridge.

He continued to advance, his wonder—and his

concern—growing. He saw no sign of the dragon anywhere. He came upon no traps. He did not wander into
any illusory passages designed to lead an intruder to
grief. The lair might have belonged to an enterprising
bear. And Draconas suddenly understood the reason why.
As a mother with a toddler will remove all sharp objects
from the child's reach, the dragon had been forced to
make his lair safe for human occupants.

Draconas calculated that he must be drawing near the
base of the mountain by now. The tunnel he walked
twisted and turned, yet always sloped steadily downward.
Rounding a corner, he saw a glow of warm, yellow-
orange light. The voices were close. The human smell
overpowering. He halted where he was to re-form the illusion, to become human once more.

He did not choose the monk's form. He had the impression, from what he'd seen and heard on the bridge,
that few of the Blessed were allowed in the cavern. Hearing among the voices raised in song the high-pitched
cries and giggles of children, he went back to being
Draca.

As always, he let go of his dragon form with deep reluctance, sighing his way back inside the fragile, frail human skin. The corridor that had seemed small and narrow
to the dragon was suddenly enormous to the human girl.
His eyes could see better than those of most humans, but
not as well as a dragon, and his hearing was so reduced
that it seemed his ears were stuffed with wax. He had to
allow himself several moments to adjust to the change.
Then, keeping near the wall, he edged his way forward.

He very nearly stepped off the edge of a cliff.

His human stomach gave a lurch and he took a hasty
step backward, painfully mindful of the fact that in this
body he had no wings to save himself from what would
have been a hundred-foot plunge straight down.

The tunnel opened into an enormous chamber. Draconas had seen something like this only once before—the
Hall of Parliament, where the dragons met. The entire
center of the mountain had been scooped out like the insides of a pumpkin. The ceiling—far, far above him—

was supported by huge columns of rock that jutted up from the smooth floor. The cavern's walls were a veritable honeycomb of small caves, built in neat, even rows around the inside of the chamber. Stairs carved out of the rock led up to the caves, opening out into walkways that were like streets.

The chamber was brightly lit. A bonfire burned in the center of what would have been a plaza in a human city. Draconas wondered at the lack of smoke from the blaze—the cavern should have filled with it. Then he saw that the fire did not feed off wood. The flames fed off stone and magic.

The child, Draca, sat down on the stone floor of the tunnel and, letting her feet dangle over the edge, gazed down in wonder at the sight beneath her.

Humans, men and women and children, clustered about the magical blaze. He listened to their songs, to the words of the songs; he watched them dance their dances, and his wonder devolved into grim dismay. Their stories were those of fighting and battle. Their songs were songs of war. He had found the dragon's army.

His roving eye took note of a group of people who held themselves apart from the others, kept their distance, stood aloof and proud. He stared at them and his dismay turned to shock.

"What have we done?" Draconas asked the question of himself and all of his kind.

"What have we done?" he asked again. "And can we ever be forgiven?"

Draconas now knew the truth about Anton and Rosa's daughter. Why she had been chosen and what for. And he was pretty certain now that he knew her terrible fate.

15

VEN SLEPT FITFULLY THAT NIGHT AND WOKE THE NEXT day resolved to leave the room that had become a prison. He spurned the monks, who urged him to continue to remain in bed. He ate breakfast with a hearty appetite and then sent the monks into a panic when he stated that he was going out for a walk. They attempted to dissuade him by murmuring that he was not well. All he had to do was point to the wound that had already closed and scabbed over. He was still a little weak from loss of blood, but he would never admit to that. If he stayed cooped up in that room with only the mad monks for company, he'd go as mad as the maddest among them.

Ven had another reason, though it was one he did not readily admit to himself. He needed to talk to Draconas. The need was grudging, for it implied weakness on Ven's part. He'd determined that he would never again ask for help from anyone. With the long night to think things over and the vision of Draconas slipping into Grald's mountain lair before his eyes, Ven had come to the conclusion that exchanging a modicum of pride for Draconas's assistance in carrying out his plot against Grald was not such a bad trade-off.

I won't ask him to help me fight Grald, Ven resolved. *I just need information about fighting dragons.*

Ven didn't dare leave the white-shielded cave of his mind

to go in mental search of Draconas—such a move would place them both in danger. But he could leave his room.

Flinging open the door, Ven found two monks standing guard outside. One of the monks jumped nearly out of his skin as the door banged against the wall. The other regarded him with a wary look.

"I'm going for a walk," Ven announced, and shoved past the two of them. "You can come, if you want."

The monk who was not quivering frowned.

"Your father—"

Ven rounded on him. "I have heard rumors that the people of Dragonkeep think I am dead, killed in the explosion. If I am to be the leader of these people, then they should see me, see that I am alive and strong and well."

Either this inspired argument carried the day, or the monk saw that he had no hope of stopping Ven from leaving, and so he gave in, though not without a whispered conversation with his fellow, who immediately darted off, presumably running to Grald with the report.

Accompanied by three monks, Ven left the Abbey for the first time since he'd gone out that fateful morning to meet his brother.

He emerged into morning air washed fresh by last night's rain and paused to gulp in great draughts. He set out to walk the streets of Dragonkeep, with no particular destination in mind, just the need to get the blood flowing and perhaps find Draconas.

Ven could not forbid the monks from escorting him— they were far more terrified of Grald than they were of Grald's son. But he could make it difficult for them, and he did. The dragon-blood gave him extrahuman strength and, even weakened, he was stronger than any of the monks. His dragon legs carried him at an easy lope through the city streets. The monks kept up as best they could—the image of Grald's fury acting as a spur—but none was accustomed to exertion of any kind, and soon they were gasping and winded.

Ven saw them falling behind and magnanimously halted to wait for them to catch up. A group of people gathered around the Dragon's Son, not approaching him or speaking to him, just watching him. Several grinned when they saw the monks come limping around the corner; one monk almost doubled over from the pain of a stitch in his side and the other two were sweating and out of breath.

"Who's guarding who?" shouted a little girl with a laugh.

Some of the adults looked stern and frowned at her. A few chuckled, though they hastily rearranged their faces as the monks drew near.

By the time the monks reached Ven's side, the crowd had melted away, all except the little girl, who stood staring at Ven with frank and unabashed curiosity.

"Begone, child," one of the monks scolded her. "Leave the Dragon's Son alone."

The little girl stuck out her tongue. The monk made an angry swipe at her, but she skipped away and ran off down the street. The monks paid her no more attention. They had their charge to consider.

"You walk very fast, Dragon's Son," said the monk, scowling.

"I plan to go on at this pace. I just wanted to let you know that," Ven returned.

"You would do well to slow down, Dragon's Son. You are not well."

Ven looked pointedly at the monks—one unable to straighten up and the other two scarcely able to walk.

"I thank you for your concern. And for your care of me." Ven's lip curled. "I feel so much safer, knowing I am under your protection."

"Ditch them," came a voice, its colors flitting about like butterflies in Ven's head.

Ven knew that voice and he could barely contain his elation. He had been right, Draconas was here. As fast as the dragon's colors darted into Ven's mind, they vanished. Ven could see them still, see the afterimages, as when one stares at the sun, but he dared not answer. Grald lurked outside his cave, waiting for him to emerge.

The monks were staring at him expectantly and Ven realized that he'd lost track of the conversation.

"You can either keep up with me or go back to the Abbey," he stated. "I need no guards. What does my father think I will do? Try to escape from Dragonkeep? The world outside is a dangerous place for me. He knows that better than anyone. Why would I want to return to it?"

The spokesman for the three monks cast Ven a churlish look. He and his two cohorts conferred in low voices, then, bowing, they turned and walked off.

Surprised and a little suspicious at the ease with which he'd accomplished his task, Ven watched the monks until they were out of sight. He kept watch for Draconas, too, but saw no sign of him. No one was about except the little girl, who was loitering in the shadows of a building.

Ven lingered in the street, searching for the man he remembered from childhood—a human male with long black hair, piercing dark eyes, carrying a staff. Several men passed by him, but they did not answer that description. He began to grow impatient and, when the little girl came dancing up to him, he tried to ignore her, hoping she'd go away.

He detested children. The sight of them brought back his own painful childhood. Adults were unkind—with their averted eyes or looks of pity or crude remarks. Children were cruel, taunting and teasing and tormenting the little boy who walked with a beast's gait.

"I wish my legs had scales like yours, Dragon's Son," the child said. "Except that my scales would be red-gold."

"Run along home," Ven told her, scowling, and he tried to shoo her away with a wave of his hand.

To his astonishment, the girl grabbed hold of his hand. She held fast when he tried to shake her loose. She was a sharp-eyed little minx, with long black hair and a spare, bony frame on which her ragged clothes hung like new-washed laundry. She looked up at Ven and grinned.

Her comment about the red-gold scales suddenly struck him, as did the long, black hair. Long ago, Ven had seen a dragon take to the air. He had seen moonlight glitter on scales that were red-gold. He'd seen the same last night . . .

"Draconas?" Ven asked softly, staring at the child in astonishment.

"Start walking," the little girl ordered, tugging him along. "No, don't look back. Keep moving."

"Is that you, Draconas?" Ven persisted.

"My name's Draca," said the girl in a loud, shrill voice. "I know you. You're Ven, the Dragon's Son. Act naturally. They're watching you."

"The monks?" Ven glanced over his shoulder. "No, they're not. I sent them back to the Abbey—"

"Not those monks. Others. Why do you think your guards gave way so easily? Look there, in the alley. And there, in the doorway of the baker's shop."

Ven cast a glance in the directions indicated. The monk in the alley blended into the shadows, but not before Ven had spotted him. The monk in the doorway of the baker's shop did not even bother to try to hide himself.

"How do you know I won't hand you over to Grald?" asked Ven, trying unsuccessfully to free his hand from the girl's grasp. He still was not certain this was Draconas.

"Because you helped Marcus escape," the child replied calmly. "He did escape safely, by the way. He and the young woman. They're on their way back to his kingdom by now."

The child cocked her bright eye at him. "Aren't you pleased?"

Ven shrugged. To his surprise, he was pleased. He didn't plan on showing it, however.

"Good for them," was all he said.

"You don't care what happens to your brother? Or to Evelina?"

"Not particularly," Ven replied. "I treated her badly and I made amends. My brother took her safely away from here. That's all that matters."

"So that is why you lured him here." Draconas nodded in understanding. "To rescue the young woman. You never planned to betray Marcus to Grald, did you?"

"No," said Ven shortly. "He's my brother."

"A brother you never knew you had."

"I knew," said Ven, remembering the small hand that had reached out to him when he was a boy, alone and crying in a cave.

Draconas was silent. Ven could almost see him rearranging impressions in his mind.

"Why didn't you take the young woman away yourself?" Draconas asked. "Why don't you leave now? You can see through the illusion. You know where to find the gate in the wall."

Ven continued walking. The girl trotted along at his side. She was forced to take two and half steps for his one, to match his long strides. They'd left the watchful monks far behind. Ven could not see any others, though he had no doubt they were there, keeping an eye on him. Now was the time to reveal his plan and ask for aid. The words stuck in his craw.

Fortunately, Draconas was able to answer his own question.

"Your name," said Draconas. "Vengeance. That's the reason you stay. You're here to kill Grald. Avenge your mother. Or maybe, that's not quite right." The girl cast him a bright, sharp glance. "Maybe you're here to avenge yourself. Take out your wrath on the father who made you what you are."

"What do you want with me, Draconas?" Ven demanded. "Are you going to lecture me on the folly of trying to slay the dragon by myself? If so, don't waste your breath. You're not telling me anything I don't already know."

"I'm here because *you* wanted to talk to me," Draconas told him pertly.

"I never—"

"Oh, not in words or even in colors," Draconas assured him. "Good thing, too, for if Grald discovered your plan, he would have your entrails for lunch. We don't have much time and there's something you need to see."

Ven drew in a deep breath, let it out. "Look, Draconas—"

"Draca," the girl corrected. "Don't say or even think my name if you can help it."

"Look, Dracon—Draca, I don't want to see anything or hear anything except what you can tell me that will help me kill the dragon."

"To help you kill the dragon? You need your brother."
Ven snorted.

"I'm serious," said Draconas. "The sons of Melisande—
both the sons of Melisande—should come together to
avenge their mother."

"That's not going to happen," Ven said, adding with a
burst of impatience, "Just tell me what I need to know,
damn it, then you can leave. That's why you've been
hanging around here, isn't it? Nursemaiding me! Like
those idiot monks! Well, you don't have to anymore. I can
take care of myself."

"You have a strange way of asking for help, Dragon's
Son," Draconas said.

"Don't call me that," said Ven.

"What? Dragon's Son? You are, you know."

Ven was silent.

"You can't keep denying it forever," Draconas said quietly. "You can kill your father, but you can't kill the
truth."

He paused, then said, "I'll make you a deal, Ven. I will
give you what help I can, which isn't much. There's no
time to teach you how to use the magic, and that is what
you truly need to fight Grald. Nevertheless, I will do
what I can to aid you. In exchange for my help, you must
agree to come with me."

"Come with you where?"

"To the palace of Grald. It's going to be a bit of a climb
to reach the entrance. Are you strong enough?"

"Palace? His lair, you mean." Ven was suddenly eager.
"Yes, I'm well enough. Is Grald there? Perhaps you and
I together—"

The child shook her head. "I would like very much to
have it out with Grald, but I have to forgo that particular
pleasure. He is strong and powerful, and he might get
lucky and kill me. And though it may be egotistical of
me to say this, I can't afford to die right now. Events
have been set in motion that must be stopped, and I'm
the only one in a position to do that. Besides, Grald is not
in his 'palace.' I made certain of that before I came looking for you."

"Just tell me what's going on, will you?" Ven said, frustrated. He jerked his hand free of the child's. "I don't like all this goose chase, run about."

"I can't simply tell you," Draca said with somber gravity. "You have to see for yourself, Ven. Otherwise, you would not believe me."

16

ON LEAVING THE MOUNTAIN FASTNESS, DRACONAS HAD searched for an easier way into the dragon's lair than the one he'd used last night. Ven's strong, scaled legs and clawed feet made him an excellent climber, but the Dragon's Son could not scale sheer rock walls. Draconas had not remained in the palace long last night. He'd seen what he'd come to see, plus much more, and there was no use risking discovery by hanging about. He'd followed a different route out of the dragon's lair, and that led him to the discovery of a back door about a half-mile lower than the one into which he'd flown. The climb was still arduous. Both Ven and the child, Draca—with her lithe and agile body and her dragon's strength—managed it easily.

Ven actually enjoyed the climb. The strenuous physical exertion took his mind off his troubles. He had to concentrate on where to put his feet and hands; he had to think about what he was doing. He had no fear of high places—his dragon-blood took care of that. He reveled in the idea that he was rising far above the world with its stink and its staring eyes and cruel laughter. When he and Draconas entered the cave that was Grald's back door, they entered the calm darkness and silent emptiness of Ven's childhood—those times he was able to slip away from Bellona and his traplines and his chores and hide himself in his own lair.

"This feels like home," he said without thinking.

"So it would to one who has dragon-blood in him," Draconas responded.

The blood burned beneath the surface of Ven's skin. He had not meant to share his inner thought aloud. He'd spoken his heart, however, and he could not very well unsay it.

"Which way do we go to see this sight of yours?" he demanded, regarding with a grim frown two tunnels that led from the main chamber deeper into the dragon's lair.

The child motioned with her hand toward a tunnel that slanted off to the left. She put her finger to her lips, cautioning silence, and walked into the shadows, her human feet padding softly. Ven followed, his claws making scraping sounds on the rock.

They advanced deeper into the massive cave, always rising. This tunnel wound round and round in a broad spiral, sometimes leveling out for a short distance, then spiraling around again, still slanting upward. The darkness was complete. Ven's dragon-sight could scarcely penetrate it. He had the dragon's instinct for moving in dark places beneath the earth, however, and he followed Draconas with relative ease.

The darkness grew lighter, as if sunlight had found its way below ground. He smelled fresh air and other smells that were distinctly human, some good and some bad, and he was reminded forcibly of the city they had just left. Sounds reached Ven's ears—sounds of a great many feet moving in unison, with rhythmic march and stamp; sounds of shouted orders and unified responses.

The sounds were loudest and the smells strongest at a four-way intersection of tunnels that formed a crossroads. Here Draconas halted and raised his hand.

"Wait," he whispered and he peered down the tunnel that smelled strongly of men. "Good," he added, after a moment. "No one's around. We can cross."

The child darted across the intersection and into the other tunnel. Ven did the same, then he looked back, puzzled.

"It sounds like there's an army down here." No need

for silence. The noise of the stamping and shouting echoed throughout the corridors.

"There is," said Draconas.

"Impossible." Ven was scoffing, dismissive. "This is another dragon illusion."

"I wish it were," said Draconas. "Unfortunately, it's all too real. Take a look."

They had reached the same tunnel Draconas had walked the night before, coming upon it from a different angle. Motioning Ven to accompany him, Draconas led him to the ledge that overlooked the vast chamber. Ven gazed down in astonishment.

Far below, drawn up in row upon shining row, was an army of humans. Except that this army was like no human army Ven had ever seen. Sunlight, filtering down through shafts carved into the cavern walls, gleamed on armor that had a strange and beautiful iridescent quality. At first, Ven took the armor for some sort of chain mail. The soldiers moved in the armor with far more ease than soldiers could move in chain mail, however, no matter how expensive or finely made. The mail coats that covered them from head to toe seemed to weigh almost nothing, for the soldiers wheeled and shifted and lunged with as much ease as if they were wearing homespun wool cloth. Ven looked from the armor down at his own scale-covered legs, and he thought he understood.

"You have judged right," Draconas said, seeing the direction of his gaze. "The armor these soldiers wear is made of dragon scales. It is lightweight and strong—so strong that I doubt if any weapon forged by human hands can penetrate it. Such armor will turn the sharpest sword."

Ven watched the soldiers drill, watched them wheel and turn in unison, and he was puzzled.

"What sort of weapons are they using? And why do they fight in pairs?"

"That is the genius of it. Think of what you know of the dragon-magic—"

"Not much," Ven muttered.

"They fight in pairs because each pair is made up of

one male, one female. Fully half the army is composed of female warriors. Not like Bellona. These women do not fight with weapons. They fight with magic. Like the holy sisters of Seth, these women use the magic to defend themselves and their partners. The men use the magic to fight. In other words, the women are the shield, the men are the sword. The weapons they are using are darts. They do not look very lethal, but they can be thrown by the hand with the force of the magic behind it. One of those darts killed Bellona.

"The man throws the dart from behind the cover of the defensive magic cast by the woman beside him. Both of them remain invulnerable to attack. And the dart is not their only weapon, I'll wager."

"But the magic drives males insane—like the mad monks. Those men don't look mad," Ven remarked.

"No, they're quite sane," said Draconas. "Like your brother, Marcus. I thought I had done something special with him. Apparently I was wrong. Over the years, Grald culled out the lunatics and placed them in the brotherhood of the Blessed. Not a bad plan. The Blessed keep watch over the population of Dragonkeep, and if the ordinary people know that they are crazed and unpredictable, they fear them all the more. Grald put the sane males into his army. He's had hundreds of years of selective breeding, and he was able to pick and choose and train only the best. This may be the second or third generation of soldiers we're looking at."

Draconas paused, then said quietly, "No human army has a chance against them."

Ven glanced at the girl sharply. "Human army. What human army do you mean?"

"These soldiers are preparing to march to war. The dragons are going to use them to launch an attack against Idylswylde."

Below them, the male warriors threw darts, while the woman chanted and sang, making circular motions with their hands, as though smoothing out the empty space in front of them. The magic of the women shaped the air into concentric circles, so the bodies behind it became shapeless blurs of purple and blue radiance, dazzling and ghastly.

Other soldiers, ranged at intervals around the pairs, played at being the enemy. They fired arrows—real arrows, not illusion—into their ranks. Other soldiers drew swords and ran in to attack on foot.

The arrows struck the dazzling, whirling, magical shields and bounced off. Swords hit the shields and were either turned aside or the blades shattered in the hands of those who wielded them. The leader called a halt to the exercise and congratulated his troops and dismissed them.

"For," said their leader, his voice ringing through the chamber, "the days of conquest are near at hand. The day we have worked for our entire lives will shortly be upon us."

"When do we march?" someone cried out.

"Soon," was the answer.

The troops dispersed, laughing and talking.

The child looked very grim.

"What are you going to do?" Ven asked. "Warn Marcus? Go fight alongside him?"

"It's not that simple," said Draconas, and the child's eyes were dark and troubled. He glanced at Ven. "For me or for you, Dragon's Son."

Draconas rose to his feet. "Come with me. There's something else you need to see."

They wended their way back down through the tunnels. Ven found that he had a sense of where he was and that he could choose which branching corridor to take nine times out of ten. He liked being here. He could walk tall and straight in these dark corridors. He liked the feeling of isolation, the comfort of the silence. He thought he would like to remain here, maybe forever.

They did not leave the cavern, as Ven half expected them to do. Draca took him on a new route, one that led deeper into the mountain's heart, deeper underground. Now the silence was heavy with the weight of the mountain pressing down upon them. Ven added these new cor-

ridors to his mental map, and it was like a corkscrew, spiraling ever downward.

They were far from civilization. Far from the world. So
far that, when Ven heard the sound of human voices, he
was severely disappointed.

"Hush!" The child caught hold of his hand and
squeezed it. Her words were little more than a distur-
bance of the still air. "We are close."

The child tugged him gently forward down a tunnel
that grew lighter with every footfall. The voices were
clearer now; Ven could distinguish words, and they were
obviously human.

"What is all this?" he asked, mouthing the words.

The child shook her head and urged him on.

The light was quite bright now. It was not the light of sun.
This light had a pure, white quality to it that Ven recognized.

The white light was his light, the light of the emptiness
that hid him from the dragon.

The voices were only a few feet away. The child
stopped and looked up at him. He could see her quite
clearly. He could see the child and, in the stark, white
light, he could see the shadow of the red-gold dragon
standing behind the child, wings spread protectively.

"Go on ahead," said Draconas. He paused, then added,
regarding Ven intensely, "If you want to make yourself
known, that is up to you. Grald will almost certainly be
informed that you were here, and I have no idea how he
will react. You might be putting yourself in danger. The
choice is yours . . . Dragon's Son."

Ven glowered, not liking the reference. He did not like
all this skulking about and mystery, either. He wanted to
ask questions, but he felt that to do so would be to play
into Draconas's game, of which Ven was growing weary.
He would not give the dragon the satisfaction. He'd go
see whatever this was he was supposed to see and then
maybe they could discuss killing Grald.

With a final, grim glance, Ven turned and left the child
standing in the tunnel. He glided forward, as quietly as
his scraping claws would permit, to the tunnel's entrance.

He looked into a brightly lit chamber, a largish chamber, in which about twenty people had gathered to hear another person speak. Here was the source of the human voices.

But Ven had been mistaken. The voices were not human. Not entirely.

Here were humans who had dragon legs, like himself. Here were humans who had human legs and dragon wings and dragon-scaled arms ending in clawed hands. There were males and females. Some were more dragon than others. One young female—the speaker—had a human head and breasts. The rest of her body was that of a dragon, though molded in a softer, human form. Delicate wings hung from her shoulders. A little boy standing beside her was almost completely human, except for a glittering scaled tail that twitched and thumped the ground as he listened.

The conversation was lively. The other half-dragons were not at all shy about questioning or challenging the speaker, who gave back as good as she got. Ven listened to them talk, but he had no sense of what they were discussing. He was too shaken.

He sensed more, then saw the child, Draca, come up to stand beside him.

"They are the dragon's sons," said Draconas softly. "And the dragon's daughters."

Ven was mute, struck dumb. He stood motionless, paralyzed by shock. He could only stare, his heart and his gut twisting together so that one was wrung and the other was wrenched.

"They are your siblings, Ven," Draconas continued. "Your younger brothers and sisters."

"They are monsters," Ven stated harshly. He felt his gorge rising. "Monsters like me. No wonder they keep them hidden down here!"

The dragon's children had their own, exceptional hearing. Though Ven had spoken in a whisper, they all heard and they all turned to stare.

"A spy!" hissed one.

"Wait!" called out the young woman. "Wait!" she called

again, and this time she was speaking to Ven. "Do not run off. Didn't you hear us? We were talking about you."

At this, a sigh rippled through the other half-dragons. "The Dragon's Son . . . the Dragon's Son . . ." The whisper went around and they moved forward, not threatening, but eager and curious.

Ven had been about to flee. He had his back turned, ready to run, ready to leave this horrible image behind.

He told himself that to flee would be cowardly. He braced himself and turned around, faced them head-on. He swallowed the bitter bile in his mouth, felt it burn down his throat into his stomach.

The young half-dragon female advanced. Her human face was lovely. Her brown eyes were large and wide open to the world. The bone structure of her face and body was delicate, yet strong. Her long, glistening hair fell to the small of her back and stirred about her like a shimmering curtain when she walked. She moved with grace and elegance that was fluid and sinuous like a reptile and proud like a human, her human shoulders back and squared. Her iridescent wings quivered. The hand she held out to him was covered in scales that sparkled blue, like his own. Her hand ended in five small talons.

She wore no clothes, as did some of the half-dragons, those who were more human than dragon. Her scales covered her body, which had a human torso and thighs and slender dragon legs with clawed feet, like Ven's. The scales ran up her stomach to cup around her bare human breasts.

Ven saw all this in a single, swift glance. Then he kept his eyes fixed on her face, because his stomach turned when he looked at the rest of her. He tried to keep his face rigid, to keep the disgust he felt from showing, but the young woman must have seen it, for she stopped walking. The hand she held out to him dropped to her side.

"I'm not a spy," he said, the only thing he could think of to say.

The young female's eyes softened. "No, of course you are not a spy. You are our brother. The eldest among us. We were told you had arrived in the city, and we were hoping that our father would introduce us. We were just discussing the ceremony we were planning to welcome you. As it is"—she blushed slightly, smiling—"you caught us unprepared. We apologize, Brother. We have looked forward to this meeting for a long, long time. You are welcome among us. Very welcome."

Twenty pairs of eyes, of every color known to humankind, stared out from faces, some of which were human, some dragon. They regarded him with admiration, with respect.

They don't see a monster, Ven realized. Looking into the eyes of the young female half-dragon, he saw pride, pride in herself. *I'm the only one who sees monsters.*

He was suddenly ashamed, for she was seeing in his eyes what he saw in the eyes of other humans when they looked at him: fear, disgust.

He couldn't help it. They were monsters—all of them. Ven felt sick at the sight of them. He started to shake. His limbs trembled. His scaled legs grew too weak to support him, and he fell to his knees on the stone floor. He wanted to say something, but he couldn't. His throat was thick with tears he refused to let himself shed. He clasped his arms around himself and curled in on himself. He bowed his head and bowed his back, bowed himself before his siblings with a moaning cry that was not human.

They gathered around him, surrounding him, supporting him. Arms that were strong and scaled and cool clasped him and held him. His sister's arms. His sister's voice, soft in his ear.

"You will not be alone anymore, Brother. From now on, you will never be alone."

17

THE CHILDREN OF THE DRAGON THEY WERE CALLED, THE half-human/half-dragon creatures that were Ven's half brothers and sisters.

Ven spent a long time among them that day and listened and watched and wondered. He thought he should be pleased to know that, as his sister assured him, he was not alone in the world, that there were others of his kind. He wasn't. He was repulsed whenever he looked at the grotesque monstrosities—bits and parts of human and dragon bodies joined together without rhyme or reason.

He tried not to stare at them, for he hated it when people stared at him, yet he couldn't help himself. He tried averting his eyes, but that was worse, for he, too, knew how terrible that felt. When a little boy came running up—his dragon's claws scraping the ground and his dragon's tail thumping the floor behind him—Ven felt his stomach heave, and he had to look away or retch.

Fortunately, the child didn't notice. He sniffed at Ven, much as a dog sniffs, and said cheerfully, "Pew! You stink!"

"It's the human smell," said his sister as she might have said, *It's the garbage.* "Their stench clings to everything."

The little boy ran off to play with other children of the dragon—some older, some younger, some with tails, some with wings and tails, some with clawed hands and no tails.

If I held up a looking glass, I would see the same expression of shock and revulsion in my eyes that I saw in the eyes of my own brother, Marcus, when Marcus first looked on me. I despised Marcus for that look, but the truth is, I understood how he felt. I feel the same way when I look at myself.

What is strange, what I can't understand, is that they don't feel that way about themselves. They are proud of what they are. They are not ashamed.

He simply couldn't fathom it.

He might have supposed it was because they had not been exposed to ordinary humans, but he was disabused of that notion when his sister, whose name was Sorrow, took him on a tour of their lair.

"My mother named me," Sorrow explained, seeing Ven's startled look when she told him. "Before she died. They say that our father, the dragon, was angry when he heard what my mother called me, for I was the first-born—after you, of course—and he was vastly pleased with me. But my name was the last word my mother spoke, and the silly human who was my wet nurse was very superstitious and said my mother's unhappy spirit would linger with me if my name was changed, and she refused to nurse me unless my mother's wishes were honored. Our father said I was to keep the name, 'Sorrow,' but he added to it so that now it is 'Bringer of Sorrow.' And so I will be known to those humans we conquer. You've seen our human army?"

Ven could only nod. He didn't know what to say, feared saying too much, and did what he was naturally inclined to do: kept silent.

"You've seen other human armies in the part of Dragonvarld in which you grew up. How does ours compare?" Sorrow asked eagerly.

"What did you call it?" Ven interrupted.

"Call what?" Sorrow's thoughts were on the army.

"The world. You had a name for it."

"Dragonvarld. Dragon World, in the human language.

Have you never heard that? It is what the dragons have called this world for centuries. I understand that the humans have some other name for it. They term it 'Dirt' or something like that. But, then, they don't know the truth, at least not yet, so I don't suppose we can really blame them."

"What truth?"

"That the dragons are the true rulers of this world and always have been. Our father tells us that the humans fancy themselves the rulers." Sorrow laughed, rippling laughter that caused the scales on her torso to glitter and sparkle in the patches of dusty sunlight filtering down through the air shafts. "All that will soon change."

Ven could have asked more. He could have found out all about the army and when they were going to attack and where, but he didn't want to know. It was easier not knowing. He didn't want to think about it for that would require him to make decisions. Sorrow wanted to talk about it, however. She persisted in her questions.

"So, we were speaking of our army and comparing them to the armies of other humans. Tell me what you think."

"There is no comparison," said Ven flatly, hoping to end the conversation. "Human armies do not have magic. They will think they are being attacked by demons from hell. They will run like rabbits. Or die of sheer terror."

"That is what our father says." Sorrow was pleased to have her information confirmed. "Our humans do very well—for humans. Of course, they have dragon-blood in them, so that is what accounts for it."

Ven's thoughts went to his mother, Melisande, and to Bellona, the woman who had raised him. His mother had dragon-blood in her; that was why she'd given birth to the monstrosity that was himself. Bellona had not, at least so he guessed. Yet, she'd been raised with those like his mother who could work the dragon-magic.

"There is one human army who would not be afraid," Ven found himself saying. He was immediately sorry he brought it up, but, oddly, he felt as if he needed to defend his race.

"What army is that? Not the army of Idylswylde?"

"No. The army of a place called Seth."

"Ah, yes. True. We will not have to fight them, how-ever. They are ruled by a dragon and so will be our allies in the upcoming war of conquest."

"They don't know they are ruled by a dragon," said Ven.

"Of course they do," Sorrow returned, amused.

"No, they don't. My mother came from there, as did the woman who raised me after my mother's death. Bel-lona told me that the people of Seth think that dragons are their enemies. They have been taught to hate and fear them."

"But every month, the people of Seth send us their strongest male children to be raised here—"

"The babies are smuggled out in the dead of night. No one in Seth knows the truth, except for one—the Mistress of Dragons. And that's because she *is* the dragon. Like Grald, she has stolen the body of a human and uses that body to keep the humans in ignorance."

"Stolen a human body! What are you talking about?"

"Grald, our father, the dragon, stole a human body—that hulking piece of excrement known as Grald. The dragon uses that body when he walks among humans. He used that body to rape my mother and bring me into the world."

"I don't believe you!" Sorrow cried angrily. "Our father would never inhabit a human body. Our father is above such things. Grald is a human who serves the dragon. A *human,*" she said, laying emphasis on the word.

Ven shrugged. He couldn't prove what he'd said. He thought it interesting that Grald hadn't told his children the truth. *Difficult to proclaim yourself human when you've taught your children to despise and look down on that race.*

Ven wondered what the people of Seth would do when they found out the truth. He'd once asked Bellona why she didn't return to Seth and tell the people what she knew.

"I will never go back there," Bellona had told him harshly. "I would see your mother everywhere." And then she had looked at him—something she rarely did, for she couldn't stand the sight of him—and she had brushed back the hair from his forehead. "That will be your task, Ven."

Ven. Vengeance. He had forgotten her words about "his task" until now. Even dead, she added to his burden.

Brother and sister walked through the "palace" in silence. He could tell by the flush on her face and the tight line of her lips that Sorrow was still angry with him. The high color on her cheeks faded, after time—when he didn't say anything more—and she smiled at him.

"Are you teasing me?" she asked. "About Grald? I've heard it's something humans do to each other. Teasing."

Ven might have been accused of many failings in his life, but teasing people was not one of them. He didn't know how to answer, and so he kept silent. Sorrow took his silence for acquiescence. "Just don't say anything to the little ones, will you? I don't want them confused."

"I won't," Ven agreed. He had no intention of getting that well acquainted with the "little ones" anyway.

All this time, he and his sister had been walking through the "palace," traveling up and down corridors and tunnels that crossed and crisscrossed, sometimes opening into chambers that were small and cozy and sometimes opening into vast, cavernous halls. They saw many of the human soldiers, as these men and women traversed the lair. When they passed these soldiers, the humans would bow to Sorrow, as ordinary humans might bow to Prince Marcus, treating her with marked respect and reverence. She received their obeisance and murmured greetings with careless dignity, making it clear that this was her due and she expected nothing less. The same respect and reverence extended to Ven, but he was as uncomfortable with it down here as he was in the world outside.

He saw, too, that the children of the dragon did not mingle with their distant cousins—the humans who had the dragon-blood in their veins, but no scales on their bodies. The children of the dragon had their own living quarters that were set apart from those of the human soldiers. If the two met, the Children held themselves aloof. Once on their tour, Sorrow came upon one of the dragon-children playing with a human. She grabbed hold of the arm of the dragon-child and hauled him off to a dark corner and scolded him roundly, then sent him off to play with his own kind.

"The only humans allowed in our part of the palace are the mothers. Those who bear us."

"I want to see them," said Ven, the first words he'd spoken almost since they started.

"Why ever for?" Sorrow was astonished. "They are humans who are strong in the dragon-magic, but, apart from that, they are like any other humans, except that they have been honored by our father."

"I just do," said Ven. He could not tell his sister. She would not understand. He wasn't sure he understood himself.

Sorrow shrugged and led him to where the women who were due to give birth to the half-dragon children were kept in isolation.

There were about ten of them. Sometimes there were more, Sorrow said, sometimes less. All of them were near the end of their time, their bellies distended and swollen, their faces haggard and pale, their bodies thin and wasted, for the dragon-child inside each was literally sucking the life out of its mother.

Ven looked at them and he saw his own mother, Melisande. She had also been "honored" by Grald.

"Do any survive the birth?" he asked.

"Not many," said Sorrow in matter-of-fact tones. "Those who do are sickly and die soon after. Why do you look at them like that? They are to be envied, not pitied! The women of Dragonkeep vie for this honor! Only the very best are chosen, and they consider themselves extremely fortunate."

"Do these women look like they consider themselves 'fortunate'?" Ven demanded.

"They are human," said Sorrow disparagingly. "I don't look at them at all if I can help it."

"The dragon lies to them, Sorrow," Ven said, repeating what Draconas had told him. "The dragon tells the girls they are coming to live in luxury in this palace. Instead, he brings them here and impregnates them and, in essence, murders them."

Sorrow was silent a moment, the flush of anger creeping back to her face. Then she said, quite calmly, "You think I should be shocked to hear that the dragon lies to them. I am not. Humans have no capacity to understand the dragon mind. You have lived among them. Do they understand you?"

Sorrow's eyes softened. "I know your story, Ven. The human, Grald, told us. He said that they put you in a cage. That they mocked you and ridiculed you. He said that even your own foster mother told you that you are the devil's spawn. And that you believe her."

Ven regarded her in grim silence.

"I am sorry, Brother. I did not mean to bring up these hurtful things. Grald told us that it might make you sad." Sorrow's fingers touched his arm lightly. Her flesh was warm, the long talons cool by contrast. "Is he wrong in what he says of you?"

"No," Ven answered, after a moment. "He is not wrong."

Grald was not right, either, but Ven couldn't explain that. His feelings were a jumble, his world turned topsy-turvy, so that black was white and white was black, good was evil and evil had been made good. Or maybe it was all just a muddy shade of gray. He envied his sister, envied her pride in herself. He envied her clear, sharply delineated view of life. He envied Sorrow her ideas about the dragon, far different from his. She had been raised to honor her father and disparage her mother. He'd been taught just the opposite. Which was right? Both? Neither?

It was all such a tangled, twisted mess. He couldn't sort it out. Life would be much easier, simpler, if he took his sister's view of it. Yet, something about her life wasn't quite right. Just as something about his own life wasn't right. Fumbling for the answer, he spoke his thoughts aloud.

"If we are taught to believe that we are better than humans because we are half dragon, then doesn't it follow

that we are viewed by dragons as being less worthy than
one of their own kind? Who knows but that, among themselves, they mock us and ridicule us the same as humans?
We are neither, you see. And despised by both."

"No, of course not," Sorrow retorted. "Our father is
proud of us! We are his greatest achievement."

Ven shook his head. Sorrow seemed about to add more,
but she clamped her lips and even managed a wry smile.
"It seems we *are* brother and sister. We have been together only a few hours and already we are quarreling."

"I'm sorry," said Ven, and he meant it. "I'm trying to
understand. That's all. I'm just trying to understand."

"Have you talked to our father about your feelings?"
Sorrow asked him.

Ven wondered what she would say if he told her he was
determined to kill the father she so revered.

Sorrow clasped his hand, squeezed it tightly. "Do so. Our
father wants the chance to try to explain. He says that the
humans have mistreated you so that you are all twisted up
inside."

Maybe that's true, Ven said to himself. *Maybe I should
hear my father's side of the story.*

"I will," he said suddenly. "I will talk to him this night.
Thank you . . . Sister." He spoke the word awkwardly, but
found it felt good. It warmed a place inside him that had
been cold almost forever.

He basked in the warmth, until one of the mothers gave
a cry of agony, her back arching with the pain. The skirts
of her dress were suddenly stained red with blood.

"It is her time," said Sorrow, pleased. "Another brother
or sister will soon be with us."

The woman was moaning and writhing with the birth
pangs. Her face had gone deathly pale, her eyes wide and
staring. Women dressed as holy sisters came swiftly to
her aid and, lifting her gently, they bore her away. The
other mothers-to-be looked after her, their faces strained,
and they placed their hands on their own monstrously
swollen wombs. One looked at Sorrow and at Ven. Tears
began to stream down her cheeks. Her crying was sound-
less and it was all the more terrible for being silent.

Ven turned and walked away, his clawed feet scraping against the stone. The sound was loud in his ears. Even Sorrow, who joined him, seemed subdued.

"Even human babies are born in pain," she said as much to herself as to him. "And sometimes they kill the mother who bears them."

"I need to get back," Ven said. He did not add that he wasn't supposed to be here; Sorrow so clearly thought that her revered father had sent him.

"I would urge you to stay with us," she said. "But you need to talk with our father. Tomorrow, you will return to us and be one of us, always."

"I would like that," Ven said, and part of him meant it. Another part of him said it only because he didn't want to hurt his sister.

18

ON THE MORNING OF THE DAY VEN ENTERED THE MOUN-
tain, Evelina was taking a stroll over to the beach area
where the boats were moored. Most of the fishermen
were already at their work; she could see the shadowy
forms of their boats slipping in and out of the mists rising
from the river. One man remained on shore, however, doing something with a net, mending it, perhaps. He wasn't
looking at the work in his hands. He had his eyes fixed on
her. He'd had his eyes on her ever since she'd walked
into view.

Evelina remembered him immediately. He had carried
her from the boat, lifting her up in his strong arms and
ferrying her to shore, so that her feet didn't get wet. He
desired her. That was obvious. He took no trouble to hide
his lust. Rather, he flaunted it. Evelina guessed that he
had stayed away from his fishing on the off chance that he
might run into her.

Evelina was glad to make use of any man who offered
himself, especially a man so strong and good-looking,
with his dark hair and eyes and sun-browned skin. Feign-
ing not to notice him, she walked closer, looking at the
sky, the river, and the crudely built, but snug, little
dwellings.

"Good morning, Mistress," he said.

Evelina gave an affected start. "Oh, you startled me,

sir. I didn't see you. Good morning," she returned, adopting a tone that was frost-rimed with just a hint that she might possibly thaw if the sun were warm enough.

His hands were busy with the net, feeling their way over the rope, his eyes busy with her, feeling their way over her body.

"What brings you out so early on this fine morning, Mistress?" he asked.

"I need a potion for His Highness's wounds that he took on our journey. Perhaps you have a wise woman here who brews up such healing liquors."

"Aye, Mistress, we do," the man answered. "The Widow Huspeth lives in the woods. Strange woman, but she knows what she's about, I guess. You'll find a trail leads to her dwelling, though I would be glad to show you the way myself."

"No thank you, my good man," said Evelina with a grateful glance from beneath her lashes. "I will find the way. I bid you good day."

"Perhaps I'll see you tonight," said the fisherman, with a smile. His teeth were white against his black beard that was cut short, so that it outlined his firm jaw.

"I don't know why you should," said Evelina. She had plans for this night. She turned to go.

"My house is close by," he told her, as she departed. "It will be the one with the candle in the window. If you feel the need of company, come knock on my door. My name is Jorge."

Evelina did not reply. She walked away, her head held high, yet she was pleased to know that she could still charm a man. What with the way Marcus had been acting around her, she'd been starting to have her doubts.

She found the trail through the wilderness and soon came upon the house of the herbalist. Evelina was expecting the usual half-mad crone, toothless and gray-haired, crouched over a bubbling cauldron, and she was considerably disconcerted to find a woman of no more than thirty years, clad in man's breeches and a man's shirt, down on her hands and knees grubbing among the plants in a large garden.

Evelina approached quietly, wanting to see before she was seen. The woman was instantly aware of the unfamiliar presence in her woods. She turned her head and rose to her feet all in one fluid motion.

"Keep to the trail," the woman said, her voice husky, as if not much used. "I don't want my plants trampled."

Evelina glanced about. She saw no signs of the woman's house and guessed that it was hidden deeper in the wilderness. The woman wiped dirt from her hands and crossed over to where Evelina stood waiting.

"I'm looking for the Widow Huspeth," said Evelina.

"You're a stranger," said the woman. "Not from the village."

"I am—" Evelina began.

"It doesn't matter," said the woman coldly. "I just want to be clear where we stand. What do you want?"

"I want the widow," said Evelina, starting to grow annoyed. The woman's eyes were hard and bright and went through Evelina like a skewer.

"They call me Widow Huspeth hereabouts. Though my name is just Huspeth. What do you want?" she repeated.

Evelina found it difficult to talk to those shrewd eyes. She gazed at some red flowers as she spoke. "I want a fertility potion. And the liquor they call absinthe."

Huspeth smiled. "Your man won't marry you, is that it? So you're going to force the issue."

Evelina's cheeks flushed, though not with maidenly confusion. "I am already married. We want a child, that is all."

The woman brushed her indignation aside and came back to the practical. "I have what you want. But it works only at certain times of the month. When did you last bleed?"

Evelina was startled and suspicious. She'd had no mother to explain such things, and basically all she knew about child-bearing was that when the monthly bleeding and cramps stopped, you had a baby nine months later. She was not all that clear on why this should be, however, or what one had to do with the other.

"Why does that matter?" she demanded, thinking this was becoming a bit too personal.

"There is a scientific explanation, but you wouldn't understand and I don't care to try to explain it," said Huspeth dryly. "Let us leave it at this—a woman who wants to conceive has a better chance of doing so in the middle of her cycle."

Evelina thought back. "A fortnight. Maybe a little longer."

The woman grunted and shook her head. "The potion still has a chance of working, but you must lie with him this night. Already it may be too late. As for the other you ask for—what did you call it?"

Evelina was accustomed to doing her business with city apothecaries. "Absinthe. It's also known as wormwood. You distill—"

"I know it. Never heard it by that other name. What have you brought in payment? I don't do this for charity."

"I have no money—"

"I have no use for money," Huspeth said, her lip curling.

Evelina unwrapped a bundle to reveal some fish she'd stolen from the rack where they'd been left to dry in the sun.

The woman eyed the fish, then gave a curt nod. "Wait here. And don't go trampling my plants!"

Huspeth took the fish and stalked off, disappearing into the forest.

"Mad as a hornet," Evelina muttered.

She stood on the trail, looking about her in bored fashion. Bees and butterflies clustered among bright red flowers in one part of the garden. The air was warm and still, and she could smell more rain coming. She fidgeted, wishing the woman would hurry. She'd passed a stream on the way, and she wanted time to bathe and scrub those telltale stains from her clothes.

Just when she thought that the widow had abandoned her, Huspeth appeared, walking down the trail. She handed Evelina two small containers made of baked clay, stoppered with cheesecloth tied neatly around the top.

"This"—the woman pointed to one of the clay vials—

"is the liquor for him. I'm thinking you know how it works?"

Evelina smiled. She had never made use of absinthe herself—she was accustomed to fending lovers off, not working to seduce them. Her father had been known to resort to the use of the green aphrodisiac on occasion, either drinking it himself to heighten his own pleasure or slipping it into the drink of some unsuspecting girl.

"And this is for you," Huspeth continued. "To help with the baby. Drink it now, so that it has a chance to work."

Evelina sniffed at it. She didn't detect anything wrong about it, and so she lifted it to her lips and drank. The taste was sweet; it had been laced with honey. She felt it slide down her, warm and soothing.

"You must lie with him tonight," Huspeth emphasized. "And no guarantees."

Evelina understood. She took the clay vial containing the aphrodisiac and tucked it into her bosom.

Turning on her heel, the woman walked back through the garden. "Mind you don't trample my plants," Huspeth added, tossing the warning over her shoulder.

Smiling to herself in anticipation of the evening's pleasures, Evelina went off to a secluded spot on the river bank to take her bath. She did not know that Jorge was discreetly following her and was watching her from the trees, and that was a pity, for the knowledge would have heightened her enjoyment of her bath immensely.

19

GRALD ROAMED ABOUT THE CAVERNOUS HALL OF THE abbey, waiting for news, his scowling face and clenched fists a terror to the Blessed, who—when they were forced to speak to him—cringed and blanched at the spark of fury in his eyes.

The monks had lost Ven, and Grald had made it plain that unless the Dragon's Son was found, some of them would pay for their folly with their lives.

At last one monk came striding across the grassy field that surrounded the Abbey, walking with the long and purposeful gait of one who bears important news. By the expression on his face, when he threw back his cowl, the news was rather good than otherwise.

Seeing who it was, Grald immediately dismissed the other monks to speak to this one in private.

He was the monk of the bridge, the monk Draconas had encountered, whose eyes were not as mad as the eyes of most. He was, in fact, not a monk at all, but a high-ranking officer in the Army of the Dragons and one of Grald's most trusted agents.

"Commander Leopold!" Grald exclaimed in satisfaction. "You have news, I see." His hulking body hunched over that of the soldier, who—though he was tall for a human—was head and shoulders shorter than Grald. "Have you found him?"

"I have, Lord," the soldier replied. "He is in the palace." Leopold paused to let this information sink in, then added, "He is with the Children."

Grald sucked in a breath through his teeth and let it hiss out in a name. "*Draconas*. The Walker found a way inside."

"Despite our best efforts, Lord, I am afraid he did. As I told you, I am certain it was Draconas who tried to talk his way past me on the bridge that night. Although then he was disguised as a monk. My shield-mate was the one who saw Ven inside the palace, and she told me that he was accompanied by a child—a little girl."

"Of course. How very clever," Grald muttered. "What idiots we have been! Searching for the man, Draconas, when, naturally, he would take on another form. What is Ven doing? Is he still there? What did he tell the Children?"

"I do not know, Lord," Leopold was forced to admit. "My shield-mate feared to come too near the Children. They do not react well to humans spying on them. You recall what they did the last time."

Grald smiled, proud of his children's ferocity. They had not actually slain the man, who had mistakenly wandered into their part of the cave. Their attack had, however, left him a gibbering idiot, and a one-armed idiot at that.

Thinking of the children brought to mind the yearly ritual when he would invite another group of young women, chosen because they were strong in the magic, into his "palace." Grald rubbed his hands in anticipation. This year would be momentous. He planned to impregnate the women using Ven's body. He hoped that the seed of that half-dragon body, mingled with the magic of himself, the dragon, would produce far better children—more dragon and less human.

It is fitting, Grald thought, *that Ven should be the one to take over this task. He proved that I was right in my theory that we could breed more like him. All I require are women like his mother, who are strong in the magic.*

"What else did Ven see inside the palace?" Grald asked.

"The army," replied the commander.

Grald ground his teeth in ire. "He will alert the humans, if he can. Warn his brother."

"What does it matter?" asked Leopold imperturbably. "I've seen human armies. There's nothing they can do against us. Whatever Ven tells them of us will only plant terror in their hearts. Fear is a fast-growing tree that bears noxious fruit."

"That may be true, but I don't trust the Walker. He must not leave Dragonkeep. I want him dead."

The commander was dubious. "Pardon me if I point out, Lord, that one of your own kind attempted to kill the Walker and failed—"

"Anora bungled it," said Grald bluntly. "She foolishly alerted Draconas instead of taking him by surprise. Or perhaps her action was not so foolish. Perhaps it was deliberate. The Walker and Anora have been friends for many centuries." His eyes narrowed so that they nearly disappeared in the shadows of his overhanging brow. "Draconas is cunning, but I am more so. This time, we will catch the Walker off guard. Ven will kill Draconas."

"Ven is hardly strong enough—"

"Not the old Ven," Grald interrupted with a grin. "The new Ven. Once I have taken over my son's body, I will go to Draconas on some pretext or other and I will slay him. As simple as that."

"Ah," said the soldier in understanding.

"We must move faster than we have anticipated, however. When my son leaves the palace, apprehend him. Make no mention of the fact that you know where he has been. Let him think he has fooled us. Bring him here to me tonight, at the hour past slumber, when all is quiet."

"And the Walker?"

Grald thought this over. "He must not be allowed to interfere with my plans. Keep him occupied."

Leopold bowed. "As you command, Lord. I have one more question."

"Ask it," said Grald.

"When may I return to my company? My shield-mate and I do not want to miss out on the battle."

"Do not worry, Commander. You will march with your

comrades. You are too valuable a warrior to remain disguised as a monk forever."

Leopold bowed at the compliment and took his departure.

Ven left the cavern by the way he'd entered. The sun was sinking into the west and the shadows were long by the time he descended from the mountain and found his way back to the city. That part wasn't difficult. He simply followed the smell, the stench of humanity. He'd never noticed it before. Now he knew he would never get it out of his nostrils.

The Blessed pounced on him almost immediately. They said nothing, but he knew they knew where he'd been without a word being spoken. Their eyes flitted to him and flitted away. Like Bellona, they never looked at him long, if they could help it.

"I want to see Grald," Ven demanded, as they wound their way through the maze of streets.

"Grald wants to see you, Dragon's Son," replied one of the monks, one who had a saner look than the others. He actually met and held Ven's gaze.

"Good," said Ven, rather nonplussed. "Then take me to him."

"Not yet," the Blessed said. "Grald is busy with the plans for war. He says that you should dine first and rest yourself after the exertions of the day. Grald bids you come to him after the hour of slumber."

"Very well." Ven did not like being "bid" to do anything, but he was ravenously hungry—he had been too distracted by his inner turmoil to eat anything beneath the mountain—and he was exhausted, not so much physically as mentally. He had a lot to think over before meeting with his father.

As for slaying Grald, his death might not be necessary. That was one of the things Ven had to think over. He was intrigued by the new way of viewing himself offered to him by his siblings. He had seen himself reflected only in the eyes of humans, and that was like looking into water stirred by the wind, so that his reflection was always distorted and warped. He'd seen himself in the eyes of Bellona, who had been ashamed of him and loathed him. He'd seen himself in the eyes of Evelina, who'd seen a freak, a beast. His siblings had lifted up before him a mirror of pure crystal, without flaw, touched by no emotion, and he'd seen himself honored, revered, a miracle of creation that combined the best parts of two separate entities to create a new kind of person, someone who was not unnatural, but had his or her own place in the world.

That this miracle came at the cost of a human's life was regrettable, but then, as Sorrow had said, many human children walking the earth this very day had come into the world at the mother's expense.

So perhaps I don't need to take revenge against the dragon. Perhaps, instead, I should thank and honor him.

Ven went to his supper and ate with a good appetite. Then he lay down on his bed, not to sleep, but to consider all the questions he would ask his father, the dragon.

Grald sniffed about the vast hall in the Abbey. Once he was certain by both sight and smell that he was alone, he walked over to a portion of the wall that was solid stone to the eyes of humans, empty air to his dragon eyes. The illusion concealed a tomb made of granite with a heavy granite lid that now rested on the floor.

Inside was the body of Grald, the body the dragon inhabited. Tonight, the human would finally receive his release in death. Grald would tear out Ven's heart and place it in the golden locket. He would seize the young, strong body, and when that was done, he would take what was left of Ven and place him inside the tomb. The dragon would lift the heavy lid of the coffin in his claws and seal Ven inside. There, the young man would continue to live, buried alive, his still-beating heart fueling the body the dragon had usurped. Ven might live for thirty or forty years, Grald calculated. The dragon would get thirty or forty years of good use from the young man's body, maybe longer. And when that body eventually aged and died, the dragon would have many more bodies of his own children from which to choose.

"My offspring will be a force in this world," he said proudly, placing his hands on the lid of the tomb and gazing at it with satisfaction. "My armies will conquer human nations. My children will rule them. We dragons will bring order to this world of humans, teach them to obey and respect their masters. I almost wish Ven could be at my side to see it."

Grald imagined what it would be like to be trapped, suffering, inside this coffin; trapped for years without end, the minutes dropping so slowly, like the blood of the ravaged heart.

"A noble sacrifice, Ven," said the dragon softly. "One that will be long remembered."

Grald made certain that the illusion was still in place, that the tomb remained hidden to all eyes but his. Then, his thoughts going on to other matters, the dragon left to apprise Maristara and Anora that their plans had changed, that Draconas had been discovered alive, and that, of necessity, the war must go forward sooner than anticipated.

He did not expect the elder females to be happy about the situation, and he was right.

They weren't.

The conversation between the three dragons was an explosion of color, blobs of anger hurled onto a mental canvas. Grald and Anora in particular went at each other, accusations sharp as claws tearing and ripping until the canvas was in shreds and came perilously close to being destroyed.

"Stop it!" ordered Maristara, her colors black as hoarfrost. "You both stink of fear."

The battling dragons went silent, their colors subdued, though still smoldering.

"Not fear," Grald returned. "Our own damnable reluctance to act."

"He's right," Anora conceded grudgingly. Her colors were gray with fatigue. "We dragons will find any excuse to keep from taking that first step off the ledge."

"The first step has been taken," Maristara reminded them. "We must now either flap our wings or fall to our doom into the pit below. You, Anora. You have said that you walk among the humans."

"I am with them now. The takeover of the latest body went smoothly. No one suspects. I find I am starting to hate this, though," Anora returned bitterly. "This killing of humans in order to use their bodies. I found this murder particularly reprehensible."

"Anora is weakening!" was the alarmed thought that flashed from Maristara to Grald.

"None of us likes it," said Grald, lying, for he enjoyed the killing. "I am going to be forced to slay my own son. You don't see me whining over it."

"And when will you kill him?" Maristara demanded. "We cannot make a move until you have taken over the half-dragon's body."

"Tonight," said Grald. "The arrangements are made."

"And the Walker?"

"Slaying him will be my first course of action once I am in my new body. I will take care of that tonight as well."

Maristara and Grald waited for Anora to object, but her colors were hidden.

"Good," said Grald. "Then if all goes according to plan, the army of Dragonkeep will make ready to march against the humans tomorrow."

"So soon . . ." Anora murmured.

"Is this a problem?" Maristara asked irritably.

"No, I am prepared to act."

"Not too precipitously, I hope," Maristara said. "The timing must be right. The humans must be made to think that this cannon of theirs brought about the catastrophe."

"You have no cause to worry," Anora returned, her colors taking on a fiery glow. "I know what I am about."

"Very good," said Maristara. "Then we will each keep the other apprised. Good fortune to us all. Tomorrow will be a momentous day for all of dragonkind."

"A day too long coming, if you ask me," Grald muttered.

"No one did," said Anora, and her colors disappeared with a snap.

20

DRACONAS HURRIED THROUGH THE STREETS OF DRAG-
onkeep, hoping to reach home by suppertime so as not to
worry Rosa. The hour was sunset, and the streets were
crowded with other homeward-bound people. Draconas
had to dodge and weave his way along the narrow streets.
His disguise as a hoyden aided him in this, for he
bumped, shoved, jostled, or pushed people as needed and
received in turn nothing more than a muttered scolding or
a threat to box his ears, whereas an adult behaving in a
similar rude manner would have ended up in a fistfight.

Worrying about someone worrying about you is not a
dragon trait. Independent, solitary beings, dragons enjoy
the freedom of doing what they please when they please
without thought or care for any other. Humans, on the
other hand, need to care and be cared for in return. That
Rosa and Anton were coming to care deeply for the
young girl who had intruded into their lives was becoming increasingly apparent to Draconas. Their caring was
an added and unexpected burden, a burden he did not
need right now.

No good telling himself he should have foreseen it. In
the split second he'd had to make his decision, he'd been
thinking only of his own survival, not looking ahead to
see how that survival might impact the lives of humans.

As a walker, he was supposed to have as little effect on

human lives as possible—a rule he'd effectively scuttled years ago when he had started on this disastrous enterprise. Since then, he'd ended up entangled in more human lives than he wanted to think about.

"It's like one of their blasted round dances," Draconas grumbled to himself as he ran down the street, his long braids flying out behind him. "You start out with one human and things are going fine, then suddenly the music changes and you're handed off to another human, then another after that, and before you know it, you find yourself a long way from where you want to be."

As if fate were determined to prove him right, Draconas's need to race home caused him to burst into the house without first doing what he would have normally done—taken a careful inspection of his surroundings. If Draconas had been paying attention, he would have seen the monk loitering in the street, and he would have known immediately that this night he should not go home. He should have let the humans worry.

As it was, Draconas was in too much haste to notice. He arrived to find that Rosa was out, and he had time to chop the carrots and the onions, ready to add to the meat that was already in the stew pot, when Rosa opened the door.

"It's good to come home to a warm house and supper already started," said Rosa, taking off her scarf and giving the girl a hug. She gazed at Draca and added, with a frown, "But what have you been up to? You look as though you've spent the day crawling about in a cave! I trust you washed your hands before you started the cooking."

"Yes, ma'am," said Draconas, exhibiting hands and arms that were clean to the elbow, if not much beyond that.

"Your face is filthy and you've even got dirt in your hair," said Rosa, scandalized. "You had best go wash up before Anton comes home. Though, poor man"—she sighed—"I think it likely he'll be late again this night."

Draconas thought so, too, since Anton was helping to make the weapons of war that the dragon army would carry into human lands. As he poured water into the crockery bowl the family used for washing, he thought of the daughter that Rosa and Anton would never see again, and he thought of the hideous grandchild that she had borne them—a grandchild that resembled the daughter they loved except with clawed feet, or perhaps wings and a tail.

He would never tell them, of course. In this dance, the music would not change. The partners would not shift. The dancers would keep dancing until the final beat of the drum.

There came a knock at the door.

"Strange time for visitors," said Rosa, turning from the bubbling stew pot, over which she had been hovering, to peer out the window. She gave a little gasp. "It's one of the Blessed!"

Draconas knew in that instant that he'd made a mistake. He should not have come back to this house. He'd been discovered. Perhaps Ven had given him away, although Draconas didn't think that likely. Ven was one to keep himself to himself. Draconas considered it far more likely that someone in the "palace" had seen through his illusion and tracked him down.

Rosa opened the door and there was the exact monk of the bridge, sane eyes and all.

"Good evening, Brother," said Rosa nervously, with a strained smile.

"Good evening, Mistress," said the monk. He was relaxed, his tone natural. His gaze, as he glanced about the house, was casual. If he saw Draca, standing at the back of the room, he took no special notice of her. "This is the home of Master Anton, the blacksmith, is it not?"

"Yes, Brother—" Rosa hesitated.

"Brother Leopold. Is your good man about?" the monk asked politely.

"No, Brother Leopold, he is working late this night," Rosa replied. "You will find him in the smithy. I can show you, if you will come . . ." As she started out the door, she was closing it behind her.

"Bless you," Draconas said to her softly.

Unfortunately, the monk stopped her. "Thank you, Mistress," he said, smiling affably. "I would not think of interrupting his work. I will wait for him here, if my presence is not an inconvenience."

Rosa murmured something and, with a frightened glance at Draca, she opened the door to allow the monk to enter.

The monk walked into the house and stood politely until Rosa offered him a chair. He sat down and his gaze went over the house again. Rosa remained standing, twisting her skirt in her hands.

"Whatever you are cooking smells delicious," Brother Leopold said, glancing at the stew pot, from which a fragrant aroma of onions and meat and spices was rising. "You wait until your good man comes home to dine, I take it."

Rosa murmured something unintelligible and then did not know what to do with herself. She continued to stand near the door, twisting the cloth. A tense silence fell—tense on the part of Draconas and Rosa. The monk appeared to be quite at home. Smiling, he settled comfortably in his chair and continued to look about, apparently quite taken with what he saw.

"You are a good housekeeper, Mistress Rosa," he said, and his gaze went at last to Draca and remained on her. "Your daughter must be a great help to you."

Rosa gulped, unable to answer.

"What is your name, child?" Brother Leopold asked.

"Draca," answered Draconas. He forced himself to meet the monk's gaze with the frank and unabashed stare of a curious child.

"Come closer, Draca," said the monk, reaching out his hand. "You are not afraid of me? Good. So many children are," he added sadly to Rosa. "It's too bad, really."

Draconas walked over to the monk. He could not figure out what was going on. One minute he thought the monk knew exactly who and what he was, the next he thought he didn't. Perhaps this *was* just business with Anton.

"You are very pretty, Draca." The monk took hold of her hand. "Smart, too, I'll wager. Are you smart, Draca?"

"I hope so, Brother," Draconas answered.

"And you like to walk, don't you, Draca?" said Brother Leopold. He patted her hand. "I've seen you walking about town, haven't I? Quite the 'walker' . . ."

Draconas stared hard at the monk. Still smiling, still affable, still patting Draca's hand, the monk gazed intently at him.

"Quite the walker," the monk repeated.

There was no doubt now in Draconas's mind that the monk knew who and what he was and that he was telling Draconas he knew. Draconas tensed, waiting for the attack, waiting to be arrested, waiting for who knew what . . . The monk released the girl's hand with a final pat and turned back to Rosa.

"Do you mind if I invite myself to dinner, my good woman? Truly, the food smells wonderful. We get no such meals in the monastery, I assure you. It would be a treat for me."

"Of course, Brother Leopold," Rosa stammered. "We . . . we would be honored. Draca, run and fetch Anton. Tell him we have a guest—"

"Oh, do not make Draca *walk* over there," protested the monk. His gaze fixed on Draconas. The monk's eyes were focused and intense and alert and in no way mad. "Draca has walked such a lot this day. She should rest. I am in no hurry. I have been working at the site of the blast," he added, continuing to look at Draca. "A terrible thing. So many buildings and lives destroyed. Fortunately, that part of the city was only sparsely inhabited. We are indeed lucky that the blast did not occur in *this* neighborhood. Many more would have died. Hundreds upon hundreds. Including Anton and Rosa and our little Draca here and other children just like her."

The monk smiled at Draconas, then added, "There are those who believe that human life is cheap. That the life of a human is not worth that of say—a dragon, for example. What do you think, Draca? Such a great walker as yourself must have an opinion."

"Some believe that," Draconas replied, meeting the monk's gaze.

"But not you," said Brother Leopold.

Draconas paused, then said steadily, "Once I did. But not anymore. I would not want anything bad to happen to the people of this neighborhood."

"Good for you, child," said the monk with a nod. "We may all look forward to a quiet evening at home this night."

Rosa stood staring from one to the other in confusion.

"Ah," said Brother Leopold, rising. "Here is our good blacksmith, now! Greetings, Master Anton."

Anton, considerably astonished, stood stock still in the door. Rosa sidled up to him and nudged him and he came to himself. Mumbling his greetings, he entered the house. When the monk resumed his seat, Anton took the opportunity to flash an alarmed and questioning glance at his wife.

Rosa shook her head and shrugged helplessly.

Both of them looked at Draca.

Draconas knew more than they did. He knew why the monk had come. The monk had made that plain. Draconas was to spend a quiet evening at home this night. If he did not, something bad would happen, not only to Rosa and Anton, but to every human living in this part of the city.

Draconas offered to go lay the table for supper. The monk sat at his ease, talking with a bemused Anton about how his work was coming. Rosa followed Draca into the kitchen to look distractedly at the stew.

Draconas spread the well-worn cloth and set out the crockery bowls and the horn spoons. As he placed the human utensils on the table and prepared to eat the human food, he realized that he had just made his decision. He had declared where he stood in this war between humans and dragons.

He sided with humans against his own kind. He felt a deep and abiding sorrow at this, but he did not regret his decision. His own kind were wrong.

The four of them sat down to the simple meal. Rosa ladled out the stew into the bowls. Draconas dipped his spoon into the broth. He was shoving aside a detested carrot to get at the meat, when Ven came hurtling out of the cave in which he'd hidden himself for all the years of his life.

Ven came running straight at Draconas. Grald chased him. The dragon's claw reached out for Ven, for his heart . . .

Draconas dropped the spoon in the bowl, splashing hot broth all over the table and startling everyone.

"Draca?" asked Rosa anxiously. "What's wrong? Are you ill?"

Draconas looked up to find the monk's sane eyes fixed on him.

"Nothing is wrong, Rosa," said Draconas, after a pause. "I'm sorry. I'll clean up the mess I made."

The irony of the words struck him. All along, it was what he'd been trying to do. Clean up the mess.

He left the table to get a cloth. He could not help Ven. He could not save him. Melisande's son would have to save himself.

Or rather, Melisande's sons. Perhaps he could do something, after all.

Demurely, keeping his eyes lowered, Draconas went back to the table and began mopping up the spill.

The monk could stop his dragon body from leaving this house. The monk could not stop his dragon mind. Draconas's colors flared, purple and gold.

"Lysira! Are you there?" he cried silently, as he kept an eye on the monk.

"Yes, Draconas," said the young female immediately.

The monk was rising to his feet. He had quit smiling.

"You seem to be deep in thought, little girl," said the monk.

"Lysira," said Draconas, knowing he did not have much time. "Find Marcus. Enter his mind—"

"Enter his mind! The mind of a human! Draconas, I'm not sure—"

"You can do it. You must! Tell him . . ."

Brother Leopold reached out his hand, placed it on Draconas's head. "You do not look well. I think now is time for rest."

Draconas squeezed out one burst of color before darkness overtook him and he sagged to floor.

"She's had such a busy day," said the monk solicitously. Lifting Draca in his arms, he carried the unconscious girl to bed.

21

DRACONAS'S PLAN TO ALERT MARCUS TO HIS BROTHER'S danger was an excellent one. Sadly, Draconas forgot his own mantra—humans are unpredictable. Even after hundreds of years among humans, Draconas could have never predicted Evelina.

Marcus woke about midafternoon from a deep sleep that left him feeling sluggish and thick-headed. Alarmed to find the day so far advanced, he hastened out to ask if young Thom had been sent for the king's men. The patriarch assured Marcus that the young man had left that morning. Due to the rain, however, the earliest the king's men might be expected was sometime tomorrow.

Marcus didn't like this news, and he was short with the patriarch, who was humbly apologetic. Young Thom did not have a horse, nor did he have wings. The road was as long as God made it and the king's men would be here when they were here. Marcus knew he was being unreasonable, but he longed for home.

Since the patriarch expected all royalty to be unreasonable, no harm was done. The good old man hinted that a swim in the river might clear Marcus's head and lift his spirits, and he offered to provide a change of clothes, although certainly not the sort of clothes to which the prince was accustomed. Grateful and ashamed of his bad temper, Marcus accepted. The swim did clear his head and left him feeling refreshed.

He was glad to discard the monk's robes, which had become hateful to him, and put on homespun breeches and a much-patched woollen shirt. After that, he idled away the afternoon, refusing to let himself think about anything. He watched the fishermen return with the day's catch and further distracted himself by talking with them about their livelihood. He asked some guarded questions about the sunken cave, wondering if these men had any idea that they were living in such close proximity to a vast city hidden inside an enchanted forest.

He found that none of the fishermen ventured past the fork in the river. The fishing was bad, he was told, and the waters treacherous. They fished the waters their fathers and grandfathers had fished before them and saw no reason to go anywhere else. Their lives were good, with the exception of the occasional flood, and when that happened they buried their dead and shoveled the mud out of their dwellings and went back to plying the river when it had returned to its banks.

Marcus also wondered what had become of Evelina. He asked around for her, and one of the women told him that Evelina had gone to the river, to an area where the women did their laundry, and that they were taking good care of her. He was not to worry about her.

Marcus didn't. He'd find a private moment to speak to her tonight. He had to explain to her, as delicately as possible, that he was not in love with her. Manlike, he assumed they'd have a logical, rational discussion and that would end the matter.

The village held a feast in his honor that night, serving up fish and onions and potatoes all boiled together in an enomous kettle hung over a roaring fire. He saw Evelina, but did not have a chance to talk to her, for the men and women ate separately, the women after they had served the men. Evelina had apparently won favor with the women of the village, for they were making much of her. Someone had given her a change of clothing, like his own—worn and patched, but clean and comfortable. She looked fresh-scrubbed and wholesome in her homespun garb, and when she caught him looking at her, she blushed and smiled. Marcus felt a pang of uneasiness. The thought came to him suddenly that Evelina might not be all that logical.

He tried to signal to her that he wanted to talk, but he could never catch her eye. She seemed to be willfully ignoring him. The next thing he knew, the sun was sinking into the river and the fisherfolk were heading to their beds. Evelina walked off with the patriarch's daughter. Marcus did not want to make a show of running after her, especially in view of the men, who were drinking and swapping stories around the fire. Marcus bid everyone good night and returned, alone, to the house.

Having slept most of the day, he was not ready for his bed. He sat by the fire, brooding over Evelina, Ven, Draconas, the dragon, his father—everything he'd refused to let himself think about all day. He made up his mind to the fact that he would never see Ven again, nor could he even dare contact him, for the dragon was always lurking about, trying to find a way inside. Draconas was dead; Marcus was certain of that. Dragonkeep would remain hidden beneath its blanket of illusion as its army marched on to conquer his people.

"Yet if I told these fishermen that there is a city of living souls not twenty miles from where they ply their nets, they would bind my arms with rope and take away all sharp objects," Marcus muttered. "I'm not even sure my own father will believe me. It's all so fantastic—"

A gentle knock sounded at the door. "It's Evelina," said her voice, speaking softly.

Marcus breathed a sigh. He didn't want to have this conversation, but he needed to set things straight, let her down gently.

He opened the door.

"No one saw me," she assured him, slipping in past him. She wore a cloak, with the hood cast over her head, and she carried a basket on her arm. Placing the basket on the table, she removed her cloak and hood, and tossed them aside.

"You should close the door, Marcus. Someone will see the light."

He hadn't realized until she said something that he'd been standing there with the door wide open. Feeling uncomfortable, he did as she bade him and shut the door. He turned back to find her removing a stone jar and a mug from the basket.

"I brought you some wine," she said.

"Evelina, I want to talk—"

"And I want to talk to you, Your Highness," she said.

She poured wine into the mug and carried it over to him. She stood before him, holding the wine in her hands. She had washed her hair; its blond curls fell around her shoulders. Her eyes were soft and warm in the flickering light.

"I'm sorry I was so familiar with you last night, Your Highness," she said. "I realize that I behaved unseemly and I ask you to forgive me. I know that you were under a terrible strain when you said all those wonderful words to me when we were running for our lives from that dreadful place and that you really didn't mean them. How could you love me? I'm nobody. Not a princess or a duke's daughter . . ."

"Evelina," he began, feeling wretched. "It's not—"

"Please, drink the wine, Your Highness," she continued, holding it out to him. Tears glimmered on her lashes. "The patriarch's daughter made this wine and she would be offended if you did not. I promised her I would tell her how you liked it. You can lie, if you want. After all, you are a prince and you can do with people what you like—"

"Evelina," he tried a third time.

She thrust the wine into his hands and then ran to a corner of the room and sobbed as though her heart would break.

Marcus gulped some wine. He was completely out of his depth, floundering in water that had been ankle deep when he waded in, but which was now up to his chin and rising. Evelina had said the very words to him that he'd been going to say to her—about how it had all been different when they were in Dragonkeep and he'd been under a strain and so on and so forth. When he'd said it, it seemed reasonable and logical. When she said it, she made him feel like a worm. He didn't know what to do now. Anything he said now would only make matters worse. Yet he couldn't leave her weeping in a corner.

He drank more wine. It had a peculiar taste to it, not at all like the wine to which he was accustomed. And it was far more potent. The warmth spread from his throat to his belly and his limbs, sweet and pleasant and relaxing. He drank more wine and then lowered the half-empty mug to the table and walked over to Evelina.

The water was no longer closing over his head. He was floating on top of it. He had wronged her. He would apologize. She had been brave and loyal.

"Evelina," he said for the fourth time, and she turned around and looked up at him with her blue, shimmering eyes. He floated on top of those eyes, floated gently along like thistledown.

"I meant every word!" he gasped. "I love you! I adore you!"

The warmth of the wine suffused him. He ached and throbbed with it, and he could find relief only by drowning in the blue water of the river of her eyes. She was in his arms, her soft flesh in his hands and her sweetness on his tongue, and he was tearing off his clothes and her clothes and they were lying on the mattress, panting and heaving and his need was hot and pain-filled and she was willing and yielding . . .

And then he had to stop to scratch his leg. He went back to her, but then his arm itched uncontrollably and he scratched at it and then, suddenly, he was itchy all over. He tried to ignore the itching, but he couldn't, and he had to stop what he was about to do to scratch at himself. Evelina moaned and nuzzled him, running her hands over his body, and he tried again, but the itching was a terrible distraction.

She opened her eyes and looked at him and suddenly pulled away.

"You . . . you've gone all blotchy," she gasped in dismay.

He scratched at his head and neck and looked down at his naked body and saw that she spoke truly. He was covered in large red blotches, about the size of a coin of the realm, growing larger and spreading rapidly. The blotches burned like fire and itched like the devil and he could do nothing now but scratch at them. He could swear he could feel them on the inside of his mouth.

"It's not the plague, is it?" Evelina cried. Covering herself with a blanket, she crawled off the bed.

Marcus groaned. "No, I think it must have been the wine. I break out in these blotches sometimes if I eat certain spices or herbs, but it's never happened with wine."

"Spices," murmured Evelina. "Oh, my God. You wretched man. You stupid, wretched man! Why can't you be normal?"

Suddenly, strangely, Evelina turned into a dragon. The dragon's eyes stared into his. The dragon seemed nervous, afraid.

"I don't know how to talk to you." The dragon's colors were tenuous and wispy. "I . . . this is so alien. Your mind is too . . . small. I feel squeezed in. Human, can you hear me? I am a friend of Draconas. My name is Lysira. He sent me—"

And then all the colors in Marcus's mind exploded.

Evelina scrambled backward off the mattress and crouched on the floor, staring in horror at the prince.

Marcus lay on his back. His eyes—gleaming wild in the firelight—rolled and roved, as if he were following the erratic flight of an invisible flock of birds. His eyes darted back and forth, up and down, back and forth. His body began to twitch. His hands curled. She'd seen the effects of wormwood on people before and she'd never seen anything like this.

"He's having some sort of fit," Evelina wailed. "First blotches, then fits. Why can't you be normal?"

She shook him by the shoulder and dug her nails into his flesh. No response. He was gasping, as though he was finding it difficult to breathe, and watching the invisible birds, not paying any attention to her. Not getting her with child.

"You're a freak!" Evelina cried. "As bad as your brother, even if you don't have the legs of a lizard."

She punched him a couple of times and then sat back on her heels and stared at him. She didn't know what to do. He was growing worse. He began to thrash about. Men died of fits like this.

And if he died, what would become of her?

"I should get help!"

Evelina feverishly threw on some clothes and, flinging open the door, she ran out into the night—straight into the arms of Jorge.

"I heard a cry," he said, and his voice was calm and his arms were strong and comforting.

Quivering, Evelina pressed against him.

"The prince," she gasped, "He's . . . there's something wrong . . . he's having a fit . . . the wine . . . I have to find the patriarch—"

"No, you do not," said Jorge. "You found me. Come back inside. Keep quiet."

"You don't understand! He might die!" Evelina struggled to free herself.

"You are the one who doesn't understand," said Jorge coolly, his grip on her firm. "If His Highness dies, they'll discover that you put the wormwood in his wine."

Evelina went cold all over. "Poison! They'll think I poisoned him! They'll hang me!"

She felt faint. Jorge put his arm around her and half-carried her back into the house. Shutting the door, he bolted it.

"Maybe someone else saw me go to the Widow's . . ." she whimpered.

"Only me," he said, reassuring.

She looked over at Marcus.

"Oh, Holy Mother of God!" Evelina whispered, shrinking back against the wall. "He's dead!"

Marcus's head lolled on the pillow. His arms hung over the sides of the mattress, hands dangling limply.

Jorge knelt swiftly beside the prince and felt for a

pulse. He put his head close to Marcus's open mouth. He examined the blotches on his body and then looked at Evelina and smiled.

"What?" she asked, shivering so that her teeth chattered. She could already feel the noose closing around her neck.

"He is not dead," said Jorge. "He is breathing easily. His pulse is strong. The blotches are already starting to fade. They will probably be gone by morning. He is asleep."

Evelina heaved a shuddering sigh and closed her eyes.

"Thank you, God!" she breathed. "Thank you!"

"He's very deep in sleep," Jorge added. "I doubt if a cannon shot would waken him."

Evelina opened her eyes. She heard Huspeth's words, *You must lie with him this night.*

With him. With some man.

Evelina was suddenly all business. "How much will he remember when he wakes up?"

"Very little, I should think," Jorge said, shrugging. He moved near her, put his hands around her waist, and jerked her close to him, so that her breasts pressed against his chest. "Or, let's say, he'll remember what you tell him to remember."

He sat down in the chair. Hiking up her skirt, he pulled her onto his lap and ran his hands up her bare thighs. Evelina's mouth closed over his and she moaned as his tongue flicked against hers. Relaxing, her worries over, she gave herself to pleasure.

Pleasure with a normal man. Not a freak.

This was all working out for the best. At least now a freak wouldn't be the father of her child.

Marcus would only think he was the father.

22

THE ABBEY WAS DARK AT THIS HOUR OF THE NIGHT, THE deepest hour, the end of one day and the start of the next. At first, when Ven entered, he could not see Grald, not even with his dragon vision. He knew Grald was here—he could hear the man's heavy breathing—but he could not locate him. Ven was not about to call out to him, like a lost child afraid of the dark. He assumed Grald was hiding deliberately, to try to intimidate him. Ven followed the sounds of the breathing and came to the thronelike chair that Grald used for his audiences.

The chair was empty. The sounds of the breathing came from the back, behind the chair.

Light flared suddenly, a torch ignited. Ven was momentarily blinded, and he squinted into the brilliance. The dragon crouched outside the cavern of his mind and, for once, Grald was not trying to scrabble or claw his way inside.

"I understand that you paid a visit to your siblings," his father said.

Grald was a monstrous mound of flesh and shadow in the torchlight, a grotesque figure.

"Splendid, aren't they? Like you, my son. You are the oldest, you know," Grald continued, the eyes beneath the overhanging brow consumed in shadow. Not even a glint or gleam was visible. "There were others before you, but you were the first to survive. Finally I came upon the right combination. This might surprise you, but I'd never used a woman like your mother in our previous breeding trials. I deemed such human females, who were strong in the dragon-magic, too valuable. They protected Seth from invasion and, here in Dragonkeep, they help maintain the illusion that hides this city and bear those children who have grown up to become my soldiers. You saw the army, as well, I think. Draconas was most thorough."

Ven remained silent. No need to speak, when all his questions were being answered.

"Draconas was the one who gave Anora the idea; ironic, isn't it? I decided to experiment on Melisande, and you were the result, turning out far better than my expectations. I decided to see if I could emulate my success, and I mated with several females who were strong in the magic. One child out of that first group of ten survived to adulthood—your sister, Sorrow. The next year, several more survived, as the holy sisters learned how to care for the infants. They are magnificent, aren't they? Your brothers and sisters?"

"For monsters," Ven returned.

He hadn't meant to say that. The words slipped out before he was aware of them. He was ashamed the moment he'd spoken. He didn't want to feel that way. He didn't want to hate them, as he hated himself.

Grald took a step nearer, moving into the light, so that his eyes seemed to kindle and catch fire. Ven didn't like anyone coming that close to him, and he almost took a step backward. He then realized that this would look like weakness, and he held his ground.

Grald's mouth twisted. He glowered down at Ven.

"I raised your siblings to be proud of who and what they are. They are the future of mankind. The future of dragonkind."

"How can they be the future of both when they are neither?" Ven asked. "And neither dragons nor men will have anything to do with them."

He couldn't understand why he was saying such things. He had not come here intending to insult his father. He'd come here to talk to him. The reason was Grald. Something about the man made Ven nervous. Perhaps it was the way the dragon lay so still outside Ven's cave, no longer trying to force his way in. Almost as if he knew it was just a matter of time . . .

"You should know the answer to that," Grald stated. "You are stronger, smarter than any human born. What's more, you have the ability to live in the human world *and* in the dragon world. You can communicate mind-to-mind, a feat no human can perform. You have the ability to wield the dragon-magic."

"No, I don't," said Ven perversely.

"You do," Grald reiterated. The eyes in the shadow of the brow were laughing at him. Grald was baiting him, and that further irritated Ven. "You choose not to. But that will change."

"I don't see how we are going to be the future of dragonkind," Ven said, ignoring the lure. "Dragons must be as repulsed by us half-dragons as humans. Maybe more."

"Some are," Grald admitted. "But they will come to see the logic behind your creation. By ruling humans, you will ensure that our future is safe and secure. Because of you and those like you, ordinary humans will come to worship us, hold us in reverence and awe. They will abandon the God of their imagination, a God they cannot see, and turn to dragons."

"Your kind will be the true rulers, then, not us?"

Grald made a dismissive gesture. "Only in the larger matters. We dragons care nothing for the day-to-day life of these worms. We might go for years without intervening. So long as the humans remain harmless. And you and your kind will see to that."

"I see. Your plan to conquer humans starts with my brother's kingdom."

"And you will lead the army against him," said Grald.

"*I* will?" Ven was incredulous. He gave a dismissive laugh. "I want no part of this."

"I know," said Grald, and he sighed deeply, his voice laden with sorrow and regret. "I know."

"Draconas did you no favors by hiding you from me,"

Grald continued. "He should have let me raise you, as I raised the others, to be proud of what you are. If he had, then I might not have been forced to . . ."

Grald raised his heavy shoulders and let them drop. "I could have trusted you. But your mind is tainted. You have turned against me. You have turned against your own family."

Ven's unease was growing. He was alone with a dragon who, even in human form, was a formidable opponent.

"There are none to help you, Ven," said Grald quietly, reading his son's thoughts. "Not Draconas, who has his own problems. Not your precious, magic-wielding brother. Ven. Short for Vengeance. Yes, I know. I have known for a long time. You should have killed me before now. You might have been able to do it—taken me by surprise. Caught me unawares. Fear held you back. Fear that is inherent in the human part of you. If I had raised you, you would not know fear. As it is, I will have to work hard to eradicate that weak part of you when—"

Grald paused.

"When what?" Ven was having trouble breathing. His chest was tight, his mouth dry, his throat constricting. Grald was right. Fear's poison coursed through Ven's veins, debilitating, weakening.

"Look behind me," said Grald. "See through the illusion. Others cannot, but your eyes can penetrate the magical veil, can't they, Dragon's Son? Just like they penetrated the wall, so that you could help your brother escape. There will be no such escape for you."

Ven saw a tomb. He had no need for the dragon to tell him whose tomb it was. Vague and horrifying memories came to him, memories of Bellona telling him about his mother and a tomb and a bleeding body sealed inside darkness and agony for years on end . . .

Ven bolted. His dragon legs were strong. He could easily outrun Grald. Ven made a dash for it, digging the clawed toes into the floor and leaping off them, the powerful thigh muscles propelling him across the vast hall toward the door.

He could outrun the lumbering human. But he could not outrun the dragon.

Grald had begun to shed his human body even as he shifted Ven's attention away from him and to the tomb. Short human arms, with their soft and flabby flesh and grasping, stubby fingers, began to elongate and grow strong and powerful. Scales ran over the flesh like gleaming quicksilver, hardening and protecting. Sharp claws replaced puny nails. The dragon's clawed hand reached out and caught hold of Ven's foot and tripped him up, sent him crashing heavily onto his stomach.

Confident he was free, Ven had not expected to be grabbed from behind, and the shock when he felt himself yanked off his feet was paralyzing. He had no time to break his fall, and he slammed into the floor hard. The impact knocked the breath from his body. His chin hit the floor with brain-jarring force that drove his lower jaw into his upper. His mouth filled with blood, either from biting his tongue or from teeth knocked loose or both. His head throbbed with pain and there was a buzzing in his ears. His vision blurred, tears sprang to his eyes.

Dazed, Ven tried to scramble to his feet, only to be slammed down once more.

The dragon held his prey pinned to the floor, pressing him to the stone, as Grald continued to undergo his transformation, crawling and squirming his way out of the human body like a maggot crawling out of diseased flesh. The emergence from the human form required time, but Grald had time.

As he had told Ven, no one could hear him. No one could help him.

Except his magic-wielding brother . . . and he was far away.

23

EVELINA CLUNG TO HER LOVER. SHE HAD NEVER KNOWN pleasure like this and, even as they relaxed after their love-making, she kissed his neck and bit at his earlobe, when a shout cracked like thunder over them both.

Marcus stood naked by the side of the bed. His torso and arms were still covered with fading red blotches. His eyes were wide and wild, his face pale and blotchy and terrible. He stared straight at Evelina and her lover.

Jorge shoved Evelina off him and leapt to his feet in the same motion, dumping her onto the floor. He grabbed at his trousers, which were down around his thighs. Yanking them up, he hastily began to stuff himself and his shirt back into them.

"Fight!" Marcus cried, his fists clenched. "You have to fight."

"I'll not fight you, Your Highness!" Jorge gasped. "Oh, sweet blessed saints! You a prince! I'll be drawn and quartered and my head hung up on spikes!"

Turning to flee, Jorge tripped over Evelina, who was huddled on her hands and knees, trying frantically to figure some way out of this disaster. Jorge pitched headlong over her and landed on the floor. Rolling onto his back, he began to crawl, crabwise, toward the door.

Marcus advanced on him. "Fight, Ven! Stand and fight him! The magic! Use the magic!"

Evelina's head jerked up. She stared intently at Marcus.

"I'll not fight you, Your Highness," Jorge babbled. He was sweating and shivering and crawling for all he was worth.

"Ven . . ." Evelina murmured. "What is he talking about? Ven's not here . . . Unless . . ."

She scrambled to her feet. Running over to Jorge, she pulled him up and shoved him bodily toward the door.

"Get out!" she cried. "Get out! Hurry up!"

Jorge didn't need telling. He flung open the door and bolted out, holding his unlaced britches up with one hand as he dashed into the night. Evelina slammed shut the door and put her back to it and faced Marcus, who was staring straight at her and, apparently, not seeing her.

Evelina waved her hand in front of his face. His eyes darted back and forth, and his breath came short and fast, as though watching some harrowing contest.

"Fight!" he cried again, then he suddenly clutched at his head and reeled backward, staggering halfway across the room.

"I was right. He's possessed. He's fighting a demon!" Evelina breathed.

Evelina knew something about demons. She'd been in a tavern once when one of her father's companions had been seized by a demon. The man had fallen to the floor, writhing and twitching and foaming at the mouth. Someone had wanted to call a priest, but his woman said that wasn't necessary. Her man fought with demons on a regular basis and he always came out the winner. She told all his friends to pin him down, and she gave him a stick to bite on so that he wouldn't choke to death. He wrestled with the demon for a short time, then, victorious, he fell asleep. When he came back to consciousness—and this Evelina remembered quite clearly—he had no recollection of anything that had happened.

Marcus gave another cry and made a swipe and a lunge at the air, as though he were holding a sword, though his hand was empty. Evelina watched for her chance, and when he moved near the mattress, she rushed at him and struck him hard in the chest, knocking him down. Evelina pounced, straddling him and holding his arms. He did not resist her, but lay there, staring up at whatever it was he was seeing—which wasn't her. His face contorted. His hands twitched and he gasped or cried out. Fearing someone would hear him yelling like a madman and interfere, she stuffed a rag into his mouth to stifle his shouts, and she swaddled his arms against his sides with the blanket.

Now, it was up to Marcus. Either he won or the demon did. At this point, Evelina was almost too exhausted to care which.

She left Marcus to his fight and went back to pour herself a cup of the strong red wine. She gulped it down and poured out another cup, drank half of it, then carried it to the bed and splashed a bit of wine onto the mattress. She examined the red stain and was pleased. It resembled blood, if one didn't look too closely. Evelina finished the rest of the wine, then stripped off all her clothes and lay down beside Marcus.

He stirred and gave a muffled cry. His arms bulged against the bindings. His body twisted and heaved.

"Freak!" Evelina muttered, shoving him over to make room for herself. "Just like his monster of a brother. I'm glad Marcus isn't going to be the father of my child. He'll just think he is. And he *will* marry me. Oh, yes, he will. I deserve nothing less, after all I've put up with."

Closing her eyes, she gave a contented belch and let the wine fumes carry her pleasantly into slumber.

Beside her, on the bed, Marcus fought the dragon.

24

THE WORMWOOD EVELINA HAD SLIPPED INTO MARCUS'S wine acted as a key on the lock of the door of his mental room, removing all fear of the dragon that lurked outside, removing all his inhibitions. He left that little room and went stumbling about into the minds of the dragons like a drunken man, weaving and laughing along a street of swirling, shimmering dragon dreams that were beautiful and horrifying, bestial, alien—like himself.

Marcus cavorted inside the minds of dragons. He didn't know how many dragons, but a lot, seemingly, for the fantastically colored images flew at him from every direction, fluttering around inside of him, like being bombarded by ribbons of rainbow. Then suddenly lightning splintered the rainbow and a voice intruded, shocked and dismayed.

"What are you doing, Human? Please, stop! This is not wise."

"My name is Marcus. Who are you?" he cried merrily.

"I told you! I am Lysira." She sounded stern and thoroughly put out, like his old tutor. "And this is not proper behavior!"

Marcus had never liked his tutor, and so he ignored her. Like a drunken reveler—or an escaped prisoner, drunk on freedom—Marcus capered into and out of the minds of the dragons. Naked, shouting his defiance, shouting his adoration, he wrapped his nakedness in the colors of their amazement and danced from dragon to dragon. He glided into their minds with the elegance of a dancer, doing a turn, singing a song with the colors of his own mind, then gliding swiftly out. He played tag with them, hide-and-go-seek, dodging and darting, evading and avoiding, all the while laughing wildly at the sheer joy of it all.

Marcus was a child again, a lunatic child, and his soul remembered what his brain worked hard to try to forget—the beautiful, dazzling, alien world of wondrous, magical beasts, whose thoughts wove silken tapestries, using the stars for needles and the sunbeams for thread. This was the reason that, long ago, he had traded madness for sanity, traded the lonely, isolated, shut-off, locked-up-tight gray world of humans for the dreams of dragons.

The dragons soon got over their shock that a human had actually managed to invade their minds. They were horrified and angry, just like his parents had been. He knew how that worked. It made him powerful.

Some of the dragons tried to catch him. Another dragon, a young female, sought to protect him. They all ended up in a bitter argument, and Marcus was forgotten or shoved aside. The flames of their passion roiled around him, but could not touch him.

Marcus kept it up, made himself a nuisance.

The young female fluttered about after him. "Listen to me, Human! You must come to your senses. Draconas sent me to warn you—"

"Draconas!" Marcus called. "Where are you, you old fart? Still alive? I should have known it. I escaped, by the way. No thanks to you."

He laughed and stumbled about in a dazzling, brilliant fog.

And then the fog shredded, torn apart by a dragon's claw.

The eyes that had found him in the cave found him again.

Marcus had stumbled into the mind of Grald.

No pretty colors here. Steel blue bars slammed down around Marcus, trapping him. He hurled himself against

Grald's mind, trying to free himself, but the dragon held him fast.

"As long as you are here, Prince Marcus," the dragon said, "you can see what I see, feel what I feel. When next you meet your brother, you'll be meeting me."

Ven stood in a dark room. In back of him was a tomb— Ven's tomb. Marcus could hear Ven's heart beating, and it was a thrilling sound to the dragon, for that beating heart was the key to the magical spell that would allow him to take over Ven's body and make it his own.

Grald opened the tomb, and there inside lay the human Grald, a look of horror on his face, his mouth gaping wide in screams of agony that had long gone unheard. The dragon held a golden locket in his hand. He opened the lock, dumped the heart into the bloody cavity of the human's chest. When the heart fell, the human gave a last, shuddering cry and died. The body lay in the tomb, eyes wide, mouth still open.

Grald discarded the human body he had worn, crawling out of it, leaving it on the floor like a snake leaves its shed skin. The dragon advanced on the new body he had chosen.

"Fight!" Marcus cried. "You have to fight!"

Ven turned to flee, but the dragon seized hold of him.

"Fight, Ven!" Marcus shouted. "Stand and fight him! The magic! Use the magic!"

Ven struggled valiantly, but he had never learned how to use the magic, and he was no match for the dragon. Grald dug his claws into Ven's breast, ripping through skin and flesh and tissue, cracking ribs. Ven screamed in agony and Marcus shuddered and tried frantically to break free of the bars of the dragon's mind. The dragon forced Marcus to watch.

"You wanted to see our dreams," said Grald. "Now you see them."

A clawed hand tossed aside broken fragments of Ven's ribcage, as he writhed in excruciating torment in the dragon's grip. The dragon wound Ven up in strands of magic, enchantment that bound his life to the dragon's and the dragon's life to Ven's. Then the dragon seized hold of the beating heart and tore it from Ven's chest, leaving behind a gaping, bloody hole in the shattered breast.

Grald held the heart in his hand and bent his will upon it, and the heart began to shrink until it was a doll's heart or that of a bird, rapidly beating. Grald tucked the heart carefully inside the golden locket that he held suspended by a golden chain on a single claw.

Then the dragon carried Ven into the sarcophagus and dumped him into stone-bound darkness. Grald lifted up the heavy lid and slid it in place, sealing Ven—bound by enchantment to a horrible life—inside the tomb.

The last image Marcus saw was his brother's face as he came to realize that he would be trapped in darkness and unceasing pain, with no escape but death, and that would come only when the human body the dragon had taken over had aged past the point of usefulness.

Grald turned to face Marcus. The dragon opened the locket he held in his claw.

"Here's a dream for you, little prince."

An army of humans wearing armor that sparkled in the sun like the glittering scales of the dragon marched triumphantly through the gates of his father's castle.

Leading the army was Ven.

Slit eyes glared at Marcus. Jaws opened wide. Slashing fangs dripped saliva. Claws, stained in blood, curled over him. The massive tail lashed and twitched.

Marcus grabbed for his sword, but . . . he had no sword. He was naked and soft and fragile, and he couldn't escape . . .

A hand—his brother's hand—thrust through the darkness. The hand was that of the little child who had reached out to Marcus so many years ago. The hand was the hand that had shown him the way through the walls of Dragonkeep. His heart aching, his thoughts floundering in confusion, Marcus grasped at the hand.

Ven clasped him firmly, and the bars of Grald's mind vanished.

Marcus stood in a vast dark hall, standing beside an empty tomb. Ven lay on the floor. Grald loomed over him.

The dragon was a grotesque monstrosity—half-in and half-out of the human body. He clutched Ven's ankle with a single claw, keeping fast hold of him, preventing him from escaping while the dragon continued to shift form.

The dragon head was emerging from the human's stooped and fleshy shoulders, the human neck elongating into that of the dragon. The human legs shifted, stretched, bent into the powerful hind legs of the dragon. Dragon wings sprouted from human shoulders.

"Help me, Marcus," Ven cried, his voice grating across Marcus's mind. "I can't fight him alone."

"You're dead," said Marcus. "I saw him kill you."

Even as he spoke, he understood. *You wanted to see our dreams . . .*

Marcus looked from his brother to Grald, and Marcus realized suddenly that he had seen what the dragon dreamed, not what he had done. The battle was not over. It was just beginning.

"Use the magic!" Marcus told his brother. "He's weak now!"

"I can't use the magic," Ven cried, struggling to free himself from the dragon's grip. "It isn't in me!"

"It is," said Marcus. "It is a part of you. Admit it."

Ven continued to fight, twisting. Trying to break the dragon's grip on his ankle, he kicked at Grald's scale-covered arm with his own clawed foot. Ven was strong and powerful, but the dragon was stronger, and every second that passed, Grald was growing stronger still. Already, there was very little left of him that was human.

Grald dragged Ven closer and stretched out the other clawed hand.

"The magic beats in your heart, Ven," Marcus told him. "It pulses through your veins. It mixes with the air in your lungs and throbs in your fingertips. It sparkles in the sunlight like the scales on your legs."

Ven closed his eyes and clenched his fists. His body shuddered. The battle that raged inside him was as desperate as the battle he was waging for his life. For they were both the same.

"Human!" called Lysira. "Marcus! You can't fight Grald. Go back inside your room! Lock yourself up safe!"

Now it was Marcus who hesitated. He didn't want to be trapped in another horrible dream. One from which he might never escape.

"Melisande's sons—both her sons—will avenge her," said Marcus.

Gripping his courage in his empty sword hand, Marcus left Ven's mind and flung himself headlong into Grald's.

The dragon had hold of Ven's ankle, the same place where, when Ven was a child, a bulldog had bitten into the scaled flesh. Draconas had saved Ven, then, but Draconas wasn't here to save him now. Ven had to save himself. He stared at the scaled leg, the leg he had stared at with loathing every day of his life since the day he'd first realized that he was different.

He had a choice. He could die—worse than die—writhing helpless in the grip of the father who had made him what he was.

Or he could fight. And make him pay.

Ven looked up at Grald, at the leering face bending over him, at the wings starting to spread wide, filling the darkness. The old catechism that Bellona had made him recite on his birthday came back to him.

"What is your name?"

"Ven."

"Your true name."

"Vengeance."

The magic roiled and bubbled and surged up from some pit deep inside him. The magic seethed and burned and twisted. Raw and unformed, mingled with pent-up rage, the magic spewed from Ven's mouth. He vomited fire and spit acid. The fire seared Grald's eyes, and the acid sprayed over the claws that held Ven's leg. The dragon roared and reared back his head. Scales bubbled in the acid, his eyes burned. Grald snatched his claw away.

Ven rose to his feet. He reached out to the past and seized hold of the power. He took hold of every sneer, every averted glance, every pitying gaze. He seized his mother's pain, Bellona's twisted love, Evelina's mockery. He grabbed his own fury and his siblings' pride, and he bundled all of it into a crackling, blazing ball. He hurled that ball with all his strength at his father.

The magic struck the dragon full in the chest and sent him crashing back against a solid stone wall. The building shook, the ground trembled. Ven collapsed.

His strength flowed from him like blood from a pierced heart. He'd given it all, everything, nothing was left. He was weak and helpless as the squalling babe lying alongside his twin, lying in his mother's blood, except that now he lay in the blood of his father.

It seemed to Grald that he'd been struck by the sun.

The molten fire that had been conjured of Ven's very soul smote the dragon full in the chest. The magic melted the armor-like scales, seared through to the flesh, burned away the flesh to attack the bone and pulsing organs beneath. The magic splashed onto Grald's eyes and head, blinding him, and sprayed over his wings, which were yet emerging, causing holes to open where the fiery blobs hit the fragile membrane. What human flesh still remained on the dragon dissolved, bubbling horribly, like fat on a hot skillet.

The full impact of the blow fell on the dragon's breastbone, right over the heart, jolting it out of its centuries-old rhythm. The dragon's heart lurched and thumped wildly, erratically. Grald could not catch his breath. Air rattled and whistled in his chest. Looking down with his half-blind eyes, he saw shattered bone and a mass of charred and bleeding flesh.

Grald was in unbearable pain. He was dying. Slain by the son. Slain by the mother.

Vengeance. Grald has always known Ven's name and been mightily amused by it.

"Not now!" the dragon raged, staggering. "Not yet!"

His son's living heart. It would keep him alive.

Grald lurched toward Ven, who lay unconscious on the floor. Grald's own heart hammered and shook. He was finding it increasingly difficult to draw a breath. He fixed all his concentration on his son. Lunging forward with a claw that yet had the strength to rip open Ven's human chest, he bent to pluck out his heart.

A human blocked his way. Grald struggled to see through the smoke that was drifting from the fire of the magic into his mind.

The prince. The brother. He stood over Ven's body, blocking the way.

The sons of Melisande.

Human flesh and bone. Fragile and soft.

Grald swiped his claw at the prince, intending to smash the puny frame to bloody pulp, cleave him open, cast him to one side, then get at his prey.

The dragon's claw passed through air, whistled through darkness, touched nothing.

The dragon's heart thudded and began to slow. Grald toppled to the floor, landing with a thud that cracked stone walls and sent tremors through the ground. The dragon never knew he had fallen over. He stared at the human, who wavered in his sight, and he kept staring into death and beyond.

25

THE DRAGON'S AGONIZED RAGE BURST AGAINST MARCUS, seeming to boil his blood. And then the darkness of death began to rush in like a rolling tide, swallowing up the rage, thundering down on Marcus, crashing, churning, and crushing.

"Run!" Lysira warned him. "Don't get caught inside Grald's mind!"

Marcus fled the dragon's mind. He stood, shivering, in his little room, and watched Grald die.

"Ven?" Marcus called.

There was no answer. His brother's mind was empty, the colors drained. He too was dying.

If Marcus had been there, physically present, he could have saved his brother. But Marcus was far away, with a river between them. And he was running out of time.

"Lysira!" he cried.

"Let him go," the young female dragon said to him, and she sounded shaken. "He should never have been born. Neither he nor the others."

"Others?" Marcus cried, grasping hold of that word. "What others?"

The dragon shut her mind and he could not find a way back in.

Desperate, searching for help, Marcus ran about the

streets of dragonkind, racing from one mind to another, battering on doors, hammering on windows, pleading for someone—anyone—to open up to him.

He carried the image of Grald holding Ven's bleeding, beating heart in his blood-stained claw and thrust that image into every mind he could find. Colors swirled around him, colors that had no name in the human vocabulary. If they existed at all in human vision, they were fleeting, transitory. Colors so beautiful his heart ached to bursting at the sight. Colors so hideous and horrifying that his soul shrank away from them.

"You can't let him die!" Marcus cried. "He is your child!"

But the dragons saw it differently. They wanted Ven to die. If he died, so did their guilt.

Raging, Marcus kicked at the doors and bashed his fist into the windows and, suddenly, one door opened so fast that he was caught by surprise and nearly tumbled over the threshold.

"Who are you?"

A voice. Words. Spoken words. A voice like his voice speaking words like his words. A human voice, yet with something of the dragon in it, for he saw it spangled with silver and radiating shining light.

"Who are you?" Marcus countered, dazzled by the brilliance.

"I am Sorrow, Ven's sister—part human, part dragon."

Marcus could see her now. The light reflected off scales and shone on her long hair.

"I am Ven's brother," Marcus replied, awed.

"Impossible. You are human," said the sister scornfully.

"I don't have time to explain. Ven is in dire peril. Are you in Dragonkeep? Can you go to him?"

"That picture you showed me, of the dragon trying to kill him—"

"That image is from the dragon's own mind. Ven fought for his life and now the dragon is dead and Ven is dying . . ."

"Dead? The dragon is dead? My father is dead?" Sorrow was appalled.

"He tried to kill Ven," Marcus returned. "Ven had no choice—"

"I don't believe you!" the sister cried in rage. "Why? Why would our father kill his own son? Ven is to be our leader."

"The dragon meant to take Ven's body. As I showed you. We don't have time for this!"

"You care about Ven, don't you?" Sorrow sounded puzzled.

"He's my brother," Marcus said. "And he's your brother, too. You have to help him."

"He killed our father . . ." said the sister slowly.

Marcus would have liked to have grabbed her and shaken her. "Look!" he said angrily and he held up the image to her mind.

The sister looked. She saw the human she had known as Grald in the tomb, the gaping hole where the heart had been torn from the chest, the man's eyes wide in death. She saw the dragon, half in, half out of human flesh. Still, she wasn't convinced.

"I don't believe that our father would take a human body. That he would become one of you. Why would he?"

"To enslave us, rule us, conquer us—" Marcus paused.

He heard the sounds of wings beating and the hissing intake of breath. A shadow passed over him, chilling him. The shadow glided over him again, larger, darker.

Lysira's colors flooded Marcus's brain.

"Human! Maristara is coming. The dragon ruler of Seth. She knows something has happened to Grald, and she is on her way to investigate. You have to leave. Now! Go back to your little room and shut and bolt the door. No more drunken reveling."

"If the dragon finds Ven, she'll kill him," Marcus argued. "She will finish what Grald started!"

"There will be no need for her to kill the dragon's son. He will be dead by the time she arrives." Lysira returned. "Now, go! Quickly! Before she catches you!"

Marcus stepped into his little room, but he did not close the door.

"The next time you see Ven," he said to Sorrow. "He

won't be Ven. He'll be the dragon. Ven will by lying in that tomb—"

The shadow of the wings covered him. He cast one last, pleading look at Sorrow and then slammed shut the door.

Ven lay stretched out, his body relaxed, in his cave in the forest. A sliver of twilight, about to be extinguished by night, trickled into the cavern's entrance through the heavy foliage of the trees that surrounded the cave. Ven heard Bellona's voice calling him, but he didn't move. She had no hold on him now. None of them did.

He heard the flap of dragon wings outside the cave, but that didn't matter. When the dragon arrived, he would be gone.

The little girl walked into the cave. She squatted down on her haunches beside him, peered into his face.

"Go away," said Ven wearily. "I did what you wanted. I did what they all wanted."

"So now you're going to give up and die, is that it?"

"What do you care?"

"And what about Marcus? You asked him for help and he gave it. He and his kingdom are in danger."

"That's his problem," Ven returned. "He has two human legs and a pretty human face. Someone will help him—"

"You saw the army of dragon warriors. You know that your brother and his people cannot win against them."

"So will it make my brother feel better if I'm standing there by his side, ready to die with him?" Ven asked, annoyed.

"I'm not asking you to die for him, Ven," said Draconas, leaning close. "I'm asking you to live. In the kingdom of Seth, your mother's kingdom, there are people who know how to fight this kind of war. People who have been fighting dragons for centuries. They've been fighting for all the wrong reasons, but that doesn't matter. Go to them, Ven. Tell them the truth. You can enter safely now. Maristara is away."

Ven smiled. "Good plan, Draconas. But it's wishful thinking. I'm dying and you know it. And you can't save me. Not this time."

"Ven—" called Draconas.

Ven closed his eyes and refused to open them, and eventually the little girl went away.

"Ven . . ." a voice spoke his name. Bellona was there. In all these years, she'd never found his cave. She was there now. Stern and unsmiling, she regarded him in silence. But he knew that he'd pleased her. For the first and probably only time in his life, he'd pleased her. Bellona gave him a brief nod and then she was gone, and Ven was alone.

He wasn't afraid.

He wasn't anything.

Ven let himself sink into the darkness. He let the darkness carry him along, as the river had taken Bellona's body to the sea.

Sorrow stared into the afterimage left behind by the human, Marcus. She pondered his words, considered what to do. She rose from her bed and went to the chamber next to hers. She sneaked inside, moving softly, but her brother's senses were acute. Lucien's slit eyes were already open.

"I heard you talking in your sleep," he said.

"I wasn't asleep," said Sorrow.

"Then who was here? Who were you talking to?" He looked closely at her face, which glimmered white in the darkness, and he rose from his bed. "What is it, Sorrow? What's wrong?"

Lucien was the most dragon of all the siblings. He had dragon arms and claws, dragon legs and feet. His torso was human flesh and bone, with a smattering of scales across his shoulders that extended up the back of his neck and over his head. His face was human. The eyes were slit eyes, like those of a reptile. He was quick and he was strong. The nearest in age to Sorrow, he was her confidant, her companion.

"Come with me," she said. "Be quiet. I don't want to wake the others."

Lucien did not ask questions. He knew her, trusted that she had a good reason for this midnight ramble.

As they walked through the labyrinthine corridors of the dragon's lair, Sorrow shared the image of Ven's human brother with Lucien. She shared his words, the pictures. Lucien was so shocked at the vision flaring before his eyes that he almost walked into a wall.

"I don't believe what he says about our father, Sorrow. The human lies."

"I don't believe it either. That's why we're going there."

"To the Abbey?"

Sorrow nodded. The cave was dark, but not to her eyes or her brother's. They moved swiftly through the winding corridors of stone. They did not speak except with their thoughts, which sometimes converged to form a river, then separated, forking off into individual streams. The dragon's children were not like dragons, who rarely give voice to their thoughts. Nor were they like humans, who are forced to do so. They blended speech and thought so that many times they had no idea where one began and the other left off.

The corridor they walked led from the Abbey to the palace beneath the mountain. The corridor was used by the dragon, to travel from one place to another. Few humans knew of the existence of this corridor. What went on beneath the mountain was secret and was meant to stay that way. The children knew it from the mind of the dragon.

The walls of the corridor were rimed with scales, marks of the dragon's passage. The sight of these led Lucien to exclaim suddenly and vehemently, "Our father would never take the body of a human. It's all a lie."

"A lie," Sorrow agreed.

She walked swiftly, confidently, certain of the outcome. The children of the dragon entered the great hall to find it awash with blood.

In the center lay their father, dead.

Sharp nails pierced Ven's human flesh, claws raked the skin of his forearm. The pain was acute and dragged him up, struggling and fighting, from the deep.

His eyes flared open. Sorrow bent over him.

"Why did you do this!" she demanded, hissing in anger. "Why did you kill our father?"

She dug her nails deeper in his arm, until the blood ran. Her fury flared through the darkness, lighting her face, blazing in her eyes, and staving off death, just for a moment.

"You wouldn't understand," Ven said weakly. He closed his eyes, tried to sink back down beneath the dark surface. "Just go away and leave me alone."

"I think he's dying," Lucien said in hushed tones.

"Oh, no, he's not," said Sorrow. "Not until I know the truth."

The hand that had drawn his blood moved to his forehead. Another hand rested, palm down, on his breast. His sister's touch was healing; warmth poured through his body, thick and viscous and sweet as honey. Ven's heartbeat strengthened. His breathing came easier. The darkness began to recede, and he was floating rapidly to shore.

Ven sat up and shoved her hands off him. His head ached and he felt sick to his stomach, but he was alive.

"You will live," said Sorrow coolly. "How long you live depends on your answers. Lucien is incredibly strong. He once tore a human apart limb by limb. He can do the same to you."

Ven didn't look at them, either of them. He stared at the carcass of the dragon. Scaled flesh, clawed and mangled. Bones exposed. Blood running in rivulets into the chinks and cracks of the stone floor. Ven's body was sticky with the blood. His sister's hands had blood on them, from where she'd reverently touched the body.

"Why did you kill our father?" she asked again, her voice breaking.

Ven looked at her, really looked at her, for the first time. He saw that she was terrified.

Grald had kept his children isolated, segregated. He kept them dependent on him. A good plan, for the dragon had never imagined leaving them. Dragons live for centuries. Grald would see his children age and die, see many generations of children die before he did. But he was dead. His children were alone and they couldn't cope.

Ven understood Sorrow's fear. He recognized it as his own. In that moment Ven, who had always felt sorry only for himself, felt pity for another.

"Why?" Sorrow shrieked, and she flung herself at him, striking him on the chest. "Why?"

He said nothing, for there was nothing to say. She knew the reason; he'd seen the images in her mind. Her terrible "why" had nothing to do with Grald's death. It had more to do with her own life, her own reason for being. She was asking herself for the first time the question Ven had been asking all these years.

She wouldn't like the answer, but he couldn't help that.

"Sorrow," called Lucien. He stood by the tomb, staring down into it. "Come look at this." He sounded shaken.

Sorrow glared at Ven a moment longer, then, her back rigid, her legs stiff, she walked over to the tomb. She cast one glance inside and then turned away.

Ven stood up, slowly and painfully. He limped over to the dragon's carcass and stared down at it. Finding what he sought, wound around the dragon's bloodstained talons, Ven removed the golden locket and carried it over to the tomb. Opening it up, he displayed the heart within. The heart had stopped beating. With the dragon's death, the enchantment was broken.

He thrust the locket in Sorrow's face.

Sorrow averted her eyes. Lucien started to gag and was sick on the floor.

"You want the truth, Then look at it," Ven insisted.

Sorrow looked. She looked at the shriveled heart and the maltreated corpse in the tomb. She looked at Grald, the human, dead, and saw the expression of agony and horror frozen on his face.

Ven could hear outside the cave of his mind the beat of wings. He could feel the hot wind of Maristara's coming. He tossed the locket into the tomb and turned to leave.

"Where are you going?" Sorrow demanded.

"Away," said Ven.

"You can't!"

"Fine." Ven turned around. "You brought me back to life. Now what are you going to do with me? Wait here to see me die again? That's all right with me. Just make up your mind."

Sorrow hesitated, wavering and unsure. Lucien had finished being sick. Though he still looked ill, he went over to her and the two conferred softly.

Ven stood waiting. It truly did not matter to him, one way or the other.

Eventually the two came to an agreement.

"You're coming with us," said Sorrow.

Lucien took hold of Ven by the arm, handling him roughly, scratching him with his claws.

Ven shrugged and went along. He didn't ask where they were going. He already knew. The dragon's children had only one place they could go, and that was back to the lair where they'd been born, where they'd lived all their lives. He didn't ask what they were going to do with him, because he didn't care.

Sorrow and Lucien held Ven between them, both of them gripping him tightly, securely, though he came along docilely enough. They talked to him and about him, but he paid scant attention. He heard only the clicking of their claws on the stone floor—three sets of claws, his claws and those of his sister and brother. They made quite a racket, none of them in unison. He listened to the clickety-clack with a kind of detached fascination.

"What are we going to do with him?" Lucien asked, as they clattered down the corridor that led from the Abbey back to the lair.

"We'll hide him," said Sorrow. "With illusion magic."

"They'll come looking for him—" Lucien began.

"Not in our chambers," said Sorrow. "They won't suspect us. Why should they? They'll suppose he ran back to the humans. They'll search the human city and beyond. We're the last they would suspect."

Lucien accepted her decision without question, and the three walked on.

"What do we tell the other children?" Lucien asked, after a moment. "About Grald . . ."

"Nothing," Sorrow returned, quick and harsh. "We tell them nothing. It would be impossible to explain to the little ones, anyway," she added, a tremor in her voice.

"That's true," Lucien said. "When we don't even understand. Our father took a human form—"

"Don't say that!" Sorrow cried, glaring at him. "Don't ever say that!"

Lucien fell silent. He looked hurt, as though she'd struck him. After a moment, he said softly, "What do we do now, Sorrow? You, me, the others?"

"We'll be fine," Sorrow said. "No, Lucien, no more questions! I have to think—"

The two stopped, freezing in place. Ven, preoccupied, kept on walking. Sorrow gave him a rough jerk on the arm. Then he heard what they'd heard.

The sounds were unmistakable—the tramping of heavy, clawed feet, shaking the floor; the movement of a massive body; the stentorian breathing of a dragon. The sounds came from behind them, from the Abbey.

"The dragon of Seth!" Lucien's thoughts whispered in Ven's brain.

"I'm going back," Sorrow said abruptly.

"To hand him over to the dragon?" Lucien asked.

He glanced uncertainly at Ven, who stood there, unconcerned, as if they were talking about someone else.

"I don't know," Sorrow said, biting her lip. "Maybe. Take him to the cave, Lucien. Hide him in that place where we used to hide when the teaching humans came to us."

"Sorrow . . ." Lucien began

She cast him an exasperated glance. "What now?"

"Just . . . be careful," he said.

She rested her hand gently on his arm. "Everything will be all right, Lucien. Now, go. Quickly."

Lucien went, tugging Ven along with him. Ven might have tackled the youngster and made good his escape, but that required effort, and he had none to give. He didn't want to hurt the boy, who'd been hurt enough already this night.

Ven walked on, his gaze on the ground, staring at his feet, listening to the sound of his claws and those of his brother's scraping and clicking on the cold stone floor of the mountain.

26

WHILE VEN WAS FIGHTING FOR HIS LIFE AND MARCUS WAS sleeping off the effects of his dragon dream, Draconas sat placidly on a stool in Anton and Rosa's dwelling and darned socks. He hoped, as he did so, that poor Anton would never have to wear these socks. He would surely get blisters, for Draconas was neither particularly skilled at darning, nor was he able to hold his mind on his work, for his mind was divided—part of it in the room, keeping watch on the monk, and part of it with Melisande's sons. The socks suffered as a result, turning out all lumpy and misshapen.

Draconas's enforced nap had lasted only an hour or so, then the monk brought the little girl out of the enchantment.

"There, now," said Brother Leopold. "Don't you feel better after a little rest? Come and join us by the fire."

Draconas dragged his stool over by the fire, where Anton and Rosa and the monk sat; the couple bewildered and frightened, the monk completely at his ease. The monk asked Anton questions about his work, asked Rosa questions about her weaving, asked Draca about her friends and what games they liked to play.

Rosa and Anton gave short and sometimes incoherent answers to the monk's questions. Both sat on the edge of their chairs, as though waiting for something to jump out of the shadows at them. After a while, however, when nothing did jump out at them and Brother Leopold seemed truly interested in hearing what they had to say, they both started tentatively to relax. They had no idea what was going on, but, reason told them, if the monk was going to do anything dire, he would have done it by now. He wouldn't have been sitting by the fire watching Rosa and Draca mending clothes and darning socks.

Eventually, bewilderment and tension gave way to exhaustion. Anton endeavored to stifle his yawns, but he'd been up with the sun and worked past sunset, and he cast longing glances at his bed. Rosa actually nodded off over her mending, waking with a jerk when the monk spoke her name.

"I'm sorry, Brother Leopold," she said, blushing deeply. "I didn't mean to be rude. I'm sitting too close to the fire, I believe. It makes me doze off." She moved her chair back from the dying blaze.

The monk said something polite and continued to talk. Eventually Rosa's head lowered, her chin sank to her chest, and her work fell from her hands. Anton had already gone to sleep in his chair. He snored and mumbled in his sleep as he always did. His hands twitched.

Brother Leopold didn't move. The bell rang for curfew, and still he stayed. He no longer talked, however. He seemed to be waiting for something.

Draconas kept darning. The sock in his hands looked like no sock in the known universe, but, fortunately, the monk wasn't paying attention. He began to grow restless. He stood up, walked to the window and peered out, his gaze going in the direction of the Abbey. Brother Leopold walked back, resumed his seat, and stared hard at Draconas.

Draconas plied his needle, his eyes on his work. The monk wanted to ask him if he knew what had happened, but he didn't dare. That would show weakness. As for Draconas, all the while he'd been darning, he'd been watching Ven work his magic, watching Marcus defend his brother. He'd watched the dragon, Grald, crash down dead on the bloodstained floor.

And now Maristara was coming. He saw her, and she

saw him. She knew he was in Dragonkeep. He couldn't help that. He'd been forced to open himself up to her and the other dragons when he reached out to Lysira and asked her to help, when he'd reached out to Ven.

She had come searching for him, and she wouldn't be as squeamish as Grald about destroying a few hundred humans to get at him.

Draconas's usefulness in Dragonkeep had ended.

"Ven is on his own," he said to himself. "I can do nothing more for him. Ven will either swim or the dark waters will close over his head. Grald is dead. The sons of Melisande avenged their mother. I've made life difficult for Maristara and Anora, but I haven't stopped them. I have delayed the hour they will attack Idylswylde, but I haven't stopped that either. Perhaps I've made matters worse. Maybe I've pushed them to desperation. Whatever the case, I have to leave Dragonkeep and I have to leave now, before Maristara arrives."

The monk was a problem. He could still hurt Rosa and Anton, and Draconas owed them too much to bring more harm to them than he already had.

Draconas dropped the maltreated sock. The little girl stood up and went up to stand next to the monk. Brother Leopold eyed her warily.

"I'll tell you a story, Brother," Draconas said. "Shall I?"

"Very well," he said, his expression grim.

"Once upon a time, a dragon had a son—half-dragon, half-human. The dragon's son grew up to be a fine, strong young man, and the dragon was well pleased, for he had decided that he would steal this son's strong young body and use it for his own. After the dragon had taken over his son's body, the dragon—in the guise of the son—would catch his foe all unsuspecting and slay him. And the dragon would live happily ever after."

Brother Leopold listened, his face set in stone.

Draconas shook his head. "That's how the story is supposed to end. But it doesn't."

"Oh?" said the monk sarcastically. "How do you think it ends?"

"Most unhappily for the dragon. He's dead."

Brother Leopold gave a tight smile. "I don't believe you. This is a trick."

"Grald was supposed to send for you when he had his new body. And he hasn't, has he?"

The monk had no answer. He walked over to the door and stared, frowning, into the night.

"Go to the Abbey. Go see for yourself," said Draconas, coming over to stand beside him.

The monk glanced around. "And what do you do then?" he asked mockingly.

"I let you live," Draconas answered.

The monk stared down at the child in front of him and his mouth twisted in disbelief.

He must know that I am a dragon. Grald would have certainly told him when he sent him to see to it that I did not interfere with Grald's plans for Ven.

But it is one thing to be told and another to see for oneself.

Draconas shifted the illusion. The shadow of the dragon, kept hidden from human eyes, took the place of the little girl.

Brother Leopold found himself staring at a huge clawed foot. His gaze shifted to a scale-encrusted belly that seemed to have engorged a house, for it held within it floor, room, fireplace, table, chairs, and the slumbering humans.

The monk fell back a step. His gaze lifted from the belly and the clawed feet to the arched neck and the lowering head of the dragon, whose scales gleamed burnished red and whose eyes sparked blaze orange. The dragon lifted a front foreclaw and held it suspended over the monk's head.

Leopold was a soldier, one of the elite of the dragon army. He'd been trained to fight from the day he was old enough to understand how to kill a man with his magic. He'd been trained to fight men, not dragons—or so Draconas reasoned.

Leopold was no coward. He did not turn tail and run. He turned his back deliberately on the monster that loomed over him. His hand steady, he opened the door and walked out into the empty and silent street.

Pausing, Leopold looked back at the dragon.

"Grald told me about you—the one they call the Walker. He told me you would side with the humans. It won't matter, you know—even if Grald is dead. The humans cannot stop us. And neither can you."

Leopold departed, heading in the direction of the Abbey.

Draconas abandoned the illusion and collapsed back down into that of the little girl. He stared gloomily after the monk's retreating figure. He thought it quite likely that the monk was right. He couldn't stop them.

He looked back at Anton and Rosa, asleep in their chairs. They would sleep until dawn, when they would wake to find the child they had taken into their homes and their hearts gone. They would think the monk had taken her. They would seek her, ask discreet questions, but they would never find out what had become of her and they would grieve her loss. Once again, Draconas had been forced to use humans. Once again, he'd been forced to hurt them.

He heard wings beating. The shadow of Maristara grew large in his mind. The little girl went over to Rosa and kissed her care-worn cheek and placed the darned socks in her hands. Draca kissed Anton and, bringing a blanket, draped it around his shoulders.

Then Draconas left the house. He walked out into the street, reached up to the stars, and launched himself into the night.

27

SORROW CREPT THROUGH THE CORRIDOR ON THE BALLS OF her feet, moving as silently as possible. She had not yet made up her mind whether to confront the dragon, Maristara, or not. She wanted to see and hear before she was heard and seen. She planned to verify Ven's story, find out if he was telling the truth. If that involved speaking with the dragon, Sorrow would do so. She wanted this to be her decision, however. Not the dragon's.

As is customary with dragon lairs, Grald had constructed several different corridors that led into and out of the main hall. Some, such as the one Sorrow walked, led to the hall from the mountain "palace." Others led to the hall from outside the mountain, with no need to pass through the part of the lair where the soldiers of the dragon army lived and worked. Some of the corridors were small, made for the dragon in his human form; others enormous, meant for the dragon in his true form. Maristara entered through one of the large corridors. Sorrow came in by one of the small ones.

She stood in the doorway, in the shadows. No illusion spell could hide her from the dragon's eyes, so she didn't bother. She kept still, kept the colors of her mind subdued. Not that it was likely the dragon would seek her out. She was just one of Grald's children. The dragon had other, far more important matters to consider.

Maristara was old, far older than Grald. The dragon's scales were so dark that they were almost black. Her head was slightly stooped, her shoulders hunched, with her wings folded at her side. Tendons creaked and bones cracked as she moved. For all her great age, Maristara was not feeble. The huge body advanced ponderously into the hall and stalked over to Grald. Maristara sniffed at the charred, maimed carcass, and her head jerked involuntarily at the stench of death.

A low growl of ire rumbled in the dragon's chest. Maristara searched around, seeking the perpetrator. Her piercing gaze roved the hall methodically and sifted through the shadows. Sorrow glided behind a pillar. The dragon's glint-eyes raked the alcove and passed over her, then their gaze shifted, along with the massive head, to the door—the human entrance to the hall. Sorrow could hear the approaching footfalls as well as the dragon—a single person, running swiftly.

The dragon lifted a claw, and there was a glint of gold. Maristara held a locket such as Grald had worn; a locket containing a human heart. The dragon's magic took shape and form in her mind, and such was the power of the magic that Sorrow, standing close to it, could see the blending, merging, dazzling colors flicker on the horizon of her own mind.

The dragon began to shift form in a process that reminded Sorrow of watching humans stuff sausage. The dragon seemed to shrink and compress and stuff her own massive body into the body of a human female. The procedure took time, and Maristara had barely completed her transformation before the door burst open, banging against the wall, and a monk ran inside.

The monk came up short, his horrified gaze going first to the grisly carcass, then to the strange woman standing over it. The woman was middle-aged, with gray hair; a taut, bony face and a lank, bony body.

"Who are you and what are you doing here?" the monk demanded.

Sorrow recognized him as Leopold, one of the commanders of the dragon's army, and she wondered what he was doing walking about the city (where the soldiers were not supposed to venture) in monk's garb. He was not rattled, but composed, advancing into the room with his hands raised.

"I am Lucretta, the Mistress of Dragons," the woman answered, haughty and intimidating. She drew forth the locket that hung around her human neck and held it to the light.

Leopold relaxed. Bowing low, he murmured, "Mistress," in respectful tones.

"What do you know of this murder?" Maristara gestured to the carcass. "Was it the Walker?"

"No, Mistress. I was with the Walker the entire time. The Dragon's Son killed Grald."

"Impossible!" exclaimed Maristara.

"There can be no other explanation, Mistress. Grald chose this night to take over Ven's body for his own . . ."

Sorrow's blood tingled. A chill rippled through her and her clawed hands clenched.

". . . I sent the Dragon's Son to him and then I left, as he ordered me, to find the Walker and make certain that he did not interfere. Draconas never left my sight the entire night. Unless some other dragon intervened . . ."

"No," said Maristara. Her gaze looked far away, probing and seeking other dragon minds. "No other dragon was here." She was silent, her eyes narrowed, prying and jabbing. "Where is he, the Dragon's Son?"

"I do not know, mistress. He must have fled—"

"He tries to hide from me, but I see the blood spattered on the cavern walls. I see his guilt. I had no idea he was so powerful."

"They are all powerful, Mistress," Leopold said grimly. "Powerful and dangerous."

"The dragon's children, you mean."

"Yes, Mistress." He hesitated. "May I speak plainly?"

"Of course. You know our secrets, I see. Grald evidently trusted you."

"I had that honor," said Leopold quietly. "I am one of the commanders of the dragon warriors. I have been in training all my life for the war against humankind. I was raised with the dragon children. I have trained to fight alongside them. I am not the only one who is made uneasy by what I have seen of them. I could say nothing against the children to Grald. He was, understandably, quite proud of his offspring."

"Yes," Maristara murmured, her narrow-eyed gaze shifting to the carcass, then back again. Her lips tightened.

"Grald raised his children to believe that they are better than humans. He taught them to disdain humans and human life. Because of this, they will kill a human without a second thought."

We would, Sorrow told him silently. *You do well to fear us!*

"We are forced to revere them, to almost worship them. This was part of Grald's plan. He intended to take over Ven's body. He would then be able to control the children, who would think him one of themselves."

Bleak dismay sickened Sorrow, made her legs tremble. She leaned against the pillar for support.

"Now Grald is dead, slain by one of his own children—the *least* powerful among them," said Leopold pointedly. "Grald told me himself that Ven had never been trained in the magic, that he refused to use it or even acknowledge it. One can only imagine what the other children, who *have* been trained in the magic and in warfare, as well, can do. And not only against humans."

"What are you saying?" the Mistress demanded irritably. "You humans—always so long-winded. Come out with it."

"I am saying that bringing these children into the world was a mistake," said Leopold grimly. "They are unpredictable, uncontrollable, and far more dangerous than anyone could have imagined." He gestured to the carcass. "As you can plainly see, Mistress."

"Dangerous to humans." The Mistress shrugged. "Grald taught his children to revere dragons. Ven was different. He was taught to hate dragons. Like the humans of Seth."

"That is true, Mistress. But news of Grald's death will spread. We cannot hide it, for someone else will have to take command of the armies. We might be able to conceal the circumstances of his death from the humans, but not from his children, who communicate mind-to-mind. Once they find out that Ven had the power to kill his dragon father, they will start to regard dragons with the same disdain that they now regard humans."

"No . . . never . . ." murmured Sorrow, her heart aching.

"I did not approve of Grald's experimental breeding of humans and dragons," said the Mistress. "I thought he was making a mistake and I told him so. He has paid for his mistake. No other dragons will do so. Still," she added thoughtfully, "the older children might prove useful to us in the upcoming war—"

Leopold shook his head emphatically. "Forgive me for contradicting you, Mistress, but, as I said, the dragon's children cannot be trusted. What if they were to turn upon us in the midst of a battle?"

Sorrow could see the dragon's thoughts, the colors swirling in Maristara's mind, and they were much in accord with her own. *You fear them, miserable human. You are jealous of them. Yet . . .* Her gaze went to Grald's carcass. *Yet you are right. Too much is at stake to take a chance.*

"Where is the Walker?" the Mistress asked abruptly.

Leopold answered reluctantly. "I . . . I do not know, Mistress. Grald kept him in line by threatening to slay the humans who had protected him. The Walker was the one who told me Grald had died. What could I do against him? I am no threat to the Walker. I saw him change into his dragon form, Mistress, and take to the skies."

"You have lost both the Walker and the Dragon's Son. Draconas discovered our plans for the war," the Mistress said, glowering. "And Grald let him live! Yet another mistake!"

Leopold was defensive. "Grald was going to slay the Walker, Mistress, as soon as he took over Ven's body. That way, the other dragons would blame Ven and not Grald—"

"Yes, yes." The Mistress scowled at the dead dragon,

her thoughts baleful. *You wretched worm. You have come close to our undoing. All our carefully laid plans and now this! It is well you are dead, or I would murder you myself!*

"Pardon me, Mistress," said Leopold, "but if you are going to deal with the dragon's children, you should do so now, while they are asleep."

"I think you get above yourself, human," returned the Mistress, drawing herself up. "I know what I am about. I do not need the likes of you to advise me."

"No, Mistress, of course not," said Leopold, chagrined. "I beg your forgiveness."

The dragon made up her mind.

"You and your soldiers destroy the dragon's children. I will take care of disposing of this mess." She cast a scathing glance at the carcass.

Leopold frowned. "But, Mistress, would it not be better if you killed them?"

"No, it would not," Mistress snapped. "Tell me, Commander, can you haul away this carcass, this monstrous lump of flesh and bone? Half the population of this city would be required to even lift the tail, much less dispose of it in such a way that no one will find out the truth of what happened."

"I understand, Mistress," said Leopold, though he did not look happy.

"Kill the children while they are sleeping. When they are dead, search for the Dragon's Son."

"Yes, Mistress," replied Leopold. "What are my orders regarding him?"

"Kill him. Oh," the Mistress added, as an afterthought, "and kill any of the human women who are pregnant."

"Yes, Mistress." Leopold bowed. "After that, I would like your leave to return to my shield-mate. I assume that war is imminent."

"You assume right."

Sorrow crept away from her pillar. She did not dare turn around. She did not dare to take her eyes off the Mistress, fearful that suddenly those eyes would shift to her.

Sorrow backed her way along the corridor, her hands out-stretched behind her, feeling for the wall. She touched it, solid and cold.

The Mistress was eyeing Grald's body, her thoughts a blur of fire and smoke and death. "I will tell the populace that there was a pitched battle between the Walker and Grald," Maristara murmured. "Grald fought valiantly. He used his magic to blast the other dragon, and that magic blew asunder the walls of the Abbey. Grald killed the Walker, but, sadly, he himself died in the explosion. The massive stone building fell on top of him, burying his car-cass beneath the rubble. This will be his final resting place."

Other images appeared in Sorrow's mind. The dragon children slumbering in their lair, the little ones in a single bed, crowded together for warmth and comfort, their arms and legs and dreams so entwined that it was hard to tell where one left off and another began. And then the dragon warriors come, led by Leopold, bringing fire, im-molating the dreams and the small dreaming bodies.

Sorrow could run swiftly, but her claws would make noise on the stone floor, and the dragon would hear her.

Sorrow flexed her wings nervously. She had never had much chance to practice flying. The dragon would not permit the children to go out into the sunshine, for fear they might be seen by the humans of Dragonkeep. Grald had promised that, in due time, he would teach her to fly, but that day had not come to pass, and now it never would.

A childhood accident with regard to flying—involving leaping off an upper level—had left Sorrow with a terri-fying memory of panicked flapping, a terrifying fall, a slashing white scar across her forehead, and a deep-seated fear. Flying back to her lair would be the fastest way to reach the children, however, and flight would be silent.

Sorrow leaned forward onto the balls of her feet, trying to keep her claws off the floor, and she began to run. As she ran, she spread her wings and felt them catch the air currents. Her wings lifted her up, carried her feet off the ground. The sensation was startling and frightening, so that she gave a little gasp and froze. Her stomach was fluttering, not her wings.

Instinct rescued her, as instinct rescues young dragons forced out of their sweet darkness into the blinding sun and fresh air. As they gasp and flail and eventually fly, so did Sorrow flail and then fly, her wings lifting and falling in a smooth, swooping motion that sent her—astonished and frightened and thrilled—soaring through the darkness.

She was about halfway down the corridor when she heard ponderous footfalls and the scraping of the dragon's belly and tail along the floor. Sorrow risked glancing behind her, fearful that the dragon had heard her and was chasing after her.

There came a blast of flame so fierce that it flared through the darkness, lighting it bright as day. After that a roar and a wave of heat and a low rumbling sound that built into a horrific crash, shaking the ground and walls of the underground passage and sending clouds of dust rolling through the corridor and cascading down from the ceiling.

Crouched in the shelter of the mountain fastness, Maristara breathed devastating magic on the Abbey. The magic blew apart the walls and brought the building down on top of what was left of Grald. Sorrow kept flying, though flight was now perilous. Dragon-sight could not pierce the clouds of dust, and she was having difficulty seeing where she was going.

She forced herself to slow down. It would take the human, Leopold, some time to make his way into the palace. Once there, he would have to wake and arm his soldiers, and prepare them for what they must do.

That part, Sorrow thought bitterly, will not be difficult. They have been waiting for this opportunity, it seems.

Waiting to kill us—the monsters.

28

SORROW REACHED THE PART OF THE CORRIDOR THAT branched off into the palace living quarters, and here she had to end her flight and take to her feet. She felt a vast sense of relief when she had solid ground beneath her claws, and also a tiny sliver of regret. Although her stomach had remained clenched in terror the whole time she was in flight, she had enjoyed the rush of air past her face and beneath her wings. She looked forward to flying again. If she lived that long.

She burst into her brother's room and found him with Ven, who was lying on the bed, his eyes closed.

Lucien looked up. "Oh, Sorrow! I was worried! What was that blast—"

"Never mind that now!" Sorrow gasped for breath. Terror and the exertion of flight had stolen the air from her lungs. "The warriors are coming to kill us!"

"To kill *me*," Ven corrected.

"No," said Sorrow. "To kill us."

Ven opened his eyes and sat up.

Lucien stared at her, confused and dismayed. "But . . . why?"

"Because Ven was able to slay Grald, Maristara fears that we are a threat to all dragons. The humans think we are a threat to them. It was Leopold, one of the human dragon warriors, who talked the dragon into it." Sorrow was bitter. "The dragon gave orders that all Grald's children must die. And the humans are eager to carry out her command."

"Kill us? But . . . what do we do?" Lucien asked, dismayed.

"We fight them," said Sorrow viciously. "I was thinking we could barricade ourselves in here. Keep the little ones safe—"

"For how long?" Ven demanded. "How long can you hold out against these warriors and the dragon? I've seen these warriors, Sorrow, and so have you. They are powerful in the magic, and they've been taught to use it in battle. There are hundreds of them and only you and Lucien. You two are the only children who are old enough to fight."

"And you," said Sorrow.

Ven shook his head. "I can't use the magic."

"You used it to kill our father!"

"I had help," Ven said grimly. He didn't say who, but Sorrow recalled the human who had invaded her mind, the human who had claimed to be Ven's brother.

"Maybe we could reason with the dragon," Lucien suggested, his voice trembling.

"There's no reasoning with Maristara or with the humans. I know," Ven said. "I've tried both. We have to get out of here. All of us."

"But there's nowhere to go!" Sorrow protested. "There are hiding places in the mountain, but, eventually, they will find us—"

"We have to leave the mountain."

Sorrow felt as if all the air had been punched out of her. "But . . . this is our home."

"If you stay, it will be your tomb," said Ven.

Sorrow shivered. Death seemed easier to face than the terror of venturing out into the unknown. Lucien moved near her. His hand sought hers, and she clasped it spasmodically. They stood holding on to each other for comfort, staring at Ven, as though he could make everything right again, make this all go away.

His stern expression softened. "I know what it is to

leave the safety of the darkness and venture into the sunlight. You can do it. I did it. And I will be with you."

Sorrow saw the little ones in their bed, waking in bewilderment when they felt the heat of the fire lick their bodies, and then the bewilderment turning to terror and pain as the flames began to consume them.

Slowly, shaking, she nodded.

"Sorrow, wake the others. Don't frighten them. Tell them we're going on an adventure, an outing. The older children must carry those who can't walk or can't keep up. Lucien, we'll need food for the journey. And rope."

"Water?" asked Lucien, starting out the door.

Ven shook his head. "We won't need it. We'll be traveling by way of the river."

Lucien left. As long as someone was in charge, telling Lucien what to do, he was content. Sorrow envied him.

"Where are you going to take us?" she asked.

"To the last place Maristara would expect us to go— her own kingdom."

The two of them entered the children's room. The little ones were still slumbering. If they had heard the noise of the blast at all, they must have thought it was thunder and rolled over and gone to sleep again.

"Seth is a land of humans," Sorrow said, her mouth dry, her throat tightening.

"Yes," Ven replied. "But they might understand."

As he stood gazing down at the sleeping children, he left his mind open to her, and Sorrow saw a little boy crouched in a cave. His legs were covered in ill-fitting woollen trousers, his feet hidden by over-large leather boots. He sat in the middle of the cave, in the darkness, his arms hugging his small body. In the distance, a woman's voice called out his name. The little boy did not answer.

"You should hurry," Ven said. "It won't take the warriors long to organize and come after us."

Sorrow hesitated one more moment, wanting, wishing this not to be. All her magic could not make that wish come true, however. She placed her hand on the youngest child's forehead, smoothed it, and said in a voice that shook, "Draga, time to wake up."

The child opened his eyes. He was about two years old, with a human head and torso, dragon arms and legs, and a small tail. He blinked his eyes and stared at Sorrow in sleepy unrecognition. His face puckered and he seemed about to wail, but Sorrow hushed him.

"It's all right, Draga. Everything's all right. Sit here quietly while I wake the others."

She went from child to child, waking them, and coaxing them out of their warm beds. She tried to discipline her thoughts, to keep them cool and tranquil blues and greens, but red fear bubbled up from beneath the surface, with the result that her colors were an ugly sludge of purple and brown. The children's thoughts blended with hers, and they were frightened, but they also sensed the danger and the urgency, and were quiet, for the most part, and did what they were told. By the time all the children were roused, Lucien had returned with several large bags containing what food he had been able to scrounge.

Ven stood back, keeping his distance. He was obviously uncomfortable around the children. Sorrow and Lucien moved among the group and soon, without fuss or clamor, the dragon's children had formed a line, the older children carrying the younger on their backs.

Sorrow lifted up Draga. The child clasped his hands tightly around her neck. Lucien hefted the last of the children. Ven carried the food.

"Move quickly now, children," Sorrow said, guiding them out the door and into the dark corridor. "Follow Ven. He knows the way."

Instead of obeying, the children came to a halt. They looked at her, their eyes wide and solemn. Humans can lie to their children. Dragons cannot. Sorrow's frightened, confused colors swirled through their minds.

"Sorrow," said a little girl with dragon legs like Ven's, "where are we going?"

Sorrow tried to think of an answer that wouldn't

frighten them. Before she could respond, Ven crouched down in front of the girl, his eyes on a level with hers.

"There are those who think that because we are not like them, we have no right to live," he said quietly. "These people want to hurt us. We're going someplace far away, where they can't find us."

The children understood. Sorrow had tried to shelter them from the cruel remarks and hurtful comments made by humans when they thought the children couldn't hear, and she'd assumed she'd succeeded. Apparently, she hadn't.

Ven glanced back into the room where the children had been sleeping. "Sorrow, can these dragon warriors see through illusion magic?"

"Yes," she said, thinking she knew where he was going. "But only if they suspect that what they are seeing is an illusion. If they think it is real, then it will be real to them."

"Good," he said and he smiled at her. "Then put all the children back into their beds."

Sorrow understood what he meant and she began casting the magic.

Ven and Lucien led the children down the tunnel.

Quickly and quietly, the dragon's children walked the corridors of the mountain palace. Sorrow and Ven led the way, with Lucien bringing up the rear. The corridors were those that Draconas had walked before them, those he'd told Ven the dragon did not use.

There was one dangerous point, however. Ven recalled that somewhere up ahead, the corridor they walked intersected a corridor used by the humans. As they drew near, Ven sent his thoughts to Sorrow. He found it odd, entering another's mind and allowing her into his. Odd, but not as bad as he'd once imagined.

"Warn the children to be very, very quiet."

Sorrow nodded.

"Stay here. I'm going to go take a look." Ven left her, walking forward as quietly as he could over the rough stone floor.

Sorrow sent her thoughts to the children. The older ones whispered it to the younger, who might not be able to fully understand the pretty colors they saw in their minds.

Draga, clinging to Sorrow, had gone back to sleep with the motion of her walking. Sorrow hoped he would continue sleeping, but he woke the moment she stopped moving. He was confused, irritated at being hauled away from his bed, and fretful.

"Put down," he demanded. "Draga walk."

His voice was deep for a child and sounded unbelievably loud.

"No, Draga," said Sorrow softly, jiggling him on her back, trying to keep him quiet. "Sorrow will carry you. Isn't this fun?"

"Draga walk!" said the child willfully. He was the baby, and he was used to having his own way. He pinched Sorrow's arm and pulled her hair. "Draga walk!"

Ven came running back down the corridor.

"Warriors!" he called softly. "Everyone crouch down! Put your backs against the wall! Hurry!"

He turned angrily to Sorrow. "Keep that kid quiet!"

"I'm trying!" Sorrow gasped. She shifted Draga to her hip and knelt down, rocking him, stroking his head, making soft, clucking sounds.

Draga was having none of it. He squirmed in her arms and kicked his feet, trying to escape her grasp. He was a hefty child, and slippery. Sorrow could hear the warriors moving at a swift pace along the corridor, coming their direction. The other children crouched down, huddled against the wall. Their eyes were wide with fear. One of the smaller ones started to whimper. The boy carrying her clapped his hand over the little girl's mouth. The warriors were coming nearer. Draga struck at Sorrow with a small fist and sucked in a deep breath, preparatory to letting it out in a howl.

Ven thrust his face next to Draga's and said in a harsh whisper, "Shut up!"

Draga swallowed his howl in astonishment and shrank away from Ven. His shock was only momentary. Tears shimmered in the child's eyes and his lower lip began to tremble. His little body quivered. Draga drew in his breath again, and Sorrow knew from experience that he was all set to pitch a head-banging, feet-kicking, lung-bursting tantrum.

"Do something!" Ven hissed.

Sorrow reached into Draga's mind and seized hold of the colors that were bright and new. She mixed them together to form a brilliant, gaudy pinwheel, and started them spinning. The colors spun, faster and faster. Draga forgot his fear, forgot his anger, forgot wanting to crawl out of Sorrow's arms. He stared, fascinated, at the whirling, dazzling colors. After a moment, his body went limp. His mouth hung open. His arms slipped from around her neck. His eyes did not blink. Drool slid from the corner of his mouth.

Sorrow pressed against the wall. Intent on their mission, the warriors hastened past the corridor in which the children were hiding. She counted eight of them—four women and four men, including Commander Leopold.

"It's about time we put an end to this," the commander was saying. "I'm sorry about Grald's death, but I think all of us knew he was obsessed with his monstrous offspring. He was losing sight of the true vision."

"Personally, I found the whole business disgusting," said one of the women. "The very sight of those scaley beasts made my skin crawl. I look forward to putting an end to them. The hardest part will be killing the mothers. Poor girls. It wasn't their fault."

"They will die swiftly, at any rate. Not the long and painful death they faced bringing those monsters into the world. For them, the horror will be mercifully over."

"True," the woman agreed. Then she added, "Speaking of death, what happened to Grald, anyway? We all heard a crash and boom that shook the ground. Someone said the Abbey had been destroyed."

"I heard something about a dragon battle," Leopold said evasively. "Maristara will tell us what we need to know. No point in wasting our time speculating. We have work to do."

Their voices trailed off down the corridor.

For long moments, no one moved.

Ven rose to a half crouch and motioned. "Quietly," he cautioned.

But Sorrow was having trouble lifting Draga. The child was dead weight, absorbed in watching the spinning colors in his mind. Ordinarily her strong arms would have made nothing of such a burden, but fear and horror had left her weak and trembling. Seeing her difficulty, Ven took the little boy from her. The child hung, a limp doll, in his hands.

"What did you do to him?" Ven asked.

"A magic spell," said Sorrow. "The monks use it on those of their brethren who get out of control."

"Well, it worked," said Ven. He slung the child over one arm, like a sack of coal and started to leave.

Sorrow didn't move.

"Sorrow, we have to go—now!"

She reached out to take hold of Draga's limp hand.

"I'm not sure I'm doing the right thing," she answered. "This is our home . . ."

Screams echoed down the corridor. The screams of human women—the mothers. The screams ended suddenly, abruptly. Cut off. Mercifully.

Then an explosion shook the corridor. Sorrow smelled the acrid smell of brimstone and saw, in her mind's eye, the illusion of herself and the other children slumbering peacefully in the chamber. The warriors stood in the corridor, the men attacking, the women defending, hurling their magic at the monsters, killing the horror.

Tears came and she couldn't stop them. Human tears, for dragons cannot cry.

"It's useless. It will be easier just to die here. We're monsters, after all."

"Are we monsters, Sorrow?" Ven gestured to the little boy, gazing raptly at the pinwheel of his dreams. "Is he?"

Sorrow shook her head. "I don't believe that. But you do. And so will all the others out there. The humans in their human world."

Ven reached out. His hand clasped hers. "I was wrong. You made me see that. Now, are you coming with me?"

Out into the world. A world that she had never seen.

Ven opened his mind wide and showed it to her.

A world that smelled of green things and blue sky and sharp, bright sunlight.

The sunlight would blind them, the Children of the Dragon, until they grew accustomed to it.

Yet, in that world, there would be room to fly.

"I'm coming," said Sorrow.

29

A DOOR SLAMMED, CAUSING MARCUS TO WAKE SUDDENLY, with the panicked feeling that the dragon was chasing him. His heart racing, he stared, baffled, at his surroundings. He had no idea where he was. Sunlight flooded in through an oilskin-covered hole in the wall. Outside, birds twittered and chatted. He looked around at unfamiliar walls and up at an unfamiliar cciling. His racing heartbeat slowed, and he closed his eyes and sighed deeply.

The dragon was gone. All the dragons were gone. Memories remained. Terrifying and amazing, they wound and curled and twined about him. He might have thought he'd dreamed it all, but he could still see and feel everything with frightening clarity. Ven lying on the floor, the dragon looming over him. The golden gleam of the locket. The strangely beautiful dragon-woman, her silver scales shining in the light of his mind.

"Your brother is safe," said Draconas. "At least, for the moment."

The man stood inside the little room as Marcus had seen him before, holding his staff, his boots covered with the dust of the many roads he had he traveled.

"Where is Ven?" Marcus asked.

"He walks his own road and I have no idea where that will lead him," Draconas replied. "But he is not your concern, Marcus. Your road lies dead ahead, and I do mean 'dead.' Return home as swiftly as you can. Ride as though demons were pursuing you, for they are. Grald may be destroyed, but his plans for the conquest of humans are not. You've seen the legions of Dragonkeep. They are being readied for war as we speak. Your kingdom will be the first to come under assault.

"I have just left your father. I tried to warn the King," Draconas added. "But Edward does not trust me, and he would not believe me. You must convince him, tell him what you have seen, add the weight of your words to mine. You don't have much time. In fact, we may already be too late."

"Where will you be?"

"Where I need to be," Draconas replied curtly.

The little room burst like a soap bubble and disappeared, along with Draconas.

Marcus sat up in bed. He knew where he was now. The fishing village. He would have to ride hard to reach his home, and he felt rotten—the after-effects of a night's carousing. His mouth tasted like the insides of a well-worn boot; his head was three times the size it should be, and his stomach kept trying to climb up into his throat.

Marcus tossed aside the blanket. He would feel better after a plunge in the cold river. As he started to climb off the mattress, a voice murmured drowsily, "My darling . . ." A hand touched his arm. "You're awake . . ."

Marcus gave a violent start. He looked over his shoulder. Sleepy blue eyes gazed up at him from out a mass of disheveled blond curls.

"Darling," Evelina repeated, and her hand ran up and down his arm. "Don't get up yet. We have the whole day before us."

She was naked. Marcus had a confused impression of heavy breasts and bare shoulders and a smooth, flat stomach and dark shadows below that . . .

His blood burned, his loins throbbed. He was aroused and, at the same time, repulsed—as by a vague memory of something ugly and sordid. Marcus wrenched his gaze away from her. Not knowing quite what he was doing, he jumped out of the bed and hurriedly walked away from it.

"Please, cover yourself, Mistress," he said, and his voice was harsh. He fumbled for his breeches that he found lying on the floor. He couldn't remember undressing. God help him! He couldn't remember anything!

"Oh, my dear," said Evelina with a gurgling little laugh, "it's late in the day for modesty." Her voice altered slightly. "After all those wonderful things you said to me last night!"

What had he said? Marcus recalled drinking wine and kissing Evelina and her kissing him back and him breaking out in blotches and the dreadful itching . . . and that was as far as memory took him, before his mind ran to the little room and Ven and the battle with Grald. Yet, there seemed to be something else and it had to do with her. If only he could think through the pounding in his skull!

He looked down at his bare chest and arms and torso and saw no trace of the red blotches.

"Marcus . . . my love," Evelina said with a catch in her throat. "I should be horribly angry at you, but how can I be angry at the man who may be the father of my child? Look . . ."

Reluctantly, he turned around.

Evelina wriggled over to one side on the mattress and pointed to a patch of blood, the mark of the end of a maiden's virginity. Marcus looked at the mattress, and he looked at her. He didn't believe her. He knew in his heart and soul that he had never made love to her. Yet he couldn't prove it. He couldn't even prove it to himself, much less to anyone else.

He hadn't made love to the maiden fair, because he'd been fighting a dragon.

"Say you love me, dearest, like you did last night. Promise you'll always take care of me, like you did last night." Evelina purred. "And come back to bed."

She held out her hand to him and slid one leg over the other, slowly opening her white thighs.

Marcus averted his head. For some reason, the sight of her like that sickened him beyond measure.

"Please, get dressed!" he said coldly. He yanked on his breeches and began to search for his shirt.

Evelina burst into loud and noisy sobs.

"You did this to me and now you hate me!" she cried, gulping. "But you won't get away with it! You'll make me a princess! You'll take care of me. Or else I'll tell everyone how you used me and then tossed me away like a bunch of stinking fish heads. I'll tell everyone in the village. I'll tell everyone I meet! I'll make sure everyone in your damnable kingdom knows what a monster you are!"

Her face was red with her fury, the ugly red spreading down to the hollow between her breasts, which jiggled with the force of her sobs and her threats.

"For you *are* a monster! I'll tell them lots of things about you, Your Highness," she cried in a frenzy, almost incoherent. "You summon up the fires of hell! You talk to people who aren't there! You wave imaginary swords and shout about killing dragons!"

She glared at him, her eyes awash.

"I've heard the talk around the village about you. Strange rumors. And I know they're true. I've seen you use demonic powers. When I'm finished, they'll be tying you to the stake and stacking the wood around your feet!"

Marcus turned his back on her and started to walk for the door.

Evelina leapt from the bed and went running after him. She flung her arms around him, pressing her naked body against his. "My love, my love, forgive me! I didn't know what I was saying. I would never, never do anything to harm you. It's just . . ." She paused. "Just that we have a baby coming . . ."

Marcus managed to disentangle himself from her grasp. "Get dressed! Please! I . . . have to think about this."

"Yes, Marcus," said Evelina meekly. "I don't blame you. It was partly my fault, too. I just wanted to make you happy . . . I'll go get dressed now. I'll do whatever you say."

She padded off, still sniffing, sobbing an occasional sob that she couldn't quite control.

What she said is true. People do talk about me. They

*have talked about me since I was old enough to hear the
whispers. They whisper that I am my father's bastard, and
all know that bastard children have a propensity for evil,
are easily ensnared by the devil.*

*And now my kingdom is about to come under attack by
forces that will be considered demonic. And I will be one
to warn of their coming. Evelina's timing, though acci-
dental, is perfect.*

"What do you want?" Marcus asked her harshly.
"Money?"

"I want your love, Your Highness," Evelina replied,
sniveling. "And a father for my child. If there is a child.
And, somehow, I'm sure there will be. Last night was so
wonderful . . ."

"I'll do what is right." Marcus drew his shirt over his
head. "And not because of your threats."

"I know you will, Marcus," said Evelina contritely.
"I'm sorry I said those things. I didn't mean them. I was
afraid of losing you. I do truly love you. And I know you
love me. You said so many times last night."

Marcus sighed deeply and walked out the door, carefully shutting it behind him.

Two knights of the Prince's Own arrived in the village
that afternoon. Marcus's personal escort had been leading the search for him, and they were overjoyed to find
their charge safe and sound. The knights were introduced
to "Mistress Evelina," and they treated her with grave
courtesy, at least while Prince Marcus was present, for he
said she was coming back to the palace with them. When
he left to go bid farewell to his host, the two men ex
changed rolling-eyed glances.

"Like father, like son," muttered Sir Ranulf.

"At least the king had brains enough not to bring his trol-
lop home to meet mommy!" grumbled Sir Troeven. "Look
at the strumpet. Preening herself like she is a fine lady."

"She's proof that the lad has something between his
legs," said his friend. "There were those of us who were
starting to wonder. The question is—what do we do with
her?"

"Bring her along," said Troeven, the commander of the Prince's Own. "Nothing else we can do. His Highness's orders."

"Speaking of His Highness, I don't think the lad looks well. He's pale and too thin, by half. He won't say where he's been or what happened to him. He claims he's not hurt, but . . ." The knight shook his head.

"He was always a strange lad," his companion reflected. "Or so I've heard for it has been years since I have seen him." A veteran soldier, Sir Troeven had been abroad for fifteen years, fighting wars for other kings, since his own kingdom was at peace. "We'll get him home and let his parents deal with him."

Prince Marcus graciously thanked his host and his wife. At his request, Sir Troeven gave them a bag full of silver coins, more than the village earned in a year's fishing. The prince rode off, accompanied by cheers and blessings. There being no spare horse for Evelina, she rode pillion with one of the knight's servants.

Evelina would have liked to have ridden pillion with the prince—her arms clasped tightly about Marcus's waist, her body snuggled against his—but when she suggested it, Marcus refused, adding that he would be riding hard and he did not want her to get hurt. And, indeed, when he left the village, he put his spurs to his horse and galloped off down the road, taking his escort by surprise, so that the knights had to spur their own horses to catch up with him. Sir Troeven ordered one of his squires to remain behind to guard Evelina.

She could have argued and probably got her own way, but, remembering that she might be pregnant, she didn't want the seed jounced out of her, and so she chose to accept the prince's decision. She would follow along with the rest of the baggage, as one of the knights remarked. Evelina heard him, but she didn't mind. So long as the baggage was carried into the prince's castle, that was fine with her.

She rode behind the servant—a young lad of fourteen who smelled of garlic and had pock-marked skin. Her escort set a leisurely pace. As they sauntered along, they came upon Jorge, sitting on a piece of driftwood, mending his net.

This time, he carefully kept his eyes on his work.

Evelina held her head high, pretending not to notice him. But when they had ridden past, she glanced over her shoulder.

He was a fine-looking man. He would give her a fine-looking son. Evelina sighed a little sigh and then set her face forward. She was pleased. She had Marcus bound by chains of iron that, if he chose, could be chains of silk. Evelina meant what she had said about loving Marcus. She did love him in her own way. Her love was a selfish love, founded on her own self-interest, but, in her experience, that was how love made the world go round. As for Marcus, he would get over his snit. He was a man, and she had never met the man she couldn't lure into her bed. She could still feel Marcus's kisses from last night, and she'd seen desire prick him this morning. He'd get over being upset and—once he'd married her—(she was aiming for marriage now, after what he'd put her through last night) she would make him glad he did.

And her son would be a fisherman's son. Not the son of a monster!

30

MARCUS MET WITH NO FURTHER UNTOWARD INCIDENTS on his journey home. He and his escort arrived back at Idylswylde in the early hours of the morning. Upon sighting the walls of the castle—black and grim against the gray light of dawn—he could not contain his impatience and outdistanced his escort. His clattering arrival at the gatehouse startled the sleepy guards. Hearing the pounding of a horse's hooves, they thought that some dire event had occurred. They were on their feet, with weapons at the ready, when Marcus came galloping up. Apprehension turned to relief and pleasure, and they welcomed the prince home, and sped him on his way through the outer walls.

As he rode beneath the battlements, he looked at the cannons, lined up in a row on the wall, etched starkly against the light of the morning, black against pearl. The cannons crouched on the walls like some cold, unfeeling beast, ready to breathe fire and death on their foe. The sight was an arresting one and struck him forcibly, so that he slowed his horse. He'd seen the cannons often enough. He couldn't think why the sight of the guns should so disturb him now.

And then he understood. He was seeing them with the eyes of dragons. He was seeing them now as he'd seen them in his wild dance through dragon dreams.

The cannons. Soulless monstrosities. Able to carelessly take what is given only once and, when lost, is lost forever.

"Man cannot breathe fire and you can," Marcus said to the dragons aloud. "We have made all things equal."

He rode on.

Word of Marcus's recovery had traveled faster. His parents had been up all night, watching for him. When he stood before his mother, safe and whole, Ermintrude flung her arms around him and clung to him, crying, and he could not help but shed a few tears himself. Edward received his son with few words and a firm embrace. The old seneschal, Gunderson, stood by, watching the reunion with heartfelt pleasure.

Ermintrude was shocked at her son's gaunt appearance and wanted to carry him off to be fed and pampered and put to bed. Marcus agreed to food, but said firmly that he needed to talk to his parents immediately on a matter of the utmost urgency.

His father, looking grim, and his mother, looking apprehensive, accompanied their son to the king's study.

Marcus had been thinking all the way home on how to convince his father of the terrible threat facing them, a threat coming from an enemy kingdom that had bordered theirs for centuries, yet one no one had seen or heard of. Even now, if the king went hunting for his enemy, he would not find them. And this was an enemy whose capacity for destruction made the armies of the King of Weinmauer look like little boys playing at war with wooden swords.

At least, Marcus thought, *Draconas has been here before me, to prepare the way. This won't come as a huge surprise.*

Eating cold meat and bread, Marcus told his tale from the beginning, mixing lies with the truth where it was apparent that not even his loving parents would believe his story.

He told about how he'd run off with Bellona, which they already knew, and how he and Bellona had met up with Draconas, who had helped them find and enter the kingdom known as Dragonkeep, a kingdom hidden by illusion, a kingdom that was perhaps already marching to the drums of war. He told them about Bellona and her brutal death, and saw tears slide down his mother's face. He mentioned Ven, and his father's face darkened.

Ermintrude caught Marcus's eye and shook her head, warning him away from that subject. Marcus understood and went on.

He had to bring up Evelina and he did so, though only briefly, speaking of her as a young woman who had been a prisoner in Dragonkeep and telling how they had escaped together. He gave Evelina credit for her courage and her resourcefulness, for he had decided to make the best of the situation. He'd realized, on the ride home, that the situation might resolve itself. She claimed she was pregnant, but if he hadn't slept with her, how could that be? If she did turn out to be pregnant, then he must have done what she said, though he had no idea how. And in that instance, he would not bring any child into the world to hear, as he had heard, the whispered word "bastard."

What he did not tell his parents was how he'd been drunk and fought a dragon and danced through dragons' brains.

He thought he got through his story about Evelina pretty well—until he saw his mother's expression. Marcus flushed and coughed and shifted back to the most urgent matter.

"You already know all this I've been telling you, Father," said Marcus, after a pause to refresh himself with a mug of ale. "Draconas said he told you."

Edward, looking grim, walked over to stand by the window. He stared out at the mountains.

"I saw the army for myself, Father," Marcus said, speaking to his father's back. He didn't mention how he'd seen it, in a wine-soaked dream. "Only the River Aston separates our nation from theirs. The river runs slow this time of year. They can ferry an army across it in no time.

"And their army is terrible," he added. "An army unlike any that has been seen before on this earth. One we can't possibly fight. But one that we have to."

Slowly, Edward turned to face his son. The king's expression was dark, but not with disbelief. Marcus knew his father. Edward had dismissed Draconas because he neither liked nor trusted the dragon-turned-man. The king had not dismissed the warning, however. He'd been thinking about it ever since. Perhaps he and Gunderson were already making plans. Marcus breathed an inward sigh of relief.

"The dragons mean to conquer all of humankind, Father. Not all the dragons. Some, like Draconas, are opposed to this. But there are others, many others, who are in favor."

It was on the tip of his tongue to add that he'd been inside their thoughts, he'd seen the vibrant colors of fear and outrage in their minds. He swallowed the words with his ale.

"We have one thing in our favor—the cannons," Marcus went on, when the king didn't speak. "This is the battle you've prepared for all your life, Father. Well, maybe not quite. You envisioned fighting dragons themselves, not humans wielding the power of dragons. No matter how strong their magic, a cannonball plowing into their ranks will leave them a mass of bloody pulp—sorry, Mother."

He turned to her, afraid he'd upset her. Ermintrude shook her head and sighed.

"All this talk of war," she mourned. "Just when there's the loveliest young woman I want you to meet."

Edward and Marcus regarded her in mute astonishment.

"She has just arrived," Ermintrude continued calmly. "Her name is Izabelle. She is the daughter of the Earl of Cantwell and a distant cousin. You played with her when you were children, Marcus. I don't suppose you remember, but she does."

With another one of her leaps, which were not so illogical as they appeared, Ermintrude added, "And when do we meet Mistress Evelina?"

Marcus opened his mouth, only to close it again as Edward broke in impatiently, "My dear! Now is hardly the time!"

Ermintrude tapped her reliquary. "There is a time for all things, Edward. 'A time for love and a time for war.' So the Church teaches us."

"So it does, my dear," said the king. "But most times, war takes precedence. And it must now. I think you have a plan in mind, my son. I would be interested in hearing it."

Marcus breathed an inward sigh. He was spared for the moment.

"I was thinking we could send a small force north to slow the dragon army's march. Then feint a retreat, draw them back to Idylswylde castle, which is their objective anyway."

Edward nodded his head, approving. "I have been thinking much the same thing."

He turned to Ermintrude. "You should pay a visit to your father in Weinmauer, my dear. If you left this evening, you and your ladies—"

"Don't talk rubbish, Edward," interrupted Ermintrude crisply.

"You would have an armed escort—"

"—of knights who will be of much more use on the field of battle than trotting along after me. I won't hear of leaving, Edward, so save your breath. Carry on with your war and leave me to my business."

Edward and Marcus exchanged glances.

"Draconas says that the dragons fear the cannons. He warned that they may attack them prior to the battle. Have they tried?" asked Marcus.

"The only dragon who has come calling is Draconas," Edward said wryly.

Recalling the loathing for the cannons he'd seen in the dragons' minds, Marcus was surprised. "I find it odd that they haven't attacked."

"So did Draconas," said Edward. "I don't, however. You have the answer—the dragons won't face the cannons. They don't have to. They are going to send these wretched humans of theirs to the slaughter."

Marcus pondered. That answer was logical, though not altogether satisfactory. His father was implying that the dragons were cowards, hiding behind humans, and that wasn't true. He found the fact that the dragons hadn't tried to destroy the cannons disquieting. He would have liked to discuss this with Draconas, but Marcus had been ordered to "stay in his room." Recalling the ancient and powerful force that lay outside that room, waiting for him, he considered this advice sensible.

His father laid a hand on his shoulder.

"You look about ready to drop, my son. Go to your rest. Gunderson and I will do what needs to be done to start this war in motion. No, my son, I insist," Edward added, seeing Marcus ready to protest. "Don't worry. I'm not going to leap into the saddle and ride off this instant. Today I'll be sending out messengers, warning the crown prince and the barons to the north to fortify their borders and prepare for an attack."

"From an invisible kingdom. They'll find it hard to swallow," said Marcus.

"Weinmauer is not invisible," said Edward imperturbably. "They'll easily believe that his troops are on the move. I've already called the muster. We'll have men and equipment set to leave tomorrow."

Marcus was amazed and, apparently, his father saw that in his face, for Edward added, with a touch of bitterness, "I may not trust Draconas, but I'm not a fool. No matter what he tells you."

"Father," said Marcus, "this army we face is like no other army on earth. The soldiers fight with weapons that are not of this world. Their armor is made of the scales of dragons. I think we should warn our people what they face."

"Should we?" Edward returned. "Won't they think we are lying or worse—raving lunatics? I encountered the mad monks. I saw one of them send Draconas flying across the highway with a wave of his hand. I saw a wall that wasn't a wall and a feeble old woman turn herself into a fire-breathing dragon. Nothing anyone could have told me would have prepared me for that."

"They'll think they're under attack by the Devil," said Marcus, shaking his head. "At least tell the knights and the barons."

"I'll discuss it with Gunderson," said his father. "Perhaps you're right. After all, even if they don't believe me, they'll know better to say it to my face. And they'll be prepared when the time comes. I will summon the messengers and prepare the letters. You spend some time with your mother."

Marcus looked at his father in silent appeal.

Edward clapped Marcus on the shoulder. "Courage, my son," he said softly and left the room.

Marcus turned reluctantly to face Ermintrude, thinking he would rather be facing the dragon.

The queen rose ponderously to her feet, her silk rustling. She clasped her hands over her broad stomacher and said briskly, "You made love to this girl and now she claims she is pregnant with your child and you must marry her or buy her off. Is that what you are *not* telling me?"

"Mother!" Marcus felt his face burn in embarrassment.

"Don't worry, my son. She cannot trap you like this. You are a prince of the realm and she is . . . What is she? What do you know about her?"

"Nothing, really," he said, keeping to himself the facts he did know.

"I thought as much. How many times did you make love to her?"

"I don't remember making love to her at all," Marcus admitted. "But there was wine . . . and she was . . . was there . . . beside me . . . when I woke up . . ."

"Do you love this girl?"

Marcus hesitated. "She was so pretty and she was in danger. We were both in danger. We had only each other . . . She was brave and level-headed and—"

"You thought you were in love with her."

"Yes," he said. "I was even tempted . . . But I don't think I did. I just don't remember!"

"Does she love you?"

Marcus's flush deepened. "I think she does. I didn't mean to lead her on. It's just—"

"You are young and thrown together in dangerous and romantic circumstances." Ermintrude sighed. "I understand, my dear. Don't blame yourself."

"But I do blame myself. I have to take responsibility and, well, she made threats."

"Did she, now," Ermintrude said, her eyes flashing.

"She was distraught and didn't know what she was saying. And I mean to take care of her anyway."

"*You* will stay out of it," said Ermintrude firmly. "I will deal with Mistress Evelina. And, yes, you will take responsibility. We'll arrange to care for her and her baby, if she's truly pregnant, which she could hardly know for certain yet."

"Mother, I don't want any child growing up under the shadow of being called a bastard. Not like—"

"Not like you?" His mother, who was really his stepmother, squeezed his hand. "I know how difficult it has been for you, dear heart. I am sorry, so very sorry. We tried to protect you, your father and I. But you are the son of a prince and people will talk. It will be different for this girl. We'll marry her off to some good man who will care for her and the child. We'll see to the child's education. In the meantime, you will meet the Lady Izabelle."

Marcus shook his head. "The last thing I need is more women in my life, Mother."

Ermintrude smoothed out her skirts and patted her jewel-encrusted headpiece into place. She adjusted her many rings and her numerous bracelets. Marcus recognized the signs. She was arming for battle, just as any knight, and he knew he'd lost before he'd begun the fight. He was the son of a king, and king's sons had no say in who they married.

"Your father and I have already agreed to the wedding," said the Queen. "The young lady is lovely and quite charming. You two played together as children. She still remembers some of the stories you used to tell her. The Lady Izabelle already knows about your magic. You used to conjure up fairies for her as a child. She told me all about it. Do you remember?"

"No." Marcus tried to think back, but memory of his

childhood ended and began in a cave with Draconas. "I don't think much about that time if I can help it."

Ermintrude patted his hand. "Go get some sleep. You're falling over on your feet."

"I told Evelina she could have new clothes. She really was very courageous, Mother, and she did help me escape from Dragonkeep. She deserves something for that."

"She'll have every comfort," his mother assured him. "She will be well treated. She can live in the castle until we make other arrangements for her, so long as she behaves herself. After you've had a good rest, you and the Lady Izabelle can take a nice walk along the battlements. She's interested in the cannons. You can show them to her and explain how they work."

Marcus did not believe for one minute that the daughter of an earl would be interested in cannons, but he let it pass. He knew what his mother was about. Ermintrude embraced him, hugging him as close as her hooped skirt would permit.

"I am so glad you are home, my dear one. I prayed to God, day and night. And now I must go to the chapel to thank Him. Sleep well! I'll send Joseph to wake you in a few hours."

Ermintrude hurried off, wiping her eyes as she went. Marcus went to his bedchamber, thinking that he would lie down and try to sort out his tangled thoughts. Weariness put an end to that. He fell asleep and, if he dreamed, his dreams were not the dreams of dragons. Just the ordinary gray dreams of humans.

31

EVELINA ARRIVED AT THE CASTLE IN A POURING RAIN-
storm, a day and a night after Marcus's return. Drenched
and exhausted, she had to be lifted off the horse, for she
was so stiff and saddle-sore she could scarcely move.
Consequently, she was in an ill humor that was not im-
proved upon discovering that the only person to meet her
was a crippled-up old retainer named Gunderson, who
had only one eye.

Her squire escort was clearly glad to be rid of her and
she glad to be rid of him, for he was forty years old,
proud and snooty, and he coldly repulsed her little smiles
and flirtations, when all she was trying to do was make
the long journey less tedious.

The courtyard was in a bustle of activity even in a driving rainstorm. Everyone seemed to be running somewhere with faces that were serious, tense, and wet. If they
weren't running, they were shouting, for the army was
making ready to march, although Evelina did not know
this. Dismayed and bewildered, she was very nearly
trampled by a knight on horseback. Gunderson arrived at
that moment to claim her, and he hauled her out of the
way, escorting her up an enormous flight of stone stairs
and into the palace.

Evelina walked into the beautiful and impressive building, gazing at the spires and turrets, the gargoyles and

leaded windows, the enormous double doors, made of wood and banded with iron, and as those doors opened for her, she hugged herself with glee and wished her father could be here to see her. She imagined herself walking past Ramone. He would humbly doff his hat to her. Haughty and cold and rich, she would throw him a gold coin. Evelina sighed with regret that he was dead.

Gunderson introduced himself with grave formality, which pleased Evelina, though she didn't like the shrewd and knowing look in the old man's one glinting eye. He led her into a huge and echoing hall. The only time Evelina had been inside a building like this was when she'd taken refuge in a cathedral, fleeing a man who claimed she'd picked his pocket.

She had never in her life seen so many beautiful things—tapestries whose rich colors gleamed in the light, chairs so heavily carved that she wondered who could possibly sit on them in comfort, long tables covered with white linen on which stood plates heaped with food. She had dreamt of what Marcus's palace would be like. She had expected to find riches and warmth and good food. She had not expected to find that it was all so big and shadowy or that she would feel so small, standing in the entryway, sopping wet, dripping onto the floor.

It was then she saw Marcus. He was some distance away, walking down a long staircase, and he was not alone. Beside him was a young woman, slender, elegant, graceful. The two conversed as they sauntered down the stairs. They did not see her. They were entirely absorbed in their conversation. And in each other.

Evelina's jealous eyes noted every detail of this woman, from her thick, rich coil of chestnut hair, tucked beneath a fine lace head-covering, to her small bosoms and delicate-boned face, her pink cheeks and large, brown eyes.

Evelina opened her mouth and drew in a breath to call out to Marcus.

Gunderson said quietly, "A proper young woman does not shout like a fishmonger, Mistress."

Evelina let out her breath in an irritated hiss. She was

forced to watch in smoldering silence as the two of them reached the bottom of the stairs and continued walking through a door into another part of the castle.

Men are such fools. To fall for a doe-eyed, pasty-faced little tart like that . . .

Reminding herself that she had every right to be here, because, after all, she was carrying the prince's child, Evelina shook out her wet curls and turned to Gunderson.

"You will tell Marcus I'm here," she stated.

"*His Highness*"—Gunderson emphasized the words—"will be informed."

"See that he is," Evelina said loftily. She made an attempt to boldly meet that single eye and found it difficult. "You may take me to my room now, my good man."

Gunderson led her upstairs and through corridors and down halls and up halls, so that she was immediately lost and confused. Once they reached her room, Evelina was vastly pleased with it. The room was larger and warmer and cleaner than any she'd known. At the sight of a beautiful gown on the bed—a gown that he said was hers, a gift from the Queen—Evelina clapped her hands. And when he introduced the servant who was to wait on her, Evelina could almost feel the royal crown being placed on her head. Later she would discover that the room was in a wing of the palace located as far as possible from the chambers of the royal family, and that the servant was not so much a servant as a prison warden. But Evelina now thought herself in heaven.

The servant was an older woman, with a face like an axe and a steely eye. She obviously disapproved highly of Evelina. The woman assisted Evelina in discarding her old clothes and drying herself off. Then she showed her how to put on the new clothes, for with the chemise and the stockings and the underskirt and overskirt and bodice with sleeves that had to be tied on, Evelina would not have known where to begin. The woman brushed out her hair and, when Evelina said she was hungry, ordered a servant to bring up a tray.

The food was a disappointment, for Evelina had expected peacock's tongues, and all she got was plain roast beef.

"And now I think I will go have a look about the palace," Evelina stated.

"That is quite out of the question, Mistress," said the axe-faced woman in an iron tone. "Her Majesty is coming to pay you a visit. You must wait here."

Evelina felt a tingle of delight. The Queen, coming to see her. She sat down in one of the chairs to wait.

She waited.

And waited.

The axe-faced woman sat in a chair in steely silence, tatting lace. Evelina felt it beneath her dignity to converse with a servant, so she also sat in silence. She spent some time admiring her new clothes and her new shoes, but one could do that for only so long.

She went from being pleased to bored and from bored to irritated. And then she heard distant sounds—music! Somewhere people were feasting and dancing. She was thinking of defying Axe-Face and walking out, going to see if she could find Marcus, when she heard a rustle of silk and footsteps outside the door and smelled a fragrance as of spring roses. Axe-Face rose to her feet.

Evelina tried to calm her racing heart. Her future would be settled in this one moment.

The Queen came alone. She opened the door, entered, and said something to the woman, who curtsied deeply and went out. The Queen shut the door behind her. She glanced about the room, as though to make certain that all was well, then turned to face Evelina.

"Well, Mistress," said the Queen, giving her a dimpled smile, "are you settling in?"

Evelina made an awkward curtsy, as the servant had instructed her. She started to sit down, then remembered just in time that the servant had also warned her that no one sat while in Her Majesty's presence. Evelina remained standing, her head lowered, all the while studying the Queen intently from beneath her eyelashes.

Evelina had always considered other members of her own sex to be weak, stupid creatures, and the Queen was no exception. Evelina saw a plump, overfed, middle-aged woman clad in bejeweled splendor, pampered and protected and silly. Evelina had no doubt at all about who would win this encounter.

"Yes, Your Majesty," Evelina replied meekly, with another curtsy. She launched into her speech. "I did not expect to be so honored. I'm not a fine lady, you know, ma'am—though I'm often taken for such. I am a good girl, however. I was given a godly upbringing by my poor father, may the saints in heaven rest his soul. If I did anything wrong, it was for love. I love your son, ma'am, with all my heart."

Evelina gave a sob at this juncture, and wiped her eyes.

"Yes, I'm sure you do love my son," the Queen said. "He is a prince. He is handsome and rich and he rescued you from a terrifying situation. That is enough to turn any girl's head."

"And he loves me, ma'am," Evelina felt bold enough to assert.

"You are quite pretty, child. I've no doubt that he did fancy himself in love with you," the Queen said gently. "And now you believe yourself to be pregnant with his child?"

"I think it is likely, ma'am," said Evelina. She placed her hand on her flat belly. "I've been feeling sickish of late."

The Queen's dimples flashed, then vanished. Evelina began to feel nervous.

"I know we made love just the once," she continued defensively, having first thought she would lie about this, then deciding she wouldn't. "But a girl knows these things, ma'am." She let a tear trickle down her cheek.

"Yes, well, we will see about that," said the Queen. "I want you to know, Mistress, that I do not defend my son's actions. They were not those of a gentleman. However, you are both young and you were thrown together in an extraordinary situation, so that I can envision how this all came about. You must understand, Mistress Evelina, that marriage to my son is impossible."

"I *don't* know that, ma'am," Evelina said boldly. "Your son loves me and I love him. True, I'm not a fine lady, but I could learn to be—"

"My son is betrothed to another," said the Queen. "The Lady Izabelle, daughter of an earl."

If the woman had knocked her down with a right hook to the jaw, Evelina could not have been more astonished. She was literally rocked back on the heels of her new shoes. The thought of this had never occurred to her.

"He never told me that, Your Majesty!" Evelina gasped and she burst into sobs. "He lied to me!"

"My son did not know himself," the Queen returned. "The marriage was arranged in his absence. This must seem harsh to you, but it is the way of the world, Mistress Evelina. You will remain here in the castle until we know for certain whether or not you are pregnant. If you are, we will care for you and your child. Marriage with some good man . . ."

Evelina had stopped listening to the woman's yammering. A rival! Evelina didn't believe for one moment that this marriage had been arranged without Marcus's knowledge. He knew! He'd used her! He'd made her fall in love with him! The wormwood in his wine was suddenly justified. Her fisherman lover faded conveniently from her mind. Marcus was a prince. He could do what he wanted. If he wanted to marry her, he had only to make it a royal decree or a royal edict or a papal bull or whatever and it would happen. Who would dare tell him no? It was this other woman. The thin, pasty-faced little slut. She was the reason he wouldn't marry her.

All this flashed through Evelina's mind in a second. The Queen was still talking, saying something about Marcus riding off to war, but that she would be safe in the castle. All the ladies of the court were remaining.

Evelina said, in a half-choked voice, "Including the Lady Izabelle?"

"Yes, but don't worry. The castle is quite a large place. The two of you do not ever have to meet—"

"Oh, I would like to meet her, Your Majesty," said Evelina softly.

The Queen departed. Axe-Face returned.

When Evelina told the woman, experimentally, that she would like to have some air, Axe-Face marched her up and down an empty corridor, never taking her eyes off her, not permitting her to speak to anyone, making certain no one spoke to her. Then Axe-Face returned Evelina to her room, shut the door, and locked it.

Evelina understood. While she was in the palace, she would be a prisoner. They would not let her talk to Marcus or even see him.

Evelina snuggled into her warm, dry bed that night and said to herself softly, "We'll see about that."

32

THE NEXT MORNING, MARCUS AND HIS FATHER AND A small contingent of knights and footsoldiers left the city. They traveled light, marching swiftly for the border that separated Idylswylde from her neighbor Weinmauer and also from Dragonkeep. The nearest outpost was Aston Castle, home of Crown Prince Wilhelm, Marcus's eldest half-brother. King Edward had sent the prince an urgent message, telling him as much of the truth as he thought his son likely to believe, commanding him to send his troops to the northwest, toward the hitherto unknown city of Dragonkeep, where the prince was to deploy his men as he saw fit.

The king's army set out beneath a gray sky, for the rain that had soaked Evelina the day before continued to fall and, according to the weather-watchers, was likely to fall all that day. They rode with their hats pulled low to keep the rainwater out of their eyes. The bright-colored standards flapped sullenly in wind gusts that drove the cold rain into their faces. There was no talking among the knights or jesting or boasting of past deeds of glory. The bad weather probably had much to do with this, though Marcus felt their silence was darker and more sinister.

He had been present when his father had tried to explain the nature of this enemy to a few trusted knights. Some were professional soldiers, others landed nobles;

all were friends and comrades of the king, men who had known Marcus all his life. He saw the shock and incredulity in their eyes as his father told them, in a calm and steady voice, about the kingdom hidden by dragon-magic, about warriors who wielded magic given to them by dragons. A few knew the king well enough to voice their skepticism aloud, asking how Edward knew all this, and—when he mentioned his son—their incredulity hardened to disbelief.

Most of these men thought privately—and some muttered aloud—that they were being led on a wild goose chase by a lunatic.

Marcus began to wonder himself if this was true. He had lied to his father. He hadn't actually seen this army of dragon warriors with his own eyes, though he'd assured Edward he had. Marcus had seen them with his mind's eye. As a child, he'd seen many terrible and wonderful sights with that eye, sights that had been the dreams of dragons. What if this was a dragon's dream? Or a drunkard's dream? Whenever Marcus thought of Evelina and the wine, he flushed in shame. What if the army marched all this way and found nothing at the end?

True, Draconas had confirmed what he'd seen, but Draconas was a dragon, and could he be trusted? He'd as much as admitted that he'd taken Marcus to Dragonkeep as bait in order to lure out the dragon. And he'd made it clear that what he did, he did for love of his own kind, not for love of humans. Perhaps Draconas was playing his own game.

Marcus knew his father had doubts, though Edward had said nothing to him. The king was taking an immense risk, believing in his son—a son who was having difficulty believing in himself. True, Edward had seen the mad monks. He'd seen illusion magic at work— Draconas had once knocked the king through what he'd perceived to be a stone wall. But that was a long way from believing in magic that could hide an entire city from sight for hundreds of years and field an army of warriors with the blood of dragons in their veins.

As Marcus rode at the head of his own force—the

Prince's Own, a troop of knights who had been rewarded for service to the crown by being given the honor of escorting the prince—he looked into a future that was bleak and gray as the day.

He did not know what to wish for. If he hoped for vindication, then it was likely that he and many of these men riding with him would die. If he wished it to be nothing more than a dream, his father had mustered his army at great expense for nothing, and news that the prince was mad would spread like wildfire. His parents would have to shut him up in a monastery to silence the outcry and keep him from further disgracing his family. Thinking of this, Marcus deemed a metal dart in the throat preferable.

He rode by himself, keeping his distance from his escorts, who—truth to tell—were not disposed to be on a friendly basis with the young man. The knights, led by Sir Troeven had vowed before God and their king that they would lay down their lives for their prince if need be. They hadn't taken any oath to be his friend.

Edward was concerned about his son. Marcus knew that, for he saw his father casting worried glances in his direction. Marcus pretended he didn't notice. He much preferred to keep himself to himself.

By afternoon, however, when Marcus had not said a word to anyone and had given away his food to a pack of delighted urchins and their dogs, Edward fell back from his position at the head of the army to join his son. Raising his voice to be heard over the drumming rain, he said, in companionable tones, "What did you think of the Lady Izabelle?"

Marcus blinked his eyes to clear them of rainwater and dragged his thoughts back from the gloomy prospect before him to wonder what he did think of the young woman who was going to be his wife. The truth was, he'd been so preoccupied and worried that he hadn't given her much thought at all.

Perhaps his father guessed as much for he added, louder still, "By your silent preoccupation all day, my son, I take it you've been thinking of little else except her lovely face."

Marcus took the hint. "She is truly very beautiful, Father," he said, trying to sound as enthusiastic as possible.

And he had to give his mother credit. The Lady Izabelle was lovely. She was sweet, gentle, and graceful, and if she wasn't madly in love with him now, she was prepared to be. He had taken her on a walk around the balustrades and they had viewed the famous cannons. There had been dinner—a grand affair, served in the great hall. There was music and dancing, with the lady as his partner.

After that, his mother had suggested that he and the lady play a game of chess, which neither proved to be very good at, perhaps because neither was paying much attention. Gunderson and Sir Troeven and some of the other knights had drifted off to one part of the hall. Marcus spent much of his time watching them and wondering what they were saying. He kept having to force himself to make polite conversation and to move his chess pieces when he was supposed to.

Lady Izabelle was likewise preoccupied. When it occurred to him that a long time had passed between them in silence, he found her staring into the fire, her expression grave. When the Queen rose to her feet and summoned her ladies to her, freeing Marcus to go to his father, the lady made him a graceful bow, gave him an enigmatic smile, and glided off to join Her Majesty without a backward look.

Edward rode closer to Marcus to have a private conversation, their words covered by the rattle and clank of harness and bridle and the crackle of thunder.

"What do you truly think of her?" Edward asked.

"She is quite nice, Father," Marcus answered, thinking, even as he said it, that this was hardly the rapturous praise of an ardent lover.

Edward must have remembered his own courtship, which had lasted a quarter of an hour, for he and Ermintrude had been introduced, wedded, then bedded all in the same day.

"No tambours and lutes playing when you speak her name, as the poets say?" Edward asked wryly.

"Everything is so uncertain now," Marcus said in apology. "I can't really think about marriage."

"Bad timing—despite what your mother and the holy book say." Edward paused, then added, "Love will come, Marcus. It may not be the love the poets sing about, but it's much more comfortable." Another pause, then he added quietly, "Your mother had a talk with Mistress Evelina yesterday evening."

Marcus's skin burned so that the rainwater running down his cheeks seemed to sizzle.

"Your mother explained to her that marriage was out of the question and promised her that she and her child—if she is truly pregnant—will be provided for."

"How did Evelina . . . what did . . . did she say anything—"

"The girl took it well enough, according to your mother. She was upset, of course, but your mother is of the opinion that she will come around, especially once she understands that any type of relationship with you is hopeless. Your mother told her about your engagement. That should end the matter."

It should, but Marcus had the feeling that it wouldn't. His thoughts in regard to Evelina were all mixed up; a tangle of desire and revulsion that he couldn't understand. He saw her lying naked beside him on the bed, and he ached and throbbed, and he saw her somewhere else, doing something else—he couldn't remember what or where—but when that vague memory tugged at his sleeve, the throbbing turned into a sickening feeling that churned his stomach and left a sour taste in his mouth.

He said nothing, however, and his father, thinking he understood, gave his son a sympathetic glance and rode on ahead, leaving Marcus to his thoughts, which immediately left wedding and/or bedding and went back to what—if anything—lay ahead.

They rode swiftly that day and made a cold and cheerless camp late in the evening. The rain ceased, but the trees dripped incessantly all night long. The ground was wet and soggy. The fires smoked and gave forth only sullen, grudging warmth. Marcus was stiff and sore from the long ride, and a night spent sleeping on the ground didn't help. They were up and in the saddle as soon as there was light enough for men and horses to see where they were going. They rode all that day, slept on soggy ground that night, and were up yet again with another gray dawn.

The clouds passed that morning, leaving a clean-washed blue sky and glaring sun that, by the time they reached Aston Castle, was high above the trees. Prince Wilhelm was not there to meet them. He'd ridden out with his troops. He had left orders for the care of his father and brother and their retinue, orders that his lady-wife carried out in an exemplary manner. Grooms stabled the horses, which were glad to rest after their wearying journey. The knights enjoyed a hearty repast, and the king enjoyed meeting with his daughter-in-law and playing with his grandchildren. There was an air of tension, however, and when a messenger arrived, riding a steaming horse into the courtyard, half the castle turned out to meet him.

"What news?" the king asked, holding the horse's bridle himself.

"Prince Wilhelm bids me to give you this message, Your Majesty," said the knight. "My lord says: 'The sun shines. The river flows. The birds sing. Our archers snore beneath the trees and our men-at-arms lose the money you are paying them to each other at dice.'"

Edward was careful not to look at Marcus. Those knights who had been lingering nearby glanced at each other, rolled their eyes, shook their heads, and walked off. The king told the messenger to come inside. Marcus followed more slowly and, when he arrived, he found the messenger and the king bent over a map.

"His Highness chose this position, Your Majesty. If enemy troops were to cross the river, we deemed this to be the likeliest place. He sent scouts across the river to search for some sign of an enemy, and we found nothing. We went upstream and down and I swear on my father's beard, Your Majesty, that there is no city there. There is no army threatening to attack us. There is naught but trees and brush and deer coming to the water to drink."

Marcus sat in a chair in a corner. His father glanced at him from time to time, as if inviting him to speak, but Marcus kept silent. He knew quite well what the scouts had seen, for he'd seen it, too—until Grald had lifted the magical veil of enchantment.

Edward said that he would like to see for himself the lay of the land and how the troops were deployed. The messenger offered to escort him in the morning.

When the man had been dismissed, Edward turned to Marcus.

"I know you are tired from the long journey, my son, especially after everything you've gone through. Perhaps you would like to remain here and rest."

His offer was well intentioned and kindly meant, and it fell on Marcus with the force of an iron anvil dropped off the top of the castle wall.

"I will come with you, Father," he said coldly, and he turned his back and walked off before Edward could say a word.

33

"DEATH AHEAD OF YOU. DEATH BEHIND YOU. DEATH above you and death below. No escape, King's Son. There is no escape."

Crouched on his little stool, in his own little room, Marcus spent the night listening to the dragon's voice hissing through the keyhole. Over and over. *Death ahead of you. Death behind you. Death above and death below. No escape, King's Son.*

The tone was harsh, meant to frighten and weaken. And it succeeded.

Marcus rose from his bed with the dull, stupid feeling that comes from fatigue. He looked out of the castle's slit windows to see the east reddening with the dawn. The castle's other inhabitants were already awake, for the king had ordered them to ride at first light. The voice of the dragon lingered. Marcus closed his eyes and pressed his throbbing head against the chill stone wall.

The words "death ahead, death behind, death above, death below" had been laid in his brain like some sort of evil eggs, and now, hatching, the dread portent of the warning squirmed and crawled around inside him.

The dragon army lay ahead of them. The dragon was above them. Death behind and death below. Did the enemy have them surrounded? Were they cut off from the castle and the cannons that were to save them? Was this warning even true, or was this the dragon's way of defeating them before they'd started?

The summons came to ride. Accoutered in his heavy armor—plate over chain—Marcus clanked into the courtyard in time to hear a messenger from his brother reporting to the king that the night had passed with no alarms.

None of the knights that comprised the Prince's Own looked at Marcus this morning as they mounted and made ready to ride. No one spoke to him either, except his father, to wish him a good day. And Edward's voice sounded strained.

Marcus mounted his war horse and rode in silence, the words writhing about inside his brain.

Death ahead. Death behind.
Death above. Death below.
No escape.

The king's messenger had galloped on ahead to apprise Prince Wilhelm of their coming, and he was on hand to greet them as they dismounted, giving his father an affectionate embrace and his little brother a cool nod. Prince Wilhelm was about eight years Marcus's senior. The difference in their ages alone would have likely prevented the two from being close. Add to this the fact that Marcus had been a very strange child, given to visions and fancies and finally going insane, and the result was that the half-brothers scarcely knew each other.

To give Wilhelm his due, he had never resented the bastard son or feared him or distrusted him, as often happened in other royal households. Wilhelm had defended and protected his little brother, mostly with words, sometimes with fists. Marcus never knew this, or if he did, it was lost in the dazzling, lunatic swirl of dragon-dreams that had comprised his childhood.

A goodly blend of both father and mother, Wilhelm had fair hair, his father's hazel eyes, and a tendency to his mother's plumpness that he worked hard to avoid. His nature had always been of a serious bent, and he took his duties as crown prince in earnest. When the king and his retinue came upon the prince, he was hot, tired, and in a bad humor. Marcus could not particularly blame his brother. The most vicious foes Wilhelm faced at the moment were fleas, ticks, gnats, grasshoppers, and clouds of ferocious mosquitoes.

As the morning sun sparkled on the distant river, Wilhelm sat his horse atop the ridge, the visor of his helm raised, trying to ignore the itching of the many bug bites that he was unable to scratch beneath his armor. He made no attempt to keep the annoyance out of his voice as he indicated to his father and the assembled officers how he had deployed his troops.

"Skirmish line out front comprised of light infantry, small numbers. They will meet the first assault, fall back, drawing the enemy with them. The archers form the next line of defense."

He pointed to where the archers could be seen snoozing in the grass, their arrows stuck into the ground around them for easy access, or stuffed in cloth bags lying beside them. Behind the archers was bivouacked the majority of the infantry, a few of whom were moving in a desultory manner about their camp, heading for the trenches that were the privies or munching on whatever food they had for breakfast. The archers, if hard-pressed, could flow back through the infantry, where they could then halt to make a stand.

"My knights and heavy cavalry will be arrayed here and here," continued Wilhelm, gesturing, "prepared to flank the enemy. All the men are ready to fight. *If* we have an enemy. One that is *not* composed of moonbeams and fairy dust."

He cast a dark and baleful glance at Marcus, who saw the look and heard the words, but only as a low murmur beneath the constant hissing of the dragon. His brother and father and the commanders continued to talk. Marcus gazed out across the grasslands spreading before him, and he watched a ripple pass through the tall stands of grass like a wave rising from the river to wash over the land, setting the heads of the grass shivering and dipping low, then rising up and rolling on. The ripple traveled swiftly, spreading across the miles of empty land until it sank away to nothing not far from the ridgeline on which they stood.

Marcus thought at first it was the wind. Then he realized that the air was still, one reason for the mosquitoes. What, then, had caused that odd motion in the grass? He refocused his eyes and stared hard.

Nothing. No movement. No sound.

They're out there. He knew they were out there.

He saw his father's mouth move. He heard, in his head, the fell words "death ahead, death behind . . ."

Marcus urged his horse close to his father's. Breaking into the conversation, he said in a low voice, "You must sound the call to arms, Father. The enemy is almost on top of us!"

His father regarded him in consternation and exchanged glances with Wilhelm, who shook his head and looked away. Edward sighed deeply and rested his hand on Marcus's hand.

"My son, there's nothing out there. You're imagining things. That's understandable. This is your first battle. You're excited, eager—"

Marcus ceased to listen.

All you can see is the grass waving gently in the morning breeze and the river in the distance, sparkling and murmuring to itself in the sunshine. That is all you can see, but not all I can see. You have to listen to me! Death ahead. Death above . . .

"Sound the call, Wilhelm," Marcus urged. "Before it's too late!"

"Barking mad," stated Sir Troeven, commander of the knights of the Prince's Own, and he did not bother to keep his voice down.

Those words, cruel words, heard from his childhood on, were a fiery sword. Anger, hot and refining, cleansed Marcus's soul, burning away fear and doubt.

Marcus came to himself and saw that his father, his

brother, their knights on their horses gathered around him, looked ill-at-ease, embarrassed.

"Marcus, my son," the king was saying, "you have to calm yourself . . ."

Marcus backed his horse, backed away from their anguished attempts to assuage the madman, backed away from their pity. *He* regarded them—poor blind humans—with pity.

"You can't see them, but they are there," he said. "And I will show you."

Marcus took firm grip on the reins and touched his spurs into the horse's flanks. The horse leapt forward. The knights and his father and his brother sat there like lumps and watched him.

It wasn't until Marcus began to ride his horse down the ridge that his father finally realized what his son intended. The king gave a shout that jolted men to action. Bearded faces beneath steel helms loomed up in Marcus's path. Gloved hands tried to grasp hold of the reins and drag him to a stop. He kicked at them and kicked at his horse, urging it on, and men fell back or risked being trampled.

The animal plunged down the steep ridge, sliding and slipping and almost foundering. Marcus hung on with fixed determination, and the horse managed to regain its footing and continued on at a gallop, heading straight for the grassy plains. The empty grassy plains.

Horse and rider rode through the camp, overturning cooking pots and knocking down tent posts. Men, half-awake, had to jump for their lives as Marcus thundered past. The king shouted for someone to stop the prince, but no one wanted to risk death beneath the horse's hooves, and Marcus rode, unimpeded, for the plains of quivering grass.

And then he heard, behind him, pounding hooves. Marcus glanced over his shoulder. Mounted knights—the Prince's Own—were chasing after him. The knights were not riding to his call, inspired by his show of courage to join him in desperate battle. They were riding to catch him, drag him from his horse, fling him to the ground, and truss him up in a straitjacket.

Marcus faced forward, smiling grimly. In truth, they *were* riding to his call. He *was* leading them into battle.

They just didn't know it.

Marcus left the camp and the army behind. He entered the tall stands of grass, and he pulled back on the reins to slow his horse's mad rush. He heard the Prince's Own coming up fast behind him. There were about thirty knights, riding hard. His horse was suddenly skittish and danced sideways, eyes rolling and ears pricking.

Marcus patted the neck. "*You* know there's something out there, don't you, boy. You know it and I know it and, now, my father will know it."

He brought to mind the sight of Grald casting the magic that banished the illusion and caused the city of Dragonkeep to materialize before Marcus's amazed eyes. Marcus had tried to do the same when fleeing Dragonkeep. He'd tried to lift the illusion in order to find the hidden gate that led out of the city. He had not been able to do it, but then he had been exhausted and panic-stricken, afraid for his life.

He wasn't exhausted now. He wasn't afraid, though he felt certain that he had only moments more to live. He was excited and eager, exalted. His first and last battle would be a memorable one. He could see the magic hanging before him—a shimmering landscape painted on a backdrop of serene blue sky and tranquil white cloud, sparkling water and golden brown grass rippling gently in the morning breeze.

Marcus rose from his little chair in his little room, and he walked to the door and flung it wide open.

The dragon, Maristara, was there, holding the curtain of enchantment over her army, ready to whip it aside at the last moment, to the shock and horror of her unsuspecting audience.

Behind the curtain were dragon warriors, a thousand strong, hunkered down among the brown grass, the sunlight shining off their scaly armor. He saw on their faces smiles of derision and disdain. He saw Maristara smug and triumphant.

Marcus drew his sword and spurred his horse and rode at the curtain of brown and blue and sparkling river. He hit the fragile fabric of magic a slashing blow with the blade of his own magic, rending it and tearing it to shreds, so that the enchantment hung in tatters that fluttered in the wind.

Behind him, the Prince's Own had been shouting for their prince to stop. He heard their shouts choked off by gasps of astonishment or garbled curses. The curtain had gone up and the knights were face-to-face with their enemy—an enemy that had not been there one minute and was there the next; a strange and outlandish enemy that looked like no other enemy they had ever encountered.

The knights were thrown into confusion by this astonishing sight. Reining in their horses, the Prince's Own milled about in consternation, uncertain what to do.

Their commander, Sir Troeven—the same who had termed Marcus "barking mad"—was a soldier by profession. He had won his title after saving the life of the former king, Edward's father, in a fight with an outlaw band who had taken it into their heads that they owned the highway between Idylswylde and Ramsgate-upon-the-Aston During the past few years, Sir Troeven had been abroad, fighting battles for other kings, since there were none to fight at home. A veteran of many wars, he swept aside all that was strange or confusing about the army in front of him to concentrate on one thing—his duty. His sworn duty was to his prince, and his prince was alone on the field of battle, surrounded by the enemy.

Drawing his sword, Sir Troeven cried, "To me!" and rode like thunder through the grass and the ranks of the enemy. One after another, depending on the quickness of their wits or the strength of their courage, the knights of the Prince's Own galloped after their commander.

The dragon warriors had been assured by Grald that they and their magic would rule the field of battle.

None will be able to see you. You will sneak up upon them like the night and smite them like the lightning. You will fight at the time and place of your choosing, Grald had told them time and again.

Unmasked by Marcus's attack, the veil that covered them unexpectedly lifted, the dragon warriors were caught completely off guard. Thirty armored and mounted knights were riding down on them, and neither magical illusion nor dragon-scale armor could protect them from the pounding hooves of the massive war horses that each weighed upwards of a thousand pounds. The dragon warriors had no time to ready their defensive magicks before the Prince's Own smashed into their front ranks. Some had only seconds to fling themselves out of harm's way. Others did not even have that. The gigantic horses knocked them down, trampled their bodies, and kept going, their hooves and forelegs and bellies splashed with blood and gore and dragon scales.

The dragon warriors recovered quickly, however, and began to shift into battle formation. They fought in pairs—one man, one woman—and they sprouted from the tall grass like some sort of deadly weed.

Marcus looked back over his shoulder and saw his knights charging after him, their swords flashing in the sunlight. He saw the blood on the horses and the dead on the ground and, most important, from the ridgeline, he heard the blaring of trumpets and the beating of drums. His brother and father could see for themselves now that the enemy was, indeed, upon them. Marcus enjoyed a brief moment of triumph and satisfaction that swiftly evaporated like the morning mist. He could tell by the motions made by the female dragon warriors and the eerie glow starting to shimmer around the fingers of the males that they were arming themselves.

"Fall back!" Marcus yelled, waving his arm. "Fall back!"

Wheeling his horse, he found his way blocked.

A dragon warrior raised glowing hands. The bluish fire of the magic roiled off his fingers. Spinning and twisting, the magic snaked toward Marcus, who had time only to

suck in a breath. The blast struck him and his mount like
a gust of wind blowing from the mouth of hell.

The horse screamed. Marcus had a sickening sensation
of falling and then blackness and pain crashed down on
top of him and buried him deep.

Sir Troeven saw the prince go down, and the knight galloped toward Marcus, using a powerful yell and a wave
of his hand to direct the other knights, who were closing
with him rapidly.

The dragon warriors did not try to stop them, but
melted away at their coming. Troeven was feeling good
about this until he happened to glance over his shoulder
to see the strange warriors flowing in behind them and
around them. The warriors had managed to cut off two
knights, who had been lagging behind, laughing at the
sight of the enemy standing to face them without
weapons of any kind. Sir Troeven remembered what Edward had told them about this army and, though he had
laughed then (when the king wasn't paying heed), the
knight wasn't laughing now. These strange warriors
might not be holding swords in their hands, but they were
armed. He knew that by the confident way they moved
and by their calm, implacable expressions and the fact
that one of them had felled his prince. He had his sworn
duty and he rode on.

Marcus's horse was dead—that much was obvious—
and it had fallen on top of him. Sir Troeven could see the
prince's head and shoulders, arms and torso pinned beneath the large animal. Marcus, encased in armor, lay still
and unmoving. Two of the dragon warriors were approaching him.

Sir Troeven received another shock when he saw that
one of the two warriors was a woman, young and attrac-
tive. He got over his shock quickly enough when he saw
the woman reach out her hand toward the prince's helm,
as her male partner looked on.

Giving a shout to draw their attention, Sir Troeven dismounted and charged straight at them, yelling for all he
was worth and swinging his sword. They both looked at

him, their faces registering no particular concern at the formidable sight. The woman began to make odd circular motions with her hands, as though she were washing windows. Troeven aimed a slashing blow at the man.

His sword struck against what felt like a shield, though there was nothing between him and the warrior but dust. The sword bounced back, the blow jarring through Troeven's arm. By this time, the other knights were riding up around him, and the two dragon warriors, seeing themselves outnumbered, withdrew, vanishing into the grass so rapidly that one moment they were there and the next he could see no sign of them.

"Why did you let them go?" one of the knights demanded. "Why didn't you slay them?"

Troeven lifted his visor and scratched his grizzled chin. The sweat trickled down his face and neck, yet he felt chilled to the heart. He had only one thought now, and that was to keep his oath.

Kneeling awkwardly in his armor beside the prince, he managed to remove the prince's helm. Marcus's eyes were closed. Sweat beaded on his forehead and his upper lip. At the man's rough touch, Marcus moaned and turned his head.

Troeven smiled grimly. The prince might be grievously wounded—probably was, with a half-ton of horse on top of him. But he was alive, and it was Troeven's sworn duty to try to keep him that way.

"You knew they were there, Your Highness," he said to rally Marcus's spirits on the off chance he could hear him. "The good God knows how, but you saw them. And you charged right into them, to make us see, too. I've never beheld a braver deed, and so I'll tell your father to his beard. And I'll apologize to you, Your Highness, and beg your forgiveness on my bent knees, and I've never done that with any man. First, though, we have to get you out of here alive. And that may be no small matter."

He looked up to see the other knights had formed a cordon of horse and steel around the fallen prince. They were watching the enemy warriors with mounting amazement. In the heat of the action, they had not yet had a chance to take a good look at them.

The enemy, though not armed, was clad in armor that was strange in appearance. It was not plate armor, nor yet chain mail, such as the knights wore. The armor of these warriors was made of what looked to be shining scales that flowed like a second skin over their bodies and their limbs. And like a second skin, the armor appeared thin and fragile.

"And look at that," a knight exclaimed in disgust. "They have women in their ranks."

"Why don't they attack us? They have us outnumbered a hundred to one."

"Perhaps because they're not armed. Say 'boo' at them, and they'll all run away."

"Next time I will leave my blade at home and bring a wooden stick. That's all it would take to puncture that sorry excuse for armor."

"I'm not so sure," said Troeven sternly. "I hit something a good solid blow with my sword and didn't even make a dent."

Silence fell. The horses, skittish, blew and bared their teeth and flattened their ears. They moved restlessly beneath their riders, so that it was all some of the knights could do to keep them under control. The two knights who had been cut off from the main force were completely engulfed by the warriors. Yet, the warriors made no move to strike.

"The horses don't like them, that's for damn certain."

"Horses are smarter than men, sometimes."

The knight who had talked about the sharp stick snorted in derision and glanced back over his shoulder. "How's His Highness?"

"Alive," Troeven answered shortly.

He took stock of the situation. The Prince's Own surrounded him and His Highness. The enemy encircled them, and, beyond, the king's forces were falling all over each other. He could hear the shouts and curses of officers and the beating of drums and the clash and clatter of an army preparing to go suddenly to war. Close at hand, the battlefield was eerily quiet. No sounds of swords thwacking against each other or banging on armor or bashing in shields. No crunch and thud of battle. No panting, grunting, swearing, screaming. Only the buzz of grasshoppers and the rustle of the dry grass as the warriors gathered silently around them, watching, waiting.

"My Lord Summerson, help me get His Highness out from under his horse," said Troeven.

His voice boomed unnaturally loud in the stillness, causing several of the knights to flinch at the sound. Lord Summerson, a bear of a man, heaved and grunted himself off his horse and lumbered over to assist.

Panting and straining, Summerson managed to lift up the portion of the horse under which the prince was pinned. Troeven gripped the prince by the shoulders and pulled him free. Marcus moaned when the knight shifted him, and Troeven judged by this that the prince had broken bones, but this was no time to try to physic him. They'd have to take off his armor to see what was wrong with him, and he deemed that Marcus was far safer in his armor than out of it—a judgment call that the next few moments would prove horribly wrong.

One of the two knights who had been cut off from their comrades suddenly raised his voice in an oath.

"By my liver and lungs, I won't put up with this!"

The knight spurred his horse at one of the male warriors, intending to ride him down. The horse would have none of this, however. The animal reared up, throwing the knight heavily to the ground. Terrified, the horse galloped off.

"Mother of God! His hands!" a knight near Troeven gasped at almost the same moment. "Look at his hands!"

One of the enemy warriors stood near the fallen knight, but did not touch him. A soft warm glow spread from the tips of the warrior's fingers up his arms.

"God save us! Demons!" gasped one of the younger knights.

Another stirred in his saddle. "We should go to his aid—"

"No!" said Troeven. He could see the eyes of the enemy watching them closely. "Every man hold your position."

Shaken by his fall, the knight lay for a moment on the ground before coming to himself and the realization of his danger. Clumsy in his armor, he rolled about on his back like an upturned turtle, fumbling for the sword that had been knocked from his hand. The male warrior began to make motions with his red-glowing hands and pointed toward the dismounted knight.

The knight could not understand what was going on. Any other enemy would have leapt on him, helpless as he was on the ground, and run him through. He managed to regain his feet, sword in hand, and took a step forward, thinking, as he did so, how the heat of the day had markedly increased. He was baking inside his armor.

The knight started to sweat profusely. His armor—plate and chain—was growing hot to the touch. So hot that it began to burn his skin.

The metal began to glow red. The knight yelped in pain and flung down his sword and tried, frantically, to rip off pieces of the armor. He could smell his own seared flesh. Screaming in agony, he flung himself to the ground and thrashed about in a frenzy, shrieking for someone to help him, as his skin bubbled and blistered.

"He's being roasted!" his comrade cried in horror. "Roasted alive!"

They could all see and hear and smell that for themselves. Waves of heat, radiating off the armor, rippled the air. There were sizzling and popping sounds, as of meat being grilled in a skillet. The stench of burning flesh and hair caused more than one knight to cover his mouth with his hand or lean over his horse's flank, retching.

The second knight could stand it no longer. Sliding from his horse, he tried to break through the lines of warriors to reach his dying comrade. Another warrior held up red-glowing hands. The knight clutched at his own armor and fell to his knees, gasping as the metal began to grow hot to the touch. He tried desperately to undo the lacings and the fastenings that held the armor in place, though he knew quite well it was hopeless. He cast one silent, pleading glance toward his fellows.

"God is mercy! I'm not going to sit still and watch this!" cried a knight, and spurred his horse forward.

One of the enemy reached down to his belt and drew from a leather pouch what appeared to be a small, feathered dart.

An ordinary-looking dart, Prince Marcus had told them. *Such as you might see in any tavern game. The dart pierced a woman's throat. It was thrown from a distance of five, maybe six hundred paces.*

Troeven drew in a breath to shout a warning.

The warrior threw the dart.

The knight gave a cry, and his head jerked. He stiffened in the saddle, hung there a moment, and then toppled off the horse. He landed on his back not far from where Troeven was standing. The man's eyes stared at the heavens, where, presumably, his soul had sped. Between his eyes was a bloody, gaping hole. The dart had pierced the back of his helm, gouged its way through his brain, and exited out the front of his head.

Troeven let go his breath in a whistling sigh.

A veteran of many battles, Troeven had seen arms hacked off shoulders, hands sliced off wrists. He'd seen skulls cleaved in two—whole men cleaved in two, entrails spilling over the ground. Over the years, he'd become hardened, inured to the sights and the sounds and the smell of death. Or so he had thought.

This was different. This affected not only the mind, but the heart and the soul, turning them all inside out and wringing them.

The young knight who had spoken of demons slid off his horse and dropped to his knees. He began to pray fervently, his voice broken and anguished. No others followed his example, but several blessed themselves. All of them edged closer together.

These warriors were armed with the most powerful

weapon known to mankind—fear. They could have attacked en masse and probably slaughtered Troeven's small force in less time than it would take to speak of it. Such an attack would gain them nothing, however. Mere death. Whereas now, his knights were shaken and demoralized. White-faced beneath their visors, they cast terrified glances at the enemy and each other, wondering who was going to fall next. And, to make matters worse, the king's army was watching with all their eyes and listening with all their ears. Some of the footsoldiers—good, stout yeomen, but illiterate and superstitious—could hear the screams and the cry of "demons." They would see their knights, their commanders, their liege lords, being picked off one by one at the enemy's leisure. Dying on their knees. Unable to fight back. King Edward would see his son captured, or, worse, roasted in his own armor like a plucked goose at Yuletide.

"No, by my soul," Troeven swore to himself. "Damn your eyes, shut up!" he cried viciously to the knight, who was praying. "And get off your knees! God Himself would be ashamed of you. There'll be no miracles here unless we make them!"

His voice snapped whiplike, and the knight fell silent.

"We swore an oath to protect our prince," Troeven said, looking around the assembled knights, looking each man straight in the eyes. "And, by God, I intend to keep that oath. Are you with me?"

There were hesitant nods from some, curt nods from others. Here and there was a firm, "I am with you, my lord."

"Good," said Troeven grimly. "Now we must all make up our minds to one thing—none of us will leave this battlefield alive." He glanced out at the enemy, watching, waiting. "Give yourself to Death and you take away Death's hold over you."

He went on swiftly, not giving them time to think, "I need the lightest man among you."

Everyone looked to Sir Reynard, a knight who had just won his spurs in the last tourney, a young man of such slender build that one of his fellows had joked only this morning that he rattled around in his new armor like a dried bean in a kettle.

"I am the lightest, my lord," said Reynard. His courage was holding firm, even under this onslaught. "What is your need of me?"

"You will be responsible for the prince. Toss away your sword and shield. You won't have use for weapons. Your task is to ride for our lines. No matter what happens around you, you pay no attention. You ride. Do you understand?"

"I do, my lord," said the young man.

"Is your horse fast? If not, take mine."

"My horse is as swift as the stooping hawk, my lord," boasted Reynard proudly. "And he can bear the weight of two of us." He gave his sword, a family heirloom, into the keeping of a friend and rode his horse near Sir Troeven.

"Summerson, help me lift His Highness."

The two men lifted the prince by his shoulders and legs and heaved him onto the horse, slinging his body over the front of the saddle. The young knight took a firm grip on the prince with one hand and grasped hold of the reins with the other.

"The rest of you, fall in around His Highness," ordered Troeven, remounting his horse. "We will form a shield wall with our bodies. If one man falls, another rides up to take his place."

He had kept sight of the enemy out of the corner of his eye, seeing them taking in all of this. He wondered if they spoke the language, if they understood the commands he was giving. Not that it mattered. They would know soon enough what was at hand. The knights took their places, forming a solid wall of armored men riding in front of the prince, men riding behind, and flanking the prince on either side.

"God save our prince," Sir Troeven said in reverent tones, and every man repeated the prayer.

"God save our immortal souls," Troeven said.

Every man repeated that prayer. Every man's voice was firm.

Troeven raised up in the saddle and lifted his sword. He touched his spurs to his horse's flanks. The animal plunged ahead, and the knights rode after him.

The Prince's Own began their race against death.

34

STANDING ATOP THE RIDGELINE, KING EDWARD WATCHED the nightmare scenario he himself had predicted (but in which he'd never in his heart believed). Edward had watched in grief and (God forgive him) shame as his poor mad son had gone haring off down the hillside, riding wildly through the army encampment, and galloping out into an empty field, waving his sword at the grasshoppers. The king had turned away from the heart-wrenching sight and from the looks of pity and well-meaning banalities of his commanders, when suddenly he heard Wilhelm gasp.

Edward whipped around to see warriors springing up out of the tall grass. Again, God help him, Edward's first thought was triumphant vindication.

"My son was right!" he cried grimly. "He was right, by heaven!"

His joy at knowing his son was not insane was quickly quenched by the knowledge that if Marcus was right about everything, the king and his army were now facing a terrible foe. In the next instant, he saw Marcus's horse lurch sideways and fall to the ground, carrying Marcus down with him. Edward lost sight of his son in the tall grass.

The Prince's Own were there, however, shocked at the sight of the enemy springing up under their noses, yet keeping their heads, keeping their oaths to guard their prince.

Wilhelm began shouting commands. Men rode off with their orders and horns blared and drums rolled. Knights who had been asleep in their tents shouted for their squires and their servants. Groomsmen flung saddles and barding onto the horses, as squires sought to lace up armor with hands that shook, while the knights cursed them for being clumsy and slow and did more harm than good by trying to help. The camp was thrown into confusion, as the soldiers ran to try to see for themselves what was going on. No one paid heed to orders, and there was chaos as the officers charged in among the soldiers, using blows and curses to restore discipline.

Edward did not move. He kept his gaze focused on the Prince's Own, and he was cheered by the sight of the initial charge crashing up against the front ranks of the dragon warriors. He could not see clearly, but he could guess at the carnage caused by the war horses plowing into their ranks. One knight won through to where he'd seen Marcus's horse go down.

"Who is that?" Edward demanded. His eyes had lost some of their sharpness over the years and he could not make out the knight's device.

"Sir Troeven Hammersmith," said one of his knights.

"Ah, a good man," said Edward.

Sir Troeven dismounted and was lost to sight amid the tall grass. The Prince's Own closed ranks around the fallen, all except for two, who had been riding behind and found themselves cut off, surrounded by an enemy that had recovered from the shock of that initial charge with astonishing swiftness.

Edward could not see what was happening with Marcus, but he could picture the knight ascertaining if the prince was dead or alive and, if alive, making a hurried determination on how best to remove him from the field.

Edward expected swift action—either his own knights attacking the enemy or the enemy attacking them—and he was surprised and uneasy over what looked to be a stalemate. The knights sat their horses. The enemy held their position. Neither made a move. Wilhelm took out his spyglass—a gift from his father, and his pride and joy. The prince trained it on the enemy.

"What do you see?" Edward demanded impatiently. "What the devil's going on?"

"It is as Marcus told us, Father," said Wilhelm, and his voice held a note of wonder. "These strange warriors are not armed, and there are women fighting among their ranks."

At that moment, one of the two knights who had been cut off from the main body began his ill-fated charge into the enemy. They watched him fall from his horse.

Unfortunately, at about this time, order was restored in the camp. The foot soldiers were taking up their positions, with the officers' shouting for silence in the ranks. When the knight began to roast alive, his screams could be heard quite clearly. And so could the cry of "demons."

"God save us!" Wilhelm breathed, shaken, and he handed the glass to his father.

Edward put it to his eye. His vision was not as clear as his son's, and he had some trouble focusing. The eerie red glow emanating from the hands of one of the warriors was easy to spot, however. And then the next knight fell.

"But how are they killing them?" Wilhelm cried angrily. "They are not armed! Father, you don't believe they are demons—"

"No," said Edward grimly, handing back the glass. "They are men like us. Or rather, not like us. They are like your brother. The blood of dragons runs in their veins."

"You believe in that and I believe in it," Wilhelm said, though he didn't sound quite as confident as he pretended. "But no one else will."

Edward looked at the ranks of foot soldiers lined up, waiting the call to battle, and sighed deeply.

"Those are brave men down there, Father," Wilhelm added, "stout and true. But how will they cope with a foe who fights with fire and brimstone?"

Abruptly Edward handed back the glass. "I can't see a damn thing with that contraption. I'm going down there—"

"Father, wait!" Wilhelm clasped hold of Edward's arm, as the king started to spur his horse. "Look! The knights have Marcus. They're bringing him out!"

"That will be my lord Troeven's doing," remarked one of the barons. "He's afraid of nothing this side of heaven *or* hell."

"God speed them and protect them," Edward prayed softly. "And protect my son."

The young knight, Sir Reynard, had a firm hold on the prince, holding him with a grip strong as death. Grasping the reins tightly, he rode with his body hunched over the prince's body, thus further protecting His Highness and making himself less a target.

The young knight rode hard. They all rode hard. The horses' flanks were bloody from the spurs raking their flesh. The knights had to keep their mounts under control, however, for—bunched close as they were—a horse stumbling or bolting would mean disaster.

Aware of the honor given him and the trust put in him, Reynard put aside the fear of death and, worse, his fear of demons dragging his soul down to hell, and concentrated on his duty. Reynard was quite certain that these were demons pursuing them, demons surrounding them, demons hurling the fire of hell at them. He gave his soul into God's keeping and, though he did not quite give himself to Death, as Sir Troeven had ordered—for it is hard, at eighteen, to think that tomorrow's bright and beautiful dawn might not come—he kept fear at bay by concentrating on his goal: the line of his own forces that he could see waiting for them.

Reynard prayed a simple prayer. "God, don't let me fall off the horse!"

The demon warriors had no intention of letting them escape. Whereas before they had held their fire, "hoping to see us piss our pants," one of Reynard's companions had muttered, the demons launched an assault. They flowed alongside the galloping horses like a stream of sparkling water, their scaled armor glittering in the sunlight. Small and deadly darts whizzed among the knights like hideous hornets.

Some of the darts went astray or clattered harmlessly off the steel plate, for the knights were a moving target now. Others found their mark. A knight riding in the vanguard alongside Sir Troeven suddenly slumped forward over his horse's neck, and then slipped off his saddle. No one stopped to see if he was dead or alive. The horses charging after him rode right over him. His own horse kept going, a wild and panicked look in its eyes. Immediately, another knight galloped up to take his place, plug the gap in the lines.

A cloud of fire erupted on Reynard's right flank, frightening the horse of the knight riding closest to the demons and sending his horse plunging into the horse of the knight riding beside him. Both horses foundered and went down, taking their knights with them. Reynard, glancing back, saw the demons standing over the knights. He heard agonized screams, and a horrid taste fill the young knight's mouth. He wrenched his head around and faced forward, back to his destination.

It seemed a long, long way off.

Another knight fell in the vanguard, and another moved up to take his place. A concussive blast behind Reynard nearly knocked him from his mount. A wave of heat rolled across him, and the death screams of horses and of men sounded almost in his ear. He couldn't think about that, for he was engaged in a panicked struggle to keep hold of the prince and maintain his seat in his saddle and urge his horse forward. By some miracle, he managed all three, and then the body of the knight riding directly in front of him exploded.

A rainstorm of blood and gore hit Reynard in the face. He was pelted with fragments of armor and bone and flesh. Sir Reynard wiped the blood from his eyes and kept riding.

Darts flew in among the knights, thinning their ranks. The giant Lord Summerson had been hit four times. He held his position in line, riding stalwartly, though the blood flowed from his wounds in rivulets down his armor. Reynard glanced away for an instant, and when he looked back, Lord Summerson was gone. The next moment his gigantic horse fell, pierced by almost as many darts as its rider.

Fewer and fewer knights were left to guard Reynard and the prince. One of the darts, its momentum spent, glanced off his helm. Pain burst in his left shoulder and he looked down to see wicked black feathers protruding from his breastplate. He gritted his teeth and hunkered down over his prince and rode on.

Reynard no longer paid attention to men falling around him. He looked neither to the right nor the left. He kept sight of the king's standard and never took his eyes from it as it crawled closer and closer.

A voice was shouting at him, thundering at him. It had been shouting at him for some time, and only now did it start to seep into his brain that the voice was yelling at him. Reynard turned his head, blinking through the mask of blood that gummed his eyes and through the pain that was so much a part of him he could not tell which part.

Riding alongside him was Sir Troeven.

Only Sir Troeven. Reynard glanced around. The others were gone.

Of thirty men of the Prince's Own who had started, only two were left.

"Ride, man!" Troeven had his visor up and was bellowing. "Put your spurs to your horse and ride!"

A dart struck the commander in the eye. His face was no longer a face. It was a bloody mass of bone and teeth and jelly. Troeven sagged on his horse and then, dragging on the reins, he turned the beast around and rode straight back into the ranks of demon warriors.

Reynard did not look to see what was happening. Another dart thudded into him. He gasped and coughed and spit out the blood that dribbled from his mouth and rode.

The king's knights galloped out to meet the Prince's Own. Some had no time to put on their armor, but had flung on helms and grabbed up sword or spear to go riding to the rescue.

The soldiers in the ranks had been cheering the Prince's Own as though they were at a horse race or tourney. When, one by one, the knights fell, the cheers became more sporadic, then dwindled out altogether, and by the time the knights swept up the lone survivor of the Prince's Own and carried him out of harm's way, a dread silence had fallen over the ranks of the king's army.

The dragon warriors ceased their pursuit and drew back among the tall grass. They left behind the dead. The bodies of twenty-nine knights formed an almost straight line leading from the field of grass to the last body, riddled with darts.

Sir Troeven lay with his shattered face turned up to the heavens. No demon would have his soul or the souls of any others of the Prince's Own. They had kept their oath and God would gather them home.

They carried Prince Marcus off the field on a litter, bearing him up the ridge to where his father waited. They brought with them, as well, the young knight Sir Reynard. Marcus had groaned when they had lifted him off the horse, which they took for a hopeful sign. As for Reynard, he was dying, and there was nothing they could do for him except see to it that he was granted the honor he deserved. Acting on Edward's command, six knights bore the mortally wounded young knight to his final audience with his sovereign. They lowered the litter bearing Reynard to a place of honor—beside that of the prince for whom he'd given his life.

The full extent of Marcus's injuries would not be known until they could remove his armor, but Edward felt his son's pulse and found it strong. His armor had not been pierced by any of the heinous darts. The only damage the armor had suffered was to the left shoulder, which was dented and bashed, probably from the fall off his horse. Those who were expert in such injuries theorized broken bones, maybe a dislocated shoulder, and a bump on the head. Nothing worse. Marcus kept repeating a dark litany, crying over and over, "Death above, death behind . . ."

Once Edward had assured himself that his son was not

critically wounded, the king turned his attention to the young man who had given his life for that of his prince.

They had removed Reynard's visor, and Edward was touched to the heart to see how youthful was the pallid face that looked calmly into his. Reynard tried to speak, but a great gout of blood came out of his mouth and he could not manage the words.

Edward knew what he wanted so desperately to ask.

"His Highness is alive," the king said, taking hold of the dying knight's hand. "Thanks be to God and to you and the others, he has taken no grievous wound."

A smile flickered on the ashen, blood-stained lips and then Reynard grimaced, his body shuddered. He gave a little gasp. The hand Edward was holding, already cold, went limp.

The king placed the young man's hand over his bloody breast and closed the staring eyes.

"Father," said Wilhelm quietly. "There is trouble."

"The enemy is attacking?" Edward asked wearily. He felt suddenly tired and old.

"No," said Wilhelm grimly. "I wish they were. The enemy has vanished."

Edward stared out across the grassy field and saw nothing. No sign of the warriors who, only moments before, had been flinging deadly darts and spewing fire from their fingertips. He saw the wind ripple the grass and the sun shimmering off the armor of the dead knights. And he could hear, like a buzzing of locusts, terror spread among his troops.

"How clever," he said softly. "How damnably clever!"

He could imagine what his men were saying to each other.

"The demons could be anywhere. They could be sneaking through the grass right this very moment!"

"Or slipping up behind us to slit our throats . . ."

"Or light us on fire, same as they did the knights."

"How can you fight an army you can't see?"

"How can you fight an army sent by the devil?"

Fear was contagious. His own knights were nervous

and uneasy. Some drew their swords. Others peered over their shoulders. It took all Edward's resolve not to do the same. He, too, could feel the prickles at the back of his neck, and he couldn't help but picture one of those fell warriors sneaking up behind him.

"We're going to start losing men," said Wilhelm. "There!" He pointed to a group of soldiers who had thrown down their weapons and were running for their lives into the forest. Officers threatened and cursed, but they didn't sound very confident themselves.

A presence at his elbow made Edward start.

"Sire," said a young lad, "your son asks to speak to you."

Edward hastened over to where men were lifting Marcus onto a wagon, preparatory to transporting him back to his brother's castle. Marcus lay on the litter, half in and half out of his mangled armor. His eyes were open and clear, though shadowed by pain.

"He insisted on talking to you, Your Majesty. Wouldn't budge otherwise."

"My son," said Edward, with a smile, "I am glad—"

Marcus interrupted him. "You have to pull back, Father!" he said, white-faced. "Retreat! You can't fight what's coming!"

Edward bent over his son and clasped his hand. Edward had made the mistake of not trusting Marcus once. He would not do so again.

"What *is* coming, Son?" he asked.

It was at that moment someone spotted the dragon.

"Death from above," answered Marcus.

Maristara soared above the treetops, coming from the north, from Dragonkeep. She flew swiftly and with deadly purpose, her neck outstretched, her eyes glaring down, her huge body and vast wingspan obliterating the sun. Leaving the clouds, she dove down on them. Her breath spewed fire as she came, setting the marshlands ablaze and showing the humans, who cowered at the sight of her, the sort of death they would die.

The king's crumbling army disintegrated. The commanders had no hope of maintaining control. Some, keeping their heads, tried to prevent a rout, while others were first to head for the rear. The cry was every man for himself, and every man made a dash for it, pushing and shoving and sometimes knifing his fellows in order to clear a path that would save him from the terror swooping down on him. The sight of "demon" warriors had unnerved them. The sight of the dragon unmanned them.

The only company to hold its ground was the archers. Led by a man of stubborn disposition who believed in neither God nor the devil (and who was worshiped and feared by his men more than either of the other two), the archers stood fast even as the dragon bore down on them. They had their arrows nocked and ready and, at the command, the archers fired.

The sky was black with arrows flying, hissing, at their target.

Six of the female dragon warriors appeared, parting the veil of magic, their scaled armor bright in the sunlight. Each woman made a graceful gesture with her hands, as though she were sending forth a flight of birds. The shafts of the arrows burst into flame and were instantly consumed, tailing downward in thin spirals of smoke. The arrowheads melted and plopped in leaden drops onto the grass. The women bowed low, as the dragon passed overhead. And then they disappeared back into the illusion.

The archers flung down their bows. They trampled each other in their mad panic. But they had lost precious time standing up to the dragon, and she was swift to exact punishment. Flying over them, Maristara sprayed them with fire, setting their clothes and hair ablaze. The hapless victims flailed and thrashed about on the ground or spread the flames as they ran screaming, trying mindlessly to escape the blaze that was consuming them. Most of these dropped dead in their tracks. Others were knocked to the ground by their comrades in a desperate attempt to save them, though to no avail. The flames were insidious, burning through leather armor and clothes and flesh, burning up bone and sinew and muscle, reducing men to piles of greasy ashes.

Marcus lay in the wagon, helpless, unable to move without shards of pain splintering his body. He had dislocated his left shoulder in his fall, and he was fairly certain, by the sharp pain and horrible grinding sounds, that he had several broken bones. There was no way to tell how severe were the wounds he'd suffered until they could get him out of his armor, and it was so dented and mangled that it would probably take a blacksmith and his tools to pry it off him.

A whirlwind of confusion fed by terror swirled around him. Knights and officers were either jumping onto their horses to make good their own escape or they were standing practically on top of the king, shouting into his face, so that Edward must have been hard-pressed to hear himself think. Marcus could not take his eyes from the dragon, from the terrible, deadly beauty of Maristara.

The dragon set fire to the woods atop the ridgeline. Stands of pines and groves of oak and maple burst into flame. Fire crackled not far from the wagon holding Marcus. Smoke billowed, poisoning the air.

The dragon was forced to pull up to avoid crashing into the trees. She soared back into the sky and then made a slow, looping turn, preparing to dive down for another pass.

Edward refused to flee. Angry and defiant, he made the argument that they should stand and fight, pointing out— quite logically—that there was nowhere to run that the dragon could not catch them, no cover that she could not burn to the ground. Some of his knights, who had the example of the courage of the Prince's Own shining before them, sided with their king. They had no intention of being found dead with their backs to the foe. Others, Prince Wilhelm among them, insisted that the kingdom needed their king and its knights alive during this crisis. A heroic death benefited only the minstrels who would later make money singing of it.

The argument was interrupted by men shouting in dismay and pointing.

Another dragon appeared in the sky, flying high above Maristara. This dragon's scales flashed red in the sunlight, which was rapidly being obscured by the smoke rising from the crackling forest fire.

A voice spoke to Marcus, calm and cold inside his head. "Get your father the hell out of here!"

Though the movement cost him agony, jarring his bones and nearly causing him to pass out, Marcus gripped his father's arm.

"Father," Marcus gasped. "That's Draconas!"

"Draconas!" Edward repeated, stunned. He stared up into the sky, shielding his eyes from the sun's glare with his hand to see.

Intent on her sport, Maristara paid no attention to anything else. She swooped down on the humans, driving them before her. She enjoyed watching the panicked little creatures skitter hither and yon in a frantic and futile effort to escape death.

Draconas dropped onto Maristara like a falcon stooping on a pigeon, his front legs extended, his wings high.

At the last moment Maristara was aware of him, warned by the dragon warriors below, who had seen him appear at about the same time as Marcus. She was flying too fast to stop her downward momentum, but she did manage to twist her body so that his sharp claws could not gain purchase. Draconas struck Maristara hard, however, catching her between her shoulder blades, knocking her off balance and forcing her to cease her chase of the humans to save herself from crashing headlong into the ground.

"This is our chance, Father!" Marcus urged. "That's what Draconas is doing! Offering us a chance to escape."

Edward was quick to see the logic in this, and he was not one to give up his life when there was no need. He gave the order to ride and, casting one more glance above at the astonishing sight of dragon fighting dragon, he spurred his horse. The man driving the wagon, who had been waiting impatiently for just such a command, shouted at the horses and slapped the reins on their backs. Already nervous from the fire and the dragons, the horses were only too glad to flee and took off at top speed. The wagon jolted and jounced over dirt clods and ruts in the road.

The royal party rode in orderly retreat, racing for the sheltering walls of Aston Castle. When they came upon fleeing soldiers, they called on them to join them there.

The jouncing ride in the wagon seemed to jolt Marcus apart, but he fought off the pain and clung to consciousness, watching in awe and almost unbearable tension the battle raging in the skies above him.

Like a cat twisting in midair, Maristara recovered, barely avoiding smashing into the trees. She clawed her way, snarling, wings flapping, to do battle with this new and unexpected foe.

After his missed attack, Draconas spiraled upward, regaining the heights, seeking advantage. Maristara, heavier and older, turned, lumbering, to face him.

"Stop!" Marcus cried to the driver of the wagon. "I have to watch this!"

"Do as he says," Edward commanded. "The rest of you, ride on!"

Reining in his horse beside the wagon carrying his son, Edward looked into the sky. Some of his knights remained with him, fascinated by a sight that few humans had ever seen. The two dragons hung in the air, wings barely moving, each one's eyes fixed on the foe, engaged in a battle that was as much mental as it was physical.

Inside the little room, Marcus opened the door a crack, peering into the minds of both. If they even noticed he was there, neither could afford to pay him any mind. Neither dared turn away from the other for even a split second.

The minds of both were gray, shifting and rolling like thick fog, so that nothing tangible could be seen. Suddenly, Maristara hurled a lance of flaring orange that sliced through the gray, fog-bound mind of Draconas, boring its way into the depths of his brain. At the same moment Maristara flew at him, streaking through the air, her jaws gaping wide, her claws outstretched.

Draconas had to defend himself on two fronts simultaneously—within and without. He flung up an iron-black shield to block the mental missile and went into a steep dive.

The missile burst on the black shield. He had saved himself from death, but only barely. If the missile had found its target, it would have exploded in his brain with mind-shattering force, knocking him unconscious and causing him to plummet from the skies. As it was, he lost control of his dive for half a moment and tumbled downward, his bellowing cry of pain echoing off the ridgeline. He pulled himself out of the fall, dazed and disoriented, his mind blotchy and swirling.

Maristara dove down to finish him off.

Marcus held his breath and clamped his own brain down on the urge to shout a warning, for he could see, boiling beneath the ugly miasma on the surface, the colors of Draconas's mind, sharp-edged and clear and cold. The dragon's seemingly confused flailings had, in reality, been bringing him nearer and nearer the elder dragon. Now underneath her, presumably defenseless, Draconas did a twisting roll that carried him out from under her slashing claws. Emerging, he flipped head over tail and then launched himself straight as a spear at Maristara.

The move caught the elder dragon completely by surprise. She had no time to evade his attack. Draconas lowered his head, so that the spikes of his mane became a battering ram. Like a ship ramming its foe, he struck Maristara on her flank.

The shock of the impact sent both dragons reeling. Draconas drew blood from his enemy and knocked her halfway across heaven, but he did not sink her. Maristara was tough and she was clever and she had fought her own kind before, something Draconas—a relatively young dragon—had not.

She was also hurt. He'd done damage to her, and though she wanted with all her being to continue the fight and destroy this dragon, she could not afford the luxury.

Damn that lizard Grald. If he hadn't gotten himself killed, she could have indulged her hatred and finished off the Walker. If she died, however, there was no one to lead her forces against the humans except Anora, who had her own important task to perform. Besides, quite frankly, Maristara didn't trust Anora. Maristara never trusted anyone.

She had sky enough left to her that she could free-fall some distance, and, keeping one eye on Draconas, she drifted back toward the river and Dragonkeep beyond. She could afford to retreat, return to the safety of Grald's lair and heal her wounds. She might have worried about leaving her army vulnerable to attack, but she knew Draconas, knew his weakness.

Draconas was injured, more badly than he'd first realized in the heat of battle, and like Maristara, he had humans who were dependent on him, the irony of which did not escape him.

Because of humans, the dragons had to stop trying to kill each other. Because of humans, they'd started. Both dragons limped away, each knowing that the battle between them was not ended, merely postponed.

"Where is he going?" Edward cried. "Kill them, Draconas! Kill the dragon warriors. Breathe fire on them! Do to them what they did to us! Marcus, talk to him."

Draconas let his colors go gray.

"You have to kill them!" Marcus urged the dragon. "You saw what they did! You know what they can do to us!"

"The laws of dragonkind forbid me to kill humans," Draconas replied.

"A law only you obey!" Marcus retorted.

"Maybe so. Maybe I am the only one. Maybe I will be the last. I hope not. Killing humans is too easy for us . . ."

"And the time will come when killing dragons is easy for us!" Marcus said angrily.

"That is what we fear, Marcus," said Draconas. "Don't you understand that yet? That is what we fear."

35

IN THE GRAY TWILIGHT OF EARLY MORNING, THE HIGH priestess of Seth walked the path that led to the Chamber of the Watchful Eye to perform the Rite of Seeing. And though she walked the path alone—for no other except the High Priestess could perform this ritual—it seemed to her that she was being watched by the ghostly eyes of all those who had walked this path before her, and that those eyes were dark with foreboding.

Most of the others were shadowy figures, seen only in her imagination, as she'd heard stories of them from childhood on. One, however, was real to her and close—Melisande, the High Priestess who had come before her, the High Priestess who, some seventeen years before, had disgraced her calling and ran off with a male lover, leaving behind Seth and her responsibilities and duties. Anna had never been close to Melisande—the twelve-year-old girl had always been too much in awe of the High Priestess to dare to even speak to her. Melisande had spoken to her sometimes, though, and always smiled at her kindly whenever they met. Anna had admired Melisande and idolized her. Her fall had devastated Anna. She had refused to believe the terrible story, as it was told to them by Lucretta, the new Mistress of Dragons.

Anna had gone so far as to openly voice her disbelief—not to the Mistress, of course, but to the other sisters. Anna had even ventured to plead Melisande's cause with Bellona, the commander of the warrior women who guarded the monastery and who was tasked with the assignment of tracking down Melisande and either dragging her back to stand trial or killing her. Bellona had struck the girl across the face, knocking her to the ground, and then walked off. Anna had seen the terrible pain in the eyes of the warrior woman, who had been Melisande's lover. The girl had crept away to her cell to weep her bitter tears in solitude. After that, Anna never again spoke Melisande's name, though she kept it in her heart.

Bellona had gone, disappearing into the night while trying to track down Melisande. Gone to be with her, the Mistress had told them disparagingly. Both of them traitors. There were stories from the other warrior women about how Bellona's arrows fired at Melisande had always missed their mark—something strange, considering that Bellona's arrows had never missed before. The warrior women set out to find both of them, and one day they returned with the story that they had located Bellona and Melisande and killed them.

They had not brought back the bodies, however, claiming that they did not deserve the honor of being buried in the homeland both had disgraced. Perhaps because of this or perhaps because the warrior women never spoke about that battle and always looked some other direction whenever anyone brought it up, Anna was convinced they were lying. And she made up a fancy in her heart, a fancy that Bellona and Melisande were alive and together somewhere and that they were happy.

That's why the eyes troubled Anna so much. She felt the eyes of Melisande upon her as she walked the path that led to the Chamber. It was a feeling, not a seeing. She did not see the ghost. She felt her, felt her concern. She had never experienced this sensation before. She had been High Priestess for a year now, ever since the previous High Priestess had fallen victim to a cancerous growth. She had walked this path every morning for a year, and it was only in the last week or so that she had become aware of the ghosts.

She did not mention the ghosts to any of the other sisters. She knew what they would say—that it was all her imagination. That she was afraid because the Mistress of Dragons was gone—an event that was unprecedented in the lives of the people of Seth. The Mistress was gone, and her parting words to Anna had been more than enough to stir up any number of dread apparitions.

"I do not leave of my own choosing," the Mistress told Anna, and her tone was one of sorrow mingled with anger. "I leave out of necessity. For the first time in many hundreds of years, our kingdom faces a threat that we cannot fight alone. I must seek the aid of an ally, our sister kingdom."

Anna was amazed. "Sister kingdom? Mistress, forgive my ignorance, but I never knew—"

"None in Seth know of it. And none would know of it now, if events in the harsh world beyond our mountains had not forced me to seek help."

The High Priestess was helping the Mistress pack for her journey, carefully folding the ceremonial robe, which she would not wear during her journey, for fear of spoiling it. Anna remembered the feel of the rich, soft woollen cloth beneath her hands as she pressed the garment into the leather scrip the Mistress would carry with her on horseback. The Mistress was preoccupied and little interested in the packing. She paced the room, beating the heels of her palms together in an absent manner, lost in thought. Occasionally she cast a sharp glance at Anna, as if taking her measure, but she did not speak.

When Anna finished, she turned to see the Mistress staring out the window. Anna received the impression that in spirit, the Mistress was already far away.

"The packing is complete, Mistress," Anna said to her. "By your leave, I will go make certain that your escort is in readiness—"

"There will be no escort," the Mistress said sharply. "I travel alone."

Anna had never before questioned any of the Mistress's decisions, but now she could not help it. "Mistress, do you think that is wise?"

"Are you implying I act foolishly?" the Mistress responded. She did not turn, but continued to gaze out the window.

"Forgive me, Mistress, I meant no disrespect," Anna replied. "If, as you say, there is danger beyond our valley, then you should have an escort that is armed and prepared to defend you. Please, let me inform the guard—"

The Mistress's tone softened. "It is I who should ask your forgiveness, Daughter. I did not mean to snap at you. I am worried, that is all. Worried and afraid. Not for myself," she was quick to add. "But for my people. I must travel swiftly and in secret, so as not to alert the enemy to the fact that I have left Seth. An escort would only slow me down and draw unwanted attention. Besides, the fewer who know I have left, the better. Tell no one that I have gone. Keep up the pretense that I am here."

"I understand, Mistress," Anna said, though she was troubled. She was not very good at keeping secrets, and she wondered how she would manage.

Her next question had been innocent enough, or so she had thought, but it had brought a startling response, one that had kept this conversation going round and round in Anna's mind since that day.

"Don't you think you should at least remove the golden locket you wear, Mistress?"

The Mistress's hand went to her throat to where the locket rested in the hollow of her neck. She grasped hold of it possessively, almost covetously, and turned to face Anna with a suddenness that startled her.

"What do you mean by that remark?" the Mistress demanded, advancing a step toward her. "Why do you tell me to take off the locket?"

"I meant nothing, Mistress!" Anna gasped, alarmed by the woman's intensity. "Only that thieves might see the glint of gold and be tempted—"

The Mistress stared at her for a moment more. Then, with a sigh, the Mistress waved her hand in what seemed weary dismissal.

"Go back to your duties, Daughter. Remain alert. Keep careful watch. I fear the dragons may choose this time to attack us. The fate of our kingdom rests with you. You have trained all your life for this moment, High Priestess," the Mistress added, seeing Anna's expression of dismay. "You and the sisters will keep the dragons at bay. I have full confidence in you."

The Mistress must have departed shortly after that, for when Anna had occasion to return to the Mistress's quarters, the Mistress was not there, and the scrip containing her clothes was gone.

Anna had gone about her duties as she had been ordered. The strain of protecting her people and keeping up the lie that the Mistress was still among them was starting to tell on her, though. She lay awake half the night, and when at last, exhausted, she fell asleep, she woke in terror, trembling, dreaming of dragons. Her lack of appetite caused such comment among the other sisters that she was afraid they would suspect something. She began to force herself to choke down her food, though it made little difference. She was almost always sick to her stomach afterward.

Perhaps the ghosts she saw along her path were due to lack of sleep and lack of sustenance. As she walked, treading on the flagstones in the very footsteps of Melisande and all the others who now surrounded her, Anna shivered in the predawn chill and hugged her cloak more closely about her. She had once looked forward to the morning ritual that marked her standing as High Priestess. Now, she dreaded it, for each new day might be the day she would see the dragons coming to attack her people. Perhaps that was why the ghost of Melisande and the others seemed to cluster more closely around her this day than they had others. This was the day the dragons would come.

Her stomach clenched, and Anna feared she was going to be sick. She must not desecrate the sacred stones of the path. The thought so alarmed her that she forced herself to stop thinking of ghosts. Emerging from the shadows of the fir trees that guarded the path, she realized that she was late. The stars were fading and dawn was already pink and yellow on the horizon. She quickened her pace.

Rounding a coppice of pine, she could see the black marble columns of the Chamber, which stood outside the monastery walls, on a promontory overlooking the valley and the city below.

The columns were guardians to the one object inside the small temple. Anna hurried up the marble stairs and reverently approached the large, white marble bowl. Only when she reached it did she remember, stricken, that she had forgotten to remove her shoes. Swiftly she kicked off the sandals and, grabbing them up, flung them out beyond the columns.

She knelt down beside the bowl and took a moment to try to compose herself. That proved impossible. Anna trembled more. She poured the holy water from the pitcher that stood beside the bowl with a hand that shook so she splashed water onto her gown. Yet another infraction.

Anna forced herself to concentrate. She gazed steadily into the water, into the lapis lazuli iris of the sacred Eye at the bottom of the bowl, into the jet pupil of that all-seeing Eye, and waited for the water to cease sloshing about. Watching the water calmed her and when the last ripple smoothed from the surface, Anna spoke the ritual prayer that she said every morning, the same prayer that Melisande had said every morning, that every High Priestess before her had said every morning in a confident and even tone.

"Open wide, you that guard our realm, and let my eye see what you see."

The Eye showed her what she always saw: the valley, the mountains, the city, the monastery of the Order of the Sacred Eye. She took it all in and breathed out a sigh of relief, only to snatch it back swiftly in a gasp that was as much bewilderment as it was astonishment.

The High Priestess of Seth did not see what she had feared and dreaded and expected to see. The Eye did not show her dragons flying toward her kingdom, bent on attacking and destroying them.

The Eye showed her a young man.

Anna rubbed her eyes and blinked and stared, wondering how the sacred Eye could have made such a mistake.

The young man came from the river. He climbed over the mountains. He walked across the valley. He was a comely young man—about sixteen, perhaps, with blond hair and blue eyes that looked straight into hers.

Anna was puzzled and confused, and then she noticed something strange, grotesque. The young man had the legs of a beast. The legs, more specifically, of a dragon.

Anna did not know what to do. Was this half-man/half-dragon a threat? It must be so, or the Eye would not have revealed him to her. Yet, how could one young man, beast-man though he was, be a threat to an entire kingdom?

Then she saw that there were more like him, coming up behind him, crossing the river and climbing the mountain: a young woman with the body of a dragon and delicate wings sprouting from her shoulders; a boy, strong and muscular, his human form covered all over with scales; and little ones with claws for feet or hands, and scaly arms and tails, yet all with human eyes that gazed, unblinking, into hers.

The young man was quite close now, and Anna realized, with a start, that he could see her as clearly as she could see him. His face, especially the eyes, was familiar to her. She had the feeling she'd known him a long time.

Anna gripped the sides of the marble basin to keep herself from sinking down into a heap on the marble floor.

"Who are you?" she cried.

In his answer, though she did not understand it and did not, at first, believe it, Anna heard what would prove to be the destruction of the peaceful tranquillity of the people of Seth.

"We are your children."

36

"OUR CASTLE AT RAMSGATE IS THE TARGET, FATHER."
Marcus spoke in gasps, keeping his sentences short. He
had broken ribs, which made the drawing of each breath
an agonizing experience. "More to the point, the cannons. We have to ride back there at once."

Prince Wilhelm's physicians would have doused Marcus with poppy syrup to ease the pain, but he needed to be
clear-headed, at least until he had convinced his father of
the danger. He had already lost a night, for he had passed
out from the pain when the physicians wrenched his dislocated shoulder into place. They'd given him the poppy
syrup when he regained consciousness and refused to let
him speak to anyone until he'd rested.

Even drugged, he'd spent a restless night, slipping into
and out of strange dreams. In one, experienced just before
waking, it seemed to him that a gigantic eye was staring
down at him. He might have thought it a dragon's eye and
been afraid, but he felt the watcher's awe and wonder,
sorrow and dismay. When Marcus woke, he insisted on
talking to his father, refusing to take any more physics or
even let the leeches into his room until his command was
obeyed.

"Those dragons could destroy the cannons with ease,"
Edward remarked. "Why don't the beasts attack the castle?"

Marcus heard the note of respect in his father's voice, and that warmed him more than the poppy syrup. His only deep regret was that the lives of thirty good men had been sacrificed in order to gain it. Marcus had taken a solemn vow, with his hand on the Holy Scriptures, that if he survived this battle, he would build a chapel and dedicate it in their honor, as well as form a new order of knights in their memory, an order that would be known as the Lions of God.

"I don't know the answer, Father, and neither does Draconas. He believes, however, that this attack was a feint, a ruse, to draw us away from Ramsgate," Marcus said. "Draconas thinks the dragons have something more devious in mind." That long speech cost him two pain-filled gasps.

Edward frowned at the mention of Draconas, but he could hardly say anything disparaging, since the dragon had been responsible for the fact that the king's army had not been utterly wiped out.

"Where is Draconas?" he asked.

"Keeping watch over the movements of the dragon army."

Edward rose abruptly to pace the room. "He could destroy them with a breath."

"Father . . ."

"Oh, I know what you told me about him. How he will not kill humans in cold blood," Edward said impatiently. "I suppose I must honor him for his stand, but it is damn hard on us!"

Marcus tried to raise himself off the pillows. "Father—"

Edward saw what he was about to do and hastened to his side. "You must not move, Marcus. You'll undo all the work that the leeches did for you. Lie back and rest easy. I agree with you and with Draconas. I will ride to Ramsgate with all haste. I'll leave this day."

Marcus propped himself up on his good elbow. "I'm coming with you," he said through teeth clenched against the pain.

Edward looked down on him with affection and some amusement. "My son, you cannot even sit up in bed, much less ride a horse."

"Then fill a wagon with straw and haul me back like a sack of wool," said Marcus. "You need me, Father! I may not be able to lift a sword, but I have another weapon—the magic."

Edward said nothing. He glanced away from his son and looked out the window. Marcus saw a nerve twitch in his father's jaw, saw his face go dark and closed, as it always did whenever Marcus brought up his magic. In the past, Marcus would have let this ugly subject drop, let it fall to the floor, then kick it into a corner, so that both could pretend it wasn't there. Now Marcus held fast to it, held it up so that his father had to look.

"When I was a child, you locked me away in that little room and hid me from sight and made up a story that I was off visiting relatives. I know that was for my own good," he added, speaking in gasps and fits and starts, but never thinking of stopping. "But it was for *your* own good, as well, Father, because you didn't have to face the truth about me. And when I came back with Draconas, with the magic so bright and beautiful in my hands, you forbade me to use it. You made me feel that it was something of which I should be ashamed. Even Mother, though she loves me dearly, wishes it would all just go away . . ."

Marcus had to pause. Sweat rolled down his face, and he bunched the sheets up in a great wad beneath the blanket in order to keep the pain at bay as he plunged ahead.

"Father, if I can use my gift openly, to save the kingdom, so that all the people can see it, then you and mother will never have to be ashamed of me again."

His strength gave out. He fell back among the pillows. Edward remained standing in silence, his face averted, so that his son could not guess what his father was thinking. Edward had his hands clasped behind him, and the fingers clenched and opened and clenched. He glanced back at Marcus and then walked out of the room.

Marcus would have sighed in bitter disappointment, but it hurt too much. Outside the room he could hear raised voices, among them his father's. Marcus assumed the king was giving orders for the knights and what was left of his army to return to Ramsgate, though it did sound as though someone was daring to argue with the king. His father's voice grew cold with anger, and that ended that. There was silence.

Marcus's shoulder throbbed. Every breath hurt. Add to that the pain in his heart, that no amount of poppy syrup could ease, unless he took enough to ease him out of this life. Realizing he was thirsty, he was eyeing the water pitcher and thinking in frustration that he would have to summon a servant just to fetch him a drink, when the door opened and the court physician entered, accompanied by several assistants bearing rolls of linen bandages.

They all bowed to the prince, then continued a conversation started before they had entered the chamber.

"We will bind His Highness's arm tightly to his side," the leech was saying, the wide, full sleeves of the gown that marked his office billowing around him importantly as he walked. "And wrap the bandages tight around the rib cage. That *might* keep His Highness from puncturing a lung," the physician added with a sniff that indicated he'd be shocked if it did.

"What's going on?" Marcus demanded.

"We're making you ready to travel, Your Highness," said the physician, his mouth pursed and his face pinched. "His Majesty's command. Against *my* advice." He sniffed again. "If this journey kills you, Your Highness, don't blame me!"

"I won't," Marcus promised, jubilant.

They filled a wagon with straw, hoping to cushion the journey for Marcus as much as possible. The roads were rough. He would be bounced and jolted unmercifully. To protect him, the physician wrapped Marcus in so many layers of bandages that they would have probably stopped an arrow better than plate armor. The leech handed him a cup filled with a honey posset, liberally spiked with poppy syrup. Marcus eyed it, but didn't immediately drink it. He knew he would probably need it eventually, but he didn't like the feeling it gave him of stumbling about in a dreamy haze.

Though the physician had warned against movement, Marcus forced himself up and out of bed, grimacing not only at the pain of his injuries but also at trying to move while swaddled like a newborn. He was struggling into a shirt, trying to pull it over his head with one good arm and his teeth, when he felt a hand touch him. Warmth flowed through his body. Warmth that healed, not dulled.

Marcus couldn't see—the shirt was over his face—but he recognized the touch.

"Draconas," he said, thankfully. "Where did you spring from?"

"Hell—if you believe the gossip that is running rampant through your populace," Draconas replied grimly. "Hold still and let me work my magic on you. I can only give you ease. I cannot heal you fully. There is not time."

"Thank you for that, at least."

"Don't thank me. My motives are purely selfish. I need you and I can't have you dying on me."

"At least you're honest." Marcus managed to poke his head up out of the shirt collar. "Now that you're here, you should speak with Father—"

"I haven't time. Besides, Edward does not trust me much, and he's going to trust me less after he hears the news I bring. I cannot find the dragon army."

Marcus paused with his arm half in and half out of the sleeve. "What? I don't understand. You should be able to see them clearly from the sky."

"You are right. I *should* be able to see the army from the air, but I can't. I have spent the night searching for them. My dragon eyes should be able to detect them, even in the dark. I know they are out there, but I cannot find them. And it is not due to Maristara. She has retreated back to Dragonkeep, to nurse her wounds and save her strength for the final battle. My guess is that the female warriors are responsible for hiding the army from my sight. They have the dragon-magic, and they are as strong in it as your mother and the other priestesses of Seth. They used such magic to fend off my kind for hundreds of years."

Marcus slowly realized what this meant. "The army

could be anywhere—right on our doorstep—and none of us would be able to see them—"

"*You* can see them, Marcus. That's why I'm telling you. I believe it is because the magic they use is akin to the magic you use. It is the human factor in all this that plays havoc with my ability to penetrate the illusion. I will continue to search. The women who cast this magic have to rest sometime. The magic weakens them—the 'blood bane,' Melisande called it. The magic will take its toll, and if their spells weaken or falter, I may be able to locate them. In the meantime—"

"I will keep careful watch." Marcus tried to sound confident, though his heart sank. That heart sank still further, as he watched Draconas's expression grow darker. "Yes, what other bad news do you bear?"

"I was not going to tell you this, Marcus, because I did not have enough information to give you. I have to tell you, now, however, even though my fears are vague and ill-defined. There is another dragon involved in this plot to conquer humankind. She is powerful, one of the most powerful of my kind. Indeed, she was, for many years, our leader, honored and respected. Fear changed her. Fear consumed her. She is your most dangerous enemy, Marcus. Far more dangerous than the late Grald or the wounded Maristara."

"And let me guess," said Marcus. "You can't find her, either."

"I'm still looking for Anora, and so are others," Draconas said. "But, in the meantime, you must remain vigilant and on your guard, both in your little room and out of it."

Draconas picked up the draught of the opiate and tossed it into the slop bucket. "Sleep if you must, Marcus, but keep one eye open and one ear uncovered. And ride to Ramsgate as swiftly as you can."

37

INSIDE THE CASTLE OF THE KING, SURROUNDED BY EVERY luxury, fed three meals a day—or more, if she wanted them—Evelina was not happy. She paced back and forth, back and forth inside her chambers. A cage—even a gilt one—is still a cage.

The axe-faced woman dogged Evelina's every step. She was not permitted to go out of her room except in the company of Axe-Face, the reason being that no proper young *unmarried* girl—and it seemed to Evelina that the woman spoke that hateful word with a relish—would think of venturing into public without a chaperone. Evelina chafed against this. She was certain at first that she was being singled out for punishment. She was forced to concede, however, that whenever she caught sight of the Lady Izabelle (which was as often as the jealous Evelina could manage), the lady was always in the company of an older woman.

Evelina was not permitted to speak to any one, particularly any man, which stricture she considered extremely harsh and unfair. There were several very comely men—particularly among the Her Majesty's knights—who would have been glad to amuse her. Although the Queen's Guard were preoccupied with news from Aston Castle, receiving daily reports from the messengers who were riding back and forth, some found time to take note of the pretty girl who, it was bruited about, had caught Prince Marcus in her web of golden curls, amongst other attractions.

One or more of these knights had taken to being on hand whenever Evelina was outdoors for her daily walk in the garden. She was, of course, stalked by Axe-Face, who actually pinched Evelina's arm when she smiled at a handsome young lord who had first smiled at her. The unsightly bruise pained her for days, and Evelina never picked up a knife to slice her meat but that she indulged in fond thoughts of slicing up her chaperone.

Evelina was not permitted anywhere near the Royal Quarters, and thus she was forced to give up a notion she'd entertained of chumming about with the Queen and endearing herself to her. Evelina saw the Queen or the ladies-in-waiting only from across a vast expanse of lawn or at the end of a mile-long hallway she wasn't allowed to enter.

The only other person Evelina was allowed to talk to was the serving girl who brought her meals to her. This was also the only time Evelina ever escaped Axe-Face, who dined with other high-ranking staff members of the Royal Household. The serving girl loved to gossip, and Evelina was an avid listener, so they got on well.

At first all the servant could talk about was the war. The news was good at the start. The king had ridden off to Aston Castle merely to humor Prince Marcus, who everyone knew was mad. ("Begging your pardon, m'lady, but that's what Cook says an' she's worked here for nigh on twenty years and the stories she tells, you wouldn't believe, and it's only proper you should know, seein' the horrible way they're treating you, which isn't right, you being a fine lady yourself, if you *are* down on your luck . . .")

Then something went wrong.

According to the servant, a messenger arrived in the middle of the night. They woke the Queen, and she and Gunderson and some barons who'd been hanging about eating the king's food and drinking his wine held an emergency meeting, after which the barons looked grim, the guards on the walls were doubled and the local militia was drilling in the courtyard.

The next day, dark rumors started. A stable boy overheard a groomsman who overheard one of the barons saying that the king's army had been defeated by an army of demons who had the fires of hell at their command. By that night the rumors had spread into the city—Satan's army was on the march. This was the Apocalypse.

Shops closed. Inns emptied. Churches filled. The atmosphere around the castle grew increasingly tense. So pervasive was the mounting tension that it roused all Evelina's instincts for self-preservation. Her interest in Marcus waned considerably as she heard horror stories from the servant about castles under siege, cut off from food supplies for months, so that the people inside were forced to eat rats, until they ran out of rats and eventually ate each other.

"If the demons don't eat us first, m'lady," said the tearful servant.

Thus it was that when Axe-Face made Evelina the offer, Evelina jumped on it with both feet.

"The ladies-in-waiting are being sent home under guard," the woman told her. "Her Majesty has most graciously offered to dispatch you to a place of safety, as well."

"Under guard?" Evelina asked eagerly, thinking of several of the handsome young knights she'd seen around the castle.

"Of course," said Axe-Face coldly. After all, Evelina might be carrying the king's grandchild.

Evelina was ecstatic. Not only would she escape the drudgery and dullness of her life in the castle, she would be furnished with male companionship for the journey. She didn't care where she was going, and she was packing for the trip when the serving girl shed new light on the matter.

"So you're leaving us, are you, m'lady?" the serving girl said, plunking down Evelina's food-laden tray. "I can't say that I blame you. I'm to leave, as well. They're paring down the serving staff to the bare bone, so Cook says. Cook volunteered to stay. She's ever so brave. The Queen had tears in her eyes when she thanked her. Cook says she's going to see to it them demons don't make a mess of her kitchen."

Evelina, flinging clothes into a bag, scarcely listened.

"Prince Marcus is coming home and it seems he isn't mad at all. He turned out to be a hero, though he's bad hurt, we hear. The Lady Izabelle is going to stay on to nurse him. I call that romantic, don't you?"

Evelina halted and turned around, silken chemise in hand.

"Prince Marcus is returning to the castle?"

"Yes, m'lady. I thought you knew."

"The Lady Izabelle is staying here with him? Is that what you said?"

"Yes, m'lady. The Queen wanted to send her away with the others, but the lady said that she had agreed to be his wife and that this, in her eyes, was the same as wedding vows. She wasn't going to desert him in time of danger."

"The prince is a hero, you say? Not mad?"

"No, m'lady, not a bit of it! He led the knights against them terrible demons himself. Men fell all around him, and he rode on and slew a lot with his bare hands and then he fell and all the knights rushed to his rescue and he managed to escape, though he's grievous hurt, or so I hear. Cook's fixin' her special healing broth for him right now."

Evelina began to take her clothes out of the leather bag. "Then I'm not leaving either."

"Oh, my lady. How brave!" The serving girl gasped.

"How could I?" Evelina asked, her voice soft. "If my prince is ill, he might call out for me, and then the Queen would *have* to let us be together. She wouldn't be so cruel as to keep us apart!"

"I suppose that's true, my lady," said the serving girl, though she sounded skeptical. "But won't you be afraid?"

"Not with my prince at my side," proclaimed Evelina. " 'If I must die, at least let it be in his arms.' " She'd sung that line many a time in taverns. It never failed to set all the drunks to sobbing into their ale.

The ladies-in-waiting and most of the serving staff departed, Axe-Face among them, to Evelina's joy. Her Majesty had not been at all pleased to hear Evelina's refusal to leave and was going to order her away even if it meant tying her to a horse. Before that could happen, however, the king and his knights and soldiers and Marcus arrived at the castle, turning everything upside down. King and Queen had far more urgent matters on their minds than Evelina.

She was on her own, free to do as she pleased. Overlooked in the turmoil, Evelina was forgotten.

She recalled one of her dear, departed Papa's maxims. "Wars are for fools who want to be heroes. The sensible man will have nothing to do with them. At the first sound of the trumpet, look to yourself."

Considering this sound advice, Evelina began to make plans.

38

KING EDWARD AND HIS FORCES SAW NO SIGN OF THE dragon army on the road from Aston Castle to Ramsgate. Marcus could not find them, and Draconas remained unable to locate them. City and castle braced for an assault. A week passed and none came. No army laid siege to the walls. No enemy appeared at the gates.

People can remain in a high state of tension and excitement for only so long. When the threat that they'd been promised did not materialize, those who had fled returned to their homes, reopened their shops, and grumbled about how much money they'd lost. Smart young apprentices now scoffed at the tales of demon warriors. Only a week ago, they'd been shaking beneath the bed covers or on their knees in church.

Edward wasn't scoffing. His tension did not diminish, nor did that of his commanders or the soldiers who had seen with their own eyes the terror of the enemy.

"They're letting us stew in our juices, sire," said Gunderson. "They're not through with us yet."

Far from relaxing his vigilance, Edward redoubled the guards on the walls and drilled the gunners on a daily basis.

The peaceful interlude gave Marcus a chance to rest from a journey that, despite Draconas's healing touch, had been difficult. The dragon-magic had mended the broken bones enough so that it no longer felt like someone was stabbing him every time he drew a breath. But he was still sore, and the rattling and bouncing of the wagon over the rough roads added to his discomfort. He endured the pain without complaint, afraid that his father might stop if he said anything—and at this point, Marcus's mental distress was far worse than his physical.

He was not much better when he reached home, for he could find no relief in sleep. The dragon's voice boomed loudly through his dreams as the dragon's eyes searched for him and the dragon's claws tried to dig him out. He would wake, soaked in sweat and breathing hard, and the voice would die away, only to be replaced by whispers that dogged his waking hours.

Sometimes Marcus would hear from Draconas, but the dragon had always the same news to report, "I cannot find them."

Perhaps due to the rigors of the journey or his anxiety, a few days after arriving home, Marcus was afflicted with a mild fever. Despite his insistence that he was "not so bad," he was pale and had no appetite. His terrified mother, remembering how close she had come to losing him, bundled him off to bed and summoned the royal physicians.

They eased Ermintrude's fears by basically agreeing with Marcus's own assessment that he was "not so bad." They recommended several days' complete rest. Nothing was to be said to upset him or fret him. Ermintrude immediately banned all visits from Edward and Gunderson and provided her son with more pleasant company in the form of the Lady Izabelle. Ermintrude hoped that nursing the young man from injuries suffered in a heroic action would cause love to bloom in the lady's heart. And how could Marcus, in his weakened state, resist those warm, doe eyes and gentle demeanor?

Marcus lodged an appeal with his father. Sickness was well known to be a woman's province, and Edward was not inclined to argue with his wife anyway, for he was also concerned over Marcus's health. The king abandoned his son to a soft and perfumed captivity, though

Edward did what he could to help lift the prisoner's spirits by urging Marcus to regain his strength and quickly at that, for he might soon be needed.

Marcus swallowed the medicines and drank the broth and lay in his bed listening to the Lady Izabelle read to him or play the harp and sing. He was impressed, as his mother meant him to be, with the lady's courage in choosing to remain in the castle. He was touched by her obvious admiration for him, and he found that looking at her was far more agreeable than staring out the window at the soldiers manning the castle walls. He found, too, that her voice, which was sweet and melodic, was the only voice that could drown out that of the dragon.

He thought he might be falling in love with her.

He remembered the moment. He'd been in his little room, eavesdropping on the dreams of the dragons, hoping to stumble upon information that might help save his people, when he felt a hand touch his hand.

He opened his eyes to find Izabelle by his side.

Her eyes are beautiful, he thought. Pale gray iris surrounded by a darker gray circle. He could look into those eyes forever. The voice of the dragon faded away, and he heard only her voice, saw only her eyes.

After that, perhaps it was his illness or perhaps it was love, but Marcus couldn't seem to think clearly whenever the Lady Izabelle was near. When she wasn't, his thoughts turned to her and away from everything else. He spent less and less time in the little room.

On the seventh day after his return, Marcus was lying in his bed, his gaze resting as it always did on the lady. Izabelle finished the book she had been reading to him and laid it on the small table at her side.

Conversation languished. The lady turned to her embroidery. The fabric on which she worked was secured in a large frame so that it was drawn taut, making it easier to ply the needle. The standing frame was placed in front of her and she leaned over it, assiduously taking minute stitches, frowning slightly as she concentrated on piercing the fabric with the needle, then drawing the colorful thread through the fabric. So still was the room that Marcus could hear the thread sigh as it slipped through the cloth.

He watched Izabelle's hands. Her skin was smooth and white. Rounded, rose-tinged fingernails adorned small fingers that skillfully plied the needle. Suddenly he had the fancy that the thread she was using came not from the spool, but was sliding out of his own mind. He watched, fascinated, to see her twist and spin the colors of his magic into silken thread and then stitch them into her work.

"How do you do that?" he asked, half-laughing.

Izabelle looked up. "It takes no great skill, Your Highness. The trick is to keep the stitches small and close together—"

"No, I didn't mean that," he said. "How do you take the colors from my dreams and make them into silk?"

Looking concerned, she laid down her work on the table and walked over to him. "I fear the fever has returned, Your Highness. I will send the servant to fetch your mother—"

"No, don't. I am fine, I assure you, my lady." Marcus rested his hand on the lady's and touched her skin, cool and smooth. "See? No sign of fever. Please, go back to your work. I'm just teasing you. What is it you are making?"

"Teasing me?" she said, flushing and giving a little laugh. "I'm afraid I take everything much too seriously. As for what I am embroidering, it is a portrait, Your Highness. Are you certain you are feeling well? You look flushed. Perhaps I should see for myself if the fever has returned."

Izabelle rested her hand on his forehead. As she did so, a golden locket, attached to a golden chain, slipped out from around the lace at her throat and dangled above him.

The locket swung gently back and forth; gold glinted in the sunlight. Marcus watched it, and he saw the dragon's plan. He saw the dragon army marching upon the palace. He saw his father give the order to fire the cannons. He saw the dragon work her magic, saw magical fire race from the powder kegs to the cannons. He saw the horrendous blast that obliterated the cannons and the walls and blew up castle and city. He saw thousand perished in an instant, blown apart. The blast was of such magnitude that when the smoke and flame and debris and dust cleared, all that was left of the city of Ramsgate and the castle and the king and his people was a gigantic crater.

He saw the dragon circle above the ruin to make certain that no one survived. Then she summoned her army, and, after that, every human kingdom faced with this awful threat heard the terrible history of the kingdom of Idylswylde and capitulated and, in time, nation after nation came under thrall to the dragons.

Marcus saw it all and he tried to speak, to shout, to summon the servants to fetch his father, but the knowledge slid out of his mind as the thread slid off the spool, the colors of death and terror and destruction running through the lady's delicate fingers and sighing into the cloth.

Marcus lay back down among the pillows.

I must be feverish, he thought. *I must be imagining this.*

Lady Izabelle resumed her seat. Tucking the golden locket back into the lace at her throat, she picked up her work. Marcus watched the needle pierce the cloth, watched it draw the thread after it.

"Whose portrait?" he asked.

Reversing it, the lady showed it to him.

"Yours, Your Highness," she said with a gentle smile.

A fortnight passed in peace and quiet for the people of Ramsgate. Some in the city were starting to say that the battle of Aston Castle, though first thought to be a defeat, had, in retrospect, been a resounding victory. The demon warriors had seen the power of God-fearing men and taken themselves back to the fiery regions from whence they'd sprung.

In the castle, King Edward and his army were left to simmer in the pot until they were so thoroughly overcooked that the meat was falling off the bone. Everyone was worn out from the tension. Nerves and tempers were stretched taut.

Marcus was up and about and seemed almost fully recovered, at least physically. Edward was concerned about his son's mental state, however, for Marcus was lethargic, absent-minded, and given to daydreaming.

Ermintrude wasn't worried.

"He's falling in love, my dear," she assured Edward.

"Falling in love doesn't mean a man's brain turns to mush," Edward said sharply.

"Doesn't it?" Ermintrude asked with the flash of a dimple.

One conversation in particular worried the king. He had taken his son aside to speak to him in private. "Have you received any word from Draconas? If so, you've said nothing to me. Much as I dislike depending on him, he is our eyes and ears."

"Draconas . . ." Marcus repeated. His brow puckered. He seemed to be trying to place the man.

"Draconas. You remember. The dragon?"

"I'm sorry, Father." Marcus faltered. "I don't . . . I can't . . ."

The Lady Izabelle glided up to stand beside him. Marcus smiled.

"No," Marcus said mildly. "I haven't heard anything of him in days. And now, if you will excuse me, Father, I promised the Lady Izabelle a game of draughts."

He and the lady sat at table by the fire.

Evelina, meanwhile, was proceeding with her plans for regaining her prince.

On his return, she'd managed to catch a glimpse of Marcus as they had carried him to his room. Evelina had been shocked at the sight and had known a twinge of fear. He was so pale and thin, he looked to be at death's door, and what would that mean for her? Her spirits rallied, however, on considering that, if the prince did die, she would be the mother of the only son poor Marcus would ever father. Evelina decided that she could bear the news of his death with fortitude, and she was almost disappointed to hear that he was recovering.

The serving girl who had been Evelina's source for information had left the castle, but, now free to roam about, Evelina made friends with Cook, who kept Evelina informed. Cook brought Evelina the news that the Lady Izabelle had moved into the royal chambers lock, stock, and barrel, establishing herself as Marcus's nurse and companion. Evelina seethed with jealousy.

That day, she dared to try to pay the prince a visit and walked boldly into the royal quarters. Guards, posted outside the prince's chambers, escorted her off. Evelina then tried to find a way to sneak into Marcus's room in the middle of the night. Lady Izabelle might possess talents in lute-playing, but Evelina possessed talents of her own that she was certain the prince would find far more exciting. A night spent in bed with her would clinch the deal.

Evelina eagerly questioned Cook about secret passages and hidden tunnels, such as she'd heard about in minstrels' songs, which told of forbidden lovers sneaking through passages to meet each other in clandestine embrace. Unfortunately, the architect of this palace had been totally lacking in romance, for no secret passages existed, at least that Cook knew about, and she'd lived in the palace for twenty years.

"Though," Cook remarked thoughtfully, "I do remember that there was a wing in the palace that was sealed off and no one was allowed inside. Unsafe, we were told. Bits of the ceiling fell down on people's heads or something like that."

"That's no help," said Evelina with a sigh.

"I did hear that His Highness asked about you," said Cook.

"Did he?" Evelina was vastly pleased.

"He heard that you came to see him, and he asked the Lady Izabelle to send for you and bring you in to him."

"He did?" Evelina's heart beat fast. "His Highness sent for me? When was that? This morning?"

"Oh, no. A few days ago," said Cook.

"But . . . no one came to fetch me!" Evelina cried.

"The Lady Izabelle never told you," said Cook with a wink. "She promised His Highness she would, but she never did."

Cook liked to gossip and she liked to embellish her stories. She liked being made to feel important, and she liked Evelina. There was some truth to this story, but not much. Marcus had asked after Evelina, but it was his mother he had asked, not the Lady Izabelle. She knew nothing of Evelina—Queen Ermintrude had seen to that.

Evelina believed the tale because she wanted to believe it and also because, if she'd been the Lady Izabelle, she would have done exactly the same thing herself.

She concluded it was time for drastic measures.

It was time to go shopping.

Being Ramone's daughter, Evelina had, from her first days in the palace, kept a watchful eye out for small and easily transportable valuables that could be tucked into a sleeve or dropped down one's bosom or secreted in one's purse. The hasty departure of the ladies-in-waiting provided a treasure trove for Evelina, who slipped into their abandoned rooms and helped herself to everything they had left behind. Since the women had packed in a state of panic, Evelina made a considerable haul, finding scattered pearls, bejeweled hair combs, silver hairbrushes, dropped rings, and a fine pair of small silver candlesticks.

Evelina put her cloak around her and cast her veil over her head and, acting in the guise of a servant, she ventured out of the palace and walked down the hill into the city. She went first to the pawnshop, and from there she went to another part of the city, a darker, seamier part. Although Evelina had never been in or even heard of Ramsgate-upon-the-Aston before now, she knew where to look for what she sought and found it quite easily.

She was, after all, Ramone's daughter.

Evelina returned to the palace with the object safely in her possession.

It was well that she went on her shopping expedition when she did. From that night on, life would change drastically.

Around midnight, a messenger rode a lathered horse into the courtyard. Despite the lateness of the hour, Gunderson was there to meet him; the old man was always on hand during any crisis. He took one look at the messenger and called for men with torches and sent a servant running in haste to bring the king.

The messenger was covered with the dust of the road and so exhausted he fell from the saddle. He was parched and could not speak for the dryness of his throat. Someone brought him water and he drank thirstily and then gave his news.

"New Bramfells is attacked!" he said hoarsely. "Demons came upon us three days ago, surrounded the city."

He took another drink, then spit it out, coughing.

No one spoke. All waited in grim silence.

"They brought with them hellfire!" he gasped, when he could speak. "They called down the lightning from the heavens. We could do nothing against them. The rocks our catapults hurled at the demons burst apart in midair. A flight of arrows changed into a flock of crows and flapped away. I am sane, Your Majesty!" the man cried wildly. "I swear to God I saw it with my own eyes!"

"I do not doubt you." Edward took hold of the man's shoulders, gripped him tightly. "Three days, you say? Has the city fallen? Do you still hold?"

"Hold!" The messenger laughed, brittle laughter that cracked. "There's nothing left to hold. The city is destroyed! We tried to fight the fires, but the flames were everywhere and they spread too fast."

All could now see, as they stared at him in the flickering torchlight, that his eyebrows and the hair on the front of his head had been singed off. Holes made by cinders riddled his cloak, and one sleeve was burnt away, revealing an ugly burn on his arm.

Every man there could picture the disaster. Fire was the terror of every city. Buildings with thatched roofs and wooden beams stood jammed up against each other in order to conserve space. With no effective means of putting out a blaze, once fire started, it could eat a city alive.

"Then there came a dragon," the man continued, not looking at anyone, talking feverishly to himself. "A great red monster it was. We thought we were finished, but the beast did not attack us. It flew at the demons and . . . and . . ."

The messenger blinked and faltered.

"And what, man?" Edward demanded. "What happened?"

"A whirlwind took the dragon," the man said, awed. "A whirlwind caught the beast and twisted it, so that it nearly smashed into the city. The same wind fanned the flames of the fire, causing it to spread that much faster."

"The red dragon could have been Draconas," said Edward in a low voice, taking Gunderson aside. "He must have changed his mind about killing humans. But it seems the warriors can protect themselves against him. What do you suppose is left of the city?"

"Rubble and ashes, Sire. And the dead," said Gunderson.

Edward turned back to the messenger. "Others must have escaped, as you did. Do you know how many?"

"A handful maybe, Your Majesty. Most were too afraid of the demons to leave the city. Better to lose your life than your immortal soul."

"They're not demons!" Edward said sharply. "Stop saying that. They're men, same as us—"

The messenger stared at him.

"No use, sire," Gunderson advised. "He won't believe you. No one will. The dragons are playing on every nightmare and superstitious fear we've ever harbored."

"Thousands of people in that city . . . children . . . burning to death." Edward closed his eyes and covered his face with his hand. "God help them!"

"One thing more," Gunderson asked the messenger, who was on the verge of collapse. "How did you escape?"

"God's grace maybe, sir," the man replied weakly. "I don't know. I didn't expect to."

Gunderson watched as his men bore the messenger away to be fed and doctored.

"The warriors let him go," Edward said. "They let that man pass safely through their lines. 'Always leave one survivor to tell the tale.'"

Gunderson pondered this, then said, "Aye, sire, I fear

you're right. They knew he would 'tell the tale.' They want us to hear it. Because we're next."

"At least we have the cannons," said Edward. "I'll wager the dragon warriors won't be turning cannonballs into crows—"

"Father! . . ."

Feeling a hand clutch at his arm, the king turned. "Marcus! What are you doing out in the night air? You'll catch your death!"

"Father!" Marcus said desperately. "You must not— Must not—"

"Must not what?" Edward asked, for that was as far as his son went.

"I don't know," Marcus said, puzzled and anguished. He plucked at his hair with trembling hands. "I can't catch it. It's all unraveling."

"He's out of his head with fever!" Edward exclaimed, concerned. "Where is his servant? You, sirrah," he said angrily as the man came puffing up. "What do you mean allowing your master out of his bed at this time of night?"

"I am sorry, Sire," the man gasped. "He heard the commotion and was up and gone before I knew it."

"Take him to his bed and summon the physician." Edward put his arm around his son's shoulder. He could feel Marcus's shivering. "There's nothing you can do, my son. What's done is done. Go back to your bed."

The servant had brought a blanket with him. He wrapped it around Marcus's shoulders and, in wheedling tones, he tried to persuade the prince to come back inside.

Marcus resisted. He stared into the night sky at the stars, which sparkled so sharply it seemed to Edward he would cut himself if he touched them.

"It's too late, Father," Marcus said and his voice was calm. "Death has caught us."

Death had not caught Draconas. At least, not yet. He had searched unsuccessfully for the army of dragon warriors for a fortnight, and he had almost begun to think that perhaps Maristara had called off the fight and gone home to think things over when word came from Lysira that the dragon army had reappeared. They surrounded a human city.

Draconas warned Lysira to keep well away. He then tried several times to contact Marcus, to warn him that New Bramfells was under siege and that the king should immediately send reinforcements.

As it turned out, Maristara had no thought of besieging the walled city. She had given her troops orders to destroy it, and they did so, burning out a city of five thousand people in less than a day. Even if Draconas had managed to speak to Marcus—and he was never in his little room these days—Edward's force could not have reached the city in time.

The law of dragonkind. Kill no human.

Draconas had upheld that law and defended it for hundreds of years, as had other dragons before him. He tried to save the city without killing any of the dragon warriors. He swooped down on them with no intent to kill them—though they didn't know that. He hoped to frighten them, scatter them, cause them to break and run. His hope was a meager one, for he guessed that Grald had trained them for just such an attack.

Sighting Draconas, the male warriors continued their assault against the humans, leaving the female warriors to defend against the dragon. With incredible speed, the women summoned a cyclone of magic and sent it after Draconas. He had no choice but to pull out of his dive and retreat or risk being caught up in the whirling, whipping winds.

Draconas was forced to watch New Bramfells burn, watch the smoke billow into the air, watch it rain ashes and hot cinders back down onto the ground. He heard the screams of the slaughtered and smelled the burnt flesh, and he saw, as he dove at them, the faces of the dragon warriors looking up at him, cold and calm and unfeeling, as they went about their business of killing.

"They can defend against one dragon or perhaps even two or three," Draconas muttered to himself. "But what about hundreds? I think that might give them pause."

A day later, the city still burned. Draconas again searched for Marcus, but the little room was empty. The dragon warriors vanished inside their illusion. This time, Draconas knew where they were headed, and he had the feeling that they would not wait two weeks to attack the castle. Frustrated, unable to think of a way to stop them, he watched the smoke of New Bramfells snake up into the heavens as the few survivors, tiny as mice from this height, wandered among the rubble, searching for a life they had once known and would never find again.

Draconas made a decision.

"For once, our kind is going to have to take a stand, and we're going to have to do it fast. No time for arguing or dithering, no tabling of motions or referrals to committee."

Draconas opened himself up to the minds of all dragons everywhere, letting them see into his mind, letting them see all that he had seen—the fall of the human city.

"As specified in our laws," Draconas said to the dragons, his colors red with flame and blood, "in time of dire emergency, any member may call a meeting of Parliament. It is such a time and I summon you to attend."

He closed his mind swiftly, before the flood of questions overwhelmed him, and flew to the meeting site.

39

BECAUSE HE HAD ALWAYS FELT COMPELLED TO VIEW himself as an advocate for the humans among whom he walked, Draconas had previously appeared before the Parliament of Dragons in his human, "walker" form. This day, he came before them as an equal, a dragon, one of their own. He was the first to arrive, and he did that for a reason. He wanted to greet every single dragon, look each in the eye.

The dragons entered, one by one. Some, like Lysira and, astonishingly, the old irascible Malfiesto, greeted Draconas warmly, their crisp, sharp colors flowing beneath his wings and lifting him with their support. Others, such as Litard and Arat, barely glanced at him as they entered, and they kept their colors wrapped close to themselves, sharing nothing with him, yet all the while trying to bore inside his skull.

Notable in absence was Anora. The speaker's rod lay on the floor where she had last laid it down. No one stood in her place. No one picked up the rod.

The mood was electric. Tension sparked and cracked among the dragons, who eyed each other suspiciously.

Draconas had to do the impossible. He had to try to bring them together.

"I have summoned you here—"

"Such a summons may be issued only by the Minister," stated Mantas, a young and hot-headed male.

"In an emergency, any dragon may call a meeting," Draconas returned, keeping his colors even and level. He knew he was being deliberately goaded. "In any event, you answered it."

He and Mantas had a brief eye-rapier fencing battle. Mantas broke contact, glanced away. The younger dragon rolled his eyes, indicating that he ended the confrontation merely to save time, not because he was in any way intimidated. Draconas gave an inward sigh and plunged ahead.

"Our first order of business is to elect a new minister."

"There is no need. We have a Minister," Reyal, one of the female dragons, stated in colors of ice-blue. "Anora is our Minister."

"She has betrayed us!" Nionan, a female who had always liked humans, struck in. "Anora has forfeited her right to rule over us."

"She did *not* betray us," Litard retorted. "She is trying to save us. Draconas is the traitor. He has betrayed his own kind to side with the humans who would destroy us—"

Nionan's colors flared orange. Litard snarled and a brawl of minds broke out in the Hall. Colors swirled and clashed in the center of the cavern. Dragons shifted positions, leaving their accustomed places to form factions. Lysira and Nionan hastened to Draconas's side. So did the elderly Malfiesto, who, unfortunately, took this opportunity to start lecturing the young hot-heads on their sins.

Into this miasma, Draconas dropped the image of the human city of New Bramfells. He showed the dragons the flames, the destruction, the dying humans. He held up before them the image of the dragon warriors, and he displayed their power. The dragons watched, some grieved and shocked, some impassive, and at least one grimly pleased.

"It is not ordinary humans who will destroy us," Draconas told them. "*These* humans are the enemy, these with dragon-blood in their veins and dragon-magic in that blood. Not long ago, all of you were appalled at the very suggestion that such a terrible crossbreeding might occur. Now some of you promote it."

"Such humans can be easily controlled by us," said Mantas, who had become the leader of the opposition. "We have let humans go their own way too long. It was all well and good when they were killing each other, but now they threaten us. Maristara is right. They need to be controlled. Brought under our wise rulership. Told what to do."

"No human has ever done what he was told," said Draconas dryly. "I see no reason why they should start now. Even those with the dragon-blood will go their own way soon enough, and then how will you bring them to heel? For they will fight you with your own weapons!"

Arguments broke out again, and the colors blazed hotter and led nowhere.

"Listen to me!" Draconas thundered and, though many cast him baleful glances, they subsided to hear what he had to say. "Another human city is going to be attacked and destroyed as was New Bramfells. Thousands more humans will die."

"Those with the cannons," said Mantas coolly.

Draconas drew in a breath, commanding patience. "We can stop Maristara and Anora and the dragon warriors from committing this atrocity. If we all join together and act to protect the city of Ramsgate—"

"The humans will fire the cannons at us and try to shoot us out of the sky," said Mantas.

"I will speak to them," Draconas said. "Make them understand—"

"Bah! Humans have no capacity for understanding. They are ruled by their fear—"

"In that, we're much alike," Draconas returned.

The young dragon bristled. "I say let them die! Let others of their kind see what happens when they dare to threaten those who should have been their masters centuries ago and would have been, but for some misguided thinking. You listen to me, Walker. If you side with those humans and try to save them, you will find me there to stop you."

"And me," said Litard.

"And me, as well," said Reyal.

The three dragons rose from their places, their claws scraping against the stone floor, and their wings twitching, eager to fly.

"The session of Parliament has not ended," said Draconas.

"Oh, yes, it has," returned Mantas, his head snaking around to regard those who remained. "It has all come to an end. You just don't know it yet."

The three dragons departed and, after a moment's hesitation, others followed until only four, Draconas, Lysira, Malfiesto, and Nionan, remained.

"The Parliament—" Lysira began.

"There is no Parliament," said Draconas. He had not only failed the humans. He had failed his own kind. Despite what Mantas said, Draconas knew it and he grieved the loss.

"The Parliament of Dragons is dissolved."

40

THE LADY IZABELLE SHIFTED HER EMBROIDERY STAND TO resume her seat by the fire. Marcus, sprawled in the chair opposite, had fallen asleep. She regarded him suspiciously, wondering if he was truly slumbering or shamming. The human was pale and gaunt with dark smudges beneath his eyes. He was restless in his sleep, twitching and tossing his head. He looked ill. She smiled, satisfied.

It must be a dreadful experience, Anora thought, smoothing the embroidery with her human's hand, *having one's soul pulled out and stitched into the fabric of my magic, imprisoned within an embroidery frame.*

The dragon wasn't truly stealing his soul, of course. Dragons do not believe in souls. She had merely borrowed the human term. The enchantment she'd placed on Marcus was a type dragons had concocted during the ancient wars, when they had fought each other. If a dragon could lure or trick or force another dragon to look into his eyes, that dragon could catch hold of his foe's colors and wrap them up or steal them or drain them or whatever he chose. So does the snake charm the rabbit. Anora had not been certain the spell would work on Marcus, for she had never attempted it on a human. Snagging him had been laughably easy, however.

Anora kept Marcus's thoughts wound around the spindle of her mind. Stitching them into a portrait wasn't really necessary, but it amused her and added to his torment. He knew what she planned. He'd seen it all quite clearly when her mind had locked onto his. A pity, but one of the drawbacks associated with using this spell was that the caster was forced to open his mind in order to trap his opponent's. Anora had considered the risk and decided it was worth it.

She'd severed the human's contact with Draconas, and although Marcus knew her plans, she was not worried about him revealing them to anyone. The prince might wriggle and squirm, but she had fast hold of him. He could not escape, not until she freed him. For Marcus, freedom would come only with death.

The human mother rustled into the room. Ermintrude was nearly as pale as her son. Her face was drawn and troubled. Her dimples had vanished. Going to Marcus, she felt his forehead and his pulse and she gave a deep sigh.

"I think he is improving, Your Majesty," said Anora in the guise of the lady.

Ermintrude didn't hear. She was concentrating on her son to the exclusion of all else. She smoothed back the hair from his forehead, then, seeming to remember they were not alone, she turned to Izabelle.

"I am sorry, my lady. What did you say?"

"I said I think he is better, Your Majesty," Anora repeated.

"I don't know," said Ermintrude bleakly. "I don't know."

Shaking her head, she added, "After this terrible news from New Bramfells, I have been thinking that you should return to your home, Lady Izabelle. I should never have permitted you to stay, and I would not have, if I had known the danger would be this great."

This plan did not suit Anora at all, and she was ready with her arguments.

"Your Majesty," she said, her eyes lowered modestly, "I cannot bear to leave His Highness. Perhaps I flatter myself—I am sure I do—but it seems to me that Prince Marcus has some small regard for me, and I fear my departure might cause some setback in his recovery."

Anora raised her eyes to meet the Queen's. "I am not at

all afraid so long as I am inside the safety of castle walls, ma'am. I would be terrified to leave."

"You would have an escort," the Queen assured her.

"And that would take brave men away from the fighting, should it come to that. My father would never forgive me." Anora lowered her eyes again. "I will go if you command me, Your Majesty. But I would much rather stay."

Marcus roused at that juncture. "What is the matter?" he asked, noting the lady's high color and his mother's frown.

"Your father and I decided that we should send the Lady Izabelle back to her home in Weinmauer," said Ermintrude. "The lady, it seems, refuses to go."

Anora glided over to stand beside Marcus. Her skirts whispered around her ankles. She looked into his eyes. "Do you want me to leave, Your Highness? As you are soon to be my husband, I will be guided by your decision."

She could see in his mind the red of his struggle to escape her, and she caught hold of that color and wound it around and around the bobbin of her magic.

Marcus mumbled something and sank back into his chair and closed his eyes.

"He wishes me to stay, Your Majesty," said Anora. "I love him. I do not want to leave him."

"So be it," Ermintrude said. She touched the young woman on the cheek. "I will be proud to call you 'daughter.'"

"Thank you, Your Majesty." Anora curtsied.

"I will sit with Marcus awhile," the Queen continued. "You should go rest before dinner."

Anora curtsied again to the Queen and left her alone with her son. Anora's thoughts were focused on her plans for the night, when, traversing a narrow spiral staircase, she was aware of someone coming up as she was going down.

The two women met in the center and stood regarding each other in the flaring torchlight. Anora recognized the human—a female with blond hair named Evelina, who had tried to barge in to see the Prince. The Queen, Anora recalled, had been most upset. The female was of lower

ranking than Izabelle, and she should be the one to stand
aside so that the lady could pass. Evelina did so, after a
moment's pause. Anora gathered up her skirts and
squeezed past the young woman. Evelina did not curtsy
as she should have done. She stood upright and stared
quite boldly at the lady. Happening to glance at Evelina as
she went by, Anora saw the human's mouth curl. The glint
of baleful enmity in the eyes would have chilled any human to the bone. Anora had no care for humans, however,
and she thought nothing of it, except to be annoyed at the
inconvenience of having to deal with these hoops and the
yards of silk, and a weak and fragile little human body.

The Lady Izabelle had been fifteen years old when the
dragon had waylaid her entourage in the wilderness,
killed her escorts, and dragged the screaming and terrified young girl into a cave, there to tear out her heart and
steal her body. Anora had left the girl, still horribly alive,
sealed inside the cave, blocking the entrance with a heavy
stone, so that none should find her. Anora placed the
girl's heart in the golden locket, hung the locket around
her neck, and proceeded on the journey, creating her own
knightly escorts out of illusion.

The dragon's intent had been to merely enter the castle
and gain access to the royal family. Anora was pleased
and astonished beyond measure to discover that the
young woman, whose body she'd stolen because it suited
her purpose, was actually to be betrothed to Prince Marcus. This opened up all sorts of possibilities. If dragons
had held human beliefs, Anora would have said that this
was a sign that God himself smiled on her. As it was, she
seized the fortunate coincidence and made the most of it.

Dinner that night was a glum affair. The food was not
very good, nor was there very much, for Cook was ra-
tioning what she served them. There was no music. The
musicians had been sent away. The king was not present.
He had gone to inspect the city's fortifications and super-
vise the evacuation of the populace. The few who were
present at the table did not linger over the mutton stew,
and the meal ended quickly. After dinner, Anora played at
draughts with the Prince until she was able to plead fa-

tigue and take her leave of them for the night. She carried Marcus's soul off in her work basket.

When the church bells in the city rang twice, Anora wrapped herself in a cloak of illusion, and stole out of her room. She glided down the stairs, through silent, deserted halls, out into the courtyard. From there, wrapped in the night, she made her way to the castle wall, where stood the cannons.

Soldiers were at their posts, manning the towers, keeping watch, walking their rounds. Every man was watchful and alert, for each had heard the fate of New Bramfells. Anora listened to them talk in tense, low voices as she stole past them, unseen and unsuspected.

The moon was waning from the full, yet still shed enough bright white light for Anora to see almost as clearly as by day. She welcomed the light. Her dragon eyes could see living beings in the dark—humans glowed a warm red in her vision. But the cannons had no life. They squatted black and ugly and repulsive in the moonlight.

Six grotesque monsters, with misshapen arms that they used to haul themselves around, and trundling legs. Anora regarded them with loathing. She hated them, hated the smell of the iron that reminded her of blood, hated the stink of sulfur and saltpeter, hated the all-pervasive stench of humans that bound iron and death together.

Anora walked around the cannons, not touching them, for she detested the feel of them. She knew how they worked. Prince Marcus had most kindly explained it all to her, and she'd seen them in action from a distance, hearing the appalling roar that shook the ground, and watching them belch fire and burp up stone balls. She thought back to a time when dragons had witnessed humans picking up sticks to use as weapons, and she knew from dragon lore how the dragons had laughed, amused by the sight. The dragons had laughed and had then gone back to their dreams.

"We should have known," Anora said sadly to herself. "We should have seen then that these cunning little beasts would one day be capable of producing weapons that threaten our very existence. We should have done then what we do now. We should have shown them that we are the true rulers of this world, taught them to fear us and respect us. Still, better late than never, as the little beasts say."

Soldiers walked past the dragon, so close she could have plucked their cloaks. They did not see her, though one stared straight at her. Anora kept still until they had gone. The illusion effectively concealed her from human eyes, but it could not dampen sound. While she waited for them to continue on their way, she decided she should contact Maristara.

Maristara was waiting for her, impatiently it seemed.

"Where have you been?"

"About our business," Anora returned.

"You have not heard the news."

"What news? Just tell me. Do not be so dramatic," Anora said. Maristara could be such a dullard sometimes.

"Draconas summoned the Parliament."

"Did he?" Anora found that interesting. "To try to convince the others to save the humans?"

"Of course."

"With what result?"

"As you might expect. Parliament could not agree. Some went one way, some another. Draconas has a few of the noble houses on his side, but we have more on ours."

"And how did it end?"

"The Parliament of Dragons is dissolved," said Maristara with grim satisfaction. "Good riddance, if you ask me."

Anora heard the news with shock and, oddly, regret. She thought fondly of the long debates, the interminable discussions, the Speaker's Rod being handed civilly back and forth among them. She recalled the rustle of wings and the flicking of tails and the heads turning their bright eyes on first one, then the other, as the rainbow of their wisdom shone about them and bound them together. And now all that was dissolved, as grains of salt disappearing in a glass of water, so that you could never more see them or even tell what they had once been.

Fear emptied Anora of color. For a terrible moment

she was cold and hollow and dark inside. The voices of her ancestors seemed to cry out against her, their dead eyes stared at her accusingly. In an instant she had undone the work of centuries. And where would it lead?

"To peace," she insisted stubbornly. "To stability. Once the humans are cowed and come under our rule, the dragons who have been deluded into siding with the humans will see reason. Parliament will be restored. All will be well again. Better than before."

So she reassured herself, and though doubt remained burning in the pit of her gut, like an unexpelled remnant of brimstone, she was able to ignore it and turn her attention back to Maristara. And a good thing she did.

"What did you just tell me?" Anora demanded, appalled.

"The dragon's children are in Seth," Maristara repeated, her colors murky and sullen.

"How could you let this happen?"

"I cannot be in two places at once!" Maristara returned vehemently. "I cannot prosecute this war from Dragonkeep as you insisted upon and, at the same time, chase after Grald's monstrous progeny!"

Anora caught hold of a word. "Monstrous. Yes, that is what they will seem to the humans of Seth, who have been taught all their lives to fear dragons. We have no need to worry. The humans have undoubtley slaughtered them."

"On the contrary, they embraced them," said Maristara, and it seemed she would have hidden these thoughts, but Anora ferreted them out. "I have lost contact with the High Priestess. The heart in the locket withered and turned to dust. They found the body of Lucretta and they freed her from my spell. The body I had stolen is dead. Fortunately, I was not in it at the time. I had abandoned it."

"You have abandoned your senses! One of two human kingdoms under our sway, and Seth has been lost to us."

"We will regain it." Maristara was confident.

Blindly confident—the confidence of ignorance, Anora thought, seething. All contact lost with Seth. The Mistress of Dragons unmasked. By all logic, the humans of Seth should have killed the half-dragon monsters.

Humans are so completely unpredictable! Anora fumed. She had lived among humans, disguised as the holy sister, off and on for years, and she still found them baffling.

We must destroy them, Anora realized. *Destroy them all. Only then will we finally be at peace.*

"Is all going well in Ramsgate?" Maristara was asking. "Our plan remains unchanged?"

"Yes," Anora replied. "The plan proceeds. The dragon army marches with the dawn. By sunset tomorrow, this city will be a hole in the ground, and the world of humans will have learned a bitter lesson."

The conversation between the two dragons ended, and Anora proceeded with her spellcasting. Her plan was foolproof. It could not fail. Unpredictable though humans might be, she saw no way they could escape their fate. The real army would cast an illusion of itself. The illusionary army would attack the castle. The cannons would misfire. The horrendous explosion would wipe out every living being within a twenty-mile radius. Two major cities destroyed. What was left of the kingdom of Idylswylde would sue for peace.

The dragon army would then march on the neighboring kingdom of Weinmauer.

Terms: Surrender or be destroyed.

Or maybe just be destroyed.

Anora began to work her magic.

41

THE NEXT MORNING, AS DAWN BROKE, SCOUTS BROUGHT word that the enemy army was on the march, heading for the capital. The enemy was, as yet, some miles distant, moving slowly, in no hurry. The flash of the sun off their armor could be seen for miles, according to one report. So, too, could the smoke billowing into the air, for they set fire to field and farmhouse as they passed. The warriors summoned lightning from out of blue skies, starting fires where the bolts struck, so that it seemed to the victims that God himself hurled His wrath against them. Some began to cry that these warriors were not demons but avenging angels, sent to punish them for their transgressions.

"The end of the world is coming," they wailed, and so it was, but in a way they could not fathom.

After hearing the terrible death toll in New Bramfells, King Edward had ordered the evacuation of the civilian population of Ramsgate-upon-the-Aston. Monasteries and abbeys in outlying districts took in many of the refugees. Merchants closed their shops, packed up their merchandise, and left via the river or overland. Once the city was emptied of civilians, the king pulled the troops off the city walls and brought them in to defend the castle.

Edward sought to convince his soldiers that these warriors were neither demons nor angels. They were ordinary men with extraordinary abilities. Few believed him. The king might have pointed out that his very own son could wield the same magic, and Edward sometimes wondered, in the sleepless hours of the night, if being open and honest about Marcus and the magic would have been the better course of action. He decided eventually it would have made no difference at all. The ignorant and superstitious would have thought Marcus a demon, too.

The cannons were readied for action. The gunners were in position. The gunpowder, usually stored in a bunker that had been dug into the ground some distance from the castle proper and its outbuildings, was hauled from the bunker to the castle. Edward had ordered construction of a small bunker near the guns, and this was stocked with powder barrels. Buckets of water stood by the guns and by the bunker in order to douse any spark.

Edward's cannons were different from most cannons being built by other nations. His were designed to fight not only men on the ground but also dragons in the air, and thus his cannons could be cranked up to fire into the sky. Mounted on a revolving table, they could also be swiveled about in order to follow a moving target. This day, the cannons faced the ground. He considered his most formidable foe the dragon warriors. If a dragon appeared, the cannons could always be realigned.

The sun climbed toward noon. Everything was in readiness. Archers and men-at-arms lined the walls. The gunners stood by their cannons with their ramrods, six men to a gun, each man assigned a different task from placing the charge to ramming home the cannonball to sighting the gun in on its target.

"Here they come!" one eagle-eyed youngster cried from his perch in the top of the tallest tower. "Marching across the fields!"

The enemy rippled over the land, their scaled armor glittering like the river that flowed past the castle. The dragon army marched directly on the castle itself, bypassing the city walls, flowing down into the valleys and up the hills. The warriors took their time, not yet attacking. The hands of the warriors were empty, but this time

no man laughed. Some had been present at the ill-fated
Battle of Aston and had seen for themselves that the
empty hands of the "demon" warriors carried death.
Those who had not been present had heard the stories. All
watched in grim silence as the army advanced, silence
broken only by the nervous jingle and rattle of armor, the
hissing and sputtering of the torches, and, here and there,
muttered prayers.

The army was not yet within range of the cannons. The
King himself would give the order to fire.

"Stand ready," said the cannon's commander.

Inside the palace, the few people who had chosen to remain were gathered together in the great hall where the
knights could protect them, in case the walls were
breached. Queen Ermintrude was among them. Edward
had argued and pleaded with his wife to flee to her father's castle in Weinmauer. The Queen had most indig-
nantly refused.

"How would that look, me running home to Papa, crying that my husband cannot protect me?"

"He can't protect you," Edward had replied glumly.

"Nonsense." Ermintrude had clasped his hand and
pressed it to her bosom. "We have the cannons and brave
men."

She had sighed, then said softly, "We've seen bad times
before, Edward, my love, and we've come through them
together. We'll come through this one just the same."

"I hope you are right, my own true heart." Edward had
kissed her on the cheek and she had smiled at him. He
had been glad to see her dimples flash again. He had
something else to say, however. "If anything should happen to me, the people will look to you as their queen for
guidance."

"I know." Ermintrude had spoken calmly, though the
dimples had once again disappeared. "Just don't let anything happen to yourself, Edward."

The Queen stood by a window peering out, watching
Edward, who was everywhere at once. Her guards
begged her repeatedly to come back into the center of the

room, away from the window, but Ermintrude ignored them. She chafed at being cooped up inside the castle, unable to see what was going on. She would have been out on the walls herself if she could have managed it. Edward would have had a fit, and, more important, she could not leave Marcus.

Ermintrude shifted her worried gaze from her husband to her son. Marcus had insisted on going out onto the walls himself, though his left arm was still in a sling and he was running a low-grade fever, according to the Lady Izabelle. Marcus had ordered that his armor be brought to him in his room, but he lacked the strength to put it on.

When Ermintrude went to see him, she found him sitting in a chair by the fire, watching the Lady Izabelle work on her embroidery. Ermintrude noted an odd look in her son's eyes, like those of an animal trapped, caged. The look was so very odd that she was startled and uneasy.

"He is only fretting that he cannot join his father," she said to herself. She was impressed with the Lady Izabelle, who could find the strength of character to work at embroidery at a time like this.

Hearing the Queen enter, the lady covered her work with a cloth. Ermintrude had never laid eyes on the lady's fancy work, and she was not of a mind to do so now.

"We are all to move to the great hall," she said. "The commander of my guard deems it will be safer for us there."

Marcus was established in a chair near the fire with the Lady Izabelle close at hand. He continued to stare at her, and Ermintrude thought to herself that she'd never seen a young man so much in love. She prayed that she and her beloved husband would live to see them married. At the thought, tears filled her eyes, and Ermintrude scolded herself, for she had determined in the night that she would keep such debilitating fears at bay. She had to be strong, for the sake of those around her.

One other person joined the small group in the great hall. Mistress Evelina was in attendance. How or why she came to be here was a mystery to the Queen, who remembered ordering Evelina away a fortnight ago. Too late to remove her now. And, Ermintrude was forced to admit, the girl was behaving herself. She was meek and quiet and respectful. She looked often at Marcus but, Ermintrude was glad to see, he paid no attention to her. He had eyes only for Izabelle.

"Your Majesty," Evelina said with a deep curtsy. "Some wine might give us courage. I will be glad to pour, if you sanction it."

"Yes, a good idea, Mistress," said the Queen, distracted, for, at that moment the call came that the dragon army was advancing. Ermintrude hastened back to her place by the window. She could see Edward, standing with his cannons, tall, unafraid, in command.

She had never loved him more than at that moment—a blessed state in which to enter heaven, if death should take her.

Anora, in the body of Lady Izabelle, watched Marcus, sitting weakly in the chair. He had his eyes fixed on her, hating her, knowing what she planned, knowing he was going to die in moments, knowing everyone he loved would be dead. Knowing there was nothing he could do to save them or himself.

He would die, torn apart by the blast. All the humans would die, what small bits were left buried beneath tons of stone that had once been a castle, the rubble and ruin of a nation lying at the bottom of an immense crater. She waited impatiently for Maristara to give the signal.

The illusory dragon army would launch its attack at the castle. The illusion was a mammoth work, created by Maristara, while the real army waited miles away, keeping a safe distance from the site of the blast. The illusory army could not do real damage, but it didn't need to. No human would remain alive long enough to figure out he'd been duped.

A few more seconds and Anora would make up some excuse to leave the hall. She'd established her escape route. Marcus had told the Lady Izabelle, as something that might interest her, that a passage led from the castle beneath the walls and opened into a pasture some distance away. (Draconas had taken Marcus out of the castle that way many years ago, though Anora did not know that . . . nor would she have cared.) Once outside the walls, she would slough off this frail human body and take on her own strong and powerful dragon form.

She would watch the explosion from the clouds, remaining on hand to make certain nothing and no one escaped annihilation.

"Centuries from now, humans will come to look on this site and they will shudder in horror," she said to herself in satisfaction. "We dragons will see to that. No more will any human dare to even think about creating such a destructive force!"

"Would you take some wine, my lady?"

Anora turned to see the yellow-haired female, Evelina, holding out a goblet.

Anora didn't particularly want anything to drink, but everyone else had a goblet, and she didn't want to draw attention to herself by refusing. She took the glass of wine and put it to her lips and drank a silent toast to victory. When she had drunk the wine, she would leave.

Anora then learned just how unpredictable humans can be.

The pain began in her gut—a sharp, stabbing pain unlike anything her human body had ever felt. The pain was so intense that Anora gasped out loud and clutched at her stomach. Another pain—worse than the first—doubled her over. A tremor shook the body of Lady Izabelle. A horrible taste filled the mouth and foam bubbled from the lips. The heart lurched, limbs convulsed. Writhing in agony, the body collapsed. The yellow-haired girl who had served Anora the wine caught her in her arms.

"My lady! What is wrong?" Evelina cried.

Cradling the body of Lady Izabelle, Evelina lowered her gently to the floor. Anora could not speak. The throat burned and the tongue was swelling. She stared up into the face of the girl holding her and, though the girl registered shock and horror on her face, Evelina's eyes smiled.

"You won't have him!" Evelina whispered, bending solicitously over the suffering young woman. "He's mine and he's going to stay mine. Don't worry, my lady. The poison acts very swiftly. You won't suffer long."

Poisoned! Anora's mind reeled with the shock. *The human has poisoned me! The body is dying!*

When the body died, the dragon would start to change back into her true form. There was no way to stop the process. The body was already finding it hard to breathe. The limbs were convulsing, the arms and legs jerking and twitching.

People gathered around her, and all was confusion and mayhem. Some shouted for a physician. Some cried to give her air. Some thought she'd been hit by an arrow and they ran to the window to see who fired. Others ran away from the window to see what was happening. In the midst of the chaos, Anora felt her dragon form start to flee the dying body. In moments, claws would erupt from delicate little hands. Scales would glisten in the place of smooth, fair skin. The simpering mouth would elongate and fill with razor teeth. She could not stop it. She had to accept it. She had to decide what to do and quickly, for she was in danger. It would take time to shift from the human form into the dragon. During that time, she would be vulnerable to attack.

The one weapon she had was her magic, for she could cast spells in either the human form or dragon, though the dragon was far more powerful. Yet, even using the magic required her to wait until the dragon emerged more fully.

As for the humans, she trusted they would be in such a state of shock and bewilderment at seeing the demure and gentle Izabelle developing a snout and a tail that Anora doubted they'd be able to think clearly enough to react. The only one who might pose a threat was Marcus, and she still had him in her power.

Anora was thinking all this through—the dragon mind working coolly and logically as the human mind was fast spiraling into death—when she felt Evelina's hand slip beneath Izabelle's long hair, that had come tumbling down in her thrashing. Concealing her hand in the mass of chestnut hair. Evelina stripped off Izabelle's emerald earrings. Her hand than slid down to the back of Izabelle's neck and took hold of the chain of the golden necklace.

"Seems a pity to waste your jewels by burying you in them, my lady," Evelina whispered.

Anora realized, too late, what the girl meant to do. Fear gripped the dragon, fear that almost paralyzed her. She made a desperate effort to try to stop Evelina, but the human body was in its death throes and useless to her. The dragon body was just starting to emerge.

The chain of the golden locket that held the human's heart snapped and so did the magic, lashing about like a snake with its head cut off, flopping and twisting, completely out of Anora's control.

The magic coiling about inside her, Anora shifted back into her dragon form, but the alteration wasn't happening as it was supposed to. She had no control over it, and so some parts of her body were changing and others were not. If she didn't retrieve that locket and soon, she could be trapped in this form—half human, half dragon.

Like one of Grald's monstrous children, she thought savagely. She had to retrieve the locket, release the heart of the human girl, and free herself.

Dragon jaws slavering, Anora lunged at the wretched human who had done this to her.

Evelina had been about to drop the locket down her bosom when a gigantic claw, growing out of the hand of the Lady Izabelle, made a frantic swipe at her. A monster's head, sprouting horribly from a human neck, tried to snap off her arm.

Evelina screamed and sucked in a breath and screamed again. Still screaming, her mouth wide open, she stumbled backward, tripped over her long skirts, and fell.

She was up again in an instant, half crawling, half scrambling, slipping and falling and still screaming. Yet, even while trying frantically to escape a terrible death, Evelina remained Ramone's daughter.

She clutched the golden locket fast in her hand.

Anora had one dragon leg and one human, one dragon arm and one human. Her head was neither dragon nor human, but a grotesque combination of both. Dragon scales stuck out of human flesh, dragon teeth jutted out of a human mouth, dragon wings sprouted from a human back and dragged limply across the floor. Shambling and shuffling, Anora hurled herself at Evelina and grabbed hold of the hand holding the locket. Anora tried to wrest it from her.

Evelina fought like a cornered cat, spitting and hissing, howling and kicking and biting the monstrous thing that had hold of her.

Anora squeezed, attempting to break off the girl's hand, if she had to. Evelina cried out and Anora seized hold of the locket. She started to wrest it away, when bitter pain tore through her body. She looked down to see the point of a sword emerge from her gut. The sword's point was stained with her own blood.

In her desperate need to retrieve the locket, Anora had let go of everything.

She had let go of Marcus.

Marcus yanked the sword from out of the back of the dragon. He saw the monster fall, but he did not know if he had killed it or not. He didn't have time to find out.

"Finish it!" he shouted to the knights, who had been staring at the apparition, too stunned to react. Hurling the bloody sword back to its owner, Marcus ran for the enormous double doors and slammed them against the wall with a boom. He ran down the marble stairs and into the courtyard.

"Don't fire!" he bellowed up at the walls. "Father! Don't fire!"

Startled faces stared at him. Mouths gaped. Men tried to grab hold of him. Marcus knocked them aside, paid them no attention. He kept running, kept shouting.

"Don't fire! For God's sake, Father, don't fire!"

His tone was so dire that several men joined him, crying out, "Don't fire! Don't fire!" though they had no idea why.

Marcus dashed up the stairs leading to the top of the wall where the cannons stood in a row, facing the enemy. Men fell back to get out of his way. Marcus shoved aside those who didn't move fast enough. Finding the sling around his injured arm impeded his progress, he tore it off. Fear and adrenaline ate up his pain. He could see at a glance that the dragon warriors were in range. The order to fire would be given at any moment.

Edward stood some distance from him, but Marcus could see clearly his father's lip moving, starting to form the word that would cause the gunners to touch the match to the portfire. He could see the gunners starting to react, anticipating the command.

And he could see, as well, the image in the dragon's mind. He saw the tendrils of magic wound like rope around the bases of the cannons. Stretched from one to the other, the magic wrapped around the muzzles, draped over the wheels, extended along the floor to the stone bunker where the gunpowder was stored. Marcus saw the flame leap from the cannon to the tendrils that snaked past it. The tendrils blazed with a dazzling blue-white light that arced from one cannon to the next until the entire, magical web flamed in Marcus's vision.

Then the blast, white-hot as the sun, the magic of the dragon strengthening the explosion until it was hundreds of times more powerful than a spark setting off a thousand kegs of gunpowder. Cannons, people, stone walls vaporized. Not a trace of them left. The blast expanded outward, blowing apart the castle walls, lifting gigantic blocks of granite high into the air, boring deep into the earth, spreading to the city where buildings crumbled and walls shattered.

Time slowed for Marcus, though it seemed to have speeded up for everyone around him. He could hear nothing for the roaring of blood in his ears. He could not even hear his own voice.

The stairs he climbed seemed to grow in number, so that he would never reach the end, and then, suddenly, with a great bound, he was at his father's side, clutching him and gasping, breathless, "Don't fire the cannons!"

Edward stared at his son, speechless.

"If you do"—Marcus sucked in a huge breath—"we'll all die!"

"Hold, there!" Edward shouted.

"Hold!" cried the captains and most of the men obeyed.

One, however, heard the king's voice, but not the king's words. This gunner had listened many times over to the terrifying tales of the demon warriors—how they could burn a man alive with a single look from their fiery red eyes. He'd been watching the enemy's inexorable advance with growing terror, and he was so panicked that he lowered the lighted portfire to the vent.

Marcus jumped at the man and socked him in the jaw. The man flew back against the cannon and then slid to the ground in a groggy heap. Those standing nearby watched the prince in stupefaction that was starting to harden into anger.

Marcus gasped for breath.

"I have . . . to show you something."

He turned back to the cannons and raised his hands and let the magic that he'd never before been allowed to use— the magic that they had tried so hard to suppress—flow out of his fingers and his arms, flow out of his mouth and his nose, a part of him, as the air he drew into his body.

His magic fell like raindrops on the tendrils of enchantment that wrapped around the cannons and caused the rain-bejeweled tendrils to glitter in the bright noontime sun. Men sprang back, out of the way, blessing themselves, so that eventually the glittering cannons stood isolated, surrounded by a ring of frightened and bewildered men.

Marcus walked over to one of the glittering tendrils and touched it with his hand, and the glittering rain-droplets of magic froze and changed to ice that sparkled briefly in the sun. The tendril, weighed down by the ice, broke and shattered, like ice-rimed tree limbs. The magic fell to the stone flagons and melted away.

"Sire! Look!" Gunderson pointed.

Those who could wrench their gaze from the enchanted cannons looked out over the walls to the hills and fields beyond.

The enemy was gone.

"God has saved us from the demons!" cried a priest, finding this a much easier explanation than what he'd just witnessed. "It is a miracle."

Men began to cheer. They flung down their weapons and started to dance on the walls, embracing each other, yelling with all their might.

"Where did they go?" Gunderson asked, dazed.

"No miracle, I'm afraid. It was an illusion," Marcus said. He was just thinking that this was the happy ending, when Draconas burst into his mind.

"Marcus! Where have you been?"

Draconas appeared to him not as the Walker, but in his dragon form, all teeth and eyes and gleaming red scales.

"Draconas!" Marcus was glad to see him and he was even gladder to tell his tale. "The dragon—"

"Never mind!" Draconas snapped. "You think you've won this battle, but it's not over yet. You've jumped out of the kettle, only to land smack in the fire. The real dragon army is on its way and so are the dragons."

42

THE DRAGON ARMY MASSED ON THE TOPS OF THE HILLS surrounding the castle. At some unheard signal, the warriors began to flow rapidly to the attack. Soldiers watching from the castle walls blinked and rubbed their eyes. They had seen this army once and then it had vanished, and now it had reappeared. Even the stalwart were shaken. Men cursed or trembled. Some fell to their knees. The priest who had called out that God had saved them looked accusingly into the heavens, as though suspecting some sort of cruel joke.

Leaving Gunderson in command, Edward took time to return to the great hall with Marcus, to see for himself what had occurred. He stared in horror and loathing at the carcass of the dead monstrosity that lay on the floor. Following Marcus's initial strike at the dragon, the knights who'd been paralyzed with shock had come to themselves and obeyed his command to "Finish it."

They had attacked the monster with sword and knife and spear, stabbing it over and over in their grim determination to slay it. The carcass, riddled with wounds, lay in a vast pool of blood. The eyes still held the fury of the dying dragon. The jaws gaped in a hate-filled grimace. Tragically, some parts of the Lady Izabelle were still visible, and it seemed to Edward that the dragon and the pretty young girl were locked in a lethal embrace.

"Cover it with a sheet or something," the king ordered, sickened.

"Poor girl," the Queen murmured softly, weeping. "Poor child."

"At least she is at peace now," said Edward. He put his arm around his distraught wife. "Come away."

"I didn't know she was . . . was that . . . that evil *thing*!" Ermintrude cried, sobbing into her husband's breast.

"None of us knew, Mother," said Marcus, trying to comfort her. "Don't blame yourself. Not even another dragon could have seen through the façade. She allowed me to see the truth, but only when she was certain she had a firm hold on me. Then she tortured me with the knowledge of what she planned."

A squire appeared in the doorway, seeking the king. Edward looked about for someone else to help his wife, who was shivering and sobbing.

"I'll stay with the Queen, Sire," Evelina offered in meek tones.

No one had paid any attention to her before this, and she'd taken care to keep well in the background. Now she came hesitantly forward.

Edward glanced at Marcus, who frowned and searched the room for anyone else. Her Majesty had sent most of the servants away for their own safety, keeping only one woman, who had been with her for years. That good woman crouched in a corner, laughing and blubbering hysterically, completely useless to her mistress. Evelina was the only woman remaining.

Though pale after her frightening ordeal, and far more subdued than usual, she was composed and in control. Marcus did not doubt her courage, no matter what he thought of her character. He gave a reluctant nod.

Evelina assisted the Queen to a chair by the fire and knelt down beside her, chafing the woman's hands, which were cold as what remained of the human hands of the corpse.

"Mistress Evelina," said Marcus.

"Yes, Your Highness?" Evelina looked up at him, her blue eyes wide. She tried a tentative smile.

"Don't bring my mother any wine," he said harshly.

Evelina's cheeks stained red. The smile shriveled. She lowered her eyes. "No, Your Highness," she mumbled, her response barely audible.

"Keep an eye on that creature," said Marcus to one of the knights as he and his father left the great hall. "Don't let her out of your sight. And don't let her leave the palace."

Gunderson stood atop the wall staring out eastward through a spyglass. Others were watching that direction, as well, eyes squinting, trying to see.

"What is it?" the king demanded.

"As strange a sight as I've witnessed in all my years, Sire," said Gunderson and he handed over the glass. "What do you make of that?"

"You know I can't see through that damn thing," Edward said, exasperated. "Marcus, you look."

Marcus lifted the glass to his eye and brought the amazing sight into focus.

Women on horseback raced along the road that led from the north, riding for the castle gates. The women were clad in leather armor of ornate and archaic design. They wore steel helms and carried shields with the insignia of an Eye upon them. Their swords bumped their legs as they rode. They had bows strung over their shoulders and quivers of arrows tied to their saddles.

Flanked by the warrior women, who rode protectively on either side, were twelve horse-drawn chariots. Each chariot was driven by a female warrior, and riding in each were women clad in white robes that streamed out behind them. The lead chariot was accompanied by a young man, who was not riding, but was running alongside, loping easily over the ground, keeping pace with the horses.

Marcus lowered the glass and rubbed his eyes, which were starting to tear.

"Well?" his father demanded impatiently.

"The warrior women of Seth," Marcus said.

"Do we fire?" Gunderson asked.

"No!" said Edward, and "No!" Marcus shouted at the same time.

"Sire, I don't like this—" Gunderson began.

"Neither do they!" Marcus cried, pointing.

The dragon army had spotted the riders and the chariots. A group of dragon warriors detached from the main body that was marching on the palace and shifted direction, racing at a run to cut off the women of Seth before they could reach the palace.

Those watching from the castle walls had no idea where this strange army had come from or what they were doing here, but, seeing that the enemy was trying to stop them, Edward's soldiers immediately took their side. They cried out warnings to the riders and clashed their spears on their shields and pointed urgently to the dragon warriors who were racing down upon them.

The riders saw their peril and increased their speed. They galloped over the road, holding formation, keeping themselves between the enemy and the chariots. The chariot drivers plied the whip to their steeds. The chariots rumbled and bounded over the paving stones. The passengers clung to the sides, holding on for dear life.

The troop of dragon warriors separated, some racing to cut off the women, some moving to attack them on the flank. The riders, gripping the saddle with their thighs, let go of the reins and, grabbing their bows, fired arrows at the approaching dragon warriors.

Those waiting on the walls expected to see the arrows go up in smoke, as they'd seen happen in the Battle of Aston. To their astonishment, the arrows of the warrior women of Seth penetrated the dragon-scale armor. Many attackers fell, and those on the wall cheered.

It was apparent, though, that the army of Seth would not win the gates before the dragon warriors cut them off.

Edward raced down the stairs, shouting for his knights.

The horses had already been saddled and readied for battle, and now stable-boys and groomsmen led them into the bailey near the gatehouse. The knights mounted, as did the king. Marcus ran down with him and stood near the gates, holding his father's bridle. Marcus longed to join them, but he was not strong enough to sit on a horse, and he might imperil the mission.

"If I fall, you are in command, my son," said Edward.

Marcus was in command. Not Gunderson. Marcus, the bastard son, the son he had not wanted, the son he'd never understood. Marcus saw pride and confidence in his father's eyes, and he saw something else: an apology. It would forever go unspoken between them, but Edward was saying he was sorry.

"Look after your mother," Edward added, and he put on his helm and took up his shield and rode to the gates, where men stood, ready to fling them open at his command. His knights fell in behind him.

"Open the gates!" the king commanded.

"Covering fire!" Marcus shouted. "Keep them busy."

He thought of using the cannons, which were now perfectly safe, but no man would go near them, and Marcus himself was reluctant to chance it. Catapults hurled stones at the besiegers. Flights of arrows soared through the air, and though the dragon warriors caused these to go up in smoke, the attack kept their attention on the archers on the walls and away from the sortie at the front gate.

The king and his knights rode out from the castle walls at a gallop. They raised their voices in a mighty shout. Trumpets blared from the walls and drums rolled. The dragon warriors rushing down on the chariots heard the commotion at their backs and saw that they were about to be caught between the hammer of Seth and the anvil of the king's men.

The enemy did not give up. They hurled wicked, deadly darts and blasted their foes with fire and lightning. Here a knight fell and there a warrior woman tumbled from her horse to lie bleeding on the ground. The commander of the Seth warriors urged her horse forward, shouting something to the woman who rode in the lead chariot, a woman whose robes were deep purple.

Clinging to the driver with her arm around her waist, the woman raised her other hand and pointed to the sword held by the commander of the Seth forces. Her sword burst into white flame. The commander brought it down in a fiery slash at a dragon warrior. The enchanted blade sliced through his armor and cleaved him almost in half. The commander did not waste time looking back to see her foe, but galloped on to the next.

The leader of the dragon warriors saw that his small force was about to be separated from the main body and surrounded. He had been trained to fight ordinary humans, not the female warriors of Seth, who, though they might not have possessed the dragon-magic, did possess the knowledge of how to use it and how to thwart it.

"Fall back!" he shouted, and his forces began an orderly retreat.

Some of the younger knights would have given chase, but the king ordered them sharply to return to the safety of the castle walls. The chariots rolled through the gates, their horses wet and foaming at the mouth. The knights and the women warriors galloped in behind them. The gates slammed shut.

Marcus was on hand to meet them. He searched frantically through the crowd, paying scant attention to the women warriors or the women in the chariots until he found the one he sought.

Ven was inspecting a metal dart that had lodged in the scales of his leg. Grimacing, he grabbed hold of the dart, yanked it out, and tossed it on the ground.

"Ven," said Marcus warmly. "It is good to see you!"

The Dragon's Son lifted his head.

Marcus held out his hand.

Ven straightened. He eyed Marcus with no change of expression. He made no move to take his hand.

Marcus flushed. He lowered his hand and started to turn away.

Ven took a step forward, his clawed feet scraping on the ground.

"Brother," said Ven gruffly, and he embraced Marcus—gently, so as not to hurt his injured arm.

43

THERE WAS HEADY CELEBRATION, BRIEF MOMENTS OF elation and triumph, and then the knights and soldiers of Idylswylde took second looks at the proud and fierce-looking warrior women of Seth and their pagan priest-esses and began to wonder if they'd opened the gates of the sheep fold to let in the wolf. Those in the courtyard gathered around the women, regarding them with baleful glances and muttered comments. At about that moment, someone caught sight of Ven and saw that while he was human above, the young man was beast below.

Shouts of "Devil-spawn," the clash of steel, and a rush of men put an end to the brothers' reunion. Marcus tried to reason with them, but he couldn't make himself heard. He knocked a man to the ground with a blow of his fist, as Ven lifted up another with his bare hands and flung him back to his comrades, bowling them over like ninepins.

Hearing the uproar, the warrior women drew their weapons and started to go to the rescue. The king's men rushed to bar their way, and it seemed as though the enemy might as well sit down and rest, for their work was being done for them.

A furious shout sounded. Hooves clattered on cobble-stone. King Edward rode into the fray, his knights accompanying him, striking to the left and right with the flat of their blades.

The king turned to face the mob.

"Have you gone mad?" Edward roared. He had no
need to use his sword. The fury in his voice and the rage
in his face caused the soldiers to fall back and lower their
weapons. "Last I looked, the enemy was *outside* the
walls!"

The soldiers muttered and then one spoke up boldly,
pointing at Ven, "What's this then?"

"A miracle," Edward replied. "A miracle sent by God
in our hour of need. Now return to your posts! Or, by
God, I will clap every single man among you in irons and
charge you with treason!"

The soldiers saw the king, and they saw, out of the cor-
ners of their eyes, the knights on horseback, who had
them surrounded. The soldiers were riled, their blood was
up, and they made no move to disperse. The king's face
darkened. His knights were starting as to edge their
horses forward when a man shouldered his way through
the crowd and ran toward the king.

He was stopped at spear point by one of the knights.
The man said quickly, "Your Majesty, I bring urgent
news."

Edward stared down at the man in astonishment, for he
recognized him. "Draconas!"

"Dragons are flying to join in the assault, Your
Majesty," said Draconas. "Not just one. Many."

His voice carried. A hush fell over the crowd, as they
lifted their heads to stare fearfully into the sky.

"Many?" Edward repeated in dismay. "What can we
do to fight them?"

"You spoke truly when you said a miracle had come."

Draconas held out his hand and a woman strode forward. She walked with dignity and grace, and the crowd
parted as she came.

"This is Anna, the High Priestess of Seth," said Draconas.

"Your Majesty," said the High Priestess, and she made
him a low bow. "My sisters and I can defend you against
the dragons. That is why we have come."

Before the king could reply, shouts went up from all

parts of the castle, crying that the enemy had regrouped and was launching the attack.

"Get back to your posts!" Edward commanded.

Men returned to their positions. The warrior women took their places alongside the soldiers, who glanced at them askance, but were too busy preparing for the assault to have much to say to them.

Marcus heard the command, but he did not move. News of the dragons and the enemy attack made little impact. He stared, entranced, at the High Priestess.

"She is lovely," he said softly, to himself, or so he thought.

"Yes, she is," said Ven.

Marcus looked from his brother to the High Priestess and flushed. "I am sorry, Brother. I didn't mean—"

Ven smiled. His smile was stiff, for it hadn't been much used, and he wasn't certain quite what to do with it.

"Admire Anna as much as you like," Ven said. "She and I are friends, that is all. I have a family of my own to look after now. Twenty brothers and sisters. I'll explain later," he added, his smile warming as he saw Marcus's astonishment. "Now, we had best prepare to deal with the dragons."

"There is no need to be diplomatic, Your Majesty," Anna was saying, responding to the king's delicate questions. "We know the truth about the dragon, as we know about the deceit that was practiced on our people. We know that the Mistress of Dragons, the woman we revered, was actually a dragon herself."

Her gaze went to Ven. "We know about the babies that were stolen away in the night and taken to Dragonkeep. We know about the dragon's children. We have taken them in and offered them sanctuary. And we have come to your kingdom to stop the dragons from enslaving you as they did us."

"Your help is most welcome, High Priestess," said Edward. He was glad to see that many of his commanders were standing within earshot and that they were listening intently. "Let me know what you need."

Voices cried out from the watchtowers and the walls.

The attack was commencing. Globules of fire, like balls of molten lava, flew over the walls. The flames spread rapidly, feeding off whatever they touched, be it cold iron or human flesh.

"Put out those fires!" Gunderson roared.

"Do not use water!" The commander of the warrior women shouted. "Water spreads the flames! Smother them with wet straw or blankets!"

"My sisters and I need someplace quiet to form our sacred circle," Anna replied, raising her voice to be heard, as the commotion boiled around her. "We do not fight with swords, Your Majesty. We fight with our magic."

"Marcus, take the High Priestess and her women into the palace," said Edward and, for once, his son didn't argue with him.

Marcus bounded forward with alacrity.

"High Priestess," he said, bowing. "I am yours to command."

He held out his arm to escort her. Anna rested her hand on his and Marcus felt a different kind of magic, an ordinary kind of magic, one that had nothing to do with dragons.

Marcus led the women of Seth to the king's private chapel, which was quiet, isolated, and well protected. He wondered if God would be offended at this invasion of pagan practices. Recalling what Draconas had said about the miracle, Marcus could only hope and trust that the Lord was open-minded.

"We will do our best to fight the dragon," Anna was saying to Marcus. "But I must confess to you, Your Highness, that some of us, myself included, have never battled a dragon before. And none of us have ever fought more than one dragon. I'm not sure we can do it."

"I am certain you will succeed," said Marcus, hardly knowing what he was saying.

Anna remained somber. Halting outside the chapel doors, she turned to face him. "The magic makes us very weak and ill. The blood bane, we call it. Some of us might die. I want you to be prepared for that," she added gently.

"Then you must not attempt it," Marcus said firmly. "We'll find some way to deal with Maristara—"

"You misunderstand me, Your Highness." Anna lifted her head proudly. "I say this not to try to evade our duty, but to inform you that we know our fate and accept it. This is our fight as much as yours. Maybe more so. Our nation has been held captive for hundreds of years." The sisters filed past her into the chapel. She began to push him away. "And, now, you must go. The ceremony is sacred, and it is secret."

Marcus opened his mouth to protest.

"Please, go, Your Highness. All will be as it will be. There is nothing more you can do, and your presence would only distract us."

Marcus saw that further argument would be useless and would, perhaps, only anger her. She was a ruler of her people, and she had a right to expect her wishes to be obeyed.

Marcus brought her hand to his lips and bowed. The High Priestess was the last to enter the chapel. As she shut the door, she said to him, "No matter what happens, Your Highness, we are not to be disturbed."

Marcus nodded. She shut the door, and because he did not trust any other to guard them, he took it upon himself to remain outside the chapel door. He sat down on a stone bench and that was a mistake. The moment he stopped moving, pain and fatigue overwhelmed him. His shoulder throbbed, his head buzzed. The floor tilted beneath his feet, the walls slid sideways. Marcus leaned back against the wall to wait for the dizziness to pass.

He'd been going on adrenaline alone, and that was suddenly all used up.

The chapel was located inside the palace proper, sheltered from the hustle and bustle of everyday life. Even though tumult raged beyond, the thick walls dampened most of the sound. He could hear faintly the ongoing struggle and the chanting of the sisters as they gathered in their circle.

And he also heard voices shouting in terror, "Dragons!" and he heard a blast and boom of fiery breath.

The pain and weakness were so great, he did not think he had the strength to move off the bench. His gaze lifted to a stained-glass window above him, to the myriad colors shifting in his wavering vision. "I faced the dragon before. I can do it again."

He left the little room and entered the mind of the dragon.

Maristara was furious. Her fury burned inside her like the brimstone rumbling in her belly. She was furious and she was afraid, and she was using her fury to try to squelch her fear. The dragon had always been a bully, and like most bullies, she was a coward. Her longtime companion in this adventure, Grald, was dead, and though she had despised him and distrusted him, she had relied on his brutal strength and low cunning more than she had cared to admit.

And now Anora was dead, too. Maristara had outwardly disdained the powerful dragon. Inwardly she stood in awe of her. Anora was dead, slain by the wretched humans—a fate she had predicted would come upon them all.

Maristara was left to fight this battle on her own. She had to finish what they had begun. She had to. She had no choice.

Maristara's hold on Dragonkeep was tenuous, at best. Grald's despotic rule had caused many of the citizens to question his authority. The people hated and distrusted the mad monks. Few had dared do anything about it, but then came the lethal blast that had destroyed so much and killed so many. Shortly after that, the Abbey collapsed mysteriously, Grald vanished, and an army of strange warriors that no one had known existed marched through their streets.

Maristara had flown to join the army, leaving the palace guarded by the mad monks, never dreaming that the humans, armed and led by some wretched blacksmith, would invade it. There they had discovered the bodies of the hapless young women who had been impregnated by Grald. The truth about his breeding program was revealed and now most of the city of Dragonkeep was in open rebellion.

As for Seth, Maristara had already lost that kingdom. The people there knew the truth, as well. Ven had shown them the body of the Mistress in the tomb. Once she had seen that, the High Priestess had looked into the Eye and let her gaze roam far. She had used the Eye's magic to see the past and the present. There had been nothing Maristara could do to stop it. Apparently, all these years, the Watchful Eye had been watching her.

Maristara pondered Anora's dying words. Her colors had already started to fade when the dragon spoke them.

"We are our own doom, Maristara," Anora had whispered.

And there had been a tinge of horror in those colors, the revelation coming too late.

The Parliament was dissolved. War was inevitable. Maristara's new allies were hot-headed young dragons who, if not for this, would have been out stampeding cattle for the fun of it. She couldn't stop them. They wouldn't listen to her.

And here, rising up through the mists of her rage and gloom, was a human. The Prince who had helped Ven kill Grald. The Prince who had killed Anora. He was inside her mind, trying to kill her.

Maristara was in no mood for it. Her fury boiled like the fire in her gut, and she was about to expend it all on him, searing him with the blast that would leave his brains mush, when, suddenly, the Prince was gone. He dropped out of her mind as though he'd fallen through a trapdoor. Maristara didn't have time to wonder, for there, in his place, was the Walker.

He wore his human shape, his human boots.

She saw Draconas in her mind, even as her eyes glared down on the castle below and the shadow of her wings glided over it. The women of Seth were working their magic. She could feel their power directed against her, as she had once directed that same power against others of her kind.

"So you have taken sides," she said to Draconas. "You've turned against your own kind."

One of her young cohorts dove down on the castle, spraying it with fire. She tried to warn Litard, but he did not listen. The flames hit the magical barrier created by the sisters and flared back at him, forcing him to make a sudden, violent, twisting turn to escape being toasted with his own breath.

"I don't want to fight you or the others," Draconas replied. "You can still stop this, Maristara. Your army is exhausted and demoralized. The magic they use comes with a price—the warriors grow too weak to fight. That's the true reason that the warriors waited so long between attacks, isn't it? It was not a cunning ploy to let the humans stew in their fear. It was simply that your army didn't have strength enough to do battle.

"And while it is true that your humans are powerful in the magic and well-trained as a fighting force, they were never taught how to survive in the world outside their sheltered cave. Grald never expected they would have to. He expected a swift victory, followed by capitulation. He did not foresee a prolonged war, which is what you have now. Your warriors are footsore and weary and half-starved. Many have fallen ill. They have no supplies and no supply lines. They cannot undertake a siege of the castle, and now that the priestesses of Seth are here, Edward can hold out against your army for a long, long time. Call them off, Maristara. Retreat. Go back to Dragonkeep."

"And then what, Walker?" the elderly dragon asked. "What happens then? Will your humans leave us alone now that they know where to find us? Or will they come with their armies to conquer us?"

"We can talk, negotiate . . ."

Maristara snorted. Shadowed silence fell between them.

"Anora was right," Maristara said at last. "We are our own doom."

Marcus came back to consciousness to find himself lying on the floor beneath a stone bench. He sat up, rubbing a sore jaw. His father and Ven both bent over him.

"What happened? Are you all right?" Edward asked in concern.

"Draconas hit me!" said Marcus.

Edward smiled. "He's done the same to me on occasion. Usually for my own good. Here, can you stand?"

Marcus staggered to his feet, supported by his father. He could hear strange sounds coming from outside—roars and bellows and eerie, bestial screams of wordless rage and defiance.

"Father, what is it? What is happening?" Marcus glanced back at the chapel. "Anna, the sisters—"

"The High Priestess and the sisters are all safe and well. They are resting from their labors. Your mother has taken charge of them." Edward was grim. "Come and see for yourself, son."

As Marcus walked outside, a drop of liquid hit him in the face. He thought at first it was raining, but the sun was shining, the day was clear. He touched the liquid on his cheek and drew back his hand.

His fingers were red with blood. Blood that had fallen from the sky. He lifted his eyes, tilted back his head, and gasped. He had to hang on to his father's arm for support, or he might have fallen.

In the sky above Idylswylde, dragons fought dragons.

Long, long, long ago, when humans themselves were living in caves, some far-distant ancestor of Marcus's might well have looked into the sky and been awed and terrified by the same sight. No human had witnessed such a battle since, and now both armies halted in their killing to watch the fight, which was horrible and deadly beautiful.

Scales flared green and blue, red and black and purple, as the sunlight glinted on bodies that wheeled, dove, and soared. Lightning flared and thunder split the skies and shook the ground. Flames crackled as the dragons breathed their scorching breath, trying to burn wings or blind eyes. Jaws snapped. The dragons tore at each other with clawed feet. Blood fell in a gruesome shower, spattering on the cobblestones and sliding down the castle walls.

Marcus shaded his eyes, seeking Draconas, but the sun was directly overhead, and it was hard to tell one dragon from the other. He tried to venture inside his little room, but the fury and hatred smote him and seared him, so that he had to leave or risk being consumed.

"There he is," said Ven. His dragon eyes could see clearly. He had learned to look into the sun. He pointed.

"And the big one? Who is that?"

"Maristara," Ven answered.

"And what about the smaller one? I think I have seen her before."

"Her name is Lysira. She guided us to Seth."

"She's in trouble," said Marcus.

Lysira, intent on fighting one of the younger males, did not realize that Mantas had cunningly drawn her into a trap. As he battled her, Maristara was diving down on her from above.

"Yes," Ven remarked impassively, calmly watching the battle as one might watch a bull-baiting, with no care who wins.

"You hate them all, don't you?" Marcus said. "You'd just as soon see them all die."

Ven flicked him a glance. "Do you blame me?"

"No," said Marcus. "I don't suppose I do."

Lysira breathed a gout of flame at Mantas, who evaded it. Before she could breathe again, he turned tail and flew off. Lysira's roar of triumph was cut short by a gasp of fear and astonishment as the shadow of her foe fell dark upon her.

Lysira rolled away, twisting her body, and the move saved her life, for Maristara had been about to seize hold of the smaller dragon's neck in her powerful jaws and snap it in two. As it was, Maristara managed to sink her teeth into only a portion of Lysira's neck, the sharp fangs piercing the scales and into flesh. It was not the hold she had wanted, not a lethal hold, but it would do. Maristara tightened her grip and began shaking Lysira like a dog shakes a rat with the same intent—to break her back.

Screaming in pain and outrage, Lysira writhed and struggled in the other's grip, trying desperately to break the powerful dragon's hold on her. A dark shape streaked toward her. Not knowing whether this was death or life, Lysira involuntarily shut her eyes.

Draconas had been fighting a defensive battle, hoping to prevent dragons from killing each other. Thus far, though the dragons had done a lot of damage, none had died nor was even critically injured. He had begun to hope that Maristara might be engaged in this battle merely for show and that she would soon be willing to give up and call it a draw.

Maristara might have done so, but she had suddenly seen an inviting target in the young female. Maristara owed Lysira, who had led the dragon's children into Seth. In addition, the death of the female he loved would suitably pay back Draconas for all the harm he had done Maristara and her allies. Maristara attacked Lysira, and Draconas saw that the elder dragon meant this attack to end in death.

He flew straight at Maristara, striking her with his claws extended, hitting her on the flank with all the force he could manage.

Maristara gave a grunt as Draconas barreled into her, knocking the wind out of her. Her jaws opened. She was forced to let go her hold on Lysira so that she could breathe.

Lysira was badly hurt, however, and barely conscious. She started falling toward the ground, unable to help herself. The young male, Mantas, swooped in, thinking to finish her off.

With a howl, the old dragon Malfiesto dove at the youngster and, with a flurry of claws, buffeting wings, and lashing tail, drove Mantas away. The irrascible old dragon snagged the half-conscious Lysira gently in his claws and carried her away. Draconas, seeing this, inwardly apologized to Malfiesto for every bad thought he'd ever had about him.

Draconas turned his attention back to Maristara. She was breathing painfully, and he thought he had probably broken some of her ribs. Blood dribbled from his claw marks on her flanks. Her head drooped. Smoke, not flame, came from her nostrils. She seemed about finished. The fire in her belly was doused.

"Give up, Maristara," Draconas sent his colors to her. "I don't want to kill you or any dragon. Let this be an end of it."

Nodding, her breath coming in heaving gasps, Maristara turned and started to fly away. Draconas gave a deep sigh and was looking about to see what had become of Lysira when Malfiesto's colors boomed blazing red.

"You idiot! Behind you!"

Draconas whipped about to see Maristara lunging straight at him.

"This is not an end. It is only the beginning." She crashed into him.

The two grappled, slashing and snapping, kicking and snarling, hitting each other with wings and tail. Magic sparked and crackled around them. Locked in a deadly embrace, the two began to spiral toward the ground.

"They're both dead," said Ven, and even he had a note of tension in his voice.

"God, no!" cried Marcus.

The sons of Melisande watched in pity and horror the battling dragons plummet to the earth—falling on top of the dragon army.

Shadow and blood covered the dragon warriors, who, staring upward, saw their danger. They fled, panic-stricken, running for their lives, some of them seeking cover beneath the very castle walls they had, only moments before, been attacking. The soldiers manning the walls, mesmerized by the terrible sight, let their foes come and did nothing.

Down and down the dragons fell, rolling over and over, and they were both within a heartbeat of death, when one of the dragons suddenly broke free and, shaking loose the hold of the other, began clawing and fighting and flapping upward.

"Which is it? I can't see!" Marcus cried, half-blinded by the sun, which made all colors black.

The other dragon tried to recover, but one wing was in

tatters. The dragon pitched over and crashed headlong into the ground.

The impact shook the foundations of the castle, knocking men off their feet, causing towers to tremble and sending cracks snaking up the walls. An enormous dust cloud arose, momentarily obscuring the body from sight. Men who ran to the walls to try to see were soon choking and coughing as the cloud roiled over them.

"Which is it?" Marcus cried again.

"Maristara," Ven returned. "She is dead."

Marcus raised his eyes to see the red dragon flying wearily overhead. Draconas circled the carcass of the enormous dragon that lay sprawled out over several hills. Maristara had fallen so fast and from such a height that the body had half-buried itself in the ground.

"Go home," Draconas said, speaking to the other dragons. "The battle is finished."

"For today," said Mantas, snarling, and, with a final glance at Maristara, he and his cohorts flew off.

"For today," Draconas repeated, and his colors were so dark and sorrow-laden that Marcus knew better than to intrude, and he silently withdrew, leaving the dragon to his grief.

The fight was all knocked out of the dragon warriors. The death of the dragon who had commanded them finished them off. They picked up the bodies of their dead comrades and, using what illusion magic remained, they disppeared from sight. They had no more strength to return home. Sailors and fishermen, upon returning to the city of Ramsgate-upon-the-Aston, were outraged to find that every sailing vessel in the harbor had gone missing and so the army made its inglorious way back to Dragonkeep.

The people of Ramsgate tended their wounded and buried their dead with hymns of praise, and celebrated their salvation in the church that evening. Their major concern was what to do with the carcass of the dragon, which would soon start to rot. They would have to cut down a forest of trees to find enough wood to burn it, and the smoke created by such a conflagration would smother the populace if the wind was in the right direction.

As it turned out, they did not have to worry. The day after the battle, a dozen dragons appeared in the skies, led by one dragon with flaring red scales. The dragons created a magical web that sparkled like stars as it dropped down from their claws and settled over the carcass. The dragons lifted up the body, cradled in the starry web, and bore it away with them. All that remained was the enormous crater that the body's fall had gouged into the earth.

Ever after, the site would be known as Dragon Downs.

In the days that followed, Marcus and Ven spent much of their time together, and they were often joined by Anna, the High Priestess of Seth. Ven and Anna between them told Marcus about Sorrow and Lucien and the other children. Marcus listened in awe, disturbed by what he heard, yet glad at least for Ven, that he had found something good in his life.

The three had only a few days together, for the warrior women of Seth were anxious to return to their home. They feared that dragons might attack the kingdom in their absence. Ven, too, was eager to return to his family.

The king gave the women of Seth as many gifts as they would accept, and he and his knights paid them every honor as they were about to depart.

"I thank you and your people for all you have done for us," said Edward to the High Priestess, as she prepared to take her place in the chariot that would bear her home. "Without your help, we would not have survived. And," he added, with a smile that lit the hazel eyes, "I look forward to the alliance of our two kingdoms."

The High Priestess of Seth and the Prince of Idylswylde smiled at each other. Sometimes rulers *do* have a say in who they marry.

"As do I, my soon-to-be Daughter," said Ermintrude, giving the young woman a tender embrace. The dimples were back, undaunted.

King and Queen bid a more reserved farewell to Ven. Neither of them could ever feel completely comfortable around their son's half-brother. Ermintrude, especially, had trouble knowing what to do with her eyes, which kept going, despite her best efforts, to the clawed, scale-covered feet.

"Whatever will we do with him at the wedding?" she asked her husband in a low voice, as they walked back to the palace. "My father will die of the shock."

"All in all, not such a bad thing, my dear," Edward remarked.

The warrior women mounted their horses. The drivers took their places in the chariots, along with the priestesses of Seth. Anna and Marcus and Ven lingered together, reluctant to say goodbye.

"What will you do, Ven? Where will you and the children go?" Marcus asked, for if ever there were destined to be outcasts in this world, it was these half-human, half-dragon children of Grald.

"For the time being, we will remain in Seth," Ven said. "The sisters have invited us to live among them until we feel more at ease. This time has not been easy on Sorrow and the others. They are learning how cruel and hurtful you humans can be."

"And how kind," Marcus reminded him with a glance at Anna. "And compassionate." He reached out to take her hand, loath to let her go.

The High Priestess flushed in pleasure. Her fingers twined around Marcus's.

"True," Ven admitted. "But no human community will ever fully accept us. Someday, when the younger children are stronger, we will leave Seth and find a homeland of our own."

The commander of the warrior women was restless. She did not dare say anything to the High Priestess, but Marcus could see by the restive way her horse cantered about on the stones that she was eager to be on her way. It was time to say farewell.

The brothers embraced. Marcus helped Anna into the chariot. He kissed her hand and pressed it to his heart. She bent down and kissed him on the lips, and a cheer went up from the knights and the soldiers on the walls.

The gates opened, and with a flourish of trumpets, the women of Seth left Idylswylde and headed back for their homeland.

Ven, running alongside the chariots, turned to wave at Marcus, who lifted his hand. His heart went with two he'd come to love. Sadly, Marcus turned around and nearly fell over Draconas.

"My God, you startled me! Where have you been?" Marcus greeted the Walker with warmth. "I haven't seen you since that day you knocked me out."

"Good thing I did, too, or Maristara would have made mincemeat of your brain. As it is, it seems that the lovely young priestess has done just that."

Marcus laughed. "Anna is beautiful, isn't she? We're going to be married in a month's time."

"I am glad for you," said Draconas. "Though your lives will not be easy. You both have dragon-blood in your veins. You know what your children will face."

"We know," said Marcus somberly. "We have talked of it. Still," he added, cheering up, "if we have a boy, I will ask you to come take him to the riverbank to teach him the magic."

He had hoped to make the dragon smile at the memory of another small boy who had learned the magic by the side of the river. Draconas shook his head.

"You will have to teach your son yourself, Marcus. My days as a walker are nearly at an end. I came to tell you goodbye. My people are at war and my place is with them. I am working to bring about peace, but I am not hopeful."

"We may soon be at war ourselves," said Marcus. "When Anna and I are married, our first task will be to try to enter Dragonkeep to open negotiations. But I am not hopeful, either. They have been taught to hate us."

"They aren't the only ones who have been taught hate," Draconas remarked.

"True," said Marcus, thinking of Ven. "The blame lies with us, as well."

Draconas held out his hand. "Farewell, Your Highness. A last word of advice—stay out of that little room. You're needed in this world. You should not be trespassing in ours."

"Yet, I would like to go there sometimes," said Marcus quietly. "To dream the dreams of dragons."

And perhaps, he thought as he watched Draconas walk away, his boots dust-covered and worn down at the heels, that was all it had been.

A dream of dragons.

He watched Draconas until the dragon was lost to sight, walking down the road, and the gates of the palace had shut upon him.

EPILOGUE

A FORTNIGHT AFTER THE ASSAULT ON IDYLSWYLDE, WHEN life in the city had almost returned to normal, a secret trial was held inside the castle of the king.

Long after darkness had fallen, the prisoner was removed from her room, where she'd been held under strict guard, and taken to King Edward's private study. Four guards escorted the prisoner, and her hands were bound, for she was being tried on the charge of murder.

Evelina came before the king with her head held high, her jaw firm, though her dreams hung about her in shreds and tatters. She had awakened one morning a week ago to find her mattress soaked in blood—proof that she was not pregnant. She had tried to hide the evidence from Axe-Face, who had returned, much to Evelina's ire. That, however, had been impossible.

After that, everything had gone wrong. Evelina had planned to retrieve the goblet that she had given to Lady Izabelle and rinse it out before anyone had a chance to examine it. The startling and unexpected turn of events of that day had so rattled her that she forgot about the goblet until it was too late. When she went to find it, the goblet was gone.

One of the Queen's knights, with great presence of mind, had picked up the goblet from the floor and secreted it inside a chest in his room. He had later presented it to the king, who gave it to the royal physician, who performed his tests and stated that, in his expert opinion, the wine had been poisoned. Now, Evelina faced the very real possibility of being hanged.

Yet, she kept her head high as she listened to the prosecuting lawyer recount the evidence before the king.

"Your Majesty, you have heard three witnesses here swear under oath that they saw Mistress Evelina pour the wine from the pitcher into three goblets—one which she gave to Her Majesty, one which she kept for herself, and one which she gave to the Lady Izabelle," the lawyer related, his tone stern and cold.

"According to these men, no one touched the goblets other than Mistress Evelina. You have heard the testimony of the herbalist who has identified Mistress Evelina as the purchaser of the poison a few days prior to the murder, using this ring"—the lawyer held up a ruby—"to pay for it. The ring has been identified as belonging to one of Her Majesty's ladies-in-waiting. In addition, we have recovered several other valuables that had gone missing in the young woman's room."

Evelina remained defiant, a faint smile of disdain on her lips. Her attitude appeared to exasperate the King. Edward's expression hardened.

The lawyer held up an object.

"We also found there a half filled vial containing more poison secreted beneath her mattress."

That was foolish, Evelina admitted. She should have thrown it out. The dream of feeding it to Axe-Face had been too dear to let go. The lawyer was still talking. Evelina stifled a yawn.

The lawyer called for Gunderson to take the stand.

The elderly retainer limped forward.

"Tell us, Master Gunderson, what you discovered about Mistress Evelina's background."

"She is the daughter of a petty thief and pickpocket known as Ramone, last seen leaving the city of Fairefield in company with a troupe of ne'er-do-well actors under the leadership of a scoundrel called Glimmershanks. This troupe and the young woman's father have since disappeared."

Evelina clenched her jaw and stood unmoving.

Gunderson sighed and rubbed his chin. "There is no doubt, Your Majesty, that the prince's ... er ... half brother knows the truth about this young woman and how she happened to be in Dragonkeep, but Ven refused to answer any of my questions, saying only that he was at fault for what had happened to her and he would not say anything against her."

Evelina tapped her foot, waiting impatiently for her chance to speak.

Gunderson bowed and stepped back.

The lawyer continued. "As to motive, Mistress Evelina was known to be jealous of the Lady Izabelle, for her betrothal to Prince Marcus. Both this serving girl and the cook have given witness to that." The lawyer bowed and concluded.

"Mistress Evelina," King Edward spoke sternly, "you face death by hanging if this charge of murder is found to be true and we find the evidence against you overwhelming. Do you have anything to say in your own defense?"

"I do, Your Majesty," said Evelina. "I did *not* poison the Lady Izabelle."

Before the king could say a word, she added coolly, "I poisoned the dragon.

"I knew all along that the so-called lady was a dragon, Your Majesty," Evelina continued. "I learned about such monsters when I was held prisoner in Dragonkeep. I know I should have told someone, but I feared no one would believe me. So I concluded I had to deal with her myself. It was the least I could do, seeing that you had all been so kind to me, Your Majesty."

A tear slid down her cheek.

"I saved your lives," Evelina said with a catch in her voice. "I saved your kingdom, Your Majesty. And for that I must die! But first," she added, raising her head with a flash in her eye, "I'll tell what I know from the scaffold. I'll proclaim the truth about your son!"

"Our people already know the truth about Prince Marcus, Mistress," said Edward. "We have no secrets from them, now, and neither does our son. And we find it difficult to believe your story that you penetrated the dragon's disguise. However"—his mouth twitched—"we can't prove it."

He was silent a moment, regarding her grimly, and, despite herself, her heart beat fast.

At last he said, "You will not hang, Mistress Evelina."

She felt her knees go weak with relief, and true tears flooded her eyes. She had not realized, until that moment, how frightened she was.

"But we cannot in good conscience unleash you upon an unsuspecting public. Therefore we have decided that you will be escorted, under guard, to the Abbey of the blessed Saint Elizabeth, there to spend the rest of your days in prayer and penitence."

Evelina's jaw dropped. "A nun!" she repeated, shocked. "I'm to become a nun!"

"If God will have you," said Edward dryly. "Which we much doubt. Whether you take the veil or not is entirely up to you, Mistress. You will be a prisoner in the Abbey, well-guarded, day and night, by the Abbess, who is, we understand, a woman of extremely strong character. You will remain there under penalty of death. If you should escape—and we must tell you that the Abbey is located in mountainous terrain and is, further, extremely isolated— you will be hunted down, and the sentence of death will be immediately carried out. Do you understand?"

"I would rather be hanged!" Evelina cried.

"That is, of course, your choice, Mistress," said the king gravely, and thus ended the trial.

In the end, Evelina did not choose to be hanged. She was Ramone's daughter, and so long as there is life there is hope. The more she thought about it, the better this sounded. She had no doubt but that she would be able to seduce her guards and that one or more of them would help her escape. She had her charms and the golden necklace that she had stolen from the dragon, which she'd managed to squirrel away so that not even Axe-Face had discovered it.

Unfortunately for Evelina, she had to revise her plans almost immediately. Her guards turned out to be women—the warrior women of Seth. Having learned that Evelina had poisoned one woman affianced to Prince Marcus, the warriors were more than glad to take on the task of escorting this dangerous female to her prison. Evelina was not above attempting to seduce one of the women, but that proved a failure. None of them so much as glanced at her the entire journey.

Hope dimmed still further when she found out that when the king said the Abbey was isolated, he meant *isolated*. She and her guards traveled for weeks on end through thick forests, with nary a town or village in sight. Wolves and bears and wildcats prowled the woods at night. Evelina counted ten snakes crossing her path. She thought of trying to make this journey on her own, roaming the vast wilderness defenseless, with no food, and her heart sank.

They arrived at the Abbey in a snowstorm. Evelina was frozen clear through. Her toes and fingers had gone numb. It hurt her to walk, and she was forced to hobble her way over the frozen ground. The Abbey was an enormous building made of stone quarried from the mountain. It was surrounded by a high wall, penetrated by only a single gate, that was barred from the inside. The bar was so heavy that four of the stoutest sisters were required to lift it, and it was only opened when someone needed to enter.

The warrior woman escorted Evelina safely inside, then left her to her fate. Evelina, clutching a little sack containing her belongings, including the golden locket, stood shivering in the courtyard.

The sisters took Evelina to a windowless cell with a mattress in it and nothing else. She was told that this was her room. The cell was nearly as cold as outdoors, and

Evelina resigned herself to freezing to death. She lay in bed, huddled beneath a thin blanket, and wished she'd opted for hanging. One of the sisters appeared. She took Evelina to a warming room, where there was a fire. The sisters gave her food and drink, plain but filling, and undergarments over which went robes made of heavy black cloth.

I must look like a crow in this black garb, Evelina thought dismally.

Then she realized that there were no men about to see her, so it really didn't matter what she looked like. She snuggled gratefully into the habit that was, at least, warm.

The sisters took her, at last, to see the Abbess.

The Abbess was in her late forties, stout, well-educated, strong-willed, and determined.

Standing before the woman, her hands folded in her sleeves, her eyes lowered, Evelina pretended to listen as the sonorous voice of the Abbess laid down the law and handed out the rules that were, from now on, to define Evelina's life. All the while Evelina was casting oblique glances from beneath her eyelashes around the room.

The quarters of the Abbess were simply furnished, but appeared sumptuous compared to those of the other nuns. A fire burned on the hearth, making the room cozy. The bed had a mattress of goose down, not of straw. There were chairs and a writing desk, and the Abbess had her own secretary to handle her correspondence, for— Evelina would come to learn—the Abbess was a power in the church in this part of the world.

Evelina had been doing some hard thinking. The sisters, though they might labor and toil in the fields and around the Abbey, appeared to be healthy and well-fed. Having gone to bed hungry more than once in her life, Evelina appreciated the value of always having enough to eat. Inside the Abbey, she was safe and protected. She had her own room. True, there were drawbacks—one of them being a great deal of time that she would have to spend on her knees in prayer, the other that there were no men. But prayers were easily said, and as for men, what had they ever brought her but trouble?

Looking at the Abbess, Evelina saw herself in that chair, basking by the fire, eating all the food she wanted, ruler of her own small kingdom.

And so when the Abbess concluded by asking Evelina what she thought of where she now found herself, Evelina sank down onto her knees and clasped her hands together.

"I thank God, Reverend Mother," she said piously, "that He has brought me home."

Peeping up from beneath a curtain of golden curls, Evelina saw the Abbess was touched and impressed. Inwardly, the novice looked to the future and smiled.